Sins
of the
Seventh
Sister

SINS
of the
SEVENTH
SISTER

*A Novel Based on
a True Story of the Gothic South*

HUSTON CURTISS

Harmony Books
New York

Published by Harmony Books, New York, New York.
Member of the Crown Publishing Group, a division of Random House, Inc.
www.randomhouse.com

HARMONY BOOKS is a registered trademark and the Harmony Books colophon
is a trademark of Random House, Inc.

Printed in the United States of America

Design by Lauren Dong

Library of Congress Cataloging-in-Publication Data is available upon request

ISBN 1-4000-4538-X

10 9 8 7 6 5 4 3 2 1

First Edition

To my wife, Lizzie,
who translated my handwriting and corrected my spelling
for the last fifty years.
I could not have done it without her!

∾

ACKNOWLEDGMENTS

I wish to thank my good friends Arthur and Jeanne Sexton,
Renie Tener, Felice Gordon, and Michael Wilder, for their support;
Alan Nevins, my literary manager,
who believed in my book from his first reading;
Shaye Areheart, my indispensable editor;
and Sarah Kuchelmester, my guiding light.

LIST OF CHARACTERS

THE CURTISSES

GENERAL WILLIAM BAKER CURTISS, *married Alexandria Randolph; they had two daughters, Almeda and Mary*

ALMEDA CURTISS, *never married, mistress of Senator Burton, aunt of Huston Curtiss and great-aunt to Opal, Bea, and Hugh*

MARY CURTISS, *had one son, Huston, by John Ferris (rumored to be John Wilkes Booth)*

HUSTON CURTISS, *natural son of Mary Curtiss and John Ferris, adopted by his grandfather, General Curtiss and named for his friend Sam Houston; married Virginia Channell*

VIRGINIA CURTISS, *daughter of Joseph Channell, a church builder, and Ellie Hamilton, who died bearing her; had three children, Opal, Bea, and Huston II*

EMMA AND ALVIN CHANNELL, *Virginia's half-sister and half-brother; their father, Joseph, married the rich widow Coughenour after his first wife's death*

BEA CURTISS, *married and moved to Buffalo*

OPAL CURTISS, *married four times; her first husband was Elwood Harrington III, her third, General Openheimer*

HUSTON CURTISS II (Hugh), *married Billy-Pearl Fancler; one son, Huston III*

HUSTON CURTISS III (Hughie), *married and had one daughter, Sigrid, later divorced and married Lizzie*

THE FANCLERS

PETER FANCLER, *married Elizabeth McCloud in 1880 and had eleven daughters*

FANNIE, *married Burr Goden and had seven children*

SARAH, *married John Canfield and had fifteen children*

MARY, *married Jake Martin and had three children, but she died young*

RUSSIE, *married Ryan Canfield and had one child*

SEBE (LUCEBA), *after the death of her first husband, Howard, married Kirby Conway and had four children, Lloyd, Worthy, and Harry (from the first marriage) and Pauline*

OLIE, *married Martin Wilton and had six children*

BILLY-PEARL, *married Huston Curtiss II and had one child, Hughie*

EVA, *married John Weese and had eight children*

RHODA, *married Harry Baker and had three children*

LILLY (LILLIAN), *married Blake Coughenour, son of the widow Coughenour, no children*

CUBA, *married Bob Stern and had one child*

FAMILY FRIENDS

STANLEY BLACK, *taken in by Billy-Pearl and adopted by Peter Fancler; became Stella Fancler*

LESTER ADAMS, *sheriff, and longtime beau of Billy-Pearl's*

ROSE, *Helga, and Erica, the Dutch widows*

MR. AND MRS. RUFUS MILLER, *had six children, two older girls (unnamed), Raymond, Donald, Boobie, and Handsome*

TUBA, *Billy-Pearl's housekeeper and nursemaid to the Curtiss children*

MISS LARKIN, *a retired schoolteacher who comes to live and teach at Curtiss Farm*

LEONADIS ISAAC, *antiques dealer and close friend of Peter Fancler*

RED AND MRS. THORNE, *had four sons, the oldest boy (unnamed), John, and the twins, Richie and Lou*

Note: Some names have been changed to protect privacy.

Sins
of the
Seventh
Sister

A Note Before We Begin

Since settling in Santa Barbara, California, Stella had become the patron saint of the privileged class. The whole town turned out to celebrate her eightieth birthday. It was really her eighty-second, but I was probably the only person in the world who knew that, and I wasn't going to tell. She didn't sing, of course, hasn't for years. When you've been acclaimed the voice of the century, why muddy the waters?

Stella's birthday bash lasted three days. The beautiful, classic face of her youth was plastered on every shopwindow, and sound systems from every corner blared the grandest music of this lifetime, every leading soprano role in grand opera. She had performed them all and made them her own.

All this furor had brought publishers, and Stella called me to come and ghostwrite her story. I was good at it. I had brought practically every star in Hollywood to print, but this was my story, too, and I had never been willing to tell it, except to psychiatrists at a hundred dollars an hour.

Stella's mansion on a hill was actually north of Santa Barbara, in the Goleta Heights, where the really elite dwelled. She certainly didn't look eighty or eighty-two. Her face, over those high cheekbones, was as tight as ever, thanks to multiple plastic surgeries, and her amber eyes were still clear. I suppose the gold-red hair was a wig, but it looked exactly right. She was wearing a long purple robe with gold embroidery, probably a costume from one of her operas.

She came toward me, twirling the opera-length pearls that were her trademark, so I wouldn't miss them. And the memory train that runs through my head started getting up steam.

"We're getting old, Hughie."

"I know."

"After this, the whole damn world knows. It's dreadful to have your obituary composed before you're dead."

"But Stella, you've become a living legend, an icon for the musical world."

"Cut the shit, Hughie! What this has done is bring out publishers. I have three bids for my memoirs, and I want you to write them."

"Why would you want to do it?"

"The money, honey. I want to leave a big trust fund to educate orphan singers."

"The truth or fable?"

"The truth, and nothing but the truth."

"I'm not sure I can remember the truth. I've whitewashed it in my mind till it's mostly lost."

"Upstairs in my bedroom, I have a big blue rocking chair. Remember how I used to hold you in my lap when you were seven?"

"Both of us naked?"

"Both of us naked and smelling of Lifebuoy soap."

"And you bending down and sucking my little cock."

Stella smiled. "Do you still like it sucked?"

"It's been one of the pleasures of my lifetime. I'm grateful to you for introducing me to it."

"You see, you do remember more than you thought. I'll bet you even remember how to make apple butter."

"What a combination. Sex and apple butter and all those obsessions we had."

"Don't forget murder, Hughie."

"I suppose we can even tell about the murder. Everyone involved is dead now, except you and me." Stella put her arms around me, and we rocked back and forth as if we were in a blue rocking chair until I felt a stirring in my groin. "No one's called me Hughie for a long time."

"What does Helen call you?"

"Son of a bitch."

"That's unfair to your mother. She was the only true lady I ever knew. But you can't tell our story without admitting what a little shit you were."

I began to write Stella's story with what I thought was one of the best opening lines in American literature: "When I was ten, I took a straight razor and cut my father's throat as he lay in a drunken stupor over my mother's dead body." But then I threw it out.

I knew immediately there was no way to tell Stella's story without telling my own.

IN 1929 THE CURTISSES were still rich. Well, relatively rich anyway, compared to most of the other people who lived in the Appalachian Mountains of West Virginia. My father was heir apparent to the Curtiss money, as he was the only male. He had two sisters, who didn't count. I'm sure from the outside looking in, he seemed like the catch of the season: Huston Curtiss II, with Irish good looks, pale skin, blue eyes, and black curly hair. He and my mother made a beautiful couple; she was tall and had a sense of style about her, and that blond hair that all the Fancler girls had. Those Fancler girls were quite a show when they all got together. All ten of my mother's sisters served as her bridesmaids. People were still talking about that wedding ten years later—the year I was seven. I have to start there, for that year is the year Stella came.

My mother, Billy-Pearl Fancler, was daughter number seven of the reverend Peter Fancler and the last to marry because she insisted on finishing college. She had strange tastes for a girl who looked like she should model for Charles Dana Gibson. She loved horses and guns, and she was an expert in both; at twenty-one, she was the champion shot of West Virginia.

Horses have to be the reason she married my father, as there were two or three more desirable prospects in line. My father was a drunk from the age of seventeen, but the Curtisses still owned the best horse farm in the state, and it was only five miles outside of town from her father's church.

I was born at Curtiss Farm, Huston Curtiss III, and that cemented the marriage as far as the Curtisses were concerned. Now if my father drank himself to death, at least the line was secure. Drunkenness ran in the Curtiss family, and they were used to adjusting to it. My grandfather, Huston I, had a brother who fell off his horse one night in a drunken stupor and drowned in the mud in a rain-filled horseshoe track.

My mother turned out to be a pretty good farmer. She studied the horse business as she managed all 350 acres, and she taught horses to respond to the flick of a muscle in her beautiful long legs. Her only problem, aside from losing control of my father, was that we lived in a very large house. My mother had grown up in a large family, and she couldn't deal with all those empty rooms.

She went about gathering up people — that's how Stella came to us. Of course, she was Stanley then.

MY MOTHER'S FATHER was a preacher for sixty of his seventy-seven years. He was a circuit rider in his early days and rode to as many as twenty churches over the month, churches too poor to afford a preacher of their own. But even the twenty churches did not afford him a living for his expanding family. Before they were through, he and his wife produced eleven girls and not one boy. In his later years, he said the devil owed him a debt and paid him off in sons-in-law.

Grandfather Fancler had a good farm five miles from town and a house far enough up the hillside to escape the creek that flooded the flatlands each spring. Every year or so he would hire a portable sawmill to come into the edge of his forest and cut enough poplar and oak to add another room or two, as the girls kept coming.

When there were six daughters, he started praying for a son. He began to doubt the power of prayer when his seventh child was also a girl. Like many people in the hills, he believed seven was a mystic number and that a seventh child would have mystic powers. So when the midwife lay the red-faced bit of squalling humanity in his arms, he said, "If you really have mystic powers, you'll turn yourself into a boy."

The midwife, who had heard many strange things, ignored this. "What are you gonna name her?"

"I was going to name him William Abraham Fancler after my father, and call him Billy."

"You can still call her Billy."

But the new mother heard him and cried out, "I'm going to give her a proper name for a girl. We'll call her Pearl."

My grandfather refused to budge. "You can call her Pearl if you want, but I'm going to call her Billy."

So Billy-Pearl tried to serve both sides of her name. To please her father, she learned at an early age to hunt, to shoot a wild turkey without filling the breast full of buckshot, and to cut off a rattlesnake's head clean at the neck at twenty paces. She also learned to crochet, weave, and knit, but however well she did them, there was no pleasing her mother.

To please herself, Billy-Pearl learned to play the Irish harp and sing in a rich contralto. By the time she was ten, she rode a little Appaloosa mare behind her father's great black stallion when he visited his scattered chain of churches. Quite often, if it was spring and the area had been snowed in since fall, he would preach a man's funeral, marry the widow to some new man, and baptize their new baby. Billy-Pearl would play her harp and sing "Nearer, My God, to Thee." But already she had begun to think for herself, and much of her thinking concerned the existence of God. For what kind of God would let people lead such miserable lives?

My grandmother Fancler had been a tall woman, so they said, as tall as my mother, who was five feet ten, but now she was inches shorter. She said it was having all those babies. It seemed to have drained the very bones out of her to form theirs. She walked with her head thrust forward and her thin shoulders hunched. She spent most of her time in a rocking chair in a dark corner of the parlor, eating apples scraped out of their shell with a spoon. Most of the time her ill-fitting false teeth sat in a glass of water at her side, which scared me.

The other person who lived with us was our housekeeper, Tuba. She was very big and fat and very black. The flesh on her arms and under her chin hung in folds. Her teeth should have been white in that black face, but they were not, maybe because she always kept a pinch of snuff behind her upper lip. She hated me and was pleasant only in the presence of my mother. In private she said between her yellow teeth, "You gonna grow up to be no-good trash, jes' like your father." She'd raised my father, or tried to, but every time she had asserted any discipline, my father's permissive parents defeated her. She was determined not to let it happen again. She was always saying to my mother, "Miz Pearl, you bes' take a birch whip to that boy."

In the spring of '29, my parents' marriage was winding down. I'm sure my mother knew it. Later she would tell me that she had honestly meant to make my father her whole life, and when that wasn't possible, she shifted her attention to the farm. I think she lied; it was always the farm, the horses, and maybe her son, if I fell in line properly.

My father came home later and later, if he came home at all. It was only a matter of time. I knew exactly how he felt, for I was planning to run away, too, as soon as I saved enough money. I didn't want to become the hope of the Curtiss line any more than my father had. I kept an old rubber boot hidden in the corner of my closet, where I dropped every cent I could get my hands on, to finance my escape.

I don't think my mother worried about losing the farm when my father left, for she was very much in the good graces of her in-laws, especially my grandmother Curtiss. Grandmother Curtiss had social pretensions, and Billy-Pearl was the kind of daughter one needed for that game, not the two dowdy, plump things she was saddled with. Whatever looks were in her genes had gone to my father. Her daughters, Bea and Opal, looked more like Victorian parlor maids, with their rosy cheeks and black curly hair. Their dark looks gave weight to the rumor that maybe John Ferris, who was buried up in our family cemetery, and who was admittedly my grandfather Curtiss's father, was actually John Wilkes Booth.

Papa Curtiss hated that rumor about John Wilkes Booth, even though he knew he was a bastard and that the old general who adopted him was really his grandfather. He had given the grade school a big framed lithograph of Abraham Lincoln to hang in the front of every classroom, but that seemed to have backfired, and people took it as proof that the tale was true.

I used to sit in the classroom and look up at Lincoln's picture and wonder if my great-grandfather had shot him. I knew one thing: if my mother had done it, Lincoln never would have lived long enough to be dragged across the street to die.

I NEVER SAW my father sober. He began drinking before breakfast, the hair of the dog that bit him, stirred in a glass with a raw egg; at noon he'd be feeling better and would tell jokes at lunch, especially if we had girl cousins visiting. By four o'clock he knew better than to try to drive his beloved yellow Cord Roadster, and one of the farmhands would have to drive him the five miles to town and bring the car back.

I'm not too sure what my father was like between dinnertime and midnight, for he was seldom home. He would call and say he was having dinner at the Randolph Hotel. My mother would spend the evening reading to me or playing the piano, or rocking back and forth in a big morris chair, crocheting endless edgings for tablecloths and napkins and tea towels.

I learned to stay up late, to lie in my bed and listen, until I heard my father's taxi coming up the lane to our house. My mother would quickly run upstairs and get in her bed and pretend to be asleep. My father usually had trouble fitting his key in the front door, and I would go down and open it for him and hold out my hand for a quarter.

I still remember the smell of him: the Sen-Sen he hoped would disguise his alcoholic breath; the cologne that didn't quite cover the sweet perfume of the lady of the evening, whoever she was; the brilliantine he used on his dark black curls; and something else I was not able to identify at that age. A heavy, musky animal scent not too far removed from the smell of the horses in our stable when the breeders were guiding the enormous penis of the stallion into the waiting mare.

OUR HOUSE WAS very big and old. It had once been an overnight stop on the wagon freight route from Baltimore, Maryland, up over the Blue Ridge Mountains, into our valley and along the riverbanks that led to the Ohio River and floated down to whatever destination lay below. The body of the house was made of giant logs, two stories with a broad hallway running its length. It was started in 1808 and added to by each generation. Old General William Baker Curtiss, I suppose, was its most illustrious tenant; at least he was the biggest thief. When he returned from the Civil War, he brought home four hundred wagons loaded with ill-gotten booty, each wagon pulled by four mules. He truly believed "To the victor belong the spoils."

Old General William came home impressed with the great antebellum mansions of the South, with their tall columned porticoes, so he added a row of twelve great round columns two stories high, and he sheathed the log walls with white clapboard, so the whole house looked as if it had been transformed right up from the Natchez Trace.

Somewhere around the turn of the century, indoor plumbing was installed. Gasoline pumps were added to the wells and cesspools dug. Every other room was turned into a large and stylish bath. When my parents were given the country place, as it was known, my grandmother Curtiss had all the fixtures replaced with new colored porcelain ones. We had bathrooms of nine hues. In a country and a time when most rural families used outdoor toilets or privies, this was pretentious to the nth degree.

The first fall when I went to school, there was a joke that went around the school bus: "Do you know why them Curtisses need nine bathrooms?"

"No, why?"

"Because they're so full of shit."

IN THE SUMMER OF 1929, all the talk was of "get rich quick." Even in our Appalachian town, stock tips were the subject of the day. Dairy farmers, potato growers, and moonshine makers passed on the latest inside tip. Buy as much as you can, 10 percent down, the rest on margin. Andrew Mellon is head of the federal bank, and he's buying it. Herbert Hoover says we have nowhere to go but up.

My father's father, Papa Curtiss, had eight different businesses, and HUSTON CURTISS & SON was plastered all over everything in big gold letters, but I didn't love him. I didn't even like him, except as a source of money and gifts. He was fat, round and fat, and with the least exertion he huffed; he also had asthma. I took the quarters and occasional silver dollars that he gave me and dropped them in the rubber boot in my closet, adding to my private wealth.

When my mother married into the Curtiss family, her mother-in-law shepherded her into various charitable organizations. It was the duty of the privileged class to see that the less fortunate were cared for. My mother was welcomed by the men because she was pretty, and by the female contingency because she was a well-known minister's daughter and sure to take the moral high road. But this was not always the case.

May 10, 1929
My Journal Begins*

ONE EVENING EARLY in the summer, conversation was going around Grandmother Curtiss's dinner table, as it was wont to do. Earlier dinner conversations had turned into yelling matches, with each person talking louder than the last and sometimes pounding the table. As there were always at least twelve of us at the table on Friday nights, it made quite a clamor. So my grandmother had instituted new rules.

Starting with Papa Curtiss, each person got his chance to tell what he had done in the previous week, followed by a short question-and-answer period, before the attention moved on to the next person. Papa Curtiss sat at the end of the table with his chair pushed back to make room for his expanding girth. He liked the look of my mother in the candlelight, with her long, thin patrician neck and her head crowned by a massive braid of golden hair. It had never been cut.

Papa Curtiss spoke of the wisdom of converting all our liquid assets into stock, and he named the stock of the moment. Then he made a little "humph" that meant "The master has spoken," and he nodded to my mother, giving her the floor. But tonight my mother seemed hesitant to speak. She hemmed and hawed, which was unusual for her, and we all pretended not to notice. Finally she said, "I'll stand up. I want you all to hear me." By now she had everyone's

---

* In the spring of the year when I was seven, my grandfather gave me a journal and pointed out how important it was to keep a record of the events of your life. I had learned to write when I was four, so writing for me was easy. I began with my name, Huston C. Curtiss, and the date, May 10, 1929. I didn't write every day, lots of days go by with nothing interesting at all, but I did keep at it pretty well for the year, and then off and on for several more years. I kept it hidden in the rubber boot in my closet and told no one about it until now. So when I decided to write about the beginning of my life with Stella, I had this record to jog my memory.

full attention, even that of my father, who was on his third glass of wine, in spite of my grandmother's disapproving looks.

"As you know, I've been spending Friday afternoons at the county orphanage." My grandmother nodded her approval. "The school year's almost over, and the state doesn't educate children beyond their sixteenth year. Then it pushes them out to the waiting vultures." My mother was given to dramatic turns of phrase.

Here my grandmother interrupted, disobeying her own rule. "You're not going to ask me to take in another of those children. I've already got one of your girls in my kitchen and a boy delivering for the store."

Papa Curtiss echoed, "No more; enough!"

"Let me go on. This year there are six children too old to stay according to that dreadful state law, which should be changed." Here she looked directly at our county judge, Judge Brown, who was tonight's guest of honor. My mother became more resolute and raised her voice, which was unnecessary since it carried like a deep-toned bell. "There's a boy, I'm sure you'll recognize his name: Stanley Black. He's sixteen, and I'm going to take him home."

There was dead silence. Judge Brown was the first to recover; nothing shocked him anymore. "Isn't he the kid who killed his father?"

My mother's voice now turned from a bell to a very sharp knife. "You know very well he went through your court. At the hearing, he was never even accused. He was just a ten-year-old unlucky enough to be in the room when his father stabbed his mother and then killed himself."

Now it was just my mother and Judge Brown. "The sheriff said the kid had blood all over him." It was an unfortunate time to mention blood, as Matthew's knife was just then cutting through the rare beef roast.

"Your inquest decreed that Stanley's father killed himself."

Judge Brown shrugged. "It was the easiest thing to do. What are you going to do with a ten-year-old boy, send him to the electric chair?"

My father was now unpleasantly drunk and ignored everyone but my mother. "You might have talked to me about this."

"I need someone to help train the horses for Lexington." My mother seemed to be talking to herself. "You know Zeke and Hannibal aren't up to the job."

"And I suppose I'm not?" My father's slurred words could hardly reach the far end of the table. Grandmother Curtiss pulled him back into his seat and emptied his wineglass into the floral arrangement.

"We'll talk about it on the way home." My mother helped herself to the green beans and began to cut her meat. "Assuming you're coming home tonight."

"Who's running the farm, anyway?" My father was now belligerent. My mother went on chewing her green beans.

My grandmother leaned close to my father's ear. Her lips were pulled back, and I thought she was going to bite him. "You know very well that Billy-Pearl runs that farm while you chase every whore in the county. Now, sit down and be still or leave my table." She turned back to her guests and smiled, patting the sides of her shining black hair. "I had my hair bobbed today, and not one of you said a thing." A murmur of belated compliments went around the table. "I want to look like the times and not some old fuddy-duddy, and the next time you see me, I'm going to have horn-rimmed glasses." She turned to her younger half brother, my great-uncle Alvin, for help.

Alvin had been trained by an expert to pick up the social ball. "It's just what you need to set off your raven hair." Smiling, he gave the whole table the benefit of his charm. "I've decided to have my portrait painted."

My Aunt Opal's specialty was needling Alvin. "What a surprise. Do you think there's enough gold paint in town to do it?"

For just a moment I thought everyone at the table was angry with him, jealous because he really was golden: golden hair, golden skin, golden eyes.

"I'm going to have Eddie Horner do it. He's quite good."

Papa Curtiss sputtered until the bloody beef juices ran down his chin. "I've heard he's a fairy."

Alvin kept his tone level. "His personal sex habits have nothing to do with his ability as a painter. After all, I'm not going to sleep with him. You should have him do your portrait, Billy, you'd make a beautiful subject." My mother only smiled. I knew why he admired her: it was a kind of ego, since she was golden-haired like he was, and everyone else at the table was dark-haired except for me and Aunt Emma. Emma was Alvin's sister, but she didn't count, for she was a ghost of a woman. Their mother must have saved up her color for her golden boy, for Emma had none at all. She was albino, completely white, with no pigment in her hair or skin. Even the long sweep of her lashes was white, framing the kind of blue in her eyes that you could paint with watercolors only if you added a great deal of water. Emma never went out, except for these Friday night dinners. She was afraid of the sidewalks and the streets and would not have come even here, except that she and Alvin lived in a great house on Park Avenue, back to back with the Curtiss house, and she could come through the orchard they shared.

Now my grandmother smiled at me. "Hughie." (I was Hughie, my father was Hugh, and my grandfather was Huston, so we didn't have to be one, two, and three.) "Would you like to tell us what you did this week?"

I felt my father's sudden apprehension, for quite often my recitals involved him. I stood up. It was my moment. "Yesterday I went swimming down at the cement bridge with four of my cousins." (My father was alert now, reaching for his money clip.) "We were all up on the bridge, lookin' down, when here comes a boat, just drifting, and guess who was in it?"

Opal looked impatient. "Tell us, Hughie. This isn't a guessing game."

My father was showing the corner of a dollar bill in his vest pocket. "It was Sylvia Tingler—all by herself, floating down the river."

My grandmother said, "I don't want that woman's name spoken at this table!"

I sat down. The strawberry tarts were being served. I could still feel the shame of the day before. My cousins were all lined up at the bridge rail when the boat floated under the bridge, and it was my father stretched out with his pants down, his white butt going up and down as he thrust himself into the fat, spread-eagled Sylvia Tingler. It was worth more than a dollar to keep still about that, and I knew it. I would collect later.

Alvin and Emma always left right after dinner. Emma began to feel afraid if she was away from home too long. Grandmother watched them go out through the kitchen and take the path through the orchard. They were her father's children, and yet she felt no kinship. She had never understood or liked her stepmother, who had always seemed removed, with her German accent, her pale coloring, and the vast amount of money and things, rooms and rooms of things that she brought with her. Now her stepmother was dead, and her father was gone, and these two otherworldly beings walked through the rooms like museum pieces moving through their gilded setting.

My father had had two more glasses of wine in spite of his mother and had gone to pass out on a couch in the foyer.

My grandmother Virginia did her hostess duties sitting on her green velvet recamier. She poured the after-dinner coffee from a silver pot shaped like a melon into thin little demitasse cups the size of eggshells. With it were thimble-size goblets of cognac. Billy-Pearl sat in a claret-red velvet wing chair, with the light from a Tiffany-shaded lamp falling on her in splotches of soft color. Her mother-in-law said to her, "Pearl, you really should have your portrait painted. You're quite beautiful, you know, and it doesn't last." She ran her hand along the line of her jaw, not quite as firm as it had been.

Pearl drank her liqueur and held the glass before her and studied the way the light refracted through the cut glass. She knew the social graces well enough, and she truly liked Virginia, it wasn't a sham. "We are a mutual admiration society, you and I. I was just sitting here thinking how becoming your new cut is to you. But I would like to see the sides swept back like raven's wings, to accent your eyes."

"I'll try—tomorrow."

Bea and Opal had gone into the music room, their two dark heads close together at the piano. They were practicing a two-handed rendition of "I Wish That I Could Shimmy Like My Sister Kate." They did not really like their beautiful blond sister-in-law and did not understand their mother's attraction to her, any more than they understood the worship of the "crown prince," their younger brother, my father, Hugh. They were four and five when he was born, and they were ignored in the hullabaloo over the family heir. They crept into the nursery, newly painted blue, and over to the polished brass crib.

Little Hugh was sleeping soundly and did not wake when they unpinned his diaper and examined the part that set him apart from them. That little thing sticking out of the front of him was no bigger than their little finger. Surely it couldn't make as much difference as all that. They would just get the scissors and snip that little thing off—then they would all receive equal amounts of love! They were about to carry out the deed when Tuba caught them. She took one under each of her fat arms and went to the kitchen. They were sure their little bottoms were going to be smacked with the pancake turner, but instead they were each given a bowl of fresh-picked raspberries and cream, and a warm sugar cookie.

JUDGE BROWN'S WIFE'S NAME was Daisy. She was seventy-two years old and looked every day of it. Grandmother knew her age because it had been in the church bulletin last Sunday: "Mrs. Hiram Brown was seventy-two on the 12th. Happy birthday, Mrs. Brown!"

No happy birthday, Daisy. It was as though she belonged tooth and bone to that arrogant, despicable man and couldn't even have her own first name.

Grandmother had objected to inviting him to her table, but Grandfather had said, "You never know when you're going to need a politician in power. And he does have power."

"A crooked politician, you mean?"

"Is there any other kind?"

Now Daisy sat in the middle of the couch, her voluminous pale pink dress spread out around her, as though she wanted everyone to see the large bulge over her stomach and that Cheshire cat smile. When Virginia handed her the cognac goblet, she said, "I better not." And continued to smile and pat her stomach.

"Dear Daisy, let me wish you a belated happy birthday. I read it in the church bulletin."

"Thank you. I was in hopes the little one would come on my birthday, but he's as stubborn as his daddy. I was twenty-four, you know, the perfect age to become a mother: not too soon, not too late."

Her hands made wavering motions through the air as though rocking a baby. Virginia and Pearl exchanged questioning glances with their eyebrows raised.

All the guests were leaving, and Virginia was bidding them good night at the door. Pearl was carrying Hughie out to the car, leaving Hugh to sleep fitfully. Daisy had skipped on across the portico. Virginia took Judge Brown's hand and smiled. "Judge, it looks like you are going to have to send Daisy down to Weston. She's nutty as a fruitcake, you know."*

Now the judge stared at her. Her teeth were too even and too white for a woman her age. Virginia continued walking with him to the steps, taking his arm as though concerned.

"It will be easy for you, after all the poor souls you have had committed to that place."

---

* Weston was the state hospital for the insane. It was a great gray stone pile, looking more like a prison than a hospital. It had bars on all the windows and a very high stone wall. It was the ideal place to permanently get rid of the old and unwanted. It was even better having them die there, as the state paid for the casket and the pauper's grave.

MAY 13, 1929

STANLEY BLACK CAME the next Monday. I waited at home because my mother wanted to stop by the cash grocery to buy him some clothes. The orphanage allowed children to leave in only the clothes they were wearing. I had expected a boy—my mother kept saying "that boy," maybe even a playmate—but he wasn't exactly a man, either, caught somewhere in between. He was tall, as tall as my mother, and very thin. He was a frightened colt, like the two-year-olds when they get off the truck down in Lexington and are herded toward the auction barns.

He was of a color I had never seen on another human being. My first thought was, He looks like a maple tree. He was rust and orange. His long hair was the color of the inside of an old tin can, and what you could see of his skin was blotched with bright freckles as big as thumbprints. The whole effect was aided by what was obviously a new shirt in bright orange. The pants were gray, with many ragged patches, but his shoes were new.

I watched from the porch and did not run toward my mother as I usually did, trying to outrun the dogs. Today they had a clear field, and six or seven ran to greet her. Stanley stood frozen and raised his hands over his head to keep them from being bitten. I could see my mother explaining that all our hounds were friendly, and Stanley slowly lowered his hands and allowed them to be licked, and then he wiped them hard on his pant legs.

My mother was unloading several packages from her car. Since there was the possibility she brought me something, I ran to them. Before I could ask, she said, "Yes, I bought you a Babe Ruth baseball cap." She extracted it from a bag and plunked it on my head; it came down over my ears. Up close, Stanley looked even more strange.

"This is my ill-mannered son, Hughie. Hughie, shake hands with Stanley."

Stanley seemed reluctant to proffer his hand, so I took it and gave him a good shake and began the speech we had rehearsed: "Hello, Stanley, and welcome to our home. I hope you will be happy here."

Stanley looked confused, and his voice was a hoarse whisper. "Happy? I didn't know I came here to be happy; I thought I came to work."

My mother looked startled. "Weren't you happy at the home?"

"Happy was not what the home was for. We were there because no one in the world wanted us. And the generous state of West Virginia had taken us in so we wouldn't freeze to death and starve to death."

He said it as if by rote. My mother studied his face for a second. "You sound as though you were reciting. Were you told to say that?"

"We said it every morning with the morning prayers, before we got oatmeal, at exactly ten till six."

Under her breath, my mother said, "Those bastards!" She became artificially gay and buoyant. She called out, "Tuba, come see who has come to live with us. I hope you have a good lunch ready, we're all starved."

Tuba was standing behind the screen door. "Yes'um, I can see and hear without you yellin' at me, and you know we eat lunch at twelve o'clock. It's twenty till." She was holding the door open. My mother passed in, dropping the boxes. Stanley stared first at the long row of mammoth white columns and then, unbelievingly, at the mountain of black flesh that was Tuba.

My mother was chatting on in a way that seemed most unreal for her. "Tuba, this is Stanley. And you know we don't run our house by the clock; we can have lunch at twelve, or ten till, or two, for that matter."

Tuba was staring back at Stanley as though memorizing him. "How am I going to know when to put it on if I don't know when to take it off?"

"I'll just have time to take up the waist of a pair of pants for you. I am sure you will be glad to see the last of those rags they gave you. Hughie, show Stanley where the powder room is."

I could read the confused emotions that flooded his face like a picture book. I led the way down the hall to the toilet beneath the stairs. He moved slowly, trying to take everything in and looking at the open doors as we passed the various rooms.

"She thinks you might want to powder your nose." We were at the door. I switched on the chandelier. (My mother had gotten pretentious.) He stared at himself in the wall of mirrors. "I'm just kiddin'. This is where you pee and wash your hands."

He went behind the screen and used the toilet. At least he knew how to flush it. He made a great to-do about washing; he rolled up his sleeves and heavily sudsed the soap. He soaped twice and rinsed twice. To me, who usually just wet the tips of my fingers and shook them off, all this washing seemed excessive. He faced a dilemma of what to dry on, his new shirt or his old dirty pants. I let him off the hook and pointed out the neat rack of linen with embroidered blue flowers and lace edging. "They're guest towels."

"I'm not a guest. I've come to work."

"Dry your hands, then put the towel in that basket, and I will show you your room."

On the way down the hall to the servants' stairs, we passed the sewing room. Already my mother was treadling the foot pedal of her machine and stitching Stanley's pants. The voices of my mother and Tuba rose over the clamor. I motioned Stanley to stop.

I saw the objection coming on his face and whispered, "Be still and listen. It's the only way you're gonna know what's going on. I do it all the time."

My mother was saying, "I couldn't buy him pants that were long enough, with a waist that was twenty-seven inches."

"I thought he was gonna be more of a man."

"He's undernourished. With your good cooking, you'll see a difference right away."

"He looks like a girl."

"We will get him a haircut when we go shopping tomorrow."

"Zeke and Hannibal gonna think he looks like a girl, too. You can't put him to sleep up there near them two. Why, when they first come here, they thought they was gonna pop into bed with me, till I showed 'em my fists and the flat-iron I keep under my bed. Still, I had to empty my chamber pot right over that Zeke's head one night."

"Tuba, why didn't you tell me? It's dreadful not to know what's going on in your own house."

"You didn't need to know till now. I don't know how you keeps the business of this place straight, the way it is."

"What am I going to do with him? I could put him in that blue room next to Hughie."

"No, ma'am, I wouldn't do that either, till we know more about him."

I guided Stanley into the front parlor, with all its chairs looking toward the mantel and the portrait of General William Baker Curtiss. I was explaining how my great-great-grandfather had single-handedly won the War Between the States for the North.

"Well, not quite," my mother said as she handed Stanley his new pants. "Go down to the powder room and put them on. We will throw those rags you're wearing into the trash, and then we will eat. I'm starved. We will all eat two plates of everything."

I wondered whether she would put Stanley at our dining room table. After all, he was hired help. When my father was here, he ate at one end, my mother at the other, and I in the middle of the polished mahogany board. We were too far apart to pass anything, so Tuba served. When my father was gone, which lately was most of the time, I sat in his place.

Tuba solved the immediate problem by serving us at the harvest table in the kitchen, where we never would have eaten if Zeke and Hannibal had been there, for they ate badly, talking with food in their mouths and dipping bread in everything. Tuba threatened to put their food in one big bowl with a wooden spoon and slop them like hogs.

The two of them had gone up to the high meadow about a mile up the mountainside, where we grazed the summer sheep. They were going to help Uncle Billie, who lived up there in the summer and, with his dog, shepherded the flock of maturing lambs. They castrated the young rams before their hormones got to work and they started butting each other's heads. Tuba hated this day, for the men always brought back a bucket of bloody testicles to be fried.

Over lunch Tuba declared, "I ain't gonna do it, I ain't fryin' no more of them mountain oysters!"

My mother said, "Don't worry. I sent up a big iron skillet, some lard, some eggs, and some cornmeal to Uncle Billie, with a note to fry the oysters up there."

Tuba looked confused. "You sent Uncle Billie a note? Ain't you forgettin' he can't read?"

"Lord help me, I did! When I remake the world, I'm going to make sure everyone can read and write."

We had a bigger lunch than usual, finished off with sponge cake and wild strawberries, then Tuba set a big bowl of bread pudding, covered with her cream and thick with honey, in front of Stanley. "Miz Pearl and Hughie had theirs last night. Why don't you just help finish this puddin' up so I can wash the bowl?"

My mother's eyes told me to behave myself and look away as he wolfed it down.

After lunch my mother and I took Stanley to the barn to continue his orientation. The barn was my favorite place on the farm; later in life, when I saw the cathedrals of Europe, I remembered our barn.

There was a tall silo against the barn, like a bell tower. I would not have been surprised to see Quasimodo stick his head out of the upper door. The odor of silage curing permeated the barn. There was a chain and a hoist that dumped a mixture of green cornhusks, hay, and grain. The generated heat preserved it, so in winter you could fork out animal feed from the bottom door that seemed to have retained its tender green of summer.

The guided tour left Stanley confused. He could hide nothing, every thought seemed to wash across his face. And I watched him and read him every moment.

The front of the barn behind the rolling doors was reserved for the cars. My father's yellow Cord, which was hardly ever there anymore; my mother's old Jewett touring car; a big farm truck with a crib around the bed; a tractor; and beyond that, in the strange half-light, all the equipment: mowers, harvesters, thrashers, and all the paraphernalia to run a large farm that specialized in raising horses. We had three hundred acres of bottomland, plus the hillside meadows and the use of the government parkland up on the plateau.

My father believed in keeping everything in near-new condition, and everything was sprayed with orange enamel so you would recognize immediately that this was a Curtiss possession. My mother had worked out a system of loaning our machinery to farmers less well equipped, in exchange for labor.

The heavy notched and fitted beams that supported the rafters, sixty feet above the floor, had been hand-carved by artisans one hundred years before. The barn at first seemed silent, the way a church is silent. But if you stood still, you'd hear a whole orchestra of sounds: the soft rustle of mice in the corncrib, the accompanying slither of a big brown house snake as he made his way to catch his mouse dinner, if he could get there before one of the cats. There were many cats. They were fed big bowls of warm milk from the milking machine, morning and night. They were all friendly, and purred as they circled you, and mewed when they realized it wasn't milking time yet. There were birds: barn swallows that swooped back and forth over your head, and the pigeons, the loudest of all, parading on the upper beams. Then there were the solo singers, privileged prima donnas, Ruth and Naomi, two dark red hens with long, iridescent back feathers that dragged on the ground. They were mother and daughter, fat and too old for the pot. My mother had named them because they were gleaners, walking behind the threshing machine for grain, or behind the plow for newly exposed worms and grubs. They hid their nests and laid twenty-one eggs that didn't hatch, as the white Leghorn cocks were kept in pens and could not fertilize them. In late summer, I would spy on Ruth and Naomi until I found their nests, at which point the eggs were rotten. I put them away, as rotten eggs were very useful around Halloween.

In the tack room, the brass lights were all shaded with dark green glass. A table in the center held several leather-bound books with the breeding records.

The Chippendale desk in the corner was for the buyer to sit down and write his check. Saddles and bridles hung on racks along the walls. It took Stanley a little while to get used to the subdued light. My mother waited a minute, then spread her arms and turned.

"This is the center of our horse business. This is the heart and the brain. It is not an easy business, but it is marvelously rewarding. There is nothing more delightful in the world than the sight of a sun-dappled colt running against the wind through the meadow. My husband used to help me here, but he is no longer interested, and if no one is, I will have nothing to hand over to Hughie when the time comes."

Stanley fingered the soft leather and the glazed edge of the gleaming table. My mother put her head down, as though what she was about to say was her fault.

"My husband used to love all this, or I thought he did, but he no longer does. I am in hopes you will learn to be of help to me."

Some other woman might have touched him on the hand reassuringly, but my mother was not a "toucher." Some other boy might have been reassured by the touch, but Stanley would have looked for the first opportunity to wash his hands.

My mother was turning the pages of the current records. "Right now we have sixteen mares, two stallions, and ten two-year-olds overdue to be broken to the bridle and the saddle. I always hate to bring them in from the meadow. It's like the end of childhood, and a life of earning your keep begins. We also have four geldings."

Stanley looked confused. "Horses?"

"Horses that have been castrated for some reason or other. They're gentled, we use them for riding here on the farm." Stanley's face was blank, but my mother didn't notice. "Well, Stanley, what do you think so far?"

He struggled to find an answer. I thought he might cry. "Yesterday in the orphanage I was hungry and dirty, dressed in rags and shoveling shit out of the hog pens, and here I am today standing in the swellest barn I ever saw. I have new clothes on, and I ate like a pig until I thought I would burst. I think I'm gonna wake up in a minute and be back there."

"You are not going back there." She was starting up a spiral stairway, a fancy filigree of iron that led through a round opening in the ceiling. "Come on, and I will show you my folly." Stanley and I climbed after her. "This little apartment was used to sleep the carriage drivers in the past, when people came here in carriages to see the horses. I'm afraid I went overboard—an amateur decorator gone mad."

This room was very different from the dark, somber room below. It was like the sun shining in a mirror. The ceiling beams were a pale yellow, and the walls were as bright as yellow comes. Every color from a watercolor box was here on the desk, table, bed, and chairs, all flooded with light from a giant, round window and several little square ones high on the wall, next to the ceiling.

Stanley was staring at the carpet as though he didn't believe it. It was the same color of orange as his shirt. My mother saw him comparing them in amazement. "It looks like we have the same taste for orange. I ordered this carpet from Pittsburgh. No one in Elkins would stock this color."

"It's beautiful."

I had gone to rock in the big blue rocker at the end of the room. I liked this chair. I liked to rock, and this chair was so big and heavy that once you got it in motion, it would rock with just a slight shifting of weight, since my feet wouldn't touch the floor.

Stanley was looking at the bathroom. It had a big white tub on legs and a yellow-tiled shower. The toilet was discreetly placed around the corner.

I felt it was time for a comment from me; it had been too long. I got up and walked over to him. "I like yellow tile. Most of the bathrooms in our house are covered puke pink."

"Hughie."

"Well, they are. They are just the color of throw-up when you eat too much watermelon."

My mother went over and sat in the blue rocker. If Stanley hadn't been here, I would have gone and climbed in her lap. Maybe she would forget that I was a big boy of seven and rock me.

Stanley went and stood before my mother. "Ma'am, would you consider letting me sleep out here?"

She began to rock gently, looking at him, studying him. Their eyes held. "But won't you be afraid here in the barn, all by yourself?"

"It would be nice to be by myself. I never have been. Until my mother died, we lived, seven of us, in a space half this size."

"I had not heard you had brothers and sisters."

"Oh yes. My little brother Tubby, a woman came in a Model T and took him the first day—after—after—he was cute. And my two sisters were eight and nine. A woman came and said she was our cousin and took them. I don't

think she was—she was black. My brother Elmer went into the navy the day
he was fifteen, that was the day my father beat him up and threw him out the
door. I forgot about the time I was in the county hospital. I had a room to myself
for two days."

"When were you in the hospital?"

"Right after the inquest. They did to me what you do to the horses—the
geldings."

My mother stopped rocking and shoved the chair back until it hit the wall.
"You mean they castrated you? Those sons of bitches!"

"Judge Brown said I could go to prison with the other killers, or reform
school. He said they were tough on pretty boys there. Or I could get fixed so
it took the killer out of me, and go to the orphanage until I was sixteen. But no
one would adopt me—who wants someone who killed his father? Even if the
father had choked the mother to death and was lying on her dead body. And I
didn't say I killed him."

"I don't want you ever to tell me whether you killed him or not. I'll tell you
one thing, if I had been there, I would have killed him. And I'm not sure I may
not just go into town and kill Judge Brown."

JUNE 1, 1929

WE HAD A PAIR of celebrities in our town. They came presold, as their pictures were plastered on the sides of barns and fences all over the county before
they arrived. COLE BROTHERS CIRCUS AND FREAK SHOW. ONE DAY ONLY.
There was a picture, twelve feet high, of two exotic-looking Oriental girls joined
at the hip, four legs in purple stockings but one pink ruffled skirt going around
the middle of them, as though they had a common waist. Their faces glowed,
golden and almond-eyed, under a great puff of black hair. Under their picture
was a line that read: THE MOST BEAUTIFUL SIAMESE TWINS IN THE WORLD.
They were given more space than the largest horse in the world, the black tiger,
and the twenty-foot snake.

My mother didn't like freak shows, so I was allowed to spend the night with
three boy cousins, Aunt Sebe's boys, who lived in town. Lloyd was almost fourteen and was supposed to look out for us younger ones. Lloyd liked having me

as a guest; that meant my mother would return the hospitality and invite him for a weekend. His brothers were eight and ten, and they had new books of dirty pictures every time they came: Betty Boop being fucked by the old man of the mountain and pictures of Popeye with what looked like a third leg.

I would have skipped the freak show. I, like my mother, was put off by two-headed babies preserved in a giant pickle jar. I would have gone on to the big top and the main event, but one ticket covered all, and Lloyd was determined to get his money's worth. "You'll like it, Hughie. They got a fat woman here with tits as big as watermelons."

I still remembered the year before, when Lloyd had held me up and made me look at the geek. I had been sick to my stomach and was determined not to repeat that experience, because I had vomited on my cotton candy.

We saw the India-rubber man, a strange, elongated, elastic creature who could roll himself into a ball until his head was between his legs and he was staring at his own butt. I couldn't see what good that would do you. He seemed mad to me, wide-eyed and mumbling, "They've got syphilis—both of them."

Lloyd had caught his words and leaned close. "Who has?"

"Them Siamese twins, only they ain't."

Lloyd was nothing if not persistent. "Ain't what?"

Lloyd's brothers, Harry and Worthy, hardly ever said anything—Lloyd wouldn't let them—but now Harry leaned against my ear and whispered, "He farted in his own face."

Now the man was annoyed, or maybe he was just tired of looking at his own butt. "Go 'way, boy. You bother me."

He began to unfold, and we moved on to the geek. The geek was down in a big canvas net that was deeper than my head. But Lloyd grabbed me around the middle and lifted me up to look. He knew I didn't want to see. He thought I lived a privileged life and was always trying to bring me down. I closed my eyes.

"Better open your eyes, a snake'll bite you."

I opened my eyes and looked and couldn't seem to close them again. At the bottom of the canvas sat what had once been a man but now was a geek—a creature held in the lowest esteem of any member of a traveling show. It was thought that a show with a geek would have bad luck.

He was surrounded by snakes. He would grab a handful and throw them into the air. He wore only a dirty loincloth, and you could see dozens of twin red marks that seemed to be fang marks.

The spieler was yelling over the sounds of the tent canvas, which was whipping back and forth in a sudden wind. "And now, ladies and gentlemen" (there were no ladies present that I could see), "our geek will take his life in his hands. His life is just as dear to him as yours is to you. He will, right before your eyes, thrust a poison viper—its head—into his own mouth for your entertainment."

I did not feel I wanted to be entertained by a poison viper, so I shut my eyes tight.

"He's done something for you, now you do a little something for him. You have a little loose change, I can hear it rattling in your pockets—throw it down to him, sitting there in his nest of vipers. The truth of it is, he's a drunk. It's the only way you can do this kind of job, is stay soused; he'll need a bottle to see him through the night."

There was some rattling of coins, probably pennies.

"I thank you for him. You see, once when he was doing this stunt with the viper, that evil product of the devil bit his tongue off!"

I let a dime that I had been holding in my hand slide down the canvas. I saw a big blue snake with a yellow belly eye the coin.

"And now, gentlemen, because of your generosity, our geek is going to do something very special. He is going to bite off the head of a live chicken."

"Lloyd, I want to go."

"No, we paid our money, and we are gonna see the show."

He did let me slide to where my feet were on the ground and I couldn't see over. I saw a squawkin' white chicken, fryer-size, passed over my head and thrown down into the mess. There was a scream from the chicken, a crunching sound. Then an involuntary nauseous gulp from the audience as the bloody head was thrown out, and landed in the sawdust at my feet.

The manager of my grandfather's Bluebird Market had come out to our farm this morning and picked up one hundred eight-week-old Leghorn fryers; I wondered if this was one of our chickens.

The spieler had moved to the next platform. The backdrop was a painting on canvas, like the famous poster of the Siamese twins. With a pounding of bass drums and an exotic strain from a flute, the Siamese twins were suddenly onstage—four legs in purple stockings, four arms waving like snakes, two heads, and one middle covered with a pink tutu.

I was disappointed; I had expected them to be ten feet tall, like their poster. They were barely five, and they looked like two children in dress-up.

The spieler was yelling his lies through a megaphone, saying they were daughters of the king of Siam and describing the horror of their birth, when they had to be cut from their mother's belly, ending her life.

A man in the back of the tent called, "How old are them girls?"

"Fourteen, sir. Just coming into the first blush of young womanhood."

Lloyd was just behind me and whispered, "They sure got funny-looking tits. They look like bananas."

With greater authority in his voice, the man in the back said, "There is a law in this state that you can't work until you're sixteen."

The spieler was flustered for only a moment. "Sir, when I said fourteen, I meant fourteen by the Muslim calendar. I can tell that you, sir, are Christian as I am, and by the Christian calendar, these little princesses are sixteen. Born on Christmas Day they were—the same day as our blessed Savior."

I do admire a man who could think on his feet, and I added "carnival spieler" to the list of things I might be when I grew up. At a signal from Lloyd, Harry and Worthy got on each side of me and propelled me toward the exit. "I don't want to go. I haven't seen the black tiger yet."

Worthy moved fast and talked fast. He knew something I didn't. "Everything in this place is a fake. It's probably a plain old white tiger someone dyed with shoe dye."

We looked back to see Lloyd putting his hands to his mouth like a megaphone and yelling "Fire! Fire!"

"Fire" is the most dreaded word in the circus world. It brings immediate panic to animals and people alike, so they trample each other to death. The wind in the canvas was making loud crackling noises, so the two or three hundred people in the main tent did not hear the alarm.

The spieler was yelling, "Easy, folks. There's no danger. Just move out in an orderly fashion. No need to panic."

But the Siamese twins were not listening; panic was clearly written on their faces. One was looking right and one left, and so they broke and ran. The pink skirt came apart and clung to the one going right. The one going left wore nothing but the broad piece of adhesive tape that had bound them into being Siamese twins.

Lloyd grabbed ahold of us and shoved us into the shadows behind the tent. We were stooping down to look under the tent flap and see what panic this knavery had wrought when a hand reached down and grasped Lloyd by the neck and jerked him upright. We were pushed into the light to find ourselves in the hands of Sheriff Lester Adams and his cross-eyed deputy.

I was relieved until I saw how red Lester's face was. He was a friend of my mother's and came to our house occasionally, but from the look of him, that was not going to save me.

"Do you know what you might have done?" He had Lloyd by the shoulders and was shaking him until his head bobbed back and forth like a fishing float.

Lloyd was protesting, "Nobody got hurt."

"You stupid little jackass, you might have killed dozens!" Lester suddenly became aware of what he was doing and dropped Lloyd to the ground. He looked around at me. "You know, Hughie, I'll have to tell your mother about this."

"You'll just make her feel worse. She's having a lot of trouble with my daddy just—"

"Yeah, I guess so. Now, get home, all of you."

And I knew I was off the hook. I thought I just might learn to be a carnival spieler. I was pretty good on my feet.

The next day the circus was gone, leaving nothing behind but piles of elephant shit and the fake Siamese twins. There was a disclaimer and an apology in the Elkins Inter-Mountain newspaper, for the circus planned to come back next year, and they weren't burning any bridges. It was on the front page with black lines around it. The manager swore he had no knowledge that his famed twins were just two girls pasted together, and next year, when the circus played this—their favorite—town, he would have a "gen-u-wine" set of Siamese twins, and a doctor from our town could examine them.

It seemed the king of Siam was more prolific than we had been led to believe.

Worthy called me on the telephone at home and told me the Siamese twins, who were now called the gold-dust twins for the sparkle they sprinkled in their hair, had rented rooms in the alley behind Mr. Chang's Chinese laundry. It was logical they should band together, since they were the only Orientals in our town. They were working in the laundry, ironing.

They told tales of being sold into the circus life in something they called "white slavery." But it seemed to me, if it was anything, it would have to be yellow slavery.

Sylvia Tingler also worked for Mr. Chang, and I wondered how she liked the competition. She must not, for the next week she quit and went to work at the Dew-Drop Inn.

∽

MY MOTHER WAS a crack shot with a rifle or a pistol; she had learned to please my grandfather. But it was not just to please her father that she went to every shooting match she could, and won. She liked excelling. One cynic had said, presenting her the cup, "You're the best man here."

She would not be insulted. After all, wasn't that what her father had always wanted? And you could not look at her standing there, the rifle in one hand and her silver cup in the other, tendrils of her golden hair blowing about her face, and think masculine. She was Diana at the hunt.

I was angry at Stanley now most of the time. It seemed to me he was moving into places that were reserved for when I got older. But I was Machiavellian and continued to smile most of the time. Zeke and Hannibal disliked him, too, and called him "sissy" behind my mother's back. I would have enlisted Zeke and Hannibal as allies, but I hadn't sunk to that.

Stanley was allowed to carry a rifle and go with my mother down to the great sawdust pile in the lower meadow. The lumber mill had long since moved away, leaving a rotting sawdust pile as big as our house. After a rain, when the sun came out and steam rose from the rot, snakes came out of the hundreds of holes that were their burrows, and if you whistled a sharp blast, the snakes would raise up until their heads were sometimes a foot from the ground, at which point a bullet from my mother's rifle would clip their necks in two. She said it served a dual purpose, it rid us of snakes in our meadow and sharpened her shooting skills.

And now she had introduced Stanley to this sport. He had taken to shooting with relish, laughing in loud whoops when he succeeded and saying "Oh, damn!" when he missed. My mother would not let me say "Oh, damn," nor would she let me touch a rifle, keeping them locked away, except in her presence.

By now Stanley had been with us six weeks, and he was changing every day. He had his hair cut short, and he'd gained some weight. Even Tuba said grudgingly, "He may turn into a young man yet." He had lots of clothes; more clothes than he needed, it seemed to me. He even had riding pants and boots. My mother said they were necessary if he was to learn dressage, and she needed his help there, as the dressage-trained horses were our prime money crop. A well-trained horse could bring twenty thousand dollars, and that was a lot of money in the summer of '29.

Both Zeke and Hannibal had failed to become dressage trainers because rider and horse must become one, and neither of those two could ever become one with a thoroughbred. They were crossbreeds, and they both were too heavy. First the muscle system of the horse has to be built up. To carry the weight of a man, a horse has to develop a far stronger muscular structure than nature intended.

My mother had learned dressage, the French word for "training" but much more, in college at Morgantown. She had spent weekends, evenings, and every extra moment at the horse college. She had shoveled out stalls and exercised and curried horses to pay for the training.

One morning she saddled Hannah and brought her into the ring to demonstrate with a pair of experts what this skill of expert rider and trained horse was all about. She had two dozen silver cups lined up in the cupboard to prove her skill.

My job was to manage the phonograph. It was a portable Edison mounted on a tea cart, with the records underneath. Music was a part of the horse's training. One had to get used to it, as there were brass bands at every big meet. The four horses next to be trained were in the adjoining paddock, and they stood behind the railing and watched as though they knew their adult life was about to begin. (Stanley had the same look about him.)

My mother rode into the middle of the ring on this polished bronze beauty. Her coloring fitted exactly. Her boots were a light gleaming tan, her jodhpurs were just one shade lighter, and her shirt was yellow silk. Her golden braid was a crown a queen might have been envious of. I heard Stanley breathe, "Ain't she beautiful?"

I was furious with him, so I set the needle on the record with a bang, and the Sousa march filled the air. He had no right to say anything. I knew he wasn't talking about the horse. She was my mother, and I was her only boy. My mother called, "Turn it down a little." There was no volume control. To do that, you closed the doors.

Hannah turned and, bending one knee, inclined her head in a charming little bow, as did my mother before she began. First they trotted, the horse's neck extended and her back feet reaching forward to the identical place the front feet tracked and in perfect rhythm to "The Stars and Stripes Forever."

In the second exercise, the horse is required to bend his spine and move forward at a number of different gaits. The horse receives his instruction from the pressure of the rider's legs and feet and the tension and pull of the reins. Hannah stepped sideways and crossed her legs, then moved right, left, and back, like the movement of an elegant dance. She made a turn to the right, then a turn to the left, and came and stood with her head held high and one foot pawing the ground before Stanley. Stanley asked, "Is this horse for sale?"

"Not for a million dollars. Hannah and I love each other." My mother swung down and held the bridle for Stanley. "Get aboard." Stanley wasn't quite sure how. So she said, "Use the step until you learn to mount properly."

After he was in the saddle, Mother snapped a draw rein to the bridle, like a long dog leash, so she could stand in the middle and control the circle. Stanley had grasped the reins and had his feet through the stirrups, but he looked unsure.

The record had come to an end, and I reached under the cart to open the package that had just come from New York. I hoped it had a loud, banging rhythm that would inspire Hannah to throw Stanley to the ground and step on him. It was "Lady Be Good."

Hannah listened for a moment and fell into this rhythm as readily as to the Sousa march. My mother gave me a questioning look and went on with Stanley's instruction. "Now take her in a strong trot. That music is exactly right." I wanted to take the record off and break it!

Mother kept changing the instruction, and Stanley kept responding; he was gaining confidence and sat the saddle easier, and his hold on the reins was easier. She kept saying, "Good boy, good boy," as though he was her good boy and not me.

Toward the end of the exercise, she gave some of the instruction in French, which Hannah understood: "haute ecole," a kind of floating movement, and "le vade," in which the horse sinks back on his haunches and remains motionless. It was used in the days of knights for the rider to launch his spear. My mother used it to shoot wild turkeys.

"If you're going to show a horse in the Olympics, you have to give the commands in French. That was always my dream, to go to the Olympics. Enough for today."

Stanley swung down more gracefully than he had mounted, and led Hannah into her stall to be sponged and brushed. My mother followed. "I hope you can take French your first year. I can help. I was pretty good; of course, I don't get any practice. I have Josephine Baker's records, but her accent is atrocious."

Stanley was removing the bridle and taking the bit from the horse's mouth. There was a sudden edge of fear in his voice. "What did you mean, my first year?"

"Why, high school. You can't get anywhere in the world with an eighth-grade education."

She was getting down the curry brushes and didn't hear how flat his voice had become.

"You'd want me to have a high school diploma to work here?"

"You can go in with Hughie. The bus stops right at our gate. I'll be glad to have you on the bus with Hughie; the boys get a little rowdy sometimes."

He had snapped the oats bag over Hannah's head, and she was munching away; it was her reward.

"I didn't graduate from the eighth grade."

"But they gave me your report card. You did very well—almost all A's and B's."

"Everyone gets a card like that when they leave; that place gives them to everyone. It's a lie. I had to work the gardens in the summer and the furnace room in the winter. There wasn't time to go to school."

"But that's intolerable."

"Does that mean you won't want me to stay?"

She stopped the circular motion she was making with a brush in each hand. There was a catch in her voice. "Oh, my dear, no! Those bastards. I knew you couldn't trust them when they withdrew the wards of the state from the county school system and kept the money to educate you themselves. Is there any school there at all?"

"Only for the little kids."

"Those sons of bitches. I'm going to clean house out there if it's the last thing I do."

It was two and a half months until school started, and my mother began a program to bring Stanley up to the eighth grade level by that time. He was bright and willing, but he didn't know how driven my mother could be. He soon found out. Every meal was lesson time. She knew he could not absorb all the books she had brought home, so she went through and red-penciled the parts she thought nonsense, which was a lot. Luckily, the orphanage had sent a lot of old books down to the furnace to be burned. Stanley had rescued them and read them, and that helped.

My mother discovered he could draw pretty well, and he also had a bold, open handwriting. It wasn't the current Spencerian, but it was very readable.

He had drawn the outline of a horse on the back of swapping paper from the books he found in the tack room, and printed in all the parts of the horse, and was learning them. When I saw how that pleased my mother, I decided I would do the same as soon as I learned to draw.

She was determined to get something good out of this. She planned to use the fake report card to get Stanley into high school. She also had enlisted my grandmother Curtiss's help to fire Mr. Hostetler, who ran the orphanage.

All this activity freed me to spend more time in town. During the school year, I could spend only Saturdays with my grandfather Fancler. Of all the men in my life, I liked him best, because he would quarrel with me as though I were a grown-up. And he would answer my questions as truthfully as he could.

I spent Sundays at the Curtiss house on Worth Avenue. It was about the only time I saw my father anymore. Even here I didn't see much of him, as he didn't wake up until noon and came down bleary-eyed and nasty, so I spent my time with Grandmother Curtiss. I had a plan. When my mother started teaching me to shoot, as she was now teaching Stanley, I was going to shoot my grandfather Curtiss and my grandmother Fancler, and then my favorite grandparents could marry and live happily ever after.

JUNE 15, 1929

IT WAS SATURDAY. Grandfather Fancler was an early riser, so my mother let me out of the car at the bottom of the hill at seven o'clock. She had appointments with the sheriff and Judge Brown and all kinds of secret meetings.

Grandfather was waiting for me on the bottom step. He had a paper bag full of the kinds of things hikers need. I told him at once that I'd had a bad week and I'd better pick some of the four-leaf clover that grew around his steps and house. He began to point out things he thought I was not aware of as we each found a stout stick for walking. We ate wild strawberries still wet with dew; the blackberries had pretty much gone to feed the birds, but we did find a few. I was still feeling sorry for myself, and jealous, and mean.

"You are a very lucky boy. You have a great many people who care for you."

"Name one."

"Me."

"You never hug me."

"That doesn't mean I don't care. It's just that I'm not a hugging sort of fellow."

"Okay, name another."

"Your mother. She loves you dearly."

"She doesn't hug me anymore, either."

"Maybe she thinks you're a big boy now and would be embarrassed. You have to remember, we didn't hug much when your mother was growing up. We Scots are pretty much 'don't touch me.' "

"Who else loves me?"

"Your grandmother and grandfather Curtiss. Your aunts and uncles. And I forgot your father; your father loves you."

"No, he don't. He loves Sylvia Tingler."

"I doubt that. Your father may have the same trouble you do. He's trying to see if anybody loves him."

"Well, I don't, and he doesn't love me, either."

"Your father is fighting a battle right now with that old demon rum. When he licks it, he will come back to you and be a loving father."

"I don't believe it."

As he talked, we had come down the hill from the orchard, and now we were on the bank above the railroad tracks. Grandfather extracted his watch from the end of its chain and pressed the button that opened the case. "It's just about time for the train. We better get down there."

We both slid down the embankment on the seat of our pants, and I wished I were old enough for long pants. This was something we had done before. My grandfather arranged five pennies on the railroad track for the train to run over and flatten as thin as newspaper. He wore them in his shoes to keep away the arthritis.

You could put your ear down on the track and tell if the train was near. It was, and we scrambled back up the bank so we would be level with the windows in the passenger cars and could wave. Most people waved back. We lived in that kind of time, when people used to wave to each other.

There was a pattern to my trips with Grandfather Fancler. He read widely, and he always had a new story to tell me. I would sit under an apple tree and eat green apples and listen. Whoever had planted the trees long ago had been wise enough to plant many kinds. Something always seemed to be ripening from July until snowfall. There was a Golden Delicious tree at the top of the hill whose fruit was just turning yellow. We sat there and ate. Beyond was the Baldwin, and then the Northern Spy and the Winesaps and the Jonathan. He had brought a paper bag to take some apples back for Grandmother Fancler. There were several already on the ground; I knew many of those had worms, but I didn't care.

Grandfather leaned against the tree trunk and talked. For the last year, when we had walked through these hills, my grandfather had talked about the Civil War. Most of the kids I knew had no knowledge of what had happened here. The first and last battles of the Civil War were fought in this state of West Virginia. These orchards had once been a battleground; the very hill we sat on had had trenches curving around it. Soldiers had stood in mud up to their armpits and fired musket-loading rifles at troops passing below. The troop trains had cannons mounted on flatcars, and the troops had fired at this entrenchment. If you dug around, you could find lead cannonballs the size of grapefruit. Most of the people who lived around here had collected enough to make doorstops for every door in their house.

He told me how most of the Confederates had never owned a slave, and most of the Union forces didn't care about slavery. The war had all been planned by old men in paneled offices, as wars always were. Many had been buried in the trenches where they died. Some had their names carved on rough planks, but those had long ago rotted away without being recorded. Some enterprising soul had planted apple trees in the remaining ditches, and erosion had filled them in. My grandfather pointed out that the bodies had gone to fertilize the very apple I was eating. I stared at it for only a moment, then went on eating.

He had used this hillside as a laboratory to explain the food chain to me: how the smallest bug is eaten by the next size up, then the big bugs are eaten by birds, and big birds eat little birds, and snakes eat bigger birds, and owls eat snakes.

And then we started with rabbits. He explained why rabbits were so prolific: they had no protection and many enemies. The foxes who ate them were killed by men with guns, who gave the skins to fat girls to wear around their necks. It seemed man was at the top of every progression that began and ended with death.

My grandfather was fourteen when the War Between the States ended, and he wanted to teach me what he understood about it. His was the last generation who remembered, and when they were gone, there would be no more living history.

He leaned back against the tree and closed his eyes against the filtered sunlight. "Well, let's see—last week I told you about Caesar's legions marching into Gaul, today we will go back even further."

And I knew he had just finished another book. He always said you have to understand the past. How can you know where you are going, if you don't know where you came from?

I spent two afternoons a week with him now that school was out, and he joked that he had to read widely to keep ahead of me. Today we started on the Greek myths—beginning with "A," for Achilles, and how he fought Paris for Helen of Troy in the Trojan War.

The most interesting part for me was how Achilles had been dipped as a baby in the Stygian pool to make him immortal. And he was, except for the part of his heel where his mother held on to keep him from going under. And he grew up to be invincible except for his heel. Paris found out about it and shot an arrow through his foot and killed him. Grandfather explained that this was where the expression "Achilles' heel" came from. All of us have some secret spot, in spite of our armor, where we can be gotten at and destroyed. I was wondering where Stanley's Achilles' heel was. My jealousy was festering every day, until it colored my world.

My grandfather and I had made a pact that I would give up lying, which I was really good at, in exchange for a truthful answer to whatever I asked him. But I couldn't tell him how I felt about Stanley. I didn't want him to think less of me.

This was Saturday, and I was to finish the day by taking a taxi down to my aunt Sebe's house and spending the night with my cousins Lloyd, Worthy, and Harry. I was welcome, as I was their ticket into the movies at the Hippodrome. This was another of Grandfather Curtiss's businesses. They lived only three blocks from the theater, so we could stay out until nine-thirty. In those days, little boys could walk down the street at midnight and be perfectly safe.

Lloyd grumbled because the pictures were still silent, as my grandfather had refused to invest the thousand dollars that the sound system cost. I knew it had gone into the stock market, like every cent he could get his hands on.

Behind the ticket window was a girl I had never seen before. She pressed a bell for Mr. Meeken to come down from the projection room. He knew me, of course, as I came here often. He told the new girl, "This is the old man's grandson," and he said to me, "Hughie, you already saw this Valentino picture last Christmas, and we're running the same Pearl White serial. If you want to see sound pictures, you better tell your granddaddy to put in the new system," and then he went back upstairs to the projection room.

We could read the marquee of the Grand Theatre, my grandfather's competition at the end of the block: THE LIGHTS OF NEW YORK—WORLD'S LONGEST SOUND FILM. There was a line of people waiting to buy tickets. Even old Vossie's popcorn wagon had moved from the Hippodrome and was doing business up in front of the Grand.

The girl objected when she saw there were four of us. I explained that Lloyd came to read the titles to me (a lie, as I could read better than Lloyd), and he couldn't come without his brothers, because their mother had to go and work in the Green Lantern restaurant, because her husband was dead (that part was true).

There were only about ten people in the theater and this was Saturday night. This building had originally been a Lodge meeting hall, and it still was on Sunday night, when the blue law forbid the showing of movies. The floor was flat and furnished with about two hundred chairs, part of the general's loot from the South, chairs that once graced the dining rooms of southern plantations. There were also four or five Chippendale couches down front for the people who needed to sit close to the screen to read the titles.

It seemed strange to see Rudolph Valentino and Vilma Bánky cavorting in silence like ghosts across the flickering screen. The girl who played the piano worked in my grandfather's Bluebird Market next door, and she did not come over to play unless fifty tickets were sold. That was never again to happen.

Even though it was a silent film, you were still supposed to keep quiet. Worthy and Harry had a habit of grabbing each other in the crotch and yelling and laughing, so Lloyd hit each of them in the side of the head, and they cried.

Lloyd said to me, "Does your grandfather know this guy has a floozy selling tickets? Did you get a load of that peroxide hair? Look at that Valentino goin' in that tent—what do you think he's gonna do?"

Worthy and Harry answered in unison through their tears, "Screw!"

"No, he ain't. He's a powder puff; everyone knows powder puffs don't screw girls. Guys screw them."

Mr. Meeken called down from the projector on the balcony: "That's it! You kids get out of here. Go on home."

It was a very badly scratched-up print, and I could hardly read it. I didn't know what "powder puff" meant. And since I had never seen anybody screw anybody, I did not know what I was missing, and I didn't really mind when we found ourselves standing out on the dark sidewalk. The floozy had already turned out the light in the ticket office and gone upstairs to join Mr. Meeken.

We looked up and down the street. It was eight o'clock on a Saturday night, and everything was closing up and turning out the lights.

Lloyd said, "I know where there's a show better than this. And this guy really does screw."

I said, "I think we better go home."

"You a powder puff, too?"

To prove I wasn't whatever that was, I followed Lloyd down the alley behind the Chinese laundry, with Worthy and Harry following behind giggling. Lloyd threatened to slap them silly. They were already silly.

The windows of Mr. Chang, the Chinese laundryman, were just the right height to peep under his window blind as we stood in the alley in the dark. The show had already begun. Mr. Chang was lying on his back naked. His feet were on the floor, giving him leverage to thrust his cock between the legs of the gold-dust twin who squatted over him. The other one hovered over his face, and his tongue flicked out and in.

Lloyd had been right. Their breasts did look like bananas, long and thin and hanging almost to their tiny waists. It was clear what had made them look like this: Mr. Chang had one in each hand and was yanking and pulling downward like he was milking a cow. Naked, the girls looked even smaller and more child-like, although technically they weren't naked, as they still wore their purple-spangled stockings, held up with pink garters.

They all seemed wound up and in perpetual motion, and they paced each move with grunts and groans and oohs and ahs, especially Mr. Chang, who made the kinds of grunts our boar hogs made when they mounted the sows. I had seen all kinds of matings on the farm, horses, cows, sheep, and the dogs, who always got stuck together and had to have a bucket of cold water thrown on them so they scrambled apart. But this was the first time I had seen people doing it, except for my father and Sylvia Tingler in the boat, and I really couldn't see what was going on there. I didn't know people did it three at a time.

Lloyd leaned in to my ear. "Didn't I tell you? This will learn you."

I suppose if I was going to learn about sex in all its variations, Mr. Chang was as good a teacher as I would find. He was still a young man, muscled and sleek and shining brown with sweat. His head was shaved, but the girls had long stringy hair that sometimes got in the way of seeing clearly. His cock looked extremely long, not as long as a horse's but certainly longer than a pig's. I was amazed when one of the girls took it in her mouth and he rammed it down her throat; I thought she would choke to death.

The strangest position seemed to be when one of the girls stuck her butt up in the air and he mounted her the way dogs do, and the other one got a big long black rubber-looking thing, dipped it in a pail of lard, and rammed it in his gyrating ass. He gasped. (I could not tell from pleasure or pain.) He intensified the thrusting, and his moans got louder, then, with a loud gasp that seemed to originate deep within him and force its way to the surface, he collapsed on the girl beneath him and looked for a moment as though he had died.

Then he pushed himself out of and away from her, as though she were contaminated. I thought he was going to hit her. Instead he climbed to the floor, hitting the lightbulb so that it swung back and forth, contorting their shadows, as he made his way through the door. The girls put their arms around each other and laughed and laughed like little tinkling glass bells.

Lloyd pulled us all along to the next set of windows, which looked into the washroom in back of the laundry. There were several big wooden tubs with clothes soaking. You could smell the odors of caustic soaps through the open windows. Mr. Chang climbed into a tub of shirts and collars soaking in the lye soap used to remove hair oil from the stiff collars. I knew something Mr. Chang did not, or maybe he did, the way he was scrubbing with somebody's shirt. The India-rubber man from the circus had said "syphilis." (I was to hear that word again within the month.)

On the way to Aunt Sebe's house, Lloyd was wound up. He kept saying, "Boy, did you see that chink ram her?" He thrust his pelvis in imitation. "You just wait till I get two girls like that."

Worthy said, "Don't be dumb; you ain't ever gonna git one girl."

Harry said he thought the whole thing was dumb. I agreed. I certainly didn't want to do anything that would make me go and jump in a tub of dirty shirts!

JUNE 16TH, 1929

ON SUNDAY MORNING, my cousins walked me over to Grandmother Curtiss's house. She gave them a piece of watermelon and a glass of lemonade for their trouble, plus a strawberry pie to take home. My grandmother had a fetish for baking everything from the store into pies before it spoiled. There was always an excess of pies.

We did not go to church in the summertime, as the preacher was traveling in the Holy Land, and the pulpit was occupied by young guest ministers who paused and stammered and usually couldn't be heard.

We enjoyed a brunch of waffles, creamed chicken, and cranberry juice in the gazebo that stood in the middle of the orchard. It was a folly, a fantasy, like a giant festooned wedding cake; built by my grandmother's father, Joseph, after he had married the rich Dutch lady, agreeing it no longer made any sense for him to go out building churches, which had been his lifetime profession, with all that money now in the family. She had wanted him to father babies before she was too old, though he was out of the habit. My grandmother was twenty-five and already had three children. Joseph fathered first Emma, then Alvin, in quick succession. The Dutch mother had been dead now for three years, and Joseph had gotten on a train some years ago with a suitcase of cash to go to Oklahoma and cheat the Indians out of their oil lands, and was never heard from again.

Sometimes Alvin and Emma joined my grandmother, Opal, Bea, and me, but this morning it was just Emma. It was not necessary for either of the kitchen maids to stay and serve. The waffles were kept hot with an alcohol burner, and there were candles under the chafing dish of creamed chicken and the silver coffeepot shaped like a pumpkin.

I liked looking at Aunt Emma. She was really my great-aunt, though she was younger than my father. He had called this little child "Aunt" and her cherub of a brother "Uncle." I thought it was a joke. She reminded me of one of those clocks that has a case made of glass, and you can see the movement of its works. If you looked closely at her very white skin, you could see the blood coursing through her blue veins just beneath her skin, especially on the sides of her neck and on her temples.

Emma had let the food on her plate grow cold and held her Dresden cup halfway to her mouth without drinking. My grandmother waited. She knew this strange half sister could not be rushed. If you tried, she would get up like a startled deer and run back into her house. My grandmother reported that the Maiden Blush apples would be ripe in another two weeks. It was the one truly sweet apple in this orchard and the tree that Uncle Alvin took great pride in. He had planted it when he was only five.

Emma cried out, "He didn't come home last night."

Aunt Opal and Aunt Bea watched their colorless aunt like spiders after a moth. They hated Emma because there was no way to reach her. She lived like a princess in a tower, and nothing anyone said seemed to reach her, unless it was Alvin, beautiful, golden Alvin, who peopled the erotic dreams of both Opal and Bea.

Emma was looking directly into Grandmother's eyes, a thing she seldom did with anyone. And her voice rose above her usual whisper. "It's that painter . . . he said they were going to work all night — Eddie Horner was inspired. But it's morning now, where is he?"

My grandmother tried to comfort her. "He probably was tired and went to sleep there." She didn't sound convincing.

Opal wanted to be cruel. "Everyone knows what Eddie Horner is."

Bea added, "I guess we all know what Alvin is now, too."

Emma had a way of closing off her hearing to what those two said. She still spoke only to her older half sister, who now seemed like a mother, and she needed her mother.

"I lay there all night and waited, he never came to our bed . . . I haven't slept."

This seemed to be a morning to get skeletons out of the closet, and now another one danced before us. My grandmother considered these Sunday mornings here in the orchard her one indulgence. The town and what she considered her "civic responsibilities" were still out there, but at least a block away in every direction. Birds sang, squirrels scampered through the trees. The sun filtered through the green leaves and dappled everything with light, a French impressionistic painting. Aunt Opal often accused her mother of composing little groups in that manner. Grandmother was wearing a brown linen dress with a white lace collar, and her two daughters were in blue and yellow.

I could see that Grandmother was annoyed at Emma for watching through the trees to the portico of the channel house for the arrival of her brother.

There was an undercurrent between Opal and Bea. Bea looked apprehensive, almost fearful, as she usually did, and Aunt Opal was nodding to her, urging her to do something and not just make the social conversation that was requisite in this setting. I was sitting on the warm bricks of the floor and reading the funny papers that my grandfather had given me from the Washington *Herald*. It came on the train each Sunday morning from Washington, D.C., ninety miles away, and a messenger hurried it to him.

There was a lull in the conversation, with the only sound the clicking of teacups. I had thought of telling them about last night's exposure to Mr. Chang and the gold-dust twins but thought better of it. Instead I read the latest episode of Krazy Kat and Ignatz Mouse. Krazy Kat had a new iron stove, and he explained that in the winter it exuded much heat, and in the summer he put ice in it so it exuded much cold. I suppose it was humor aimed at seven-year-old boys, for I thought it hilarious; judging from the blank faces of my lady companions, they did not.

Aunt Opal ordered me, "Hughie, be still. Bea has something she wants to tell Mother."

My grandmother took off her new horn-rimmed glasses and looked at her daughter. "Well."

Aunt Bea kept her eyes on her coffee cup and spoke in a thin little voice. "Mama, I want to get married."

"Of course you do. It's every girl's right to have a husband and a home and children."

"Mama, I'm thirty-four." Bea dropped her little-girl voice and sounded thirty-four.

Grandmother glanced around her quickly as though someone would hear Bea state her age. "Someday, someday soon. The right man—"

"I have found someone, Mama. I'm too old to worry if he's the right man; he is the only man who has ever asked me in my whole life, and I'll soon be too old."

"Who is this man? He hasn't spoken to your father."

Opal interjected quickly, "Papa would say no and order him out of the house."

"Please, Opal, let your sister tell me."

"Mama, it's the salesman from Burpee Seeds."

Grandmother said nothing for a whole minute, and then she put her new glasses back on and looked at her daughter. Aunt Bea was getting plump, and already there was a puffiness around her eyes. "I knew it was a mistake to let you work over in the market."

"I'm going to get married tomorrow afternoon by the justice of the peace and go back with him to his home in Buffalo, New York."

Again there was a silence while my grandmother considered this latest bit. I pretended to be reading "Maggie and Jiggs," but I watched their faces. No one seemed to notice but Emma when the sound of Alvin's car in the portico announced that he had returned home. Emma pushed her chair back and ran. Voices bounced against the gray walls of their brick mansion. We heard the sounds of Emma crying and a thumping as though she was beating her fists against his chest, and then he distinctly said, "Sweetheart, I'm as sorry about this as you are." No one at the table registered anything.

My grandmother chose her words carefully. "You mean that tall, thin fellow, the one with the big red mustache?"

"Yes, Mother, the one who slaps everyone on the back and shakes hands too vigorously. He's a real glad-hander. He leaves a nickel tip everywhere. The waitresses all call him the 'nickel sport'—and he says he loves me."

I thought she would cry. Grandmother reached over and patted her hand, which was unusual. We were not patters. "All right, dear, all right." My grandmother was an organizer, and she was not to be denied this. "You will get married right here. We will have a garden wedding; it's short notice, but I can do it. The garden is full of flowers. No justice of the peace. Hughie, your grandfather Fancler is in town, isn't he? And Hughie can carry the ring on a little lace pillow. He is going to give you a ring, I hope." She did not wait for an answer. "Oh, what will you wear? You're too—plump for my wedding dress."

Aunt Opal volunteered to try and let it out, she was good at such things. Bea decided she would wear a blue organdy she had once worn as a bridesmaid. She could wear her mother's veil, but then she said, "No, there is no need to veil me. He has already seen my round little face, and he will take me as I am."

At this point one of the kitchen maids came running down the path to announce that the master wanted everyone in the house, there was news.

My grandfather's study (they were not called dens then, dens were for bears) was dark and filled with acidic odors from the many batteries needed to feed his radio. They sat under the library table and dripped acid onto the bright blue Chinese rug. The radio covered the top of the table and consisted of a series of tumblers as big as two-pound coffee cans. Each tumbler had to be in perfect alignment to the others to bring in the sound. Each had a wire going out the window and up three stories to the roof. For want of an aerial, my father had attached the lead wires to the lightning rod. When a storm threatened, you had to hurry and unhook all the wires to keep the lightning from coming down to the house and catching it on fire.

I was glad to see my grandfather had not been able to lace his shoes around his swollen ankles; that was worth a nickel. We all stared into the morning-glory speaker as though that would clear up the crackling sound. Lowell Thomas, the newscaster, was saying:

> For the people of West Virginia his death came as a real shock. He had served his state well for forty-eight years. Senator August P. Burton

somehow was able to ride out the various floods of scandal which have swept the political scene many times in his tenure. It was speculated that the Teapot Dome scandal would sweep him from office, but he survived. He is survived by his wife, who resides in his hometown of Elkins, West Virginia. His constituents back home were about to honor him for his many years of service with an equestrian statue to be unveiled this fall. We regret —

Grandfather had risen with difficulty and was going out of the room, careful to not step on his shoestrings. I followed as he said, "I've got to telephone Aunt Almeda, poor dear!"

JUNE 17, 1929

THE WEDDING WAS ON Monday at three P.M. And for one day's preparation, it did not come off too badly. Aunt Bea looked radiantly happy. And Aunt Opal was very good at making flower crowns and bridal bouquets with many ribbon streamers. The gazebo was garlanded with fern and sweet peas. There were as many family members and friends as could be rallied in short order, about a hundred or so. The groom wore a yellow linen jacket that did not look too bad and was colorful with Bea's sky-blue organdy. Opal tried to borrow a white jacket from my father or Alvin, but my new uncle's arms were too long.

Grandmother looked tired, and well she might be. In lieu of the gifts that normally come to the bride at showers and receptions, she had filled two large wicker laundry hampers and a steamer trunk with linens for table, bed, and bath. Her house had a great excess of everything. She packed china and flat silver and crystal carefully between wool blankets and pillow shams, and as many of the accouterments of housekeeping as she could organize. This was not the wedding she would have planned for her eldest.

My grandfather was pleased by these limited arrangements, since he knew the kind of wedding his wife wanted would have been costly. Nevertheless, he did give the groom an envelope containing five hundred-dollar bills. He did not mean it was a mark of approval; it was just that round, soft little Bea was his favorite, and he had always thought he was her ideal, until he saw this long drink of water she had chosen to marry.

I liked my new uncle. When we were introduced, he grabbed me under the arms and whirled me around, then threw me up in the air and caught me. He kissed old ladies on the cheek who had not been kissed for years.

I was angry that my mother had brought Stanley in a new white shirt and his first necktie. Our car was full coming over, for we picked up my grandfather Fancler and, of course Tuba, who had been Aunt Bea's nursemaid until my father came along. But my grandmother seemed pleased that Stanley was there, especially when he dived in to fill the punch cups and pass cookies after the service. It didn't make him seem like a servant, as my mother was doing the same thing. Not to be outdone, I found a silver tray of little finger sandwiches and carried it around.

My father was best man, and he had remained relatively sober; the punch had very little rum in it. My mother and father stayed twenty feet apart and did not speak.

The newlyweds' train left at eight, and most of the guests went to the station to throw rice and see them off.

After we dropped Grandfather Fancler off, we drove up the road to our house. Stanley sat in the front with my mother, and I stretched out on the soft leather of the backseat with my head in Tuba's lap and was soon drifting into sleep when the clamor from the front seat awakened me. My mother yelled, "Oh, dear God, the horses!"

Through the front windshield, I could see the sky ahead lighted with a bright red flow. My mother pushed the accelerator to the floor, and we bounded forward, up and over the hills, around turns on screaming tires. As we got nearer, the sky glowed brighter. For a horse owner, fire is one of the most frightening occurrences. An intelligent, well-trained horse—unless he is restrained—will run into a burning barn, and to get a horse out, you have to cover his eyes.

When we came to the last hill before dropping down to the bottomlands where our farm lay, we could see clearly that our place was not on fire. With a quick intake of breath, my mother said, "Thank God!"

The fire was to the left of us and up the dirt road that led to the old Miller place. What had been a glow was now a fountain of flame, with sparks shooting up and dying out high in the sky. We turned into the dirt road with such force that the tires threw dust and gravel in an arc behind us.

"That old log house is as dry as a tinderbox. I hope they all got out."

At the next turn, the house was in view, and though it wasn't on fire, it soon would be. The flames were coming from their chicken house, halfway to the barn. In front of the house was that dreaded symbol of violence and ignorance that told us the Ku Klux Klan was at work.* One of their number, hiding behind a hooded mask, was running toward the house, a burning torch held high in one hand.

My mother brought the car to a screeching halt, and four more sheeted Klansmen were caught in the headlights. "Quick! Give me my rifle." Stanley had anticipated her and was pulling the gun from its pocket on the back of the car seat. She threw open the door, swung the gun to her shoulder, pulled the lever arm, and fired with what seemed one movement.

The Klansman was not more than ten feet from the house when he screamed in pain, dropped the torch, and grabbed his arm. Two black teenage boys were at the corner of their house, heaving rocks. Two women were at the well on the opposite side, drawing water. Their dark faces glowed bright red in the firelight.

Stanley had freed the emergency pistol from its door pocket and stood beside my mother. He hissed at Tuba and me, "Stay down — stay inside." One of their number was dragging the torchbearer back toward them. His hood came off; it was Zeke.

Another came toward us with a kerosene can held high, as though he would

---

* The Ku Klux Klan began just after the Civil War. The masked riders rode out across the land to frighten and harass the newly freed Negroes and force them back to the farms. The social order of the South had been destroyed. It was a lawless time, and the Klan riders soon turned into vigilante groups, and when their intimidation was not enough, they used violence.

The Klan raided private homes and sometimes whole towns, burning and murdering. The death toll of Negroes and Republicans was in the thousands. The Klan was determined to restore the old order, but it was badly coordinated, and local dens soon became uncontrollable, with each operating for its own private gains and political ends.

Grand Imperial Wizard Nathan Bedford Forrest disbanded the Klan in 1869, and martial law finally brought the Invisible Empire to an end in 1871. But the ghosts of these madmen still lingered, and every once in a while a masked rider would come out of the night and torch a black neighbor's farm, especially if he was doing well.

Not until after World War I did the Klan revive. The influx of immigrants was the target this time. Anyone who was not white Anglo-Saxon Protestant was fair game. They had the support of the fundamentalist majority and the Prohibitionists, and they now had recruits in the millions from Maine to California. Georgia was its center and Atlanta its holy city. It was logical, since nowhere was the redneck mentality stronger. They elected their members to state and national assemblies. In Oregon they were strong enough to outlaw all parochial schools. Colorado, Indiana, and states in every area elected Klan members to the U.S. Senate. In Indiana a false rumor spread that the pope burn the car. My mother put a shot through the can, and the oil splattered all over him. I heard Stanley ask her, "Shall I set him on fire?"

"No, wait."

The chicken-house flame was better than any Fourth of July display. Burning feathers floated in the updraft from the heat, and live chickens ran in every direction, their feathers aflame. They were being roasted alive. When they were destroyed, they would stop with a terrible squawking scream and fall over to convulse and continue to burn. The sound was a chorus from hell. Where each fowl fell was a circle of burning dry grass.

"All right, you bastards, take those sheets off."

The remaining four hesitated, and she fired two shots in rapid succession, making round holes in the cone-shaped hoods. One of them screamed, "You can't get us all. We can get you."

"You want to bet your life on it?"

There was a muttered conference, and they began disrobing. The first to stand in the beam of the headlight was John Rhodes. His wild red hair stood on end, and he hadn't shaved for weeks. My mother took the pistol from Stanley and gave him the six-shot rifle to reload.

"Take those sheets up there to the well and soak them and beat out those grass fires."

---

was coming into a small town there, and a group waited at the station to lynch him. Riots developed everywhere aliens had come to work. The Klan was a mysterious presence, a disruptive and eventually self-destructive force.

In 1925 the Klan paraded down Pennsylvania Avenue, forty thousand strong, in the nation's capital. They were determined to elect a president, and they did so, Herbert Hoover in 1928. The Klan had been traditionally Democratic, but when Alfred Smith, a Roman Catholic, ran against Hoover, they switched parties and were a deciding force in defeating him.

The economy of the country under Herbert Hoover took a fast toboggan ride; most insider Republicans got out with their profits intact before the market fell. The Klan's power and glory went down with the economy. The leaders had always been out for the money—the monthly fees, the cost of robes and paraphernalia. The local groups, with harder times, were unwilling to send their funds off to Atlanta, and most of them splintered off independently.

The very nature of the Klan dictated violence, which in the beginning brought them respect and members. Now the decent among them realized that the Klan was ungodly, their violence went too far, and their leaders were immoral. Members dropped away and found the fraternalism they enjoyed in organizations such as the American Legion, the Knights of Pythias, the Mystic Shriners, and the Elks and Moose lodges. The Klan in Elkins held a meeting in March 1930 to vote themselves out of the national organization. They could harass, tar and feather, and burn on their own, without having to send their hard-earned money to Atlanta. This was their last meeting.

John was obviously drunk, otherwise he wouldn't have yelled at my mother when she had a pistol in her hand. "Go to hell, lady!"

"No, you're going to hell, and it would give me great pleasure to send you there. I'm sure your poor wife would be happy to know she's been beaten for the last time. Now hurry. If these poor people's house or barn catches on fire, I'll shoot all of you."

The four of them went about controlling the fire. Zeke lay on the ground, holding his shoulder and moaning. The cross burned itself out and fell over, and the chicken house was fast consuming itself. The two Miller boys came around to my mother, giving a wide berth to the Klansmen. Mrs. Miller came out from the grove of trees, where she had run to hide with her fat little baby boy, who looked bright-eyed and delighted with the excitement.

"Where's Mr. Miller?"

"He got a job now at night, cleaning the railroad cars."

"I'll stay until we get rid of the bastards, and when I go back to the house, I'll see that the sheriff gets some men out here."

Someone else had seen the fire and sent the county fire truck. The firemen put a pump down into the well and sprayed the flames. In the clamor, the Klansmen sneaked away.

When we got back to our house, my mother was boiling. When we pulled into our yard, she jumped from the car without closing the door and slammed our front door open. I ran after her as her heels clicked down the long hall to the servants' stairway. She was still carrying the pistol.

"Hannibal! Hannibal, come down here."

He was ambling down the stairs, but at the sight of the gun, he moved faster. He was carrying a pulp magazine with nude girls on its cover.

"Are you a member of the Klan?"

"No, ma'am."

"Zeke is. He and that bunch of trash just tried to burn the Millers out. I shot Zeke through his arm."

"You shot Zeke over a bunch of niggers?"

She ignored the slur and plowed on. "Put his things outside the gate. You knew about this?"

"What Zeke does is his business, an' it ain't none a mine."

"I'm going to stop this violence around here if I have to shoot every one of those cowards hiding under dirty sheets."

Hannibal pulled his lip into what he thought was a condescending smile, but it came off like a snarl. "If you don't mind my sayin', ma'am, shootin' don't seem exactly the way to stop violence." She looked down at the gun in her hand, which she seemed to have forgotten. Hannibal stood on the bottom step to tower over her. "How you gonna get the hay in without Zeke mowin'? Got to start soon. You don't want the grass any dryer."

"I'll manage."

"He's the one that always brings the crews in."

"Do you know how hard those poor people have worked to restore that old place and make themselves a home?"

"I repeat, they're just niggers."

Tuba was standing in the dark doorway. Her voice was like a volcano erupting. "This nigger might just fix you your pancakes in the mornin' with a little of that arsenic we use to spray the roses!"

My mother went to the telephone and called Sheriff Lester Adams and told him what had happened. Tuba and Stanley and I sat around the kitchen table and drank cocoa and looked at one another with eyes so bright they seemed fevered, and wondered how we would ever get to sleep.

JULY 4, 1929

WEDNESDAY WAS THE FOURTH of July. In our town, it was the all-out biggest day of the year. Decoration Day, May thirtieth, was nice but solemn. We paid tribute to our honored dead, and everyone went to the cemetery and spread spring flowers; soldiers ten years away from the Great War read off lists of fallen comrades whose bodies were not brought home but lay in Flanders Fields across the ocean. But Independence Day was flags and bunting draped everywhere, picnics and straw hats and firecrackers. We celebrated the brave souls who had freed us from the English tyrants. Since most of our town were English and Irish and Scotch, many of us were descended from these same tyrants who had come to settle these hills rather than return to class-conscious England.

Many of the WWI survivors wore their brown uniforms and their helmets that looked like washpans. They gathered in the pavilion in the park and tried not to let their solemn faces contrast too much with the glory days when they had all sung "Over There" and marched away. A disproportionate number of them had a dazed, glassy-eyed look; they were the victims of mustard gas. The pension that veterans were promised had not been forthcoming, and those able had marched again in Coxey's army and camped in squalor along the Potomac, to no avail. Herbert Hoover and his minions would not budge.

For many years, my grandfather Fancler had led the July 4th parade on his great black stallion, carrying a very large flag with thirteen stars in a circle. He was followed by the Legion Drum and Bugle Corps, dressed in colonial garb and white wigs. The horse was accustomed to blaring trumpets, as he had gone through the training program of our blaring phonograph. What he wasn't accustomed to was the loud bang of firecrackers that little boys (and not so little boys) threw beneath the horse's feet.

At seventy-seven, my grandfather had delegated his place in the parade this year to Billy-Pearl. He pleaded lack of strength to both hold the flag erect and control the horse if he reared. None of this was true, as he later told me when we were playing "truth." He wanted to be sure my mother fell heir to leader of the parade while he was still alive to assure her position.

Mother was not sure she felt up to this parade. The last three days had been difficult. She had gotten on the phone the morning after Zeke's shooting to enlist a crew for the harvest, but more than half the men had turned her down, and she knew the Klan was already at work.

Hannibal went about his job and even some of Zeke's chores, but there was something secretive about him, even though his face seemed blank except for an occasional smirky smile. Right after his dinner, he would quickly walk up the road and not come back till midnight, when he banged the back door and stamped up the steps.

There was a general feeling of unease, and my mother responded. She moved Stanley into the blue room beside mine and gave him a pistol. The dogs who had slept on pallets in the hallway and in the barn were moved to the front veranda, and they took up their jobs like troops at the front. Outside lights were left burning everywhere. My mother felt that everyone on the party line was listening in.

As we left before eight A.M. on the Fourth, pulling the big black stallion in a horse trailer behind the Jewett, a deputy from the sheriff's office pulled his car into our drive. My mother waved, so it had obviously been prearranged.

I sat in the reviewing stand set up on a little triangle of park in front of what had been my grandfather Fancler's church. This would be the last time there would be a reviewing stand here, since this was the planned location for the equestrian statue of old Senator Burton. Both of my grandfathers were on the stand. Bright shafts of sunlight broke through the clouds just before the parade began, and with just enough breeze to elevate the flags, it was exactly the right kind of a day for a parade.

There were a few scattered reports of firecrackers, but the stringent controls of sales had had results, at least until that night, when the city sponsored a fireworks display over in old man Simmon's meadow, which had just been mowed.

There were about thirty people in the stands, and they were apprehensive, muttering, expecting some sort of display. Someone had said, "I don't think so. Those cowards only come out at night."

Nevertheless, when the parade reached us, my mother was leading and sitting astride the shining black stallion, dressed in a white sailor suit and holding a giant flag aloft. The sheriff walked on the curb beside her, with his first deputy on the other side. Each walked with his hand on his gun. If my mother was afraid, it didn't show. She turned her head from side to side and smiled at her friends.

My grandfather Curtiss said, "Times like this, I wish I believed in God. I would pray."

And my grandfather Fancler said, softly enough that only I heard, "So do I."

The officers watched the rooflines of the business section with special interest. When they came to the park at the end of the parade, Lester Adams was wet with sweat. As he helped her dismount, she realized how afraid he had been for her. Their faces were close. She whispered, "Thank you, Lester, it will be all right now."

But he answered, "It will never be all right—until I run the last of those bastards out of town."

We didn't stay for the fireworks. We had a picnic lunch in the park and went home. When you have a farm, you need to get home and milk your cows, feed your livestock, and gather in your eggs. You can't just pile out enough oats and fodder for the horses for two or three days; they will eat it all at once and, with the addition of water, burst open their stomachs and die.

When we came to our driveway, we found two of the Miller boys waiting at the gate. They had come to help with the chores that Zeke might have done, since we had lost him on their behalf.

They brought the cows up from the meadow and guided them into the milking barn. My mother was surprised to find they knew how to attach the tubes of the milking machine to the cows' teats. They were an improvement over

Zeke in one area: They patted the cows on their sides and said, "Good girl. Good girl," where Zeke usually cussed. It seemed they had all sharecropped on a Kentucky dairy farm before they came up to West Virginia two years ago.

The deputy gathered up the eggs and fitted them into the counting racks and announced proudly, as though he had laid them himself, "There are ten dozen."

My mother told Tuba, as she served her new corn and her graveled potatoes with peas in the shell, "We just may get through this after all."

The deputy ate two slices of ham and took two thick slices home with him for his wife and his boy.

Stanley shook me awake the next morning. There were only the first rays of morning light coming through the curtains, so I knew it was early.

"Someone is coming up the driveway. It's a strange car. Go down by the phone in case we have to call the sheriff."

But the occupant of the rusty little black Ford turned out to be the sheriff himself. My mother was already dressed for the stable when she let him in the side door under the porte cochere.

"I couldn't get you on the phone."

"I know, it's out."

"I'll bet that bastard cut your line."

"We don't know that. The line goes out at least once a month." She had a cup of hot coffee in her hand and invited him to join her.

"This is not a social call, I got to give you this. It's the law."

She sat at the end of the table, and Tuba filled his cup anyway. "What is it?"

"It's a warrant. Zeke McCoy is charging you with attempted homicide, and there is a court hearing on Friday before Judge Brown."

"I wasn't shooting to kill, I didn't even know it was Zeke under that hood. I just wanted to stop him from burning the Miller house."

"If someone swears out a warrant, regardless how ridiculous, you have to answer, you have to post bond. I set it at a dollar. Have you got a dollar? Here, I'll loan you one. He's hired old Slim Middleton as his attorney."

"That slimy snake is a member of the Klan."

"How many times have you told me snakes aren't slimy?"

"I apologize to all snakes for the comparison. Where'd you get that old car?"

"That's the one I use to sneak up on bootleggers. I didn't think it seemly for the sheriff to be calling on a lady at dawn. After all, you are a married lady."

"Haven't you heard? My husband has left me."

"I heard. I just didn't want anyone to catch me celebrating."

Stanley started to come in the dining room entrance. The sheriff looked up, and Stanley turned and hurried around the house and went in the kitchen from the back. My mother looked confused. "What was that all about?"

"He remembered me. I'm the one who found him sitting there by the two bodies, with blood on him clear up to his elbows and a bloody straight razor in his hands."

"So that's why he washes so much."

"You can't wash guilt off."

"Lester, he was a ten-year-old boy, and isn't it possible his father cut his own throat?"

"Clear through to the spine? His head was almost severed."

"He needed killing! Horror is that it was left to a child to do it, if he did, which I choose not to believe."

"Billy-Pearl, you can't just go around killin' people because they need killin'. Promise me you will remember that the next time you see a sheeted Klansman."

"If I had meant to kill him, he'd be dead."

"Well, I think that will have to be your defense."

Tuba stuck her head through the door and called, "Who wants oatmeal?"

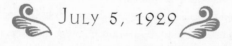

July 5, 1929

The trial was a day away, and the hay had to be gotten in. There were several pleasant surprises: four men showed up, older men who had been here year after year. The younger ones, those who were Klan members or intimidated by the Klan, stayed away. Three Dutch women came. We hardly knew them beyond a nodding acquaintance. They lived on a little farm halfway to town. My mother had picked them up several times and given them a ride home, but the language barrier had stood between them.

The three Dutch women looked exactly like the Dutch women in my geography book: round, rosy faces with blue eyes and yellow hair. One of them still wore wooden shoes in her garden. We had thought they were sisters, but we discovered that mutual tragedy had brought them together. They were war brides whose husbands had died within five years of coming home. That was the pattern for mustard gas.

Now two of them urged a third forward, who we later learned was called Rose. It seemed she had learned a little English. "We come to hay." The other two nodded. "You need help?"

My mother smiled. "Well, I'm not one to look a gift horse in the mouth."

Rose did not understand. "We have no horse, we can work yours. We are from farms."

And so they could and, to my mother's surprise, they did. On the tractor, Hannibal had already cut several swaths through the meadow. The Dutch women expertly hooked the dray horses to the hay rake, and one of them climbed aboard and snapped the reins. The other two grabbed pitchforks and followed her. The hay rake was about twelve feet wide, and each time the tines were full, the driver pulled a lever, the rake raised and left the hay behind in a neat roll. It was then turned onto a sled and pulled by another horse to the haystack.

Lloyd had come out to ride this horse and earn a dollar a day. Worthy and Harry were also hired to carry around buckets of ice water and lemonade to the workers. Things were going well, and I could see my mother was relieved. By nine o'clock, two big haystacks had been carefully built to the north of the chicken houses and the barn. By the time evening came, there would be fifteen haystacks forming a solid wall against the cold north winds of winter.

Every day a new chore. My mother had completely forgotten that weeks ago, she had contracted to have a new cesspool dug. Our old cesspool had been there ten years, and there was a limit to how much sewage quicklime could consume.

The cesspool diggers had a backhoe on a flatbed truck, and they unloaded it and began to dig in an area where the seepage would not leak into any of our wells. My mother was always pointing out to people the danger of putting their outdoor privies in areas that would drain into their drinking water. Even when diphtheria swept the valley, few people were convinced. Some people said behind her back, "That's what comes of sending a girl to college."

Stanley was not exposed to the haymaking. He went on with his usual chores. Nor were any of the thoroughbred horses, who were not workers. I helped Tuba pick the first green beans of the season, and I watched with fascination as the young pullets lost their heads to her ax. The muscle reflex would leave them jumping up and down several times, their necks spouting blood, even after their white heads with the glassy yellow eyes lay on the ground. It didn't increase my appetite for fried chicken, and it was many years after I left the farm until I could eat it again.

If my mother was worried about tomorrow's trial, she didn't let on. There were several conferences that day that I supposed were preparation. My grandfather Curtiss came, driven by the delivery boy from his store. He brought several loaves of bread that I suspected were a day old, a big box of glazed doughnuts, and a whole stalk of bananas that were too brown-spotted to sell. He sat in the wicker glider on the veranda beside my mother. I don't know what they said, since I followed the doughnuts to the kitchen. He had not been gone twenty minutes—surely they passed on the road—before Grandfather Fancler came in a taxi that did not wait. He would stay the day.

By the time seven big stacks of hay had been tramped down and their sides raked smooth, the sheriff's car pulled up to the barn. He looked around at what seemed like a flurry of business as usual, did not see my mother, and went in through the side door without knocking.

Mrs. Miller came, and my mother gave her a black straw hat with a veil so she could sit in the back of the court unrecognized unless my mother needed her. She also brought a funny-looking bundle in a pillowcase. My mother gave her a big basket of eggs and drove her home.

I heard her tell my grandfather as he got in the car after dinner, "I can't take Stanley into the courtroom tomorrow; his memories of that place must be hell."

"You may need all the help you can get." And he closed her door and went around to the other side.

I was already in the back with a young hound dog named Spot, whom I had promised a ride to town.

July 6, 1929

ON FRIDAY, THE HARVESTING crew was in the fields by six o'clock, including the Dutch ladies. As they worked, they sang what must have been funny songs in Dutch, for at the end of each one, they laughed loudly. When we left for the court at eight o'clock, everyone waved and wished my mother well except Hannibal.

Judge Brown looked out over his crowded courtroom and remarked that he hadn't seen his court this full since the trial of Billy Webley. A kind of dirty laugh went around the room. Everyone remembered. Even the reporter from the Wheeling newspaper, one hundred and sixty miles away, had been here, and was again today. Billy Webley had been caught having intercourse with a horse. The mare had fallen on frozen ground, broken her leg, and had to be killed; that trial was the circus of the year. There was anticipation that this would be circus number two.

The room seemed to be packed with my mother's friends and supporters: both of my grandfathers, my grandmother Curtiss, and eight of my mother's sisters. She was never sure whether they were on her side or whether they just wanted to witness her comeuppance.

In the row across the back were the four scroungy-looking Klansmen who had tried to burn out the Millers.

Lester Adams was sitting at the defense table with my mother, as she had chosen not to have an attorney, a move that all her friends disapproved of.

The bailiff read the charges: "Billy-Pearl Curtiss is hereby charged with attempted homicide against one Zeke McCoy." Judge Brown looked at Slim Middleton and instructed him to state his case. He began. Ever since he came back from watching the famous Scopes monkey trial, he felt he needed to use his best Clarence Darrow voice, coloring every line, pausing for effect.

"Zeke McCoy says that on July first of this year, he and a group of friends were taking a stroll near the farm of Rufus Miller when they saw the chicken house afire and hurried to help extinguish the blaze. At which point Billy-Pearl Curtiss did drive up in her limousine, jumped to the ground with a rifle, and begin firing.

"She attempted to kill one Zeke McCoy, even though he was employed by her, the motivation being to burn out the Millers' egg business and eliminate the competition.

"She shot him through his upper arm, missing the back of his head by only a foot. If this woman had been a better shot, my client, a poor honest workingman, would be dead."

Slim lowered his head and was silent for a moment for effect. Then he sat down.

My mother certainly did not look like an attempted murderess. She looked more like a schoolgirl in her soft white eyelet dress, her pale hair pulled up to her crown with a blue ribbon and falling loosely down her back. (I'm sure she knew the effect it made.)

Judge Brown looked at her as she rose. He could not bring himself to say

"Mrs. Curtiss," as my grandmother was sitting in the front row willing him not to.

"Billy-Pearl, how say you?"

She stood just to the right of Lester as though she needed moral support, which I doubted. She began in a clear, sweet voice, as though she were going to sing in church. She intended to beat Slim Middleton at his own game.

"Last Monday night, I was driving home from my sister-in-law's wedding—" She was now before the bench and added softly, "I believe you were there. I was driving home with my boy and my housekeeper when we saw a bright glow in the sky from a fire. I feared at first it was my house, but it was not. It was the home of my neighbors, the Millers."

The four in the back mumbled, "Niggers!"

"Those poor people, who had worked so hard to restore that old farm, were being burned out by the despicable, cowardly Klan. A cross was burning in the front yard, and five of them, hiding in their sheets, carrying torches, were about to burn that old historic log house which had survived the Civil War and now faced destruction by this trash. I did not know it was Zeke until he pulled off his hood in pain . . . and I threatened to shoot the other four unless they put out the fire."

Several people in the audience clapped. It promised to be a pretty good show.

Zeke was sworn in and took the witness stand. Slim led him through a rehash of his original statement. He recited his lies as though reading from a page. And when he was finished, my mother began her questioning.

"Zeke, how long have you been a member of the Ku Klux Klan?"

Zeke exchanged quick glances with Slim and began to intone: "I am not now nor have I ever been a member of the Ku Klux Klan."

My mother went on as though she had not heard. "And when you pull those hoods down over your heads with just slits for your eyes, you'd want to be sure you got your own and not breathe in somebody else's foul breath."

He had been following her question, wondering where she was going, and automatically nodded yes.

"I thought so."

She went to the defense table and brought out the pillowcase Mrs. Miller had given her. She emptied it on the bailiff's table and began sorting through it, holding up one Klansman's hood after another.

"Oh yes, here it is." She held up a hood for the room to see. She read the printing inside: "Zeke McCoy. That's your name, I believe, and this is your writing. I'm very familiar with it, since you were once employed by me."

Slim said, "I object. That doesn't mean he was wearing the hood that night."

"Mrs. Miller gathered those hoods up in her yard, after the cowards ran away at the approach of the fire truck," my mothered answered.

"So he is a member of the Klan—half the county is. That doesn't prove you weren't trying to kill him. That's the charge."

She walked over to his table. "I don't believe half the county are Klansmen— surely there are not that many vile arsonists in our county. But, Mr. Middle-ton, you should know better than I, since you are the grand vizier." She walked back before the judge.

"Do you have anything else to ask this witness?"

"It's a waste of time. You can't believe a word he says anyway. Get down, Zeke."

The judge kept his voice low and his eye on the many influential faces before him. "Billy-Pearl, I'm the one who says 'witness excused.' Do you have any witnesses who saw him with a torch?"

"Yes. Mrs. Miller is in the courtroom, and so is Tuba."

"I mean, do you have any white witnesses?"

She raised her voice just enough to be threatening but not enough to be widely heard. "That remark isn't worthy of you."

Zeke was halfway back to his attorney when she remembered. "Zeke, when were you last paid?"

The judge objected. "You already dismissed him."

"I forgot something . . . this charge that I would shoot him to keep from pay-ing his salary."

The judge recognized that order had already gone out of his courtroom. "Go ahead."

"Zeke, when were you last paid by me? And remember, I have the canceled check to prove it."

"The last day of June."

"So you worked one day in July—five dollars due you."

I heard someone in the audience say: "A hundred fifty dollars a month; that's a lot of money."

"Does anyone in this courtroom believe I would kill a man for five dollars?"

There was a murmured no.

She went to her table and got a five-dollar bill from her purse. "Here."

The judge stopped her. "Bailiff, let's go by the rule around here. Give that five dollars to the plaintiff's attorney."

The bailiff did so. Judge Brown had a habit of making up rules as he went along.

My mother called the Reverend Raymond Sycamore to the stand, and the court leaned forward. Why on earth would she call him? She was a Presbyterian and he was Baptist. Even Grandfather Fancler looked confused. At least no one would doubt his testimony, whatever it was.

After he was sworn in, she began as if greeting an old friend. "Reverend Sycamore, how long have you known me?"

"Well, I guess since you were about fourteen, and even though you don't look much more than fourteen, I guess it's been twelve, maybe fifteen years."

"And on what occasions did we meet other than the religious revivals when my father joined to help you in your church?"

"That was real nice of him, too, since he and me are in competition, kind of."

The judge was annoyed. He was a Presbyterian. "Get to the point, please."

"Reverend, I want you to tell the judge about the turkey shoots."

"Well, I'm sure he knows all about them—everybody does. It's one of my church's best moneymakers for Thanksgiving. We put up targets and charge to shoot, and the one that hits the bull's-eye the most gets the turkey."

"And how many times have I been that winner?"

"Oh, almost every year since you were fourteen, up till a couple of years ago, when I had to bar you or the men said they would stop coming. We gave geese to the runners-up and chickens to thirds, but everyone wanted the turkey."

"Thank you."

She was surprised when Slim stood up. "I have a question. Was there ever a time when Mrs. Curtiss failed to hit the bull's-eye exactly?"

"Not many."

"But some? Maybe ten inches off?"

"There was once when all the men were yellin' at her and sayin', 'Annie Oakley, go home!' When she is under stress, she don't shoot as well. She still hit the second circle three times in a row, it was still the best shootin' of the day."

"So Miss Annie Oakley does miss under stress. I repeat, in trying to shoot my client in the head, she shot him in the arm. That's about a ten-inch miss."

"Mr. Middleton, where's that five-dollar bill I gave you? Did you pocket it?"

Slim waved it in the air. "It's right here!"

My mother was standing on the right of Lester, and before anyone could see what she was doing, she pulled his pistol from its holster and fired, taking the five-dollar bill from Slim's hand.

He yelled, "You crazy bitch!" He made a grab for the bill, but not before Lester beat him to it and, with two long strides, laid it on the judge's desk. There was a bullet hole just to the left of Lincoln's picture.

Lester was laughing. "Your Honor, this proves that if Billy-Pearl had meant to kill this skunk, she could have done it. She almost got Lincoln. The sight on my pistol is just a hair's breadth off."

Slim was beating on his table and screaming, "She might have killed me!"

My mother was calm and smiling. "If I had meant to kill you, I would have. I'll admit the thought crossed my mind." She looked down at the gun still in her hand. "But only for a moment. None of you scum are worth a charge of murder."

Slim would not be silenced, though Judge Brown was pounding with his gavel and shouting, "No, it's you attorneys with bogus charges that have turned my court into a circus. What we should be dealing with here is arson."

The four Klansmen in the back of the room lunged for the door.

The judge went on, "It is the opinion of the court that the charge of attempted homicide has not been proven. Case dismissed." There was a loud cheer. "As to the charge of arson, we will take that up next Friday when court convenes, if any of the five involved are still in the county. Billy-Pearl, leave those hoods with the sheriff so he can copy down all the names."

On the way out, my grandfather Curtiss asked the Wheeling reporter what his headline would be, and he showed him his pink pad: "Annie Oakley of Elkins Takes on K.K.K."

My grandmother Curtiss invited all the people who had come to support Pearl for a late lunch, and about twenty people took her up on it. Later, as they ate and drank, they reenacted the courtroom drama several times. Grandfather warned my mother, "If you don't watch it, you are going to go down in the annals of folklore."

She wanted to know if he had seen my father, and he had, at the back of the courtroom, but he didn't know where he went. She was worried that their bank account was going down at an alarming rate. Grandfather said my father was probably covering his stock margins. The market was up and down, but it would be back up next week. Andrew Mellon said so, and President Hoover backed him up.

She reminded him there would not be any more income from the farm until she sold the two-year-olds in November. He promised that my father would sell enough stock the next time the market fluctuated upward to cover the farm expenses for the year, but it would be a shame, for it was going to hit the sky.

The Evening of July 6, 1929

It was sunset when we got home. My mother seemed exhausted, and no wonder. The crew had finished for the day and gone home. My mother pulled the car up to the side entrance, and Stanley opened her door. He seemed to be the only one around. He already knew, by phone, that we had won. He reported that everything was in order, so my mother went to have a hot bath and lie down. Tuba said she would bring up dinner, but my mother said she would just have tea.

I went upstairs to take off my good yellow linen suit so Tuba could soak a raspberry stain out of it. I had collected various nickels and dimes from friends and relatives today, and I wanted a secret place to count my money before I put it in the rubber boot in my closet.

The Dutch women had cooked for the harvesters in Tuba's absence, and there was a lot of delicious chicken pie left. I was careful not to praise it as I ate two pieces, or it would make Tuba mad. She was mad at me most of the time, anyway. I had taken a third piece on a plate for Spot, the hound pup who slept in my room, and was just at the head of the stairs when I heard screaming from my mother's room and a man's voice say, "Shut up, bitch!"

I ran to my window and yelled down: "Stanley, someone is hurting my mother."

He looked around frantically for a weapon. He started to pick up a brick that bordered the flower beds but thought better of it. The car door still hung open, and he quickly grabbed the pistol from the door pocket and ran inside. I met him at the top of the stairs but could not keep up as he raced to my mother's room and slammed open the door.

My mother was making gasping sounds, kicking, fighting, trying to dislodge a naked Hannibal as he sprawled over her body on the bed. He held her hands down on either side of the pillow and was pressing his face to hers. She was tossing her head from side to side and attempting to bite him. My mother was not a frail little woman, but she was no match for a big, well-muscled man who had spent a lifetime at hard work. His broad ass was moving up and down, attempting to thrust himself into her. "Be still. Ain't nobody gonna help you. You're gonna like it!"

Stanley paused only a second. I was still standing in the doorway, unable to realize what was happening, when he reached the bed. If he felt any hesitation, it didn't show, for he raised the pistol to the side of Hannibal's head and shot him through the ear.

The bullet must have gone through his brain and come out the other side, for it hit the bowl of a lamp on my mother's dresser and shattered it. Hannibal's whole body seemed to shudder, the way hogs do when they are shot in the head.

Stanley was like a madman. He grabbed Hannibal by the hair and rolled his dead body over onto the floor, where he jumped on his chest and kicked him in the head. I joined him in jumping up and down on Hannibal.

My mother clambered out on the other side of the bed and smoothed her gown into place and ran around to us. She grabbed Stanley with one arm and me with the other and pulled us away. "It's all right, it's all right. He's dead." She put her hands on both sides of Stanley's face, held him close, and kissed him. "Thank you, thank you." Then we three stood frozen, staring down at the body. A stream of dark blood trickled out of Hannibal's ear and onto my mother's beloved blue Chinese rug.

Tuba appeared in the doorway, holding a tray with a teapot and a plate of chicken pie. We stood, not moving, as Tuba moved around us. She put the tray down on the tea table as though this were a normal event and came over to his feet and stared down at the ugly dead body.

My mother's voice was little more than a whisper. "He tried to rape me. Stanley saved me."

Tuba pulled off a pillowcase and put it on the floor to catch the fast-congealing blood. "I been tryin' to get up 'nuff nerve to poison him. I guess you saved me the trouble!" And she laughed in Stanley's stricken face.

Tuba took charge as my mother sat down in a chair and stared into space. Tuba ordered me to go to the linen closet and get the rubber sheets that used to be on my bed when I was still wetting. She sent Stanley to cut down the rope clotheslines and bring them. She held out the cup of tea to my mother and made her drink it and brought her an old cotton robe.

"We got to get rid of this son of a bitch."

My mother's shock seemed to pass, but Stanley still seemed stricken and moved like a mechanical man as we rolled the dead body onto the rubber sheets and bound him up like a mummy. Tuba was the calm, firm voice who directed the proceedings.

My mother was suddenly aware that I was in the room. "Oh, dear God, we are letting a seven-year-old child participate in a murder!"

But Tuba soothed, "This ain't no ordinary seven-year-old child."

Tuba had never given me a compliment in my life, and I was not sure this was one. But she smiled at me when she sent me downstairs to get my big new red Radio Flyer wagon. I had only had it a week—I'd outgrown my old one—but I still wasn't sure Hannibal could fit in it.

He was too heavy to lift, even when we all tried. My mother turned a straight chair on its back, and we used it as a ramp to roll his body onto my wagon. His feet dragged on the floor. The wagon banged each step on the way down. Twice his body fell off, and finally it went rolling to the bottom of the broad stair. We had to use the same chair ramp to load him up again.

Outside, we stood in the yard and tried to weigh our options. There was a beginning moon that didn't help much, and the hound dogs kept coming around sniffing. My mother snapped on all the outside lights and walked around the outbuildings, surveying the possibilities.

Stanley said nothing when Tuba complained, "It will sure be hard to dig a grave big enough to keep this bastard down."

My mother had just returned, holding a long flashlight that held eight batteries. "We won't have to. Come on."

We all pushed and pulled under her direction until we came to the cesspool. There was a great pile of dirt where the new one was being dug and walled up, and when it was finished, the dirt would be used to fill up the old cesspool. There was a trapdoor on top of the old one, which opened to pump it out and feed it the quicklime that ate the sewage.

The door was now open. When Tuba saw what my mother had in mind, she laughed. "That's 'xactly where he belongs, down with the other shit."

After we dumped him and heard the splash as his body slid under the thick slime, we watched in the flashlight beam until he was gone. The brown rubber sheets were the color of the sewage. Even if anyone looked in this mess, they wouldn't see him, and tomorrow there would be twenty feet of dirt on top of him.

We then did what we always did in an emergency: we sat around the kitchen table and drank cocoa. Stanley still looked as if he had two glass eyes. My mother reached over and touched his hand.

He looked down. "I was just wondering if we ever do get used to killing."

"I don't really know how to give you an honest answer."

"This time I didn't think about it, I just did. The other time—"

"Stanley, you don't have to talk about that."

"Yes, I do. Please."

"You were only ten years old."

"And this time I was sixteen. I started planning, trying to figure out a way to kill my father, when I was eight. Every time he beat my mother, I wanted to— and I didn't do it until she was dead . . ."

"You may have saved my life tonight. He was a madman."

"The detective stories say it's easier each time."

"Pray to God, there will not be another need."

Tuba said, "Hallelujah!"

Stanley seemed unable to let it rest. "I thought you didn't believe in God, even if your father is a preacher."

"It's just an expression that seems to surface out of habit."

Tuba added, "Or out of need."

"I just don't believe in that do-gooder God who would make such a terrible world," Stanley said.

Tuba was putting the cups in the sink. "Well, there ain't no hell, I'm sure of that. We don't need one, we already got one right here." My mother was wiping the table, and Stanley was pushing the empty chairs back under.

That's the way it was. We cleaned up each day's mess and got ready for tomorrow.

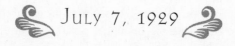

July 7, 1929

SATURDAY MORNING I WOKE up earlier than usual. Always there was the sound of birds chirping, fighting, looking for that night-crawling worm that the sun had not yet driven into his hole. Today they were even louder, moving in droves, gleaning the fallen grain heads where the meadows had been mowed. I went to the window and looked out. Somehow I thought the world would be different this morning. But nothing was changed. The early morning sun was burning away the mists. Cows were moving out of the milking shed. An old horse named Teddy Roosevelt, who was supposed to be thirty but no one knew for sure, had come up from pasture where he was retired and waited at the paddock gate in hopes that someone would give him a carrot and a handful of sugar cubes; it was his pension. My mother and Stanley were in the paddock, working at getting the two-year-olds used to the bridle and bit. They were each wearing a white shirt and tan pants. My mother's hair was braided tight and covered with a riding cap like Stanley's; they were about the same size and looked alike from my window. Nothing was really wrong, though it seemed to me it should be.

I had slept in my shorts, and I kept them on to run barefoot down through the wet grass to the paddock. I was careful not to look toward the old cesspool cover as I climbed the fence and sat on the top rail. After a while, my mother came to me, leading a roan horse she called Pretty Boy. She came to where our faces were level and studied me.

"Are you all right, Hughie?"

"Yep. Are you?"

"Yes, I think so. I wasn't too sure when I woke up."

"Neither was I. I thought I'd had a bad dream."

"And so we did, all four of us, a very bad dream. But it's morning, and we're awake, and life goes on. You go to the kitchen and have some breakfast."

She turned back to the practice ring, and I quickly got off the fence. The young roan was impatiently kicking up his heels.

I saw Tuba in her kitchen garden. It was a small patch, mostly salad-green things. She had a brick in one hand. She would put it under the leaf of her tomato plants and use the wooden mallet in her other hand to mash big green tomato worms until their yellow innards squirted out.

I didn't ask her if she'd had a dream last night. Always when I had a nightmare and screamed her awake, she would say, "If you wasn't such a bad little boy, you wouldn't have bad dreams."

"What do you dream?" I'd ask her.

"Oh, I dream I'm goin' home to the Lord. I'm eighty my next birthday, I think, maybe older. The Lord takes one look at me, and he says, 'Tuba, where you been? We been waitin' for you.'"

She was frowning to herself this morning, and I wondered if she still thought the Lord was waiting for her.

"Hughie, you get your oatmeal. It's on the back of the stove. No, you wait. You might burn yourself. I'll git it." And she started up the back steps.

I wanted to forget she hated me and I hated her, and take her elbow up the steps, as my mother had taught me, but I was afraid she would hit me. We were both up on the porch when we heard the passenger train to White Sulphur Springs that went right through our bottomland. The tracks followed along the river. It was a very informal train; you could get on by standing on the track and waving your arms, or get off by pulling on the conductor's cord. Only there wasn't any conductor most of the time. One of the two firemen who shoveled coal into the boiler—for this was a steam engine—would come back and collect the money.

We turned when we heard the whistle, then the screech the wheels made on the iron rails. My mother came to the house and waited with us to see who it was. I could have run for my spyglass, but I liked the anticipation as they slowly came into view. There were four of them: a tall, thin one in front, two shorter in the middle, and a round one in the back. My mother recognized them first. "What on earth is Sebe coming out here for, so early on a Saturday morning?"

"That sister of yours is the worse tattletale I know. She knows somethin' that jes' won't keep. I better go put on the coffeepot."

"Maybe you better make another pan of oatmeal and heat the doughnuts. The boys will be hungry."

The Miller boys were just coming in with a bucket of warm milk and a basket of eggs. My mother was surprised; she did not know they were working here after the haying. I saw a question pass between her and Tuba, who mumbled, "We gonna need a little more help now."

"Tuba, are the Dutch girls coming, too?"

"Yes, ma'am. 'Round noon. They got to git their own chores done first."

My mother laughed in spite of herself. It was her first laugh since yesterday, after the court's decision.

We all sat around the long kitchen table and ate and drank until I thought Lloyd would develop a protrusion in his skinny frame from all the doughnuts, but he didn't. Harry and Worthy and I were still young enough to eat oatmeal on demand. Sebe had loosened her blouse across her ample breasts and was fanning herself.

"Sebe, what is it? You didn't come all the way out here on a Saturday morning just to drink hot coffee and fan yourself."

"Can't a woman come to see how her younger sister is? After all, you had quite a time yesterday. The whole town's talking."

"I'm sure they are. Out with it."

Sebe looked around the table to dismiss us boys. Her three were glad to go to the barn.

"It's all right. I have no secrets from Hughie," my mother said.

"Well, you may have to pay him to keep quiet about this." (She knew of my penchant for money.)

My mother nodded her approval of Tuba's back at the sink, and Aunt Sebe began. "You know I work the dinner shift now, over at the Dew-Drop Inn, and Sylvia Tingler works the bar."

"Well, I didn't know that."

"She's not such a bad girl."

"I'm sure." Mother was sarcastic.

"You want me to go on?" My mother nodded. "Well, who should come over to the bar side about eight o'clock but that Zeke feller who took you to court. Sylvia was jokin' around with him, and he had three or four shots of moonshine, and I hear Sylvia say, 'How about one on the house? Let me fix you my special.' I didn't know she had a special. But he drank it, and she stood there watchin' him the way a fox watches a rabbit, and in a little while he nodded and just leaned over and went to sleep on his arms. Well, Sylvia went to the phone, and guess who comes in through the back of the bar? Your Hugh. Between them, they loaded him into the backseat of Hugh's little yellow car and drove away. And that wasn't the last I saw of them, either. It was closing time, so I locked up and went out the front. You know I go along the railroad tracks on the way home, and what should I see up there on the loading platform beside the boxcars but Hugh's little yellow car and the three of them. You could tell the train was about to take off, there was a hissing of steam, and the empty cars sort of trembled.

"I hid behind a wagon and watched. Them two struggled, 'cause that Zeke is a heavy man, but Sylvia ain't no lightweight. Well, Hugh put the car right up to the open door of an empty boxcar. They rolled him in, and pulled the door shut, and latched it, and put one of them tin tags on it that says 'Inspected, Do Not Open.' And the train, with a couple of chugs and false starts, pulled away. Them two hollered and laughed. That Sylvia laughs a lot."

"Where do you think the train was going?"

"It said on the side 'Louisiana Sugar.' I reckon they were going back to Louisiana to get some more. Them sugar cars are just creepin' with red ants.

"I think I'll have another cup of coffee now and maybe a doughnut."

"You've earned them. I was afraid Zeke would come back here."

"Maybe you ought to give Sylvia a present."

"I already have. My husband."

Sebe didn't say anything for a little while. There were just the sounds of her drinking and eating. My mother, too, was silent, caught up in some private thoughts of her own. She was brought to immediate attention when her sister asked, "Where's that Hannibal? I didn't see him, and you know he's as danger-ous as his friend Zeke. I never understood why you kept them two here."

Tuba answered. "I think he's gone off. He didn't show up this morning. But we gonna do jes' fine without him. I expect he's done took everything he owns and hit the road. Hughie, you go up to his room and see didn't he take all his things and go . . ." She looked at me with her narrow mean look, which meant, "You get the message and bring back the right answer."

Hannibal's room was a mess. His dirty clothes were on the floor, and his bed was half off the frame. The pants he had worn yesterday were inside out, lying by the door, and his drawers were in the hall on the way to my mother's room. His closet was almost empty except for a few things on the floor. Only his new sheepskin coat from Sears & Roebuck was on a hanger, and his new high-tops were still in their box.

I started throwing his belongings in a pile so I could stuff them in a pillow-case for Tuba to burn. His old brown wallet fell from a pants pocket. It was more like a pouch with a snap at the top. Inside was a roll of five-dollar bills. He had drawn $150 last month, and most of it was still here. I counted twenty-eight fives and rolled them back up and put them in the pouch. When the horses were sold in Lexington in February, everyone involved got a percentage of the profits, and all he had bought was a sheepskin coat and some high-tops. I began to pull the room apart. I found it—a big, old, dirty canvas money belt under his feather tick, and I ran quickly down the hall through the door to the family side and into my room, where I made the largest deposit of my young life into the rubber boot, which was now a respectable bank in the corner of my closet.

July 8, 1929

SUNDAY MORNING. MY MOTHER and I were driving back home after taking Aunt Sebe and her boys back into town. Sebe went to church and dragged the boys with her.

My mother and I could always say things to each other in the car that were difficult across a table. We had not talked since Friday night, and she knew, and I knew, there were things that needed saying.

She began with "Where shall we begin?"

I said what was on the top of my mind. "How come you kissed Stanley?"

"Hughie, don't you realize what an emotional moment that was? This sixteen-year-old boy had killed to keep me from being raped by this dirty son of a bitch—I've got to stop saying that—he was a madman. He might have killed me, and if he had, he surely would have killed you, Tuba, and Stanley to keep you quiet. You may very well owe your life to Stanley."

"I don't want to owe Stanley for anything. I want him to owe me. Why did Hannibal want to rape you when he could go into town and buy a girl for two dollars? Lloyd knows lots of two-dollar whores."

"I'm sure Lloyd knows everything. I think you may be spending too much time with Lloyd."

I persisted. "Why did he want you?"

"He couldn't stand being bossed by a woman. He had to bring me down to conquer me, and bad men think sex is the way to do it."

"Do you think I will grow up to be a bad man?"

"I hope not. You're my only child, and if I failed with you, I won't get another chance. I worry sometimes, since you have a lot of women around you and no male role model."

"I have Granddad."

"And I'm grateful for that. Now, you are not to tell him about Hannibal."

"What if he asks me and we are playing truth?"

"He's not going to ask you. It would make your grandfather very unhappy to know what we have just gone through. He loves me. And you."

"How do you know when someone loves you?"

"You don't always, not for sure. Sometimes people say it who don't know the meaning of the word."

"Are you talking about my father?"

"Yes."

"I could send Stanley to the electric chair."

"When they strapped him in, you would have to sit on his lap. When someone is killed, everyone involved in the murder and the disposing of the body is guilty. All four of us were. In fact, I remember it was your red wagon we hauled him on. All four of us are equally guilty."

"I just wanted to have something on Stanley, just in case."

"In case of what?"

"In case you get to like him better than me and I have to get rid of him."

"I will never love him better than you. You are a very lucky boy, you have a great many people around you to love you and protect you. Poor Stanley has never had anyone. Here he is at sixteen, and he has had to kill two men. Life is really rotten to some people. A little tolerance, Hughie, please!"

"Okay, a little tolerance—whatever that is."

"Now, Hughie, when we get home and I put this car in the barn, that's the end of it, we will never speak of Hannibal again. Promise?"

"I swear to God."

"Don't swear to God—just promise me."

"Cross my heart and hope to die."

"And don't hope to die, either. Hope to live, to grow up and be a good man I'll be proud of." We were pulling into the barn, and that was the end of that.

The next Monday, Great-great-aunt Almeda came home, and that was the beginning of a whole new world for me.

JULY 9, 1929

MONDAY MORNING. MY MOTHER was going to town on business that she kept secret from me. She dropped me off at the Curtiss house on Worth Avenue and wouldn't even give me a hint. As she opened the car door, she reminded me, "Don't forget your promise."

"Don't worry."

"All right, I won't worry. I've got enough problems without that." And she was gone.

My father's car was in the back drive, which meant he was upstairs asleep, although it was ten o'clock. And my grandfather Curtiss's car was gone, which meant Matthew had driven my grandparents to the train station to pick up Grandfather's aunt Almeda, who had taken the ten o'clock train from Washington. I had heard a lot about Aunt Almeda from the women in my family, all bad: she was immoral, indecent, an old whore, a mistress—all kinds of invectives. My curiosity had grown by the day. Only Aunt Opal was home, laying a very nice luncheon table with yellow roses and daisies in the middle.

I asked, "If she is such an old cat, how come you don't just give her a saucer of milk?"

"She is not an old cat. I stayed with her in Washington last year, and she is charming. Hughie, I want you to promise me you will be nice, too."

Being nice to Great-aunt Almeda was the easiest thing I ever did, and no one had to pay me.

I went out on the front porch to wait, and when I saw a taxi coming, I stood behind a column and watched.

We had two taxis in our town. She arrived in the older one. It ran on batteries, and the front seat was much higher than the back, almost like riding a wagon behind a horse. On that front seat with the driver sat a fascinating figure who might very well have been riding a horse; she was dressed for it. The back-seat was filled with a big black trunk. They pulled into my grandmother's drive and came to a stop that sounded like letting the air out of a balloon. The old driver came around and helped her down from the high step.

Aunt Almeda swept up the steps toward me, and I thought, She's a magician, and she's making magic every moment. She looked more like a clown, but I knew that was just a disguise. Her costume was bright enough for the circus, although it was designed for riding to the hounds.

She was tiny, not a whole lot bigger than I was. Even in her high-heeled black boots, she was barely five feet, though the great mass of hennaed red hair and the black derby hat atop it helped her height. Her jacket was a brilliant red called huntsman pink. She wore a full black riding skirt that fell past her knees, with one hem hooked over her wrist, and she swung it back and forth as she came toward the door, clicking her heels. Naturally, she carried a riding crop. She had seen me in my hiding place from the corner of her eye as she turned the doorknob.

"You can come out now, little man."

I came toward her. "I'm almost as big as you are." I had never seen anyone with their face painted like this, except the gold-dust twins.

She made a graceful little curtsy with her red head bowed and one hand extended to me.

"I'm Hughie," I said as I reached out and took her hand.

She raised her head and looked into my blue eyes with her shining brown ones, and without preamble, instant and breath-stopping, I was in love. And as though she knew it—I suppose she was used to making men fall in love with her, even little men—she took my hand and we went into the hall together.

She had forgotten about the cabdriver with her trunk. He was dragging it up the steps. She rushed back out and fumbled into a little velvet pouch on her belt and found a dollar. She looked but found no more, kissed it good-bye and gave it to the driver, and then she came in.

"Where's your grandmother?"

"She and Grandfather went to the station to meet you."

"Oh, dear."

After some initial shock at Almeda's appearance, Aunt Opal came and hugged her and led her up the stairs to her room, leaving me deserted and forgotten in the front hall.

I always hid behind the door and listened a minute before I came out, and I did it now as I heard my grandparents coming in. It was getting harder and harder for Grandfather to get up the steps, and what he said came out in huffs. Usually when they were alone together, they quarreled; they were quarreling now.

"Look at me. I went all the way to the station with my apron on."

"No one saw it, you didn't get out of the car."

"What if we had been hit by a train?"

"Then you would have been such a bloody mess you wouldn't care."

She was taking off the apron and throwing it on the floor, and I knew she was mad about something besides an apron. Then she began to yell. I never heard her do that except with Grandfather.

"A bloody mess. That wouldn't have been any worse than being a bloody fool waiting down at the station for your old aunt who never showed up. She could have sent us a telegram."

He sat on the green velvet lounge and loosened his shoes. She liked him to sit here; she could stand before him and he couldn't escape. I waited for them to go on a little more before I told them she was upstairs.

"If you hadn't made us late by making the girls put pies in the oven—"

"Hugh, I do believe you would let everything in the market just spoil and go out in the garbage. Cash-strapped as we are, we need to make every cent we can."

He didn't answer that but began to speak softly because of his asthma. "Aunt Almeda, Aunt Almeda . . . are you here?"

There was no answer from upstairs. Maybe she, too, was going to let them fight a little more. He reasoned on. "When there was no one to meet her, she probably stayed on the train to Pittsburgh and Cousin Natalie."

She sat down beside him on the couch, their backs to the stair landing over their heads. Aunt Almeda stood there and listened.

"Glory to God, she probably did. All I need now is that old whore in this house."

"Mama, I want you to stop talkin' about my aunt like that. What if Hughie heard you?"

"What else do you call her? She lived with old Senator Burton forty years without marriage."

"Old Mrs. Burton would not divorce him, and you know as well as I, you can't get a divorce in politics."

It was hard for him to get enough breath to talk, and when Grandmother retorted, "Mrs. Burton is a decent woman who doesn't believe in divorce," his voice was down to a whisper: "It was the same as a marriage."

"Then why isn't she the rich widow instead of a pauper who has to go around begging for a home?" She didn't want an answer. She got up and started toward the morning room when Almeda's voice stopped her. It cracked like a snake whip.

"I never begged anyone for anything. I will get on the train and go on to my niece Natalie, where I am welcome."

Grandfather huffed to his feet and went toward her with hands outstretched as she descended the stairs rather grandly. I came out from the doorway to watch. I had hoped she might wash some of the paint from her face and maybe pat her hair down a little. I thought she looked wonderful, like a marvelous clown, but I knew what Grandmother would think. If anything, Almeda had added another layer; the circles of red on her cheeks looked brighter, and the black lines that circled her eyes were more pronounced. She had removed the derby hat.

Grandfather was holding each of her hands and saying, "Aunt Almeda—you have every right."

"Of course I have every right. My father built this house, I grew up here. I see someone is in my old room."

My grandmother was staring at the painted face, trying to find the woman she had known. "Aunt Almeda, you moved out of that room more than fifty years ago."

She clicked on her high heels over to the hall mirror. "Oh, yes. The greater world called me."

My grandmother could not resist. "And you made yourself available."

Almeda turned and faced my grandmother, and her voice softened and asked for pity. "Why don't you just add 'for a price,' and we're back to where I came in. I was not a whore."

Even I recognized that whatever else she was, she was a pretty good actress.

Old Matthew had found the trunk on the porch and was struggling to get it in the front door. Almeda stopped him. "Leave it out there. I won't be staying."

My grandmother went to her and patted her on the shoulder. "Now, now, Aunt Almeda. I'm sorry—of course you're welcome."

Aunt Opal echoed from the landing, "Of course."

"I have fixed up the little apartment on the third floor for you. From the balcony there, you can see all over town." (She might as well have added, and no one can see you.)

Aunt Opal tried to take the other end of the trunk from Matthew. "We will just get this up, so you can change for lunch."

Almeda tapped her riding crop against her palm and told her sad tale. "I was out riding when the executor of the senator's estate, Judge Brown, had the sheriff padlock the doors. I have nothing but the clothes I stand in. They wouldn't let me get out my own clothes. I have nothing until the will is read."

Grandfather sounded unsure. "Have you seen the will?"

"You know he wouldn't leave me high and dry."

Opal could not lift the end of the trunk. "What on earth is in here, the senator's dead body?"

"Oh, no, the senator's wife came and took him from me, something she could never do in life. These are my notebooks, forty years of notebooks. I've been keeping a journal all my years in Washington."

Grandmother wanted to know, "What on earth for? Were you writing the kinds of things you could blackmail people with?"

"You do think the worst of me, don't you? I thought someday, when all the villains are dead, I might publish my journals. It's true, only the good die young. Most of them will outlive me."

Grandmother took over, as usual. "Well, let's just put your trunk in this closet here, under the stairs."

Aunt Opal took Almeda by the arm and guided her toward the dining room, and Grandfather followed close behind.

"I was able to borrow enough from my cook and my maid to buy a train ticket and a little makeup," Almeda said.

They were almost through the door when I heard the first hint that she was not going to fit in too well here. Grandfather said, trying to smile, "You could have saved the money on the makeup. You won't need it here."

Opal added, "It's true, these sticks-in-the-mud just don't wear much."

Grandmother could make it clear that she was the mistress here only by playing hostess. "At least not so it shows. Most of the women around here haven't even cut their hair, but I have tried to keep up with the times."

They went in to sit around the table in the morning room, and I went in search of my father. He was standing in front of the mirror in his bathroom, shaving with a long straight razor.

"I've come to spend the day with you," I said.

He looked at me reflected in his mirror and carefully scraped his pale face. "What if I have other plans?"

"My mother said you don't see me much anymore, and if you have other plans, you can change them."

"Yes, your mother would say that. What were her plans for today?"

"I don't know, it's her secret." And I sat on the side of the bathtub.

"You don't know, or you want a dollar?"

"I told you, it's her secret."

"I don't know how anybody'd keep a secret from you. What have you heard about me?"

"You mean about Sylvia Tingler, and the Chinese laundryman, and the gold-dust twins?"

He turned with such surprise that he nicked a place in his cheek. "What the hell are you talkin' about?"

I saw that his eyes were red, and he had a look about him that I had learned to hate. He also smelled bad.

"I'm talkin' about when my cousins and me were standing on the concrete bridge, and we saw your boat going under with you fuckin' Sylvia Tingler."

He squinted at me, and I knew he didn't like me any better than I liked him.

"And the Chinese laundryman fucked the gold-dust twins. I saw him under the window blind in his alley. Lloyd took me."

"Does your mother know?"

"Of course not. This is men's stuff, you don't tell your mother."

"What does this have to do with Sylvia Tingler?"

"You know she irons collars for Chang sometimes, and Lloyd saw it, I didn't, but if you stand by his door in the alley, you can peek through the crack, and she was sitting on the counter with her dress pulled up, and Mr. Chang went up and put his big horse cock right in her. His cock is this big"—I held my hands apart with great exaggeration—"and she liked it."

For a moment I thought he might cut me with the razor. I remembered Stanley had cut his father's throat, and I wondered how much bigger I would have to get to bring that off; though I was big for my age.

He splashed cold water on his face, and dressed, and acted like I had just got there. "Well, what would you like to do?"

"I would like to go over to the little park where they are putting up the statue to the senator and watch them. They were starting when my mother and I came by, but she wouldn't stop to let me watch."

MY FATHER HUGGED Aunt Almeda and seemed to like her, and I thought maybe we had something in common after all. I knew, here at my grandmother's table, my newly beloved great aunt was in alien territory, but you would never have known. She ate her nut bread and cream cheese and strawberries and drank tea with all the chatting, smiling social graces of Queen Mary herself.

When my father had finished his whiskey pick-me-up and said we'd better go, she suggested she might like to ride along. Every face at the table clouded. Grandfather was the first to speak.

"You know, the senator's widow is liked in this town."

"And you think maybe his mistress should keep out of sight?"

She was looking at my grandmother, but Grandmother had decided to let her husband muddle through. After all, Almeda was his aunt.

"It might be a good idea if you stayed in for a little while. You know the nickelodeon is just about closed down, and if people stopped coming to the store—"

My grandmother added, "Hugh has every cent we have in the market."

"The smart money in Washington got out weeks ago. Hugh, I told you over the phone."

Grandfather looked befuddled, and I decided to change the conversation for him. "There's gonna be a big horse, twenty hands high, over there in front of the church, an' they got a derrick, they're gonna raise this statue of your senator up and sit him on the iron horse."

"I didn't expect it to be erected so quickly. He had it made a couple of years ago, but I thought they would wait awhile."

My grandmother had a way of saying "his wife" like driving in a nail with one blow. "His wife is not well, and she wanted to see the dedication while she still could."

"She's not well?" In spite of herself, Almeda giggled.

And I liked her even better, but my father had already had two shots of whiskey in his iced tea and looked like he needed air, so I pulled him out the door and toward his car. Almeda called after us, "Tell your mother to come and see me."

"My mother says you're one of the women of Babylon."

"I forgot, is your mother a Baptist?"

"She's Presbyterian. But Grandpa Fancler is a preacher—you know how they are?" I didn't mean it, of course.

She followed me to the front door. "I knew your grandfather Fancler long ago." She bent down to kiss me dryly on the cheek. "Well, honey boy, it looks like it's just you and me against the world."

Later, my father and I sat on a park bench watching the workmen wrestle the iron horse onto his pedestal. It didn't look like an iron horse yet, as it was completely bound up with wide strips of white muslin until the dedication.

"I know a secret."

"How much is this going to cost me?"

"This one's free. Lloyd says you need to know this. The gold-dust twins have syphilis."

"How do you know that?"

"The India-rubber man said it when they all worked in the carnival together."

"I suppose Lloyd told you that?"

"No, I heard it myself. I told you about the gold-dust twins and Mr. Chang, and then about Sylvia Tingler."

"What has this got to do with me?"

"Lloyd says you probably have syphilis and will go blind, and your dick will fall off."

"Did Lloyd say what I ought to do about it?"

"Lloyd doesn't know everything."

"I'm glad to hear it."

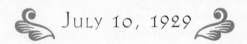

July 10, 1929

ON TUESDAY MORNING by nine o'clock, there was a big green truck in our drive with a high crib around it. I didn't like it. Pimberton Farms had been here last month and bought ten of our hound pups. I knew they had to go, but I didn't like it. Now here they were again. Our hound bitches had whelped a great many pups this last spring. Each bitch had produced nine or ten pups, a few eleven. They were all thoroughbred hunting dogs.

I liked nothing better than to lie down in the lawn and have thirty or forty half-grown pups climb on me, licking, nipping, barking, each hardly able to contain his energy. They were almost identical, with liver-colored spots on cream coats. They would run across the lawn in packs; with earsplitting yelps, one would tumble down, and twenty more would fall on him. At this stage of the game, they were fun, but a little later, when they had become teenagers and were stronger, all energy and no discretion, they would stream across the meadow in packs and bring down a lamb. They would rip out its soft belly and pull it apart. Inventing new games, they ran from sheep to sheep. They could destroy dozens in an afternoon, and once the old racial memory that burned in the back of their brain, passed down by their ancestor the wolf, was aflame, the only way to extinguish it was to get the shotgun and blow their brains out. It didn't seem to happen when their number was kept down to a reasonable amount and the mature stable dogs outnumbered the pups.

The truck from Pimberton Farms in Virginia was here to collect them. They would pay a hundred dollars each and turn them into foxhounds that would lead the chase, running before sleek brown jumpers, ridden by people in costumes identical to Aunt Almeda's. But I still didn't like it.

I went to the kitchen to get a cookie and a glass of milk and sit down with the second-grade reader. My mother had promised that if I read through the books of second grade, she would try to get me skipped to third, since I was so tall. I heard the pups all yapping with glee, like kids going on a picnic, and I remembered Spotty, and I ran. Where was he now? I went yelling through the house and out to the yard.

The truck driver was just latching the truck frame, and all the dogs were barking their anxiety to be about this great adventure. My mother was saying good-bye to Mr. Pimbrook, holding her check for two thousand dollars in her hand. I began to scream and grab the man's arm as he locked the truck gate. "Spotty, Spotty, you've got Spotty!"

The man grabbed me around the waist and held me up to where I could see in the truck. "Pick him out."

I could not. They were all jumping up and down against the side, grabbing one another's tails, rolling over, and not one of them even glanced my way. Spotty had a brown spot right between his eyes but then so did at least ten others.

On the farm, you get used to losing animal friends. Snuggly little lambs raised on a bottle grow up to get their throats cut and become mutton. Little bulls with liquid brown eyes get hit on the forehead with a mallet and end up as steaks, roasts, and hamburger. Cute little pink pigs, bearing ribbon leashes and chasing you around the yard, become nine-hundred-pound porkers, then chops, hams, and sausage meat stuffed back into their own gut. On the farm, everything is on a kind of conveyor belt that keeps moving through the seasons, and there is no tragedy, unless you call a full belly a tragedy. But Spotty was different. We had promised each other our loyalty and our love, something to hold on to when the seasons changed.

I took one last look, but he hid his face. "The little shit, the liar, the coward!"

And it took me several days before I could wish him well, chasing foxes over the hills of Virginia.

I had brought a deluge of rabbits on myself, and I was beginning to regret it. When the mowing machine passed over the meadows, it exposed dozens of rabbits' nests dug just beneath the surface. The bigger ones, and the parent rabbits, ran before the horses and escaped, leaving the defenseless ones on their own. Worthy and Harry and I had followed the mowers and picked them up until we had basketfuls. We were not intrigued by the tiny ones, cute as they might be, for we knew they would have to be bottle-fed. It was bad enough in the late winter, when we had to bottle-feed lambs, but I wasn't going to do it for two or three hundred rabbits. We picked up only the ones who could eat on their own and left the rest to the snakes and owls and red foxes; Grandfather Fancler had taught me that everything has to eat. We put them in the pens where we had raised baby chicks. Worthy and Harry went home and left me to do the feeding and the watering.

We had planned to fatten them and sell them at the butcher shop. Lloyd said he knew how to tan the skins, and we could sell those to Sears & Roebuck. They had lots of rabbit-lined garments in their catalogue and must need a big supply. When I called Worthy and Harry to come out and help me, they were busy. The only good thing was that the sleek little brown bodies looked like they doubled in size every three days. But it took bushels of green grass, and carrots, and little ears of corn. One day I gave them a peck of apples, and they were gone in twenty minutes.

My mother and Stanley went about the horse business, breaking the colts while they recited the multiplication tables, the rules of grammar, and how to spell every word in the eighth-grade speller. There was no help there.

The Dutch women reached in and tickled the rabbits' bellies, oohing and aahing the way silly people do over babies, and said something in Dutch that meant I'd have to do this job on my own. Tuba was a little more practical: she said the carrots and the white onions were big enough, and she thought she could find a recipe for rabbit pie somewhere if I would kill and skin a few.

I couldn't do it. And I couldn't just turn them out, as they would eat up our garden. When Grandfather Fancler came at the end of the week to exercise his horse, I thought I had a solution.

I smiled at him, took him by the hand, and led him down to the potting sheds where I had the rabbit cages, and I explained that I had a present for him, since he and I were such good friends. He looked from me to the rabbits. I was smiling, trying not to let my anxiety show.

"How many, about one hundred fifty?"

"I counted two hundred and nine, but they keep movin' around."

He said, "A lot of work, I guess."

I tried to look very casual. "Oh, not so bad."

"I couldn't take them home, of course."

"Why not?" I was desperate now.

"Well, they're a lot of work. For a young fellow like you, I'm sure that's nothing, but I'm getting up there; judging by the way their water pan is low, you better fill it. You see, your aunt Lillian and uncle Blake have just come to live with me and help with your grandmother. You know your aunt Lilly is young, and she might get the foolish notion to keep all these, and they would eat us out of house and home. And you know, without their natural predators, I'm sure they would multiply to at least a thousand by Christmas. Hughie, I'm sure you didn't mean to give me a white elephant."

"No, just two hundred and nine cute little bunnies."

And then he told me the story of Indian men who would give their enemies a sacred white elephant that they had to feed and care for and could get no work out of because it was sacred.

"Grandpa, what am I going to do? I'm tired of pullin' grass and scrapin' out rabbit shit."

As he let me stew, I could hear two hundred little mouths munching away, little beady black eyes looking through the wire for more. The cages were up off the ground a couple of feet, so you could see the manure pellets raining down. Already it was three inches deep on the ground, and I had just shoveled it up this morning.

"All right, Hughie, I'll help you. I thought I had taught you not to upset the balance of nature. We have to put it back."

He hitched up an old tired mare who was used only for light loads to a wagon, and we piled on the rabbit cages and went slowly down across the stubble-filled fields toward the river. There was little that was new and green here, so we went to the river. Along the riverbanks were great clusters of water-cress and crisp green grass, and we emptied the cages here and watched the rabbits scamper in every direction.

He said, "So your venture won't be a total loss, I'll give you a dollar apiece for those four bushel baskets of rabbit manure you have collected."

"Sold." I didn't tell him Tuba had offered me only a quarter for the lot, nor did I get a chance to collect. The dinner bell on the back porch began to ring: four rings and stop, four rings and stop, and my grandfather hurried the mare as fast as her tired old frame would move.

My mother was running down the lane toward us. She swung up on the seat beside us and took the reins from her father's hands. He looked apprehensive and knew whatever it was had to do with him.

"Lilly called. Mama's gone."

He didn't understand. "Gone where? Can't Lilly find her?"

"She's dead." Mother pulled the horse to an abrupt stop and jumped down and began unstrapping the harness because she didn't want to look at him as she told him.

He sat on the wagon seat and stared ahead, and after a while he said, "I'm not surprised. Your mother hasn't had much interest in living for some time."

My mother and her nine surviving sisters did what people in West Virginia did at that time. By the next morning, the undertaker was doing his magic, making Grandmother Fancler look like a sweet old lady, which she was not, and her daughters were cleaning her house from top to bottom. Usually this was done because, by the time the body was ready for viewing, a stream of people would begin arriving "to pay their last respects." The daughters cleaned and scraped and painted with a vengeance. It was as though they wanted to remove every vestige of her presence. They pulled the paper from her bedroom walls and hung a white and yellow stripe, a color Grandmother had hated. They took down the white iron bed frame and replaced it with a heavy oak one from the attic. Aunt Sebe took the oak rocker her mother had died in up behind the root cellar and chopped it into bits. The sisters kept up a running, laughing commentary, topping one another in a manner that had nothing to do with mourning or grief.

Only Aunt Olie occasionally had red eyes and asked to keep this or that which had belonged to her mother. No one argued, and in the end she took it all: twelve pillowcases full of a lifetime, with nothing else to show for it, except ten grown women who guarded their conversations so as not to speak her name.

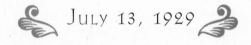

JULY 13, 1929

FOR THE NEXT THREE DAYS, until Grandmother's funeral, the farm had to get along without my mother's guiding hand. Not that there weren't a lot of hands now. The Dutch women were here almost full-time; they had taken over the gardens and the chickens. The Miller boys were in charge of the cows and shared in the return of the milk and butter sales. The dairy truck came at six each morning for pickup, and the boys didn't seem to mind starting their day at dawn. They sang church hymns as they attached the milking machines, and the sound seemed to soothe the cows. Mrs. Miller helped Tuba in the house. Her little girl was given my tricycle, reluctantly by me, and she rode up and down the broad hallway. Even the Millers' older two girls, who were seventeen and eighteen, came and polished silver, cleaned and dusted furniture, and ate blueberries and sponge cake. They were afraid to stay home alone since the Klan incident. Their little brother was named Handsome. He was learning to walk, but he hung on to his mother's apron most of the time. Of course, Stanley was now a horse trainer, and when the two-year-olds saw him coming, they would go to nuzzle against his skinny neck. He would have to give up that job when I got a little older.

My mother would drop me off at Worth Avenue and drive away without coming in, whether to avoid my father or Aunt Almeda, I never knew. It was kind of hard to avoid Aunt Almeda—she seemed to be everywhere. This morning she was sitting in one of the wicker chairs on the veranda with the remains of her breakfast. Grandfather sat on the glider opposite. He was getting too fat for a single chair. They were obviously in the middle of a conversation. After a greeting and the last cinnamon bun, I sat on the glider with Grandpa to listen.

"Huston, there is something I have to ask you."

"About the money?"

"No, not about the money. I will have plenty of money when the senator's will is probated. Huston, I had nowhere else to go but to you. I have to feel wanted by somebody. I know how Virginia feels, but you tell me the truth: do you really want an old aunt with a bad reputation?"

This was the kind of conversation that interested me, and I waited for his answer. He was slow. "How can you ask after all you've done for me? If it hadn't been for your money, I never could have started the store or the theater."

She was wearing a dressing gown that I recognized as Aunt Opal's, and she pulled it tightly across her throat, and her tone went up one pitch. "I'm not talking about money, Huston, I'm talking about love."

He went on as though he hadn't heard her. "I can soon pay it back. I'm well invested—I'm on a narrow margin, but good, sound stock."

He might have been forewarned by her tone. "Love, Huston, love."

"Aunt Mede, you know I can't say things like that. I have never been able to say that word to Virginia—oh, maybe once or twice in the beginning, when she was crying."

"The senator used to say it to me every morning and every night." She rose and looked away and didn't seem to see the beds of calla lilies that led to the street. "He could say 'love' as easy as 'good night.' I got addicted. It's like opium."

Grandfather would have gotten up as well, but it was too difficult. "I offer you a home. That has to say it."

She went over and looked down at him, and then she bent and kissed him on his bald head, leaving a red print. "If that is the best you can do, I'll have to accept it."

I don't know what made me do it, but I held up my face and said, "You can kiss me." Then I suddenly got shy and put my head down.

"Never take back the offer of a kiss. Do you know how often a seventy-five-year-old woman gets kissed? It's sad." She was gathering up the tray. "Huston, you should sell what you can now. The scuttlebutt in Washington says the bottom's about to drop out."

"This is my chance. I've got all my money and yours in Freemont Limited. And the blue chips. It went up three points yesterday."

"There is nothing to sustain anything. It's all artificial."

"There are enormous profits out there."

"Joe Kennedy told me last week that he had pulled out and was putting his money in the new talking pictures. Take my word, Huston, sell quickly."

She kept starting to go, but his voice would stop her. "I can't. When I bought Freemont, everyone thought you gave me an inside tip from the senator, and my friends bought it, too."

"Where did you get the tip?"

He said reluctantly, "From the Ouija board." I added, "The spooks spelled it out." She began to laugh, then sat back down.

"If I sold now, my friends would follow suit, and when Freemont doubles, they would crown me."

"They're going to crown you, all right."

He was a middle-aged, fat, balding man, but now she talked to him as though he were a teenager. "I was always sorry I didn't take you to Washington with me when I left with the senator. You were seventeen, old enough to be on your own—and too old. People might have thought you were my son."

"You were more my mama than she ever was, and after she left—"

She stopped him with her hand on his face. "I always lied about my age—a woman has to—and when you get older, you do it with hair dye, rouge, and tight corsets."

She went through the door and toward the stairs. I followed. Aunt Opal was in the hall. "Aunt Almeda, I laid a few of my things out in your room. I took up the hems. Maybe you can use them until you get back in the Washington house."

Before Almeda could answer, my grandmother came through the dining room door, carrying her white parasol. "I hardly think the clothes of a twenty-year-old girl would be suitable."

Aunt Opal was instantly angry. "Mama, you know very well I haven't been twenty for a very long time."

"Well, you had better not let anyone else know it, or you'll have to settle for the kind of man your sister got."

Almeda was now on the landing looking down on them. "Nothing changes. Fifty years ago, my mother was standing right there saying, 'Almeda, you're twenty-five, this is your last chance to get a husband.' So I got one. Unfortunately, he belonged to someone else."

Grandmother did not answer; instead, she went out the front door. Opal was going up the stairs. "Aunt Almeda, do you know how to shimmy? Could you teach me?"

"I certainly do. I saw Gilda Gray's show at least four times. She demonstrated and sang 'If I Could Learn to Shimmy Like My Sister Kate.'" They were laughing together. "You need a dress with fringe, I'll buy you one as soon as things are settled." They were singing together as they went up, "'And trembled like jelly on a plate.'"

I was forgotten, so I ran after my grandmother in hopes she would go to the store. But she did not. When she got to the sidewalk, she turned left and went around the block to the home of Alvin and Emma. I did not go there often because I wasn't asked. No one was. But it was a fascinating place, as good as a museum, with many things to look at.

Grandmother always said the same thing: "Now, Hughie, I don't want you to touch anything."

"You shouldn't say that to me now. I'm bigger, I'm not going to break anything."

"I'm sorry, I keep forgetting."

"Why are we going here?"

"Emma has sent me a note."

It began getting solemn and mysterious before you even got to the front door. There were two great carved lions on either side of a dark oak door that was twice as high and wide as a door ought to be. The kids in our town had dubbed this mammoth house Fort Pittsburgh. I never knew why, except that the Civil War cannons in the park across the street that were lined up in a row aimed at its great gray stone walls were the cannons that had been used to fire on Fort Pittsburgh. No one I knew would have tried a thing like that, except Cousin Lloyd, and even he could not have gotten the cannon balls loose from the pyramid they were cemented into.

The door was ajar, so I did not get to ring the bell that sounded like a Chinese gong. Aunt Emma was just inside, and she opened the door and motioned us in.

After the bright sun, it took a minute in the dark hallway to see clearly. The little light that came down from the stair landing at the end of the great hall was yellow and purple where it filtered through the stained glass.

Emma's mother had called her a white moth and dressed her accordingly, in long shimmering white gowns with loose falling sleeves, and Emma had taken on the role. She moved with a kind of gliding motion, as though her soft slippers did not even touch the marble floor. She held her finger to her lips and glanced upward with her pale eyes to tell us Alvin was upstairs. She led us into the library and closed the doors behind us silently.

Now we could talk. In this immense room with its insulating wall of leather-bound books, you could scream and not be heard. There were rows of long, thin tables up and down the middle, topped with glass cases. Emma tripped a switch, and a glowing armada set sail. There were dozens of models, mostly sailing ships. She had lit them for my benefit, for she said in her breathy whisper, "Hughie, you look at the boats while I talk to your grandmother."

The two of them sat on a puffy red velvet thing in front of the dark fireplace. Its depth was filled with masses of green ferns, but I would not have been surprised to see a fire. Whatever the time or the season outdoors, nothing was affected in here.

I pretended to be engrossed in the ship models but slowly worked my way closer so I could hear what they said. "Alvin just got home a little while ago. He's been gone since yesterday morning." I could tell she was going to cry.

Grandmother used her dry, even voice that was supposed to keep other women from crying. "Did you ask him where he had been?"

Emma was dabbing at her eyes with a silk handkerchief, and the crown of lavender flowers she wore had slipped to the side, making her look like a drunken fairy. "I didn't have to ask him, he told me, he always tells me. It's the evil painter, that Eddie Horner. Alvin says he paints best with artificial light. He says his portrait is going to be wonderful."

"I thought painters needed northern light."

"Mother always said she wanted Alvin to be painted very dignified and hang here in the library, and she wanted me to be painted like a big white moth and hang in the atrium above the potted lilies." Now she was really crying and hard to understand. "I don't think this man will paint Alvin dignified."

I didn't think so, either. Alvin looked like the bronze statue of Eros that stood on the knoll post. Slender, with his arms stretched upward, as though he were about to fly, but not dignified.

"And he is certainly not going to paint me. Alvin says they are both naked the whole time, that it frees up the artist."

Grandmother was patting her on the shoulder and saying what she always said. "He would have been better off if your mother had not brought all that money with her. Alvin would have had to work."

This was not an idea Emma liked; work would have taken him away from her as surely as the Eddie Horners of the world. What she wanted was for him to stay here in this house with her, safely out of the light.

"He does work. He goes down to the newspaper every week and talks with the editor and looks at the account books."

Grandmother proceeded with her own line of thought. "That money destroyed our father. Without it, he would still be a stonecutter, and happy building churches, instead of going out to cheat the Indians of their oil lands."

"We don't know that he is dead."

"Of course he is. Do you think in five years he wouldn't write?"

This was something I understood, so I said, "Maybe he is ashamed to come home without his hair after the Indians scalped him."

Grandmother had forgotten I was there. "Hughie, go down to the end and count the sails on the *Flying Cloud,* and I'll give you a dime."

Even at the far end, I could hear Emma's hoarse whisper. She said the thing nobody in our family talked about. "If he thinks he is going to loll about all night naked, then come home and have me go upstairs and climb in bed with him—well, I'm not, I'm just not." She was crying like a two-year-old, and I couldn't understand the rest.

She ran over to the corner and got a buggy whip she had left there. She put it in Grandmother's hand. She seemed suddenly wide-eyed, energized, her voice sharp, like she had turned into somebody else. "With Mama and Papa gone, I don't have anyone else. I want you to go up there and whip the skin right off his back."

Grandmother stared at the whip in her hand, and at this pale ghost of a half sister who suddenly was acting like a half-wit. Grandmother usually did not say things like "Now, now, dear," but she did this time. "I'll come over tonight, and you and I will walk around in the orchard for a very long time."

It was now Emma's turn to look at Grandmother as though she had lost her senses.

July 14, 1929

My grandmother Fancler's funeral was Saturday morning at ten, and by nine-thirty the church was packed. This was a Presbyterian church my grandfather had built forty years ago. It was framed with tall, thin Gothic windows whose yellow glass raised only a couple of feet from the bottom. With this many people, the air was close, damp, and hot. People had come early because there was an occasional rumble of thunder, and they wanted to get here before it started to rain.

It looked as though everyone had stripped their flower beds and banked them against the front of the church. The odor of wilting roses and stale water hung thick in the air. A steady stream of people walked down the aisle and back to look in the gray casket that sat before the altar. My grandmother's ten surviving daughters, seven sons-in-law, fifty-four grandchildren, and six great-grandchildren sat in front. I was at the end of the second row between my mother and father. I whispered to my father, "What are you doing here?"

"You know I like your grandfather—your mother gave me an ultimatum."

You could hear the comments when people came back down the aisle: "Ain't she pretty? Don't she look nice? I wouldn't know it was her." When we had gone to Runner's Funeral Home yesterday, none of her daughters knew it was her, either. Mr. Runner's new son-in-law had just come back from the morticians' school in Pittsburgh, and this was his handiwork. She looked like one of those old bed dolls made of pale pink wax that soldiers brought back from France, and her white hair was tinted a soft blue, just right with the high-necked silver-gray lace of her dress. Her false teeth wouldn't hurt her now, and they filled in the mouth so there was just a hint of a smile.

Grandfather sat in a straight chair over by the window and stared out over the pews without really seeming to see. The minister was little more than a gawky boy, and he had whispered to my grandfather for some kind of reassurance but was ignored.

Aunt Lilly usually played the organ, but today she turned it over to Mrs. Dilworth. Mrs. Dilworth was pumping the bellows with her feet and holding her hands over the keys, preparing to strike the first notes, when the thunder did it for her. There was an enormous ear-shattering clap, followed by a nearby splintering sound, as though a tree had been struck. The sky darkened outside the windows, and the room was cast into shadow.

Mrs. Dilworth was not going to be put off, and she began as loud as she could. " 'Shall we gather at the river . . . Gather with the saints at the river.' " People didn't know whether to try to sing along or not. Mrs. Dilworth's thin, quivery voice could hardly be heard. She started again.

The ten Fancler girls had spent their lifetime singing in their father's church. Their strong, full voices soared up through the high rafters, battling with the thunder and lightning as though it were a kettledrum's accompaniment. Grandfather seemed suddenly aware of the heat and smiled at his daughters. And now the rain came, giant drops pounding against the roof, the walls, the windows. Men who had been standing in the open door crowded in and shut it, and the air seemed even closer.

All those people standing squeezed tight added to the sour odor of dead flowers and the farm smells of bodies seldom bathed. The palm-leaf fans on the backs of the pews were all in frantic motion.

The young minister went to the front and put down the lid on the casket, then stood at the altar behind it. He looked frightened. The giant drops of rain were splattering on the windowsills and wetting the people standing there. There was nowhere to move, and the wet probably felt good.

Mrs. Dilworth next played "The Old Rugged Cross." My father chose this time to lean over me and whisper in my mother's ear, "I am going to Baltimore tomorrow."

She turned and looked at him with a face that said nothing.

"I am going to Walter Reed Hospital." He didn't seem sure she had heard, with all the clamor.

Mrs. Dilworth raised her hands from the keys to turn the pages of her hymn, and God in His wisdom stopped the thunder and the rain for one moment, and in it, my father with his hoarse whiskey voice said, loud enough to be heard over the entire room, "I have syphilis!"

And Mrs. Dilworth sang alone, in her thin quiver: " 'I will cling to the old rugged cross and exchange it someday for a crown.' "

My mother said, "Did you put the top up on your car?"

"I forgot. It's probably too late."

"It probably is, but I'd go do it anyway, if I were you."

He looked at her and leaned over to me. "Good-bye, Hughie," he said, and went out the back door behind the altar. And that was the last we saw of him until Grandfather Curtiss died at Christmastime.

Lloyd had been sitting behind me; now he moved into my father's seat. The rain gave up its pyrotechnics and settled into a steady, drumming downpour.

The young minister held in his hand the obituary he had cut from the paper. "I didn't know Mrs. Fancler well, I had visited a few times, but—" (He didn't say that he and Grandfather had played blackjack, and Grandmother had rocked and fumed.) "As I stand here and look out at her ten very attractive—beautiful daughters, I have to know this was a house of love."

He stopped when he looked at the ten women before him. No one nodded assent, not one smiled; his smile looked foolish. Each of the ten blond women pulled their lips into the same firm line of disbelief and raised their eyebrows. He didn't know how to go on.

Grandfather rose and put his hand on the minister's shoulder. "Charles, thank you, but Elizabeth really doesn't need anyone to guide her into the hereafter. No one of us do, really, or could we. 'The life we live is the death we will know,' that's pretty good. I should have put that up over the altar when I built this church."

His voice did not fight the sound of the rain as Charles's did, but rather rose rich and full above it. There was a loud roll of thunder, and he raised his eyes toward heaven. "Sure sounds like Lizzie has arrived and she is cleaning house."

There was general laughter, and the tension eased, but the air didn't smell any better. An old sexton came in from the back and whispered to my grandfather, who announced, "The sexton says the stables behind the church are flooded. If you put a horse in there, you better go get it out."

Several men rose and went out the back. To relieve the crowding even more, Grandfather suggested that small children might want to go down into the basement Sunday school rooms and play. Several children got up, and a few mothers with babies started down the stairs at the front of the church, but they soon came back and announced there was three feet of water in the basement. Babies who had hoped they were going to get their diapers changed began to cry.

Grandfather spoke over it. "When we were cutting the oak for the beams of this church, I did not think that we might be building an ark." There was a slight moan from the congregation.

"Now, if you had listened to me when I preached about Noah, you would know there is not going to be a second deluge. That first one was to wipe out all the evil on the earth. I look around me, and do I see a feeling of relief for that?

The Lord said, 'I will not destroy the earth again on account of men, no matter how bad they may be,' so you relax. Noah was penned up in that boat for a solid year. The smell must have been horrible, he certainly earned salvation."

He looked up as though asking for a little more quiet, and the Lord obliged. Though his voice still carried to the back, it was more on the level of a conversation with a friend.

"There is really no way to say good-bye to a life's partner. How do you sum it up? Maybe by what you leave behind; whoever says the parting words for me, that's the standard I want used. Lizzie and I leave behind ten—count them, ten wonderful women. I used to wish for a son and kept trying. How foolish. Sons get up and go out the door, and that's the end of that. But daughters—see how they have rallied 'round. And the real bonus is my grandsons. I have forty-two to keep me company in my old age, and I am proud to the point of sinfulness."

I knew he was talking about me, but then I glanced at Lloyd beside me, and he was beaming like the cat who ate the canary. The idiot thinks it's him, I thought. I turned around to see Worthy and Harry, and they had the same looks, and Bob down at the end of the pew and Russell and Peter and Edsel. I could keep a secret; I wouldn't tell them how deluded they were.

"We won't be going to the cemetery today. I am sure Lizzie's grave is full of water. It's slacked up a little, so some of you men may want to go and see if your batteries are flooded."

The women would not move until every drop had stopped, for they were all wearing their best straw hats, though some of the piles of silk flowers on them had wilted in the humidity. Grandfather looked to his daughters. "Girls, help me out here."

Aunt Lilly rose from the end of the aisle and walked to the organ. There was a murmur of appreciation, for she was truly beautiful, tall with a lovely long, slender neck, a pale Gibson girl. She was the next to the youngest at twenty-two. Where the other girls were golden-blond, ashen, and deep gold, Lilly was pale silver. Her dress was white eyelet and clung to her figure before flaring out in a sweep of skirt. She sewed well and knew the effect she wanted to make. She took off her big leghorn hat with the black silk poppies and laid it on the top of the organ as Mrs. Dilworth moved away.

Lloyd hissed in my ear, "Did you see them knockers on Aunt Lilly? Oh, man!"

(In the years to follow, Eddie Horner would paint Aunt Lilly's portrait no less than thirteen times.)

If the congregation thought they were in for more church hymns, they were surprised. Lillian's nine sisters joined her around the organ and sang song after song in wonderful harmony, all their father's favorites. He sat in his chair and smiled and knew how foolish he had been to wish for sons. "Buffalo Girl (Won't You Come Out Tonight)," "We're Tenting Tonight on the Old Campground," their whole repertory of Civil War songs, and just to finish off, "Bill Bailey."

At this point the rain stopped. A breeze blew through, and the room smelled better.

My mother and I were stopped several times on the way home by drifts of mud across the road, and once by a tree that had fallen out of the Oddfellows cemetery and was being pulled away by a farmer with a team of horses. Everywhere there were puddles, and standing water in the low places. It had rained for over an hour, the hardest downpour in anyone's memory. We came to Woolwine hollow, where Craven's Run was usually a narrow stream that drifted from springs high up the mountains, through one shallow pool to the next. Today it was a surging force that pounded through the bridge under the road, carrying tons of debris. The opening under the bridge was obstructed by a mountain of splintered wood that had once been someone's house. There were only three houses up this ravine, and one of them belonged to the Dutch ladies.

Before we could wonder, we saw them looking like three drowned rats, scrambling up the rocky bank of the road, pushing and dragging a wheelbarrow. They had a couple of crates of chickens and were pulling a rope at the end of which was their cow, who was having trouble climbing up the slick bank. They also lugged bundles of wet clothes tied up in sheets. The cow made it to the top and began to bellow. The three exhausted women sat down in the road.

We got out of the car and went to them, so as not to frighten the cow. The three of them sat there like idiots, laughing through their tears. They stared at my mother, and she stared back, trying to find words they would understand. They pointed to the great pile of broken wood, and Rose said, "Our house." Then they all laughed as though it was the funniest thing in the world.

They were going to our house, for they had nowhere else to go, but they would not get in the car because of the mud. They piled their wet bundles on the trunk rack and indicated that they should follow.

My mother said, "The first thing we have got to do is teach those women to speak English."

We came to the road that led to the Miller house and were relieved to see it had not floated down to the main road. It might as well have, for we ended up with all the Miller family in our house. We caught up with Mr. Miller, walking down the road, and he told us their roof had collapsed under the weight of a tree struck by lightning. He wanted to know if they could sleep in our barn until they could repair their roof.

My mother pointed out that we had nine guest bedrooms, and Mr. Miller pointed out the color of his skin and said that he didn't want the Klan coming down on us. My mother pointed out that she was a champion shot and owned a large assortment of guns. Mr. Miller pointed out that a black man was not allowed to have a gun. Another law pushed through by the Klan.

"You're not only going to have a gun, you're going to have four guns: one for you, one for your wife, and one for each of your two grown sons. I'll begin your instruction in the morning. If we're going to have a war here, I want some firepower on my side."

I asked, "If, when we go around the turn, our house is gone, what will you do?"

"We live on high ground, and the house is solid."

I persisted, "But what if it did fall down?"

"Well, we would just get busy and build it back, just as it was. I couldn't live without the farm. I knew the first time your father brought me here, I wanted this for my world."

"Is that why you married him?"

"That was part of it."

"Dad doesn't want to be a farmer."

"I thought when we put in the electric generators and our gas well came in that we'd be on the way to being self-sustaining, having a world of our own."

"Dad says there is a great big world out there, and someday he will show it to me."

"I'm going to make this into the finest farm in West Virginia for you—someday."

I wanted to say "I'd rather move to Pittsburgh" but didn't. She was too earnest. "Why do we need a big place? There's just you and me now, we don't need all those other people. You know Dad isn't coming back."

"I had a feeling his good-bye there in the church was really good-bye."

"You could tell all these people to just go on down the road. Stanley, too."

Our house came into view, washed clean and white and drying in the afternoon sun. There were new lakes in the meadows, and the corn stood in a foot of water, but most of the stalks were still upright. We didn't drive to the barn for fear of miring in the gravel road. We parked on the Rob Roy, which was an area with logs sunk under it.

Stanley and Tuba were coming up from the truck garden, carrying a bushel basket of tomatoes between them. Tuba was wearing muddy galoshes, and Stanley was barefoot with mud up to his knees. My mother and I both pulled off our good shoes, because the flagstones on the way to the house sank when stepped on and water bubbled up around the edges.

"Is there much damage?" my mother asked.

Stanley and Tuba answered in union, "Nope," and Tuba elaborated, "The tomatoes that were ripe got beat to the ground. There's a couple more bushels down there. I'll make ketchup tonight."

"Why don't we make a lot of spaghetti sauce. We are going to have quite a few people for dinner. The Dutch ladies got washed out, and the roof on the Miller house fell in. They are all on the way."

All Tuba could say was, "Lord A'mighty help us!"

Stanley reported that he had gotten in all the horses and cows at the first thunder. Not even the chickens had gotten wet. Only the hogs rolled in the mud up to their necks and loved it. My mother was watching the sky up above the sheep meadows. "Any sign?"

"No, ma'am."

Tuba sounded worried. "I been watching all afternoon. Maybe he can't find anything dry enough to burn."

Uncle Billie was guarding the sheep on the upper meadow. They had worked out a smoke-signal arrangement: yellow if all was well, blue if trouble, and red if dire emergency, like a cougar or a rattlesnake bite. Billie had bundles of dry leaves and grass to throw on the fire and produce each color.

"Stanley, please saddle Black for me while I change my clothes. I could never get up to the meadow with the truck."

I stood there in the yard and watched the sky, and I was the first to see a thin wisp of yellow, followed by several round puffs that looked golden in the afternoon. I began to yell. I took off my good suit on the porch and went in my underwear to help Stanley gather more tomatoes and cucumbers and whatever else was edible. I counted fifteen for dinner. I didn't know Lester Adams would be there—he made sixteen—and my mother gave him my chair at the end of the table.

I enjoyed, more than I thought I would, wading around in the mud with Stanley. At one point I sank in to my knees between the cucumber vines and yelled, "Quicksand. Quicksand!" Stanley stooped down and grasped me under the arms and pulled me out. I was surprised how warm he felt, pressed against my bare skin. By the time we had brought three bushel baskets of vegetables to the back porch, we were both covered in red mud.

My mother was getting a ham from the smokehouse when she saw us and warned, "You boys wash up down at the barn before you come in the house."

I would have dunked into the horse trough, but it felt too cold, so I followed Stanley up to his room. He turned on the water to warm and pulled off his shirt. "You can go first."

"It's a big shower. Didn't you shower with other boys at the orphanage?"

"Yes."

"I never did."

I pulled off my pants and stepped into the steaming water. It streamed down my face until I couldn't see, but I felt him move in behind me. He took the sponge and soaped it and rubbed my back, then I turned around, and he sponged the front of me.

My cock was sticking straight out. It had grown about three inches long and had often, in the last year, become erect. Stanley touched me and whispered, "I can't do that; you're lucky."

"Why not?"

"They cut my balls off."

I looked. His cock hung flaccid, no bigger than mine, and there was nothing behind it. He stepped out of the water and moved away from me, afraid. I had liked his touch, even though it was tentative. No one touched me anymore, and I was starved for it. He gave me a big towel and took one himself and wrapped it around his body as though to hide in it. He went and sat in the big blue rocking chair and bent forward to dry his feet.

I toweled my hair, and when I saw him sitting in the rocking chair, I went and climbed up in his lap and said, "I want you to hold me and rock."

"Hughie, I'll give you the chair."

"No, I'm cold. Put your arms around me." I snuggled against him with my face on his neck, the way I had with my mother until she decided I was too big for that.

He held me close and then tighter, and he rocked the chair gently, and he said, "Are you as lonely as I am?" And then he kissed me. He kissed my chest and my stomach, and then he took my cock in his mouth and rolled it around on his tongue. I felt warm, the kind of warmth I had been lonely for. I held his head between my hands as I had seen Mr. Chang do, and I thrust over and over into his mouth.

Then I pulled away and stood up and looked at him, and he panicked. He began to cry. "I'm sorry, Hughie, I shouldn't have done that. I'll have to go now. Please don't tell your mother until I'm gone."

I knew now I had in my grasp the weapon I had been looking for to rid myself of Stanley, his Achilles' heel. I also knew I would never use it. That missing thing in my life, that close warmth—I had found it.

I went and put my arms around his heaving chest. "I'm not going to tell. I liked it. We will do it every day."

And we did, almost every day, and when we missed a day, I felt a terrible need and wondered if maybe I had found my Achilles' heel.

 AUGUST 1, 1929

GRANDFATHER CURTISS'S CONTRACT with the film distributor was up on the first of August, and he did not renew. Not enough people were coming to see silent movies to pay the projectionist's salary, and Grandfather couldn't afford to buy the new talking machine. The film booker found a religious group in Louisiana who would buy the old projector for eight hundred dollars, and Mr. Meeken, the projectionist, said he would drive it down in one of the pickup trucks from the old Bluebird Market for half of the money. He did not say he was going to take his little peroxided floozy ticket seller with him, nor did he tell his wife. The floozy hid down under the dashboard and did not come up until they reached the south Elkins bridge. No one would have known it then, except that Lloyd, Worthy, and Harry were fishing for catfish from the bridge rail and saw her just as she climbed up into the seat. And that was the last anyone saw of Mr. Meeken, his floozy, Grandfather's truck, or the money.

It was a bad time for money, all going out and nothing coming in. There was tension in the air, as though a storm was approaching. And always the threat of loss, the promise of gain from the market. The economy seemed on a roller-coaster ride. The fact that Herbert Hoover kept saying "We are just going through an adjustment, all is well" didn't help much. After the fiascoes of the past few years, no one believed politicians anyway.

Aunt Opal was determined not to let that big empty theater just sit there. The two rentals a month for lodge meetings would not pay the taxes. Aunt Almeda knew the name of an agent in Washington who booked live performances, and she called him, and that's how we got that venerable Scotsman Sir Harry Lauder, on his third farewell appearance.

His fee was five hundred dollars, and Aunt Opal was sure she could sell tickets at ten dollars each for twice that amount. With Almeda's help, she painted a banner on a strip of muslin and hung it across the front of the marquee: SIR HARRY LAUDER, THE MOST FAMOUS SCOTCH SINGER IN THE WORLD, IN HIS FAREWELL APPEARANCE, SATURDAY, AUGUST FIFTEENTH.

She was banking on the fact that at least a third of the residents in our town traced their origins back to Scotland, and many people owned the big round thick Edison records of "I Think I'll Get Wed in the Summertime" with, on the flip side, "I Love a Lassie." She did not bank on the tenor of the times and the fact that when you get back to the roots of the race, the Scotch really don't like one another very well and are truly dour. About their only real interest was to look up under their kilts to see if the men were wearing drawers. Only fifty tickets sold.

In August, the canning on our farm began in earnest. With all the rain, there were bumper crops of everything. The farm provided most of the produce that was sold in the Bluebird Market. We left them on consignment and were paid 50 percent of the sale. But this year everyone was charging, and not 50 percent were paying their accounts, so my mother took her share in two thousand pounds of sugar, a thousand pounds of salt, a barrel of vinegar, assorted jars and lids and rubber rings, sealing wax, and all the paraphernalia for a major assault on the canning season.

When Grandfather Fancler saw all the preparations, he wanted to know if Billy-Pearl had had a dream about the seven lean seasons to come, as the Pharaoh had. "You may be right. The way the economy is going, we may have seven lean seasons."

"Given a choice between the ant and the grasshopper, I intend to be the ant."

"Daughter, there is a limit as to how many grasshoppers you should have at your table."

"Do you think I ought to push some of them out into the road?"

"Of course not. What can I do to help? Now that Mama's gone, I don't have to hurry home anymore—I feel guilty to be so relieved."

"Mrs. Zucker will be here in the morning, and you can direct traffic from the fields."

We could not can without Mrs. Zucker, the canning expert. She came on the first day of canning and stayed to the end. For her effort, she took home enough canned goods to last her mother and her through the winter. Today she had arrived with her old horse pulling a wagon full of empty canning jars. Green beans are hard to can and dangerous if they spoil. They could develop botulism, as could tomatoes and several other vegetables, but not when Mrs. Zucker was there.

Mr. Miller had taken the glass windows down from the summer kitchen, leaving only the screens and the tables and the sinks that had been scrubbed with lye soap. There was a battery of gas burners down one side and several boilers to sterilize jars. My mother had not remembered that Mrs. Zucker's mother was Dutch. When she met the Dutch ladies, they laughed and squealed and pounded one another on the back, and we knew a formidable canning team had been formed.

So it began. Wagonloads of truck produce were brought to the kitchen. The end product was shining jars of bright-colored vegetables and fruit, packed on the shelves of the winter cellars. The walls of the cellar rooms were three feet of earth, and two feet more with growing sod held it in place for a roof. The temperature in here, winter and summer, changed not two degrees. The by-products of all this, the peelings, cores, and cobs, were loaded on wheelbarrows and dumped into the hog pens. Their time would come in November.

We were the only farm in the area that had a refrigerated room for cooling milk and butter, and holding fresh meat. This was one of my father's contributions at the beginning, when he was still enthusiastic about his farm and his marriage. When my mother saw with what relish the Miller children ate, she knew we could never put up too much food. Also, she had drawn a plan and had a load of lumber delivered out by our gate, and Mr. Miller was starting to build a shelter for all of us to await the school bus in inclement weather.

I once thought all of her efforts were just for me, but I wasn't so sure anymore; she seemed to have embraced the world. More and more, when I felt excluded, I found respite sitting naked on Stanley's lap and rocking gently in his arms in his big blue chair.

My mother had not gotten permission for the black children to ride into town on the school bus, but she was working on it. She also found no record of Stanley's birth and decided she would make him fourteen instead of sixteen, so he would be the same age as the other freshmen.

She had invited my grandfather out for a devious reason, which she did not suggest until they were sitting on the veranda in the twilight, with a decanter of elderberry wine between them. I sat on the steps and played mumblety-peg with Boobie Miller, but I could hear. Boobie was pretty good with a knife, for a girl.

Grandfather leaned back and put his feet up on the railing. "You know, Billy, when I see how you have organized this place—you're a wonder, you really ought to go into politics. You could run this whole state."

"The secret is delegation. Let everybody do what he does best. By the way, before I forget, Opal gave me tickets to her Harry Lauder concert on the fifteenth, do you want to go with me? There will be five of us."

"I'd like nothing better. I've played 'Roamin' in the Gloaming' until I've about worn it out. Five? Your family has grown?"

"There will be you and me and Hughie, and I thought I'd ask Lester Adams and, of course, Stanley."

"Have you adopted Stanley into your family?"

"No, but I'd like to. What I'd really like is for you to. In name, anyway."

"I'm a little long in the tooth for that."

"He's going to high school this fall, and too many people remember the name Stanley Black. He needs everything he can get going for him, a name that has built-in respect. I want to register him as Stanley Fancler."

I lost hold of the knife and barely missed my big toe.

"I'd have to think about that. I haven't passed my name down to anyone, and that one out there is a strange bird. I'll tell you one thing, he's good with horses." He paused, then whispered, "Billy, I read the papers, too. That kid killed his father."

I thought, You only know the half of it.

She said calmly, "Maybe Stanley Black did, but Stanley Fancler did not. You could say he was an orphan son of one of your cousins."

"You never quit, do you?"

"Not until I get everything in order."

AUGUST 17, 1929

AUNT OPAL HAD to provide overnight lodging for Sir Harry Lauder and his accompanist. With the poor ticket sales, she couldn't afford to put him up at the Randolph Hotel, so she was preparing to house him at home, and Grandmother was not happy about it. His agent had sent a formidable list of his requirements, and she had read that he was an irascible and immoral man who associated with the likes of Charlie Chaplin. Nevertheless, being a hostess had built-in requirements; she had two rooms polished to perfection and carefully checked the list. Since the whole thing was an exercise in frustration and a losing game, she did not do it with enthusiasm.

Sir Lauder came in Saturday on the noon train from Washington, and Aunt Opal met him in Uncle Alvin's touring car, as it was the newest and fanciest in the family. I was not allowed to ride with her, so I spent Friday night at Aunt Sebe's with Lloyd, Worthy, and Harry, and sat on a luggage truck to watch his arrival.

Two rather grizzled-looking little men in their late fifties were standing on the back of the observation car. One was carrying a big leather pouch that contained a bagpipe, and the man in front was looking over the platform as though he expected a welcoming crowd. They were dressed too warmly for August, in dark greens and rust, and they each wore a tam. As Sir Harry came down the steps, even the baggy cut of his pants could not disguise the fact that he was potbellied and bowlegged, both of which drew Lloyd's comment, "I thought you said they wore dresses."

Aunt Opal hurried forward and, at the sight of her, Sir Harry turned on a light inside and began to sparkle. His eyes twinkled, his lips spread wide in a wonderful smile. As he held her hand, he said, "I've used the term 'bonnie lass' all my life, but at last I've found someone to whom it applies." He probably was happy that she didn't tower over him, as so many women did. She was small enough to smile up into his eyes.

He wasn't so congenial when they got to the theater. He began by complaining about the size of his name on the banner, the acoustics of the hall, the small stage, the lights, and the tone of the piano; it seemed the tuner had tuned it a half note high.

Lloyd and I had followed on his bicycle, me on the handlebars, with Worthy and Harry running behind. We listened from the foyer. When Sir Harry discovered his requirements for whiskey and warm beer were already in place, he had a stiff drink and tried out his voice. He sang "Roamin' in the Gloaming" with all the warmth of a fire in winter.

Even Lloyd was confused. "He sure runs hot and cold, don't he?"

Sir Harry continued to run hot as he pointed out to Aunt Opal that he was not married and did fancy himself a lassie now and then. Aunt Opal lied that her husband was in training to fight Max Schmeling and didn't fancy her philandering. Worthy wanted to run home and get his mother, as she had told the boys to help her be on the lookout for an eligible man to marry, so she could quit working at the Dew-Drop Inn. Lloyd explained that this old man didn't want to get married, he wanted only to fuck. Both Worthy and Harry thought Sir Harry was too old, but Lloyd explained that men never got too old; women stopped when they were forty, but men went on forever. Lloyd quoted the Bible: "Methuselah lived nine hundred and sixty-nine years, and he went on fuckin' to the last day."

I didn't think the Bible said that, and I was going to remember to ask Grandpa tonight.

The delivery boy from the Bluebird Market drove me home to get ready for the concert. My mother had bought me a blue linen jacket and my first grown-up tie, in red. She had bought an identical outfit for Stanley. She came into my room and stood behind me at the mirror to tie my tie. I caught her eyes in the mirror, and I knew her bland smile was to wipe away the anger I felt, and before I really thought, I said, "Mom, there's something I want to tell you." (Paris, take aim at Achilles.)

She smiled as she struggled to get the knot even. "Women never quite get the knack of this. What did you want to tell me?"

Then I realized I didn't want to tell her. I might feel cold for the rest of my life, but still there was an edge of anger.

"I'm not mad at Stanley anymore, and I don't want him to leave. But I don't want us to dress like brothers, because we're not. And Stanley is not Grandfather's cousin, either."

"I know, I wanted him to wear a blue coat tonight. I want him to feel inside the circle. I'm not pushing you out, Hughie, I need you to help me. That poor boy had never been inside any circle in his whole life. He needs that if he is going to get well."

It was the first I had thought of Stanley as being sick, that other kind of sick.

My tie was smooth, and she held my jacket for me. I wondered if he got well, would he still have a hungry mouth that wanted to devour me.

When we got in the car, I saw Stanley had a new tie, too, but it was stripes in two shades of blue. It was tied smoothly, and I wondered if she had tied it or had he managed it by himself. My mother was wearing her dark red silk, the one she kept for very special times. We had picked up Grandfather Fancler, and he was wearing a plaid tie in the tartan of his ancestors.

Lester was waiting in front of the theater. He, too, wore a tartan tie in a black-watch plaid and a blue linen jacket. It looked like everyone was Scotch tonight. Why hadn't they all bought tickets?

We sat in the front row, and I thought I would be able to tell Lloyd whether Sir Harry wore drawers under his dress, if he kicked high enough.

The room was packed by eight o'clock. Every chair was occupied, and a lot of people were standing in the back. Gertrude Gracey, who managed the Blue-bird Market, played the piano until it was time for the performance to begin. She pounded out a kind of fanfare, and Aunt Opal came out on the platform.

I hadn't realized Aunt Opal was so pretty until I saw her standing in the spot-lights. Her shining hair was curled back into a dark halo. She wore a ring of blue flowers around her neck. And in her flowing white dress, she looked like a lit-tle girl. I thought Grandmother Curtiss was probably right, maybe some nice man would think she was twenty-one instead of thirty-four and marry her. Unlike me, Aunt Opal did not lie very well.

She introduced "the most celebrated Scotsman in all the world, and rightly so—Sir Harry Lauder." Gertrude began "I Love a Lassie," and then the most dreadful moaning, howling sound I have ever heard in my life began, and the lit-tle man with the bagpipe marched on like it was a military drill and went around twice in a circle. He was wearing kilts, a tam, and a white shirt that looked like a woman's blouse with its full sleeves.

The audience was not sure whether this was Sir Harry or not, and there was only a spattering of applause that you couldn't hear anyway. The man backed to the rear of the stage, leaving the spotlighted space clear, and Sir Harry came prancing into it. If there was any doubt as to who was the star of the evening, he banished it. He was wearing a red velvet coat with lots of gold buttons and braid over a white lace jabot. His kilts were green and red, as were his kneesocks. He leaned on a twisted lacquered stick and looked out over the audience as though counting the house, and he said, "It's a bra britt evenin', it is."

Then he went into his songs. One after another, he sang like a singing machine that had been wound up and turned to full volume with an energy that belied his years and his grizzled look. He sang and danced for exactly ninety minutes. Then he bowed and said good night and walked away so abruptly that some people were too startled to applaud. And then they did—clapping and cheering and whistling.

Opal was at the stage door when he passed. "Are you going to do an encore?"

"No, ma'am. My contract calls for a ninety-minute performance, and I've done it. I will take two bows."

This he did, and then, as the crowd grew louder, she said, "I thought you were a showman."

He turned the twinkle back on and took her by the hand. "Are you?" And he led her onto the stage and began to sing to her, " 'I think I'll get wed in the summertime, I think I'll be wed in July.' " He led her through a soft clog, and she followed him step for step, and the crowd grew so loud you couldn't hear the piano, let alone that howling bagpipe.

" 'I think I'll be wed when the roses are red, and the weather is lovely and dry.' "

And when he got to "Hand in hand, together we stand, divided we never shall be," he grasped her around the waist, almost swung her off her feet, then kissed her. He bowed like a mischievous pixie, and off he went, out to the alley, and waited impatiently to be driven away.

Aunt Opal came back onto the stage, quieted the crowd, and said, "I thank you all for coming, and remember, next month our attraction is the famous Italian opera singer Galli-Curci."

On the front sidewalk, my mother waited with Grandfather Fancler for Lester to bring the car, and I went to wait with Grandmother Curtiss and a strange little woman in black silk, a black pot hat, and a veil who turned out to be Aunt Almeda. I was going to spend the night. Stanley stood over against the wall and didn't seem to know what group to join until my mother took him by the arm and guided him to Grandmother Curtiss.

"Mother Curtiss, could Stanley come with Hughie and spend the night? I have discovered that Stanley is really my cousin, and I think it might be interesting at your house tonight."

Lester was pulling up with our car, and Matthew was just behind him with the Curtiss limousine. Grandmother was not fooled, but she did truly like my mother. "Of course," she said and made Stanley a little nod of greeting. She leaned to my mother's ear and whispered something. For a moment my mother looked startled, and then my grandmother gave her one of those strange smiles that never seemed to get beyond her eyes. I could not hear what she said, and years later I asked my mother. She had said, "I got a letter from Hugh today. He says he will probably never come back, and you're a young woman."

I don't know when I had seen the Curtiss house on Worth Avenue looking more festive, except at Christmastime. Every light was on, from the big lanterns at each side of the gate and even through the front hall. The doors stood open. Grandmother took Stanley's arm and Aunt Almeda took mine as we ascended the steps. I wondered who had taught Stanley to do that — my mother, naturally.

Inside there were candles and flowers, and big silver serving pieces that I had never seen before. The two serving maids looked like they were out of a French movie, with their black uniforms and little lace aprons. Alvin was playing "Clair de Lune" on the piano in the drawing room, and a man was sitting on the bench beside him. Alvin came toward Grandmother, and where he had stopped in the phrase, the man picked up and continued to play. Alvin was wearing a pink ruffled shirt and black velvet pants.

"Virginia, I knew you wouldn't mind. I brought Eddie Horner. He finished my portrait today, and we are celebrating."

Eddie Horner got up and came toward her. She had never seen him before, and I am sure she was surprised at the look of him. It took her a moment to extend her hand. Stanley was still holding on to her elbow. Mother apparently had not taught him when to let go. He, too, was staring at Eddie Horner.

No one had told us that Eddie Horner was black, very tall and very black. Not black like the people we knew, with heavy lips and kinky hair, but black like the pictures of an Egyptian pharaoh with shining black hair combed straight back. All of his facial features were sharp and seemed to tilt up at the edges. He was polished and composed and totally in charge of the room, or any room, for that matter. He bowed at the waist and kissed my grandmother's extended hand. She was flustered. "No one has kissed my hand for a very long time."

"It's the years I spent in Paris," he said. "When I meet a lady, old habits return."

I pulled Stanley toward Grandfather's study. My mother would have to teach him to stop staring at people. Now he was looking at Aunt Emma, who sat in the corner behind a Boston fern.

"Come on, I'll show you the grizzly bear Grandfather shot." Everyone jumped back when they first saw the bear. There was a spotlight on the row of sharp teeth and the red tongue, and the bear towered almost to the top of the twelve-foot ceiling.

"If you want to look in his mouth, you have to get up on a chair."

Stanley didn't want to. I had not seen Grandfather over in the corner behind his desk, and he hadn't heard me, for he was wearing the earphones to his radio set. The weaker stations could not be heard on the speakers. When he saw me, he said, "I've got Chicago." Then he took off the earphones and wearily sank back into his chair.

"This is my mother's new cousin, Stanley."

Stanley didn't know whether to extend his hand or not when Grandfather gave him only a tired nod.

"Aren't you going to come out to the party?" I asked.

"This is no time to be giving a party. Do you know that twelve stock investors jumped out the window this week? And that was just in Chicago."

"Did you tell Grandmother it was bad business to give a party now?"

"Of course not. Women don't understand business."

The earphones were making crackling noises, and he put them back on with "Enjoy your evening, young man."

Stanley and I started for the door, but there was another question I had to ask. I went around the desk and lifted the earphones from Grandfather's head and whispered, "You're not going to jump off the roof, are you?"

"No, we're only three stories high. I would need to be much higher to splatter all this fat!" He laughed, but it was not a fun laugh.

I was at the door when he called after me. "Hughie, tell your mother to come see me Monday. I have some business with her."

"I thought you said women didn't understand business."

"There are a few exceptions, very few."

When we got back to the dining room, Aunt Opal and Sir Harry were there, and several other people who had wanted to meet Sir Harry, including the editor from Uncle Alvin's newspaper. An elegant buffet had been set up, and people were moving down the line holding Grandmother's best Haviland china. The French doors to the patio were all open, and the new floodlights Alvin had had installed in the orchard were all burning, and the trees glowed, especially Uncle Alvin's favorite, the Blushing Maiden. It had a ring of light all around it, and the little pink apples glowed like bulbs on a Christmas tree.

I put a plate in Stanley's hand and went before him in the line; he was unsure.

"It's easy. The dry things, the chicken, the ham, the beef, the cheese that you can pick up with forks, you help yourself, and the things with gravy in the chafing dish, you hold out your plate, and the maids will dip for you."

We were behind Alvin and moving slowly because he was quarreling with the newspaper editor, or rather, the editor was quarreling.

"You might have discussed it with your staff before you made the decision."

"I would think you'd be happy to be a part of the Hearst chain. They can do a lot more for you than I can. You can tap in to an international news line."

"Of yellow journalism, you mean? They have a whole staff that just sits down there in Washington and makes up lies."

Aunt Almeda was in front of them, and she couldn't help but hear. She added, "Young man, I have lived in Washington for the last forty years. Lies are the major by-product of government."

Alvin introduced her. The editor turned and studied her face. She had taken off the black hat and the veil and added just a little color. She looked charming.

"Oh, yes, Miss Curtiss. I've heard about you. I'd like to do an interview sometime." His voice was cold.

"Why don't you do that—sometime? I know William Randolph Hearst very well; I'm sure you will fit right in." She turned and helped herself to the melon balls in crème de menthe.

The silver flat service was wrapped in pink linen napkins and tied with a ribbon in Sir Harry's tartan. I knew this was Aunt Opal's work, as was the beautiful long green scarf Aunt Almeda had added to her costume since she came home.

People were finding places to sit and rest their plates. There were small tables everywhere. Grandmother had taken a plate into the study and closed the door behind her, so Grandfather wouldn't be tempted to come out and discover Eddie Horner. He wouldn't insult someone in his own house, but he wouldn't be gracious, either, to what he thought was a nigger faggot.

Grandmother whispered to me, "Hughie, run in and take off your grandfather's shoes."

I knew why. I hurried, and without him asking, I unlaced and pulled them off. "I thought your feet might hurt. Don't worry, this is for free." I pushed his shoes back under his desk and ran.

I put my plate on the mantel and went back to the table to get cream puffs before they were all gone. This was one of Grandmother's party treats that she made herself: a pyramid of small cream puffs each the size of an egg, stacked up and glued together with caramel sauce until they came to a point, with caramel poured down over the outside. I got a plate for Stanley and me.

Alvin and the editor were still arguing as they moved to the drawing room. "You could have learned the business. Your mother did. She bought the business not knowing a thing about it."

"My mother was obsessed with influencing the world around her, and she thought owning a newspaper was the way to do it."

"I wouldn't say obsessed—she was a guiding spirit."

"Obsessed, Mr. O'Connor. Control, control. Do you see that poor white ghost of a girl over there behind the fern? That's my sister, the result of my mother's total control. With my mother gone, she is hardly able to get up and go through the day. She's like a trained monkey waiting for the watchword, and her trainer is dead." Alvin moved away.

I had found Stanley a spot near Aunt Bea's harp in the bay window and gone to get my plate from the mantel. Eddie Horner was standing before the mantel, looking up at old General William Baker Curtiss's picture. It had been painted when the general was fifty, at the height of his masculine arrogance, and the painter had caught every facet of it. Horner was examining the signature. Aunt Almeda was behind him.

"It was painted by Whistler. The general was my father."

He looked at her and back at the painting. "That's a Union uniform?"

"What else? This is West Virginia, we had withdrawn from the South. As a matter of fact, it was painted in Washington in eighteen and sixty-six. My father thought he was going to be appointed by President Johnson to the Supreme Court, that being a license to steal; but someone raised another inquiry into the assassination conspiracy, and my father thought he had better get out of town for a while. So he brought his portrait and me back here. I was eighteen at the time. I wouldn't be held in a little backwater for long."

"You're like a walking history book."

"You make me sound ancient. I'm only seventy-five."

"I'd like to paint your portrait."

"Oh, no. I've been painted many times, but now my eyesight is fading, and I can't see my wrinkles, thank God, and I certainly don't want them immortalized on canvas."

Horner persisted. "When you see the painting I've done of Alvin, I think you'll change your mind. It will hang in a museum someday."

He turned to watch Alvin, who had brought a plate of food to Emma and was urging her to eat.

Almeda admitted, "He is certainly handsome."

"No, he is beautiful. I stood and looked at him for six weeks. There was no way the light could fall on his body and render him less than beautiful."

Almeda was surprised. "Did you paint him naked?"

"Nude full-length, standing before a mirror, as much in the round as though he were sculptured."

"Well, that will cause talk in this town."

"Everything causes talk in this town. Sometimes I think I should have stayed in New York."

"You may be right." And she moved away.

Sir Harry's man was called Stoker. I don't know if that was his first or his last name. He was examining Aunt Bea's harp. Grandfather had bought it for her as a teen, in hopes she would learn to play, but she hadn't gotten much further than "Three Blind Mice." The harp was a beautiful thing, with its figure of a woman on the front of it, very much like the figurehead on the prow of a ship, except it gleamed in its gold coat against the red brocade walls. Stanley and I watched Stoker as he ran his fingers tentatively over the strings.

Grandmother was following Matthew around, refilling the wineglasses, he with a carafe of red and she with white.

"Mr. Stoker, do you play the harp?" Grandmother asked him.

"Did yuh think, now, that that screamin' goat gut is the extent of my musical ability?"

"Oh, do play." And she sat down on a big velvet puff in front of him.

He was adjusting the harp, trying the strength of the pedals, when Stanley said to me, "People used to give the orphanage old copies of *Vanity Fair,* filled with stories of people who lived like this, but I thought it was just made up."

Stoker settled in his chair and tilted the harp forward against his shoulder. At the first sweep of sound, I heard Stanley gasp and lean forward with rapt attention, as did everyone in the room.

First he played "Flow Gently, Sweet Afton." Stanley was making a kind of humming sound under his breath, as if tuning a pitch pipe. Then Stoker said, "And now for the Irish among you" and began "Believe Me if All Those Endearing Young Charms," and Stanley sang with him under his breath.

My grandmother said, "Stanley, you know this song, don't you?"

"My mother used to sing it a long time ago, before—"

"Please sing it for us."

"Oh, I couldn't."

"I have a feeling your mother wants you to." She looked in his eyes and smiled. "Mr. Stoker, play it again, please."

He began the introduction, and Stanley tried to begin a couple of times, but broke off.

"The trouble is, I haven't given you a proper introduction." Stoker brought a great rolling sound out of the harp and then two high, clear notes that Stanley tried his voice against.

Grandmother whispered, "Your mama's listening."

He closed his eyes, and the sound from his throat began to build like a bell, a bird, Jenny Lind, anyone who had a beautiful, clear, ringing soprano voice. Every face in the room turned toward his, unable to believe that such a sound was coming from this frail boy. Even Sir Harry, who had been sitting with Aunt Opal on the stairs, was drawn into the room. My grandmother was turned to him, and tears were streaming down her face.

Stoker had turned into the perfect accompanist and was underplaying each note just enough to accent this unbelievable performance. Stanley sang all three verses, and his clear true tone seemed to stir the glass in the chandelier. When he came to the end, there was complete silence. He opened his eyes, afraid he had made some terrible social faux pas, and looked like he was going to run. And then they began to applaud. Stoker played rounds on the harp, and Alvin at the piano played fanfares.

Sir Harry came forward. "Lad, where did you learn to sing like that?" Stoker added, "He's got perfect pitch. Twice he hit high 'C' as clear as a bell."

Stanley seemed as amazed as everyone else. "I didn't know I could."

Sir Harry wanted to know if he knew anything else, and Stanley said it was the only song he knew. And then Sir Harry asked, "Are you from a musical family? Your father, your mother, have a voice?"

"My mother used to sing that song before my father killed her."

No one knew quite where to look. Eddie Horner slid onto the bench beside Alvin, and they began to play four-handed ragtime to an earsplitting beat. I took Stanley by the hand and started up the stairs to our room, but Sir Harry seemed determined to keep at him. "Lad, do you know how rare a voice like that is? I haven't heard anything like it since the Vienna Boys' Choir came to London. How old are you?"

I answered for him. "Fourteen."

Sir Harry considered. "I'd like to take you on the road with me. Your voice is liable to change any minute, you haven't much time."

Stanley turned and ran up the stairs. I turned to Sir Harry in case he was tempted to follow. "My cousin does not want to be a singer. He thinks it's a low-down, cheap way to make a living. He is going to be a horse trainer!"

Stanley was leaning against our bedroom door, breathing heavily. Once inside, he quickly ran into the bathroom and turned the water to splash in the tub full force.

"Hughie, please, I have to get in the tub quickly." He was squeezing out of his clothes and not bothering to unbutton. He sat in the tub. The water looked hot, the steam rising around him.

"You don't have to do that."

"Yes, I do. The singing made me remember a lot of things I don't want to remember."

He sat in the water until it was cold. When he got into bed, he pulled his knees up against his chest and held them tight and was almost immediately asleep.

I had forgotten to pull the blind down, and the first morning light hit me in the eye. Stanley was still rolled in a ball on the far side of the bed, where he had gone to sleep. I slipped out and pulled on my pants. I pulled down the blind and went downstairs.

It was only about five-thirty in the morning, but I knew Grandmother would be up, even if no one else was. She slept very short nights. She was just taking a pan of oatmeal from the stove. "Good morning, Hughie. I'm glad you're up. I like company for breakfast. Let's eat out on the screened porch."

All the tables in the kitchen were stacked with dirty dishes from last night. I got the silver and the napkins, and Grandmother brought two bowls of oatmeal.

"Can I have maple sugar?"

"Of course."

We pulled high wooden stools to the marble table that Opal and Bea had used in their teens for taffy pulls. It was pleasant to look out into the orchard, still heavy with the morning mists; the sun had not yet burned away. Then we heard the screaming: *"No, No, No!"*

"It's Emma."

"Someone is trying to kill her!"

Grandmother looked around for a weapon. There was nothing. I had unlatched the screen door and was halfway down the steps when Grandmother passed me carrying the meat cleaver. The screams were coming from near the gazebo. Emma was under Uncle Alvin's apple tree.

I heard Grandmother breathe in, "Oh, my God."

Alvin was standing on the tips of his toes, and Aunt Emma had grasped him around the legs and was trying to lift him. He could stand like this because there was a rope around his neck, tied to a limb of the tree. His weight had pulled the limb downward but not far enough. His head was bent at a strange angle, and his tongue had turned purple and seemed to fill his whole mouth. The golden boy was broken, and all the tugging, lifting, and screaming Emma and my grandmother did would not help.

Grandmother got the chair he had stood on and kicked it away. She sawed through the rope with the meat cleaver, and the body crashed down, and the limb flew back up, raining apples down upon us. Emma threw herself upon his body and was kissing his blue, blotched face. Grandmother pulled her off, fighting and scratching, and finally gave her a sharp slap across the face. She crumpled in a heap on the ground. Grandmother sent me to get a blanket and went into Alvin's study to call Lester Adams, but he wasn't home. Then she called Runner's Ambulance to take Uncle Alvin to the funeral home. He obviously was beyond the need of a doctor.

On the desk beside the phone was an envelope addressed to Emma. Grandmother tore it open and read:

Dearest Emma,
   Good-bye.
   Virginia will take care of you now. Last night I indulged in the final indignity—I let that nigger painter fuck me, and you know I can't live with that.
                                                                 Alvin

Alvin's body had been taken away, and the doctor had come to give Aunt Emma a sedative. Her housekeeper was sitting beside her, watching her sleep. Grandmother and I walked through the orchard, trying not to look at the Maiden Blush apple tree, and back up the steps to the screened porch.

There was a big school clock on the kitchen wall that said seven o'clock. The maids were washing dishes. In the dining room, Matthew had polished the table and arranged in the center a big bowl of nasturtiums from the cutting garden.

Grandmother sent me upstairs to put on a shirt, and put a tape across my mouth. As I passed the study, I looked in at my grandfather. The lights were still on, and Grandfather was still sitting at the desk, fast asleep. I put out all the lights, including the one on the grizzly bear, and tiptoed out, closing the door softly behind me.

Aunt Opal had come down to prepare the Philadelphia scrapple that was on Sir Harry's breakfast list. I passed her on the stairs. She looked tired and older than yesterday.

"I have to take him to the train at eleven, then I will drive you and Stanley home." She didn't wait for an answer.

Stanley was sitting on the side of the bed fully dressed, with his blue tie tied.

"Why didn't you come on down?" I asked.

"I don't want to see that man again."

Grandmother passed our door on the way to the third floor and Aunt Almeda's apartment. I went to wash up and get Stanley to tie my new red tie. By the time I was dressed, I heard the two of them coming down, and I motioned Stanley back until I could hear what they were saying.

My grandmother: "But I do need your permission to bury him there. As the oldest living Curtiss, you own the cemetery."

"Then you have my permission."

"I know he's not a Curtiss, but I want him close."

"Do the others know?"

"No, let's let Opal get rid of her guests before we tell her. I'll just change my clothes." She went into her room, and Almeda slowly descended.

I bragged to Stanley, "Someday I will be the oldest Curtiss, and I will own the cemetery."

"What would you want with a field full of dead people?"

Stanley and I went to the screened porch where I had started my breakfast three hours ago. He was afraid the kitchen maids would recognize him, even though they had left the orphanage three years before he had, but the wall that stands between the masters and the servants blinded them, and they served French toast and orange juice in total deference. One even asked, "Are you old enough for coffee, sir?" Stanley answered, "Yes, thank you. Lots of cream and sugar." He was getting the hang of it.

I got the best parts of the Sunday paper from the front hall, and Stanley and I went out to the gazebo to read the funny papers.

On the way to the station, Stanley and I were in the front seat with Opal, and the two Scotsmen were in the backseat. Sir Harry was in an expansive mood, laughing and slapping his knees.

"I'd say my appearance here has been a rip-roarin' success." (Opal kept her eyes on the road.) "Eh, lassie?"

"From your viewpoint, I suppose so."

"You had a full house and at least fifty standees. In view of the same, I was thinkin' perhaps you would increase my fee."

"You think fifty percent more would increase you by fifty percent?"

"That would seem equitable."

"And if I had taken in fifty percent less, you would reduce your fee fifty percent?"

"Aye—but that not being the case—"

"Aye—but that is the case. I had exactly forty-five paying customers. All the rest were freebies to give you a good house. Pass the account book back to him, Hughie."

I found the book on the floor and handed it back. He looked it over. It listed every name and whether they had paid. There were forty-five paid.

"No one needs to paper the house for Sir Harry Lauder."

"I'm sure it's not the first time."

Stoker started to say something, and Sir Harry stepped on his foot. I heard Stoker whisper, "I wasn't going to say it."

Opal pulled the car up in front of the train station. "Now, in view of our miserable ticket sales, would you care to refund half your fee?"

"You're angry because of my performance last night."

"Do you want the truth?"

"You might as well."

"I think you're an arrogant, egotistical little—very little—pip-squeak."

The two men got out quietly and unloaded their bags without saying a word more, and we drove away.

"Don't say anything, either one of you, I'm off of men for the rest of the day. I'll have to get you home. Alvin will be yellin' for his car."

"No, Uncle Alvin won't be yellin' for his car. He wants you to keep it."

"That will be the day."

"This is the day." I couldn't tell her any more than that, for the secret was still in force.

"Hughie, sometimes I don't understand you."

"Sometimes I don't understand you, either. Why did you call Sir Harry all those names?"

"You'll find out everything somehow, you might as well know this: he came into my room last night, braggin' like he was God's gift to women, and he wasn't."

Stanley giggled.

"That's all?"

"That's all I'm going to tell you."

At least it made Stanley laugh, and I had thought he wasn't going to laugh anymore.

August 20, 1929

Alvin wasn't going to be buried until Tuesday morning. It was a very short obituary for someone who had owned the paper up to the week before. But then Alvin had never done anything except get his picture painted and hang himself, and the paper lied about that. It said he had died of a heart attack, that he had known he had a heart condition for some time.

The funeral service was private. It didn't say Aunt Opal got to keep his car, which she did, or that Aunt Emma wouldn't come out of her room, which she wouldn't, even for the funeral.

We were standing at the grave in the Curtiss family cemetery by eight o'clock. The sun was breaking through the morning mist, and there still was a pale feeling to it. I don't know why we were there so early, maybe to get it over and done with. That was the feeling that Grandmother gave out. People had called, but she had stuck to immediate family only. She had given Eddie Horner an emphatic "No!" and hung up the receiver without explanation. And so there were just four women in black and me; my mother, my grandmother, Aunt Opal, and Aunt Almeda.

There was no church service, and Grandfather Fancler had been asked to conduct at the graveside, since he would make it simple and ask no questions. The undertaker waited by the hearse, and the two men who would lower the casket and fill in the grave sat on a tombstone. The whole thing didn't take more than five minutes. Somehow it was all wrong, and the only way to make it right would be to open the lid and help Uncle Alvin out and say, "Sorry, a big mistake," and he and I would climb over the fence and run down over the cow pasture all the way home.

Aunt Almeda stayed afterward, and I stayed with her. She hadn't been here for a long time. She said she wanted to get reacquainted with her family. We sat on a marble slab that covered her mother and watched the grave diggers fill in the grave, and tamp it down, and spread the blanket of white roses that had covered the casket. When they were gone, we pulled the roses apart and dropped a couple on all the graves. It seemed only fair, and Alvin would never know.

"Do you think Uncle Alvin went to hell? Emma's housekeeper says he did because he killed himself."

"If there's a hell, I'm sure it is reserved for nosy, tattling busybodies like Mrs. Kessner."

"Is there a heaven?"

"I'm not so sure anymore. I used to think it was all nonsense. That just lying there in the senator's arms was as close as heaven was going to get. But now, with him gone, I find myself wishing to see him again, and if that's the only way I can do it, I'll pray for heaven. This marble's cold. My bones are getting stiff. Let's walk."

We stood and looked at the towering column that the Daughters of the American Revolution had erected to General William Baker Curtiss. There was a commemorative plaque and a big garland of roses cut out of stone. Almeda put her hands on the smooth round stone of the column; it rose at least twenty feet high.

"Daddy, they did right by you, just one big phallic symbol," she said.

"What does that mean?"

"It means he was just one big dick. He ruled his whole world from his pants. Women were just a commodity, something to be traded around. No less a slave than the very slavery he pretended to fight against. He didn't even care which side he was on, as long as it was the winning side. 'To the victor belongs the spoils.' At the end of the war, my dear father the general returned from the South with four hundred wagons of booty, each pulled by four mules. You know that silver tea service your grandmother is so proud of? Stolen from some southern gentleman. That's what generals do; they rape a man's daughter and steal his teapot. That's war."

She went over to a space that had only a small blank headstone, and she lay down on the ground and stretched out and folded her hands.

"This is where I'm going to lie someday, right here beside my sister Mary. She was your great-grandmother. Hughie, will you come up here sometimes and sit on my grave and talk to me? I won't answer, of course, maybe I won't even listen, but you come and tell me how the world is treating you. And don't forget to joke about it a little."

August 24, 1929

The next Saturday, Almeda began my painting lessons. We spread newspapers out on the table in the gazebo. Aunt Almeda did not believe in little scrunchy drawings; we had big pieces of paper, big jars of watercolor, and nice fat brushes.

"There is no sense in watercolor unless you learn to let the water work for you."

So we did big blue washes and dabbed some off, and they miraculously became clouds.

"In watercolor, you define the world by the shadows it makes."

She added darker blues and purples on the underside of the clouds. I had always thought shadows were gray and black, but I learned a shadow can even be green if the light is right.

We did several versions of Uncle Alvin's apple tree. I was surprised, looking at it, that it could be so unchanged. The only evidence that he had died there was a rope burn on one of the limbs. The apples were turning a deeper pink each day. Next lesson, we were going to put some in a bowl and paint a still life.

I couldn't seem to look away from the tree, and Aunt Almeda asked if I wanted to go and paint somewhere else. I didn't, but I did think that somehow this tree ought to be changed. The apples ought to turn purple or brown or something.

Since Aunt Opal was making Aunt Almeda a dress, she had to go in for a fitting. "Hughie, you spread out a new set of papers, and we will try again next week." And she went into the house.

I was just soaking the paper in a pan of water when I heard "Shhh, shhh." I looked up to see a strangely shrouded little woman hiding behind a tree. She wore a long linen duster, the kind from the pictures of the first automobiles, and a big hat with a veil. She was giving me the "come here" signal with her finger, and I went.

I knew from the hoarse whisper that it was Aunt Emma. She sounded as though she wasn't through with all her crying yet.

"Hughie, do you want to earn twenty dollars?" She waved twenty dollars at me. "Ten now and ten when we're done."

I asked, "What do I have to do?" I didn't really care. I would do anything for twenty dollars—well, maybe not anything. There was a boy in my first-grade class who would eat a fishing worm for twenty-five cents. I wouldn't do that.

She led me around to the porte cochere where her limousine was waiting. It was a huge old hupmobile with a glass partition between the seats. It had been out of the garage maybe twice since Emma's mother died. Old Alex, the chauffeur, held the door open. He was wearing his brown jacket with a high collar and cap that matched the car. Now that I was a watercolor artist, I was paying more attention to shading.

We climbed in, and Alex closed the door. There was room enough in the backseat to set up a card table. The glass partition was the same dark green as leaves on an apple tree. Aunt Emma laid out a pouch purse on the seat, and it rattled. When she opened it, I saw why. She had a gun, a knife, and a big pair of scissors, and if it wasn't for having to give back the ten dollars, I would have jumped out of the car, even though we were now purring down the road like twenty kittens.

She saw my expression and announced, "I'm going to get even with Eddie Horner." (That didn't make me feel any better.) "We are going to play parts, like in a movie."

Apparently it was going to be a talking movie, because she gave me lines to say. We pulled up in front of Eddie Horner's studio and watched. He had moved into old Mr. Fergerson's photography studio after Mr. Fergerson died. His door was brightly varnished, and there was a polished brass plaque that read:

EDWARD HORNER, A.M., M.A.
OIL PORTRAITURE BY APPOINTMENT

There was only one work displayed in front of the green felt curtains over the windows, a small color sketch of Uncle Alvin's head. It was in an elegant gold frame, but it looked like a study for a larger work or a memorial.

Emma opened her coat, and I saw why she was wearing it. Her dress was ripped clear down the front, and there was a recent cut across her middle that looked like it was still bleeding.

"Now, I'll go in, and you wait just inside the door, and when I take off my coat and start to scream, you run outside and yell, 'Help! Help, a nigger is raping my poor aunt!' Be sure they hear on both sides of the street. Yell until men start running in."

On one side of the studio was the Randolph Hotel. I looked to see how many people were sitting out on the veranda; there were several. On the other side was McKenney's Saddlery. Since it was Saturday, several farmers were milling around there. I didn't think we would get much response from across the street. It was the retirement home for veterans of the Civil War. They were all over eighty, but I would yell loud enough for them to hear anyway.

Aunt Emma put her hand on my knee. "Remember, this man killed your uncle Alvin!"

She buttoned up her duster and adjusted her veil over her face and got out. Alex was holding the door.

"Remember, Alex, cover it well with the sheet. Rope is in the backseat."

She went through Eddie Horner's door with me just behind her. I had thought it would be dark inside, but Horner had installed a skylight, and the room glowed. There was very little in the room—a leather couch and a few chairs, a pier glass and a large easel, with whatever was on it carefully draped.

When he heard the door, Eddie Horner came out of a little room in the back. He was obviously shaving, as there was still white foam where he was trimming his mustache. He was bare-chested, and his suspenders hung down at his sides.

He was annoyed. "I see clients by appointment only."

"This won't take a minute. I just came by to pick up the painting of my brother."

"Who are you?"

She lifted her veil. "I'm that very, very white woman, the sister of the late Alvin Channell."

He stared at her for a moment. I knew he was thinking, with her colorless face and her blue lips, that she looked as dead as Uncle Alvin.

"All right, all right, you're welcome to it." And he went to the window and removed the portrait sketch.

"Oh, no." She smiled. "I think it is this one." And she pulled the cover from the big painting on the easel.

There stood beautiful golden-boy Alvin, life-size and standing before the same gold pier glass that stood against the wall. He was standing partly turned from the viewer and looking back with a half smile on his lips. The light fell on his golden hair and bathed his cheekbones and his shoulders, and the soft curves of his ass were painted the colors of a ripe peach. The front of his body reflected in the mirror had no discreet drape. He did not have an erection, but the painting had not stinted on his manhood.

Emma cried out like a stricken child. "That's what I came for."

He was arrogant. "It's not for sale."

"Oh, but it was. I have already bought and paid for it with my brother's life. You killed him, and I get the painting."

"You're a crazy woman. He died of a heart attack. I am going to exhibit that painting in New York and make my reputation."

Emma was fumbling through her bag, and I wondered whether she was looking for the gun or the knife. She came up with Uncle Alvin's farewell note. She held it up for Horner to see and read it aloud. And then she added, "You raped him!"

His arrogance growing by the minute, he walked around like one of the roosters in our chicken coop. "My dear lady, take a good look at that painting. He stood right over there naked every day for six weeks and looked at me with that look: that is invitation. I think that's what I'll call the painting."

"I, too, know that look. He slept with me every night of his life. That look was for me."

She was fumbling in her bag again, and this time she brought forth the gun. He backed against the wall. "You're crazy! Put that thing away. You're liable to hit somebody."

"I'm very likely to hit you. I'm a good shot—Hughie's mother taught me—though I am a bit nervous, but I still think I can shoot you through that part I find most offensive. Would you like to drop your pants, or do you want a hole in the front of them? They seem like a good fabric."

He was beginning to sweat, and his forehead was shiny. "Take the goddamn painting and get out of here!"

She held the gun level without moving as she said to me, "Hughie, tell Alex to come in."

Alex was not sure when he saw the gun. "Are we robbing the place, miss?"

"Are we, Mr. Horner?"

"No, no, it's a game."

Alex tied the painting on the trunk rack with the covering over it and waited by the open car door.

"For Christ's sake, put that gun down," Horner pleaded.

"You're right, Mr. Horner, it is a game, and we're not quite through yet. All right, Hughie, play your part."

She threw her hat on the floor and stripped off the duster. She looked more violated than she had in the car.

"Do you know, Mr. Horner, we haven't had a nigger lynching in this town since nineteen twelve. And they cut off his cock and nailed it to a telephone pole. All right, Hughie, yell loud. A nigger is raping my aunt—"

"Help, help, a nigger is raping my aunt!" I threw the door wide. I had gotten in the spirit of the thing, and I was preparing to yell it out loud.

There in the doorway stood Lester Adams. All I could see was his sheriff's badge.

"Well, Hughie, what are you doing here?"

I glanced back. Emma was getting into her duster, and Horner was escaping into his bathroom. I saw the sketch of Alvin's head, and I lied quickly. I had sworn off lying for a while, and I guess I was energized for it.

"Aunt Emma and I just came by to pick up Uncle Alvin's picture." I went and got the drawing and walked out to the car. Emma was standing in front of the pier glass, adjusting her veils. "Uncle Alvin's dead, you know."

"Yes, I know." Lester had a quizzical look.

"We thought it would be a nice thing to keep."

And so it was. I took it home and hung it on my wall. Aunt Emma took the full-length portrait and hung it in her bedroom where she could look at it as she lay in bed.

AUGUST 30, 1929

THE LAST WEEKEND in August was my mother's tenth reunion at Morgantown University. She and Lester Adams had graduated together, and they went on a Friday afternoon to be there over Saturday and Sunday. When Lester came to pick up my mother, he brought my grandfather Fancler. My mother had announced that she was bringing him out to stay with me while she was gone. But I knew it was something else; twice in the last month, there had been a paper in our mailbox that said "Nigger lover."

A month ago, my mother had moved the targets for shooting practice to the front lawn and held her shooting instruction for everyone but me and Boobie there, so that anyone going down this road would see we were well defended. We heard that word had gotten around.

The house seemed more festive with Grandfather here. He gave his black horse a good workout down through the meadow, with Stanley close behind on the back of a promising three-year-old. We ate in the big dining room with candles and the good silver. My mother had left instructions. Stanley and I had on our linen jackets with white shirts, which were enough without the ties.

The three Dutch ladies had been busy in the sewing room, and they were wearing the results of their efforts. The dresses were all in the same blue, with differences in cut and lace collars. With their yellow braids coiled on top of their heads, they looked like sisters. Grandfather seemed charmed, and though they didn't understand everything he said, they grasped his gracious manner and his smile.

"I'm reminded of an old song from the Civil War: 'Three little girls in blue,' or was it two?"

We had white gooseberry wine with the trout from our pond, and with the blackberry cobbler, we had ruby-red port. The rule was that I could have my goblet one-quarter full, Stanley could have his half full, and Grandfather and the ladies could fill them to the top, and this they did two or three times, and Grandfather laughed more than usual, and the ladies got pink in the face.

By the time we moved into the front parlor, Rose and Helga were singing in German, and Erica, who never seemed to talk in any language, was singing in French. Stanley recognized it from the horse-training manual, and he was fascinated. He said to me, "Why didn't she tell me?"

And I answered, "Why didn't you ask her?"

He was too pleased to be annoyed at me. "She can help me when I go to school."

Something strange had happened to Grandfather. He seemed to have grown younger. There was no real difference in appearance — he was still long and lean, he had a good full head of ash-gray hair, and there was still a wide white streak over each ear. Maybe it was the smile. He had big white teeth, but you usually didn't see this much of them. I was reminded to brush.

One of those times when my father was playing around with the electricity, he had installed a spotlight so that it shone down on whoever was playing our old, square mahogany grand piano. Grandfather went and sat down in the glow and began to play. He didn't play well, but he kept the loud pedal down, so you couldn't tell the difference. He started to play "Rose of Washington Square," and Rose came with a little giggle and sat on the bench beside him. He had a pretty good singing voice, which he had passed on to his daughters, but this wasn't the way he sang in church. This was fun singing, laughter and good times. The other two Dutch women went to the card table in the corner and began to play blackjack. They looked toward the piano only occasionally and smiled as though they were checking progress, then went back to their game. He sang all the Rose songs he knew, and I was surprised at how many there were.

She said, "I have not been close to gentlemen for six years, since my husband died." And then so she could be sure he understood, she said, "I have been widow for six years."

He stopped playing with his right hand and kept only a slow rhythmic beat with the left. He touched her hand. "I have been a widower for a short time. No, I take that back; my wife has been dead for a short time, but I have been a widower for a very long time."

I didn't recognize this grandfather, and I didn't want to see him like this, so I went to the kitchen where Stanley was playing dominoes with the Miller boys to see if Boobie wanted to play Chinese checkers. I thought she cheated, because she won more often than I did, but I could never catch her at it.

On the farm, we went to bed early and got up early. On the way to bed, I passed the parlor door, and Grandfather and Rose were still at it, only now they had moved to the card table. If there was a language difficulty, you would never know. Maybe laughter is the universal language. The port decanter was on the card table, and they had half-filled glasses.

I went up to bed feeling deserted. I wondered what my mother and Lester were doing. When he had picked her up, he said, "It will be like old times. We will just go back ten years and start over."

She said, "I wonder what they will all look like."

"Stop worrying. You were the youngest one in the class, that won't change." As he put her bag in the back and closed the car door, he leaned over and whispered, but I heard him, "I was in love with you then, and that hasn't changed."

I wondered what had changed. Me. She didn't have me then, and she didn't have the farm then, and I wondered if these were enough to keep Lester Adams out of our lives.

I had been asleep maybe an hour when I awakened to the sound of singing. My window was wide open, and I could see the horse barn and hear the sounds coming from Stanley's window. I knew he had bought records this week with his spending money. Each week he had ten dollars to spend and ten dollars to put away, and this week he had bought ten records of Irish tenors. I thought he wanted to learn something besides "Believe Me if All Those Endearing Young Charms." But what he didn't realize was that he didn't have a tenor voice like Chauncey Olcott's; he was a soprano and could reach C above high C. Not until he learned to imitate bird sounds from the Audubon records did he realize his true range.

Tonight he awakened me to how lonely I really was. I knew there was a chance I was going to lose my mother to Lester Adams, and maybe even Grandfather to Dutch Rose. I was sure of it when I was on my way down the hall to have Stanley hold me. Maybe he would even let me spend the night in his bed. When I came out of my room, there was Grandfather going barefoot down the hall, in his green silk pajamas my mother had given him for Christmas.

I said, "Where are you going?" at the same time he said, "Where are you going?" And then we both said, "Truth."

"I am not sure where," he said. And I told him the Dutch women had the three pink rooms at the end of the hall. They each had a pink door, and Rose's was the first.

"How did you know I was going there?"

"Lloyd told me you never get too old. He said Methuselah was nine hundred sixty-nine and fucked every day."

"I'm going to have a little talk with Lloyd. He knows things that I don't know. Where are you going?"

"Sometimes, when I'm lonely, Stanley holds me and rocks me in his rocker. Nobody else will hug me, and sometimes I need to be hugged."

"I know how you feel."

"Secret."

"Secret." And he went down the hall, and I went down the steps.

Everyone kept busy on Saturday; I don't know if it was to prove to my mother how responsible we were, or maybe that the world could go on without her and she could go off and fool around with Lester Adams. I hoped not.

Fifty years ago someone had planted a circle of apple trees at the far end of our back lawn and put down a big round of flagstone for a picnic area. The Dutch women had chosen this spot to serve dinner to my grandfather. I should have been invited, since I was the one who had spent two days painting all the wicker tables and chairs with the same orange enamel we used to paint the farm equipment; but I was not. It looked like they were still romancing Grandfather, with fried chicken and German potato salad, with too much dill weed for my taste.

It looked like French Erica was the designated widow for tonight. Although they were all wearing white dresses and looked like a French postcard, Erica had red poppies like a crown on her head, and her yellow braids were combed out loose down her back. She was also playing the mandolin and singing.

Stanley wanted me to come down to the training ring and manage the phonograph. He had a record of "Darktown Strutters' Ball," and he was trying to train a beautiful three-year-old gelding named Leopold to do a kind of two-step as a surprise for my mother. It got too dark to see, and the string of lights over the ring brought masses of bugs, and the bugs brought the bats down from the barn ceiling. Stanley gave up and hugged Leopold and rubbed him down and put him in his stall, then went upstairs to stand in a hot shower and practice singing with the Irish tenors, in an effort to deepen his voice.

Back at the house, the Millers were all down in the kitchen, popping popcorn and listening to the new Atwater Kent radio my mother had bought. My grandfather did not approve of the radio, except for news. He was afraid people would stop reading. I didn't really like all that singing through their noses from the Grand Ole Opry, and I didn't want any popcorn, so I went up to the third floor and out on a little balcony at the end of the house, where I could look down into the picnic area. It looked more like a French postcard than ever, with the citronella candles burning in hurricane globes. Grandfather was stretched out on the glider, and Erica was sitting on a cushion on the ground, playing her mandolin. Rose and Helga were playing cards.

I didn't realize how sleepy I was. I lay down on my bed and fought sleep. I wanted to be awake when Grandfather came up, but I knew I would never make it, so I got a pencil and a piece of paper and wrote, "Erica's room is the second door from the end," and put the note on Grandfather's bed and went to sleep. The world would have to go on without me.

On Sunday we all tried to sleep an hour later, but the cows didn't have a clock and were bawling to be milked by six, so they could head to the meadow and get started on the clover. A cow has two stomachs, and it takes a lot of munching to keep them both filled. Grandfather did not come down until nine, and then he just took a cup of coffee and went out on the veranda.

Boobie and I brought in the eggs, and I went out to the road to get the Sunday paper. I got the funnies out of the paper and went to ask Grandfather to read them to me. I could read perfectly well, but I liked the way he changed his voice, especially for "Maggie and Jiggs." He was leaning back on the chaise with his mouth open, sound asleep. I thought, I hope a fly flies in your mouth; it would serve you right.

We had a big freezer in the milk room that made ice. It had a funny ammonia taste, but it was good for cracking up with a hammer and packing around the ice-cream freezer with rock salt—somehow that made it colder—and if you turned the ice-cream freezer handle steadily for an hour and kept pouring in the ice, you could make three gallons of ice cream, thick, creamy, and wonderful.

The Miller boys were working at it when I saw Grandfather and the Dutch ladies going up to the chestnut grove, carrying buckets and a hoe. The buckets were for the blueberries that grew in the grove of dead chestnut trees, and the hoe was to stir in the berry bushes and dislodge any poisonous snake that might be waiting for a bird to come and feed on berries. The business end of the hoe was to chop his head off. We had both copperheads and rattlesnakes, but mostly they were just big black snakes who lived on field mice and were good for scaring a girl but did not really bite. I didn't really like the chestnut grove. It was up on the first plateau above our meadows, and it was a ghost of a grove. All the trees had died the year of the chestnut blight. The bark fell off, and the towering limbs had bleached white, like old bones. The waxen green leaves of the blueberry bushes seemed to do very well under their protection, but I didn't like the skeleton trees, and I always let somebody else pick blueberries; not that they asked me.

They brought back three gallons and dumped them in the sink to wash. Helga and my grandfather were holding the handle of a bucket together, and they smiled at each other. They both had eaten blueberries until their lips were blue. I supposed Helga was the romance of the evening; after all, she, too, had been a widow for six years, and it was her turn. I got a cupful of berries before they were added to the ice cream and the dinner muffins.

Grandfather shared the bed of the third Dutch woman Sunday night. I knew something that Lloyd didn't, but it was a secret, so I wouldn't be able to tell him. But I would hint; I would tell him he probably was right about Methuselah.

My mother and Lester got back about one on Monday, and she gave me a tight squeeze that I wasn't used to from her. When he went to leave, Lester kissed her, not a quick "see you sometime" kiss but a tender, lingering kind of thing, and then they put their cheeks together and whispered something I couldn't hear.

There was an Indian burial mound in Moundsville, and souvenirs were sold there. Lester brought me a book called *The Mound Builders of the Appalachians,* and my mother brought me three Indian arrowheads. When Lester was driving out the gate, the three Dutch ladies were standing there waving to Grandfather, like those paintings of women waving to their husbands going out to sea. And I thought Grandfather must be a Mormon sailor.

SEPTEMBER 2, 1929

THE TWO OLDER Miller girls got jobs as upstairs maids at the Randolph Hotel, and Monday was their day off. Mr. Miller would take the farm truck on Sunday night and go in to get them. All the Millers went along for the ride, as they didn't see the town very often. The kids all sat in the back of the truck and looked through the slat railing, and sometimes I went with them. We parked on a side street waiting for the Miller girls to come out.

I had ordered *Uncle Billie's Joke Book* and was telling the latest bad joke, and they were all howling and laughing, when a man climbed up the side of the truck and looked down. He was a bleary-eyed drunk, you could smell enough alcohol on him to make you throw up. We all knew him. It was John Rhodes, who lived up the road from us, and one of the KKK my mother had routed from the Miller house.

"You're a white kid! What you doin' down in there with that mess of niggers?"

Kirby Conway came roaring up on his motorcycle, and John Rhodes dropped to the ground and ran up the alley behind the hotel. Kirby asked if we were all right. "That bootlegger is going to really get himself in trouble one of these days." He gunned his motorcycle and went on down the block to the Dew-Drop Inn. He was courtin' my aunt Sebe. Lloyd was hoping he would marry her because he owned a coal mine. Also Lloyd said he was going to let him ride the motorcycle by himself, but I didn't believe that.

On Tuesday there was another of those dumb notes in our mailbox. This one was written with a crayon on a paper bag, and it said: DEATH TO NIGGER LOVERS.

We were to see John Rhodes again by the end of the week. It must have been close to midnight, since there was a full moon, but it was already going down behind Bickles Knob when the hounds began to bark and we heard the sound of someone kicking at them and throwing rocks. My mother turned on the lights across the front porch and rang the alarm bell, then she was out the door. Mr. Miller pushed me aside, trying to catch up with her. He held the gun my mother had taught him to shoot. My mother had a pistol and a flashlight, and caught in its beam was John Rhodes. He carried a cross about ten feet high, two beams wrapped in burlap bags, and you could smell the kerosene. He had been propping it up and trying to strike a match on the sole of his shoe. My mother's voice carried: "You're trespassing on my land. If you strike that match, I'll shoot you."

"You nigger-lovin' bitch, you ain't gonna shoot nobody!" His voice was blurred, and he kept striking the match until it caught, and with an insane sneer, he reached it toward the cross, but he didn't make it. At the crack of the gun, he fell forward on the burning match, extinguishing the flame. His body had not hit the ground before a second shot convulsed him. The two of them stood over him with guns handy, in case he moved. Mr. Miller said, "Shall I shoot him again just to make sure?"

The beam of Mother's light was on Rhodes's face, which was pretty much gone. "I don't think it's needed."

Mr. Miller was beginning to shake. If my mother was disturbed, it didn't show. After all, this was her second body this year.

"We did this together, Mr. Miller, and together we are going to bury him. We have rid ourselves of another piece of scum. It's a shame we can't shoot them all."

She saw me standing behind a porch column. I asked, "Do you want me to get my red wagon?"

Stanley stuck his head out the upper window of the barn and yelled, "Is everything all right?"

My mother called, "We were just shooting at foxes that were after the chickens."

They got a piece of canvas and wrapped and roped Rhodes into a roll and put him on my wagon. Mr. Miller said he could dig a grave in the morning, and he pulled the wagon down to the far end of the cornfield, where the ground was sandy and easy to dig.

My mother pushed the cross over and went looking for John Rhodes's truck. It was parked around the bend, and the keys were in it, so she brought it up beside the cross. She was just trying to lift it into the back of the truck when

Mr. Miller came to help her. There was a five-gallon can of kerosene in the back. Mr. Miller drove the truck at least a mile up the road before he got out and set it on fire and walked back.

The next day I found fifty-seven cents on the ground. It had fallen out of John Rhodes's pocket. It wasn't much, not nearly as good as the last time by a long shot. But what was it Benjamin Franklin had said, "A penny saved is a penny earned." So I dropped it down in my rubber boot.

My mother also gave me five dollars for the use of my wagon and said, "Now, remember, Hughie, this is not your secret."

And I knew that's what the five dollars was really for.

SEPTEMBER 3, 1929

MAPLE SUGAR IS PROBABLY the first crop of the spring. Its harvest begins when there is still snow on the ground, but the tree has some ingrown knowledge of when it is March, and its sap rises. Before the first thin red leaf of the honey maple shows, you go through the grove and bore holes in the tree trunks, about three feet from the ground. You insert a hollow pipe and hang a bucket on it, and the slow, steady drip-drip of the sweet water begins to fill it. Twice a day you come by with a big sled and fill the empty barrels on it. You are not bleeding the tree to death; you take only a hundred gallons of sap to boil down to one gallon of maple syrup, and twenty gallons of syrup crystallizes into five pounds of maple sugar. Endless loads of hickory have to burn night and day under the big copper kettles for two weeks. We wouldn't cut down hickory trees and deprive ourselves or the squirrels of hickory nuts, we cut up only trees that had fallen in storms.

The hot sugar is poured into oiled crocks, allowed to harden, turned out, and the crock used again. The half circle of sweetness is wrapped in cheesecloth to keep the ants out and laid up in the pantry shelves. This year we had done pretty well. It was near the end of summer, and we still had ten or twelve molds of sugar.

It was corn-fritter time, and Tuba had gone to get a mold of sugar to break up for syrup, and all the way from the dining room, I heard her yell. When I got to the kitchen, she was dumping four of the maple-sugar mounds on the table, only they weren't mounds, they were more like bowls, and one of them broke. They had been scraped out with a spoon until they were a shell not more than half an inch thick.

Mrs. Miller was kneading bread in the bread trough over by the window, and Boobie was standing on a stool beside her with a small loaf of her own in a bowl. Boobie was six now and played "little mother" most of the time. Mrs. Miller came to see what all the fuss was about, and Boobie climbed down and cowered back in the corner under the bread table.

My mother and Stanley had been working the horses since dawn and were just coming in for their breakfast. When my mother saw Tuba's accusing finger pointing at me, as usual, I began to yell, "I have a whole tin of maple-sugar bunnies in the sideboard, left over from Easter. I don't even like maple sugar anymore."

Boobie's action was a sure sign of guilt, and Mrs. Miller reached under the table and pulled her out. I would have to give Boobie lessons: when you are accused, you just stand there and smile and look people right in the eye, especially if you're guilty. But I had never had a younger sibling to pass the blame to, so I thought I had better not make Boobie too adept at denial. I could use her.

My mother was saying, "That's an awful lot of sugar for a little girl. Don't you know your teeth will all fall out?"

Boobie grinned widely. She knew the time for a fast smack from her mother was already past. She had lost most of her baby teeth and had two big ones in the front, just like a chipmunk, and just right for chomping down on maple sugar.

Stanley had gotten two cups and saucers from the cupboard, put them down on the end of the kitchen table, and went for the coffeepot. Tuba beat him to it and filled the cups with a look that said "This is my kitchen."

I decided to see if my sugar bunnies were still in the sideboard. I opened the tin and found one lone bunny in the bottom. Boobie was standing very close, smiling her chipmunk smile. "I left you one." I held the tin out to her, and she snatched him quickly. The truth was, the last bunny looked as though he had been licked.

My mother was halfway through her second cup of coffee. "Tuba, you better put on some pancakes and eggs. The Miller boys will be up from the meadow soon, and they will be hungry. Mrs. Miller, those boys of yours are wonderful. Milk production has increased a third since they came."

Mrs. Miller pounded the rising bread. "It's all that good red clover since the big rain."

"I don't know what we will do when school starts."

Mrs. Miller turned around, confused. "Ma'am, the boys done got through the eighth grade at the plantation school a'fore we came up here. That's why we was on the way to Detroit when our old truck broke down an' left us here. We was gonna send the boys to high school."

"There is no reason on earth they couldn't go to high school right here."

Tuba slapped the table with her hand. "Miz Curtiss, you are a right good woman, but you ain't livin' in the real world. They ain't gonna let no nigger go to white schools, and there ain't no black high school."

"Tuba, I wish you would stop calling yourself 'nigger.' How are you going to get other people to stop when you won't say 'black'?"

Boobie was sitting at the table beside me, drinking buttermilk. She extended her hand and looked at it and said under her breath, "I not black, I brown." I agreed, a light russet brown, mixed with a little ocher.

Mrs. Miller had divided the bread into twelve loaves, put them in the pans to rise, and was greasing the tops with lard. "I thought being in West Virginia, things would be different, but it's no different from Virginia or Kentucky. The Klan is just as bad here; we got to keep movin' north."

My mother put down her cup too hard. "I won't accept that! We're going to change things right here." And she went out through the screen porch and slammed the door.

Tuba made clucking noises. "Like I said, that woman just ain't livin' in the real world."

Stanley and I, who were both very white, sat at the table and ate pancakes and eggs with the Miller boys, who were both very black, and I suppose that in itself was the beginning of change.

SEPTEMBER 6, 1929

ALEX KESSNER DID NOT seem to have much of a mind of his own (though his wife, Nora, did). The poor man waited to be ordered around by Emma. Aunt Emma had changed since Alvin's death. Where she had been shy and quiet and sat in corners, she now screamed and threw things. She would order Alex to bring the car around and then say, "What are you doing with my car?"

When he would say, "But madam, you said to bring it around," she would scream, "Why would I do that? I'm not going anywhere. Alex, you must be losing your mind. If you keep this up, you will have to be committed."

Grandmother Curtiss was worried that Emma might have to be committed. The doctor had said, "Give her a little time. She's had a shock." But as time passed, she got worse. She still owed me the other half of my promised twenty dollars. I supposed she thought she didn't, since we had not succeeded in getting Eddie Horner lynched, but we did get the painting, and I felt that ought to be worth twenty dollars.

I was out in the gazebo eating apples from the Maiden Blush. They were ripe now, and every third or fourth one had what we called a sugar heart, a moist, juicy space around the core that tasted like honey. I had a kitchen knife and was cutting the apples in two and sucking out the sugar hearts, pushing the rest of the apple through a crack in the floor, while I watched the house for Grandmother. She couldn't stand waste, and I didn't want her to catch me. I didn't hear Emma until she was behind me.

"Hughie, do you think Alvin went to hell?"

"No. I don't believe in hell."

"Mrs. Kessner says there is a purgatory where you have to sit and wait, sometimes years, when you kill yourself, for some kind of a trial to see if you can go to heaven."

"I don't believe in that, either, but I'm not really sure."

"I stayed up with the Ouija board most of the night, and I didn't get one clear answer, it just kept spelling out 'chance.' What do you think that means?"

I didn't know, but I said, "Maybe like mumblety-peg, two out of three, three out of five. Like these apples, some have sugar hearts, some don't."

"If three out of five did, do you think that would be a sign?"

"Sure."

I had spoken too soon. She lined up five apples on the table and said, "Cut them in two."

I looked around and Grandmother was nowhere to be seen, so I whacked the five apart. Only two had sugar hearts.

"Oh my God, that means he's in hell."

"No, it doesn't. That was just practice. One for you, one for me."

She ate the sugar heart without being aware it passed her lips. "Do it again."

I went over and shook the tree, and apples rained down. This time only one had a sugar heart. We did it five or six more times, with negative results each time, and Emma was getting more agitated by the moment. So was I. I was afraid Grandmother was going to come.

"What could I expect from a lying, deceitful tree that killed my brother? Liar, liar!" Emma grabbed a stick that lay on the ground and began to beat the limbs. I ran.

We were sitting at the dinner table and through with the potato soup when we heard the sounds of a crosscut saw. The doors to the orchard were open, and you could tell where the noise was coming from. Grandmother was annoyed, but Grandfather was slicing the roast beef and passing the plates, and he didn't want his ritual disturbed. "Emma is probably having some logs sawed to use in the fireplace this winter."

"Emma doesn't even know there is going to be a winter."

"Virginia, please. Let's eat our dinner in peace."

"There hasn't been any peace around here since my brother died." She pushed her chair back.

I looked at Grandfather for permission to follow. My roast beef was too rare anyway.

"Go ahead, and come back and tell us what it is. The way things are going, your grandmother may never return."

Just when Grandmother and I got to the Maiden Blush, it began to fall toward us with a crashing sound, and we jumped back as its trunk splintered with a wrench like a breaking heart. Apples rolled everywhere. Alex was standing there, his saw caught in the cut of the tree. I thought he was crying, or maybe it was sweat. He was old.

"Why, Alex, why?" Grandmother demanded.

"Miss Emma ordered me to, ma'am. I work for Miss Emma."

"Not anymore, you don't. I'm her guardian, and I'm taking over. You work for me."

"Thank you, ma'am."

"Now, let's get a basket and gather these apples." She hurried on to the Channell house, careful not to fall on the apple-covered ground. I followed.

When we came in the kitchen door, Mrs. Kessner was standing at the wall phone. She put it back in its cradle. "Oh, Mrs. Curtiss, I was just calling you. You've got to do something about your sister. She's at it again."

"At what?"

"Abusing herself with a stick and staring at that painting." Then she saw me and clasped her hand over her mouth.

"It's all right. We don't keep anything from Hughie. We couldn't if we wanted to." We were out in the hall.

"But ma'am, there's blood everywhere."

It was too late. I was in the elevator with Grandmother, and the doors were closing. She opened Emma's bedroom door, and when she looked in, she gave me a shove backward and pulled the door shut, but not before I had seen around her.

Emma lay on the bed in a pool of blood. She looked like a sow's carcass stretched on the butcher table. There were long cuts from her neck to her knees, and a round stick of wood stuck out from between her legs, and she was smiling a sick terrible smile.

From behind the door, Grandmother was yelling at me, "Hughie, go tell Mrs. Kessner to have the hospital to send their ambulance, and go get your aunt Opal."

I didn't get a glimpse of Uncle Alvin's portrait, and I wondered if he was still smiling. I went to get Aunt Opal, and I warned her it was nasty.

Aunt Emma was in the hospital eight days before they transferred her to Weston, the state hospital for the insane. Judge Brown signed the order. She had been in Weston exactly thirty days when Grandmother got a call from the director there. It seemed Aunt Emma had soaked the spiraling flypapers that hung from the ceiling in water and drunk it, and the arsenic that was meant to kill flies killed her.

September 10, 1929

Miss Larkin had a cow, and one day she stopped at our house to see if my mother would buy it. She drove a little old Model T Ford that made strange farting noises from the back. She drove as close to the house as she could, since she walked with a cane. I went out to help her up the porch steps because I knew my mother was watching, and also, Miss Larkin was really very pleasant, even if she was a schoolteacher.

Early September was still hot, so my mother guided her back to the dining room, which seemed to be the coolest room in the house. Plus, my mother always felt she had to feed Miss Larkin because she was so thin. Miss Larkin always resisted as though she was receiving charity, and that wasn't so. But by the time she had a muffin with strawberry jam and iced tea, and I went to the kitchen to get more ice, she was able to say what she had come for. She admitted she had not been able to have the cow bred, so she was dry and there was no milk, but if she was turned in to a good meadow like ours, she would fatten up enough by November.

Then she said, "Evelyn could be butchered," but the very thought was more than she could deal with, and she began to cry and pat her eyes with a ladylike little handkerchief.

My mother was looking for an alternative to tears. "Why don't I have Evelyn bred for you, and then you will have a calf and a milk cow. I have a very good bull."

But it wouldn't work. Miss Larkin finally got around to telling us that she no longer could teach, because the little one-room school where she had been for thirty years had been consolidated into the city system, and her pension of thirty dollars a month was not enough to pay rent on her farm and live.

"But you own your farm; I remember your father owned that farm."

"Oh, yes," Miss Larkin said. She had won over the tears now. "And do you remember my brother? Well, you know men leave their property to their sons. Martin lives in Pittsburgh, and I send him fifteen dollars every month, but I just can't do it anymore."

Miss Larkin was also planning to sell her old Model T to a neighbor boy for twenty-five dollars.

"But when you have no cow and no car and no farm, where will you go?"

"They will take me in at the county farm for my pension. I don't know what they will do those three months in the summer when I don't get a pension."

She called it the county farm, but we called it the poorhouse. My mother was sitting there staring at her, not knowing quite what to say. But I knew she was working at it in her head. First she said, "Miss Larkin, we never give a name to a cow we intend to butcher, it doesn't work."

Miss Larkin thought she was being dismissed. She put the other half of her muffin on her plate and started to rise. "I'm sorry."

"No, no, please. We are going to find a solution, and it won't be going to the poorhouse."

"It's not really so bad. Lots of teachers end up there, since we are not allowed to marry and have children and teach."

"That's something else that needs to be changed."

I added, "My mother's making a list."

"The only thing there I'm afraid of is the hogs. I'm afraid that with the arthritis in my feet, I might fall and not be able to get up." We had all heard the stories of old people who fell and got eaten by the hogs. When hogs forage free, they get vicious, and a hog's jaws are strong enough to snap through a thighbone.

Just then the kitchen door swung open, and Handsome Miller came tottering through. He was learning to walk, but when he wanted to make a getaway, he dropped down on all fours and hopped like a rabbit. Boobie was right behind him. He stopped at Miss Larkin's feet. She was new, and he studied her, and she studied him.

Boobie was apologetic. "I'm sorry, Miz Curtiss. I watch Handsome for Mama while she cans green beans. I think I have to tie a cannonball to his foot."

Handsome was holding on to Miss Larkin's knee and trying to pull himself up on her lap. She reached down and gave him a boost. Boobie assured her, "He's dry, I just changed him." He was wearing bright pink rubber pants over his diaper. Miss Larkin and Handsome kept studying each other, their noses only a foot apart. My mother started to lift him off, but Miss Larkin waved her away. "You know, I have never been this close to a black child before. Handsome certainly is the right name for him."

I supposed it was, if you liked your kids shiny brown like a wet chocolate bunny, with the biggest eyes I ever saw.

Boobie came for him to climb on her back and gave Miss Larkin her chipmunk smile.

"And what is your name, little nursemaid?"

"I'm Boobie, and I'm six."

Handsome was grabbing her tight around her neck and said, "Go," as though he were riding a horse, but not before Miss Larkin had bent forward and kissed him on the cheek. They went outside playing horsey.

"I suppose she will be going to school soon."

"I'm afraid, Miss Larkin, you live in the same dream world I do. You, of all people, should know better. I have just had a fight with the board of education. They say they will cancel this bus route before they will let a black child ride."

Miss Larkin was sitting very quietly, staring down at her hands, which mercifully had escaped arthritis so far. "I just realized how much I am going to miss the children. Everyone at the farm is so old. The homeless children all go to the county orphanage."

"Let me get us another cup of tea while Hughie runs down to the barn.

Hughie, you know that walker I had when the horse stepped on my foot? Get
it, please."

I ran and got it. I knew she was going to give it to Miss Larkin, but I didn't
know what else she had in mind. The walker was like four canes. You stood in
the middle, and the back two had little wheels. Miss Larkin got the hang of it
immediately, and she laughed. "I could race Handsome with this."

"Can you follow me?" my mother asked.

Miss Larkin did, and so did I, through the breakfast room, the servants' dining room, and down a back hall that was seldom used by anyone. At the end
was a big room that still had the original log walls. It was mammoth, with a fireplace big enough to walk in. It had had a lot of uses in the past. When the house
was a freight-transfer station, the room had been a barroom. The year my father
was married, when he was still ambitious, he had turned it into a billiard room
and installed two pool tables. He had strung lights with green glass shades, all
along the high beams.

My mother snapped them on until she could raise the blinds on the windows.
There were windows on two sides, frosted over with dirt.

"What do you see here, Miss Larkin?"

"A pool hall?"

"No, no. Put a new top on the tables, bring in some chairs and a blackboard,
and this is a schoolroom. It's bigger than that one you taught in for thirty years.
And we have indoor plumbing."

"I don't know what to say."

"Don't say anything until you see the rest."

My mother opened a door into a hallway that led to a bathroom and a bedroom at the end. Though walled with the same logs, it was painted yellow and
furnished with a curly-maple poster bed complete with a feather tick.

"Now, come and sit."

There was a split-bottom rocker, and Miss Larkin came and sat in it, and my
mother and I sat on the bed. Miss Larkin stared as my mother explained, "I
need a teacher here."

"Just for that little girl?"

"No, for everybody. Everybody here needs help. I have a boy who is going
to high school; he will need help every night. They gave him no foundation in
the orphanage. I have three Dutch ladies who need help with English. Boobie's
two older brothers need math and English. Do you object to teaching black
children?"

"Of course not."

"And Hughie here is going into town on the bus to the third grade, that is, if the board of education will let it stop here after what I called them. He will need more time at night than I can give him. It doesn't look like I'm going to have much cash, but I can give you room and board, a home for as long as you want it, and you can keep your pension and your cow."

Miss Larkin was having trouble opening her mouth.

"You sit here a little and think about it."

"I don't have to think about it. God bless you!"

We left her sitting there and went down the hall.

"Hughie, go find Mr. Miller and get him to bring down Miss Larkin's cow and whatever furniture she wants to move."

"Grandpa says you can't manage the whole world."

"I'm not trying to manage the whole world. I'm just trying to do the best I can in the little part of the world that is mine."

My mother had finished the workout of a beautiful golden palomino she called El Dorado. She removed his saddle and was preparing to rub him down. I was putting away the records and the phonograph when Mr. Miller came in. He picked up a towel and sponge and began on the opposite side of the horse. He was not a tall man, not quite as tall as my mother. Their eyes met over the horse's golden flank.

"Mrs. Curtiss, I was wondering, are you all right? You know, about—well, the other night."

"Yes, I am, Mr. Miller. I was wondering the same thing about you. I'm grateful, you know, that you came to help me."

"You're grateful to me? How often do you think a black man gets to even the score, just a little bit?"

"Mr. Miller, it's not something I'm proud of, but given the same provocation, I would do it again."

"And I'll be there to help you."

"Thank you."

"Don't worry about the end results. I dug a very deep hole."

"I think this is going to be a very good horse. He's smart and he's steady, and he knows he doesn't have to worry about anything."

"He has you."

SEPTEMBER 11, 1929

AFTER HER EXPERIENCE with Sir Harry Lauder, Aunt Opal did not attempt to bring in another celebrity, but she continued to search for a way to earn income from the theater. She found a group who would rent it on Saturday night for a square dance, but they wanted her to remove the chairs. They would build benches, lined up along the wall, that could be dragged to the center and placed in rows for the Sunday church group.

Aunt Opal called my mother to see if she wanted any chairs. My mother did. The night of the concert, she had sat on a chair she liked. The afternoon she came in to look, she found eighteen, and she thought they were original Chippendale. After all, the southern families from whom the old general stole them could afford the very best. The theater looked different in the daylight with the blinds on the back window up. Aunt Opal had rolled up the movie screen and didn't know what to do with it, so my mother took it home. The eighteen chairs had once been in the dining room, for they still wore remnants of the same blue-green brocade as the drop-in seats.

Leonadis Isaac was the man in our town who knew more about the value of antique furniture than anyone else. He ran a little shop with a sign that said: ANTIQUE FURNITURE AND FINE ARTS — BOUGHT AND SOLD. People said that when he found a really fine piece, he didn't tell anyone what its value was. He shipped it off to New York and sold it for thousands. Since Aunt Opal didn't want to pay an appraisal fee, my mother said we would just offer him the chairs and turn down his offer, as it would be only half what they were worth.

Mr. Isaac turned out to be a surprise. We had only three Jewish families in our town, and I had never been close to any of them; so I expected something strange of Mr. Isaac. He was very much like Grandfather Fancler; about the same size, maybe not as tall, and appeared the same age. He wasn't wearing a long black robe or a fur hat, and he didn't try to cheat Opal out of her chairs. He did tell her that three sets were very fine, including the eighteen my mother had chosen. He thought they were original and, in the right market, would bring a very good price. Two of the couches were original, and several of the other chairs, if not original, were very good Philadelphia reproductions and would do well in New England auctions. He said he could not afford this class of furniture, and no one else in this town could, either, but he would give her names and addresses of dealers in New York where she could send photographs. One couch, he said, belonged in a museum. (And to think it had sat in the theater for years, holding sprawling kids watching Pearl White serials.)

My mother said, "Mr. Isaac, I don't know how to repay you. Will you take a percentage of the sales for your fee?"

Mr. Isaac sat down on a lesser couch. "Mrs. Curtiss, aren't you the daughter of the reverend Peter Fancler?"

"Yes, I am."

"Well, I'll tell you how you can pay me. You can introduce me to your father. I had thought to just go up and knock on his door, but it would be so much nicer if his daughter introduced us."

"Why do you want to meet my father?"

"He and I read the same books. He read Karl Marx."

"You want to meet my father because you think he's a communist?"

"No, no, I want to meet him because I think he has a brain in his head. If I don't find someone in this town to talk to, I may go mad. He and I take the same books from the library—Plutarch and Henry James, Thomas Hardy, Virginia Woolf, the whole spectrum—quite often he and I are the only ones who ever read these books. He would seem to be very liberal-minded."

She laughed. "That he is."

"I looked up his card number, and all those books he gave the library."

"He has a friend in publishing in Pittsburgh who sends him the overruns, and there is just no more room in his house for books."

"I was up on the hill one day, and I saw him walking with this boy here. They were laughing and having such a good time, I didn't have the nerve to approach him. An open mind in a town like this is a rare thing."

"Mr. Isaac, do you know where my farm is?"

"Oh, yes, of course."

"Come to dinner on Saturday night around five-thirty, and I'll have my father there."

Saturday turned out to be a very full day. My mother had planned to go into town with her truck to pick up the eighteen chairs from the theater next to the Bluebird Market, which was still open, though every week, the threat of foreclosure grew stronger. There was now a sign across the front that said CASH ONLY and another that said 50 PERCENT OFF—GOING OUT OF BUSINESS.

The people who had sold the building to Grandfather Curtiss were going to foreclose for want of three thousand dollars. He either could not come up with it or didn't see the point. He knew Grandmother had the money, but he wouldn't ask her, and until he did, she wouldn't volunteer. They were going through the motions right to the end, and so were we. At dawn, when the vegetables were still wet with dew, our whole adopted family went into the truck garden to pick. We picked three bushels of green beans. The late summer ones were easy to pick, as they grew on long poles and you could stand up and harvest, unlike the early bush variety.

We picked two bushels of beefsteak tomatoes, scarlet and dead ripe. All the summer rains had brought us a bumper crop, and there didn't seem much point to canning any more, except for ketchup and green tomato relish and mincemeat. We added a couple of bushels of sweet corn, though of course not precooked, and went in to breakfast. Tuba had made piles of French toast, and it was warming in the oven. Mrs. Zucker had just finished two big kettles of jam, one gooseberry and one black raspberry. She added a big dipper full to each of the pans of boiling syrup, so we had a choice.

My mother announced that we were going to have a distinguished guest for dinner, so we would do what Tuba called "putting on the dog."

"Well, let's at least polish silver and set the table with a full complement," my mother said. She didn't have to ask, for Miss Larkin had taken it on as her obligation to sit at a kitchen table each Saturday morning and polish the silver with ammonia and baking soda. She had retrieved old pieces, trays and mugs and coffeepots that were corroded completely black and hadn't been polished for years.

The Miller boys bragged that they were probably the only niggers in the world who drank cocoa from a silver mug, and Handsome's mother spooned oatmeal in his mouth with a silver spoon, just for luck. Miss Larkin would hold up a fruit bowl and look at her reflection and say, "You know, I never owned a piece of silver in my life." Her smile seemed less forced, easier each day, and her arthritic feet did not seem to pain her as much. She was wearing copper pennies in the new shoes that Grandfather Fancler had sent her.

My mother reminded Stanley that he and the Miller boys were to take supplies up to Uncle Billie when she got back with the truck. It hadn't rained for over a week, and the old road should have dried out enough to get pretty close to the sheep meadow.

Then my mother and I were off. I liked riding in the truck, but it had heavy springs to carry heavy loads, and when it was empty, it was like having no springs at all. I could hear the gears clanging as the differential turned, and feel every bump in the road through my tailbone, as my mother sped along.

I wasn't going to Grandfather Fancler's house today, since he was coming home with us and would spend the night. I was not as comfortable visiting his house since Aunt Lilly had taken over, though I didn't really understand why. I liked Aunt Lilly, and I think she liked me, and she certainly was pretty to look at, even prettier than my mother; she was younger, twenty-two, and always perfectly groomed. If a tendril of silver-gold hair fell across her forehead, she had planned it that way.

I don't think Grandfather was too comfortable, either. He had moved his bed down into the study at the back of the house and left the whole upstairs to Blake and Lillian, so they could have a private bathroom, he said. I thought it was because she had painted the bathroom bright pink and hung prints everywhere of the girls in Charles Dana Gibson's drawings because she thought they looked like her, and they did.

Aunt Opal was waiting at the theater with the key. She had taken a proprietary interest since Grandfather Curtiss had put the building in her name. We drove on around to the back, where the delivery boy could unload our vegetables. When we had stacked the chairs in the front of the truck bed and roped them tight, we went in the market to pick up supplies. There were only two people in the store, and for a Saturday morning, that was bad. There were trays in the front window of a penny candy that had a ring in each piece, set with different colors of glass. Since I was Grandfather's darling, I could take all I wanted, but Gertrude Gracey, the manager, would not let me pull out the rings unless I ate the candy. To eat enough of those sugary marshmallow pillows to put rings on all my fingers, out to the end, always made me sick enough to throw up. But today Gertrude said, "Hughie, why don't you just take the whole box?" And I did; in fact, two boxes.

Gertrude said she didn't see any point in staying open longer than a couple more weeks, and she regretted that Grandfather had not let her run the store on a cash basis from the very beginning. Also, there was never any need for the two extra girls. All they did most of the time was stay behind the bread case and practice back bends and putting their foot up behind their head. They were sisters, and they were double-jointed, and they were planning to join the next carnival or cooch show that came to town, whichever was first. They would hold on to an iron post that supported the ceiling and rub their stomachs on it and sing: " 'He's my handyman, handiest man I ever had to hang around, when my furnace gets too hot, he turns my damper down.' "

Gertrude didn't think she needed a delivery boy, either, if she ran cash and carry. As it was, he spent most of his time down in the basement, catching big, hairy spiders that crawled out of the stalks of green bananas that hung from the ceiling to ripen. Today he gave me in a pickle jar a spider as wide as my hand. I planned to take it home and scare Boobie with it.

We loaded all the supplies we would need, the things we couldn't grow: sugar, salt, and pounds of spices; turmeric, pepper, cloves, and lots of nutmeg and cinnamon, as it would soon be time to make apple butter. There were three big empty barrels, so we took them to make sauerkraut. The three Dutch ladies loved kraut. We took the whole rack of seeds, since Aunt Bea's new husband had left them on consignment, and we knew he wouldn't be back. Besides, by the next spring, the second year, only half of them would sprout.

Just as we were loading the barrels of flour and a whole stalk of bananas and the candied fruits for fruitcake, the truck from the Nabisco bakery at Morgantown pulled up. Aunt Opal quickly asked, "Do we owe him anything?"

Gertrude was sharp. "No, and we're not going to. When people can't pay their bills, I am certainly not going to sell them cookies."

It seemed the salesman had met the same response everywhere he had stopped.

"I've been on the road three days. Out of thirty-eight hundred in bills, I have collected exactly three hundred and seventy dollars and sold three cartons of cookies, and I'm not going back to that office and get fired. This is the end of the line."

Both my mother and Aunt Opal were interested to know what he meant by that.

"This is what I mean," he said, and he dropped the keys to the truck in Aunt Opal's hand. "I'm going down here to the freight yard and find myself an empty boxcar that's going somewhere, hopefully California. You're looking at a knight of the open road."

Aunt Opal walked around her new truck in a proprietary way and decided she would paint it blue a little later, and she did.

"Well, Sir Knight, if you are going to hit the road, we had better pack you a lunch."

She went into the little kitchen where Gertrude ate and slept, and made several ham-and-cheese sandwiches. She added sardines and baked beans, wooden spoons and paper napkins. She put them all in a shopping bag and wished the new knight bon voyage.

We drove over to Worth Avenue so my mother could have the business meeting that Grandfather had wanted weeks ago, before Alvin's funeral interfered.

Aunt Opal parked her new truck in the carriage barn. She and I opened the back of the van to see what prizes were there. The truck was packed almost full, dozens of cartons four wide and about two high and almost up to the door. Aunt Opal was suddenly silly. "Hughie, if we're going to have this many cookies, you better run in and get a gallon of cold milk!"

There were Fig Newtons, my favorite, and Coconut Crisp, Aunt Opal's favorite, and just about everyone else's, too. We began to unload them carefully, as each carton weighed about fifty pounds, and we didn't want to drop and break them. I went in and got Matthew to lift out about twenty cartons for my mother to take home. Aunt Opal was planning what bequests she would make with the balance before they got stale, but she was more excited about the truck than the cookies.

"Do you realize last month I had no transportation, and now I have a fancy red touring car and an enclosed truck?"

She also had 112 cartons of cookies, and we stacked them up on the workbenches against the wall, then took the truck back to the theater to pick up the rest of the chairs and put them in the carriage barn. I went along without asking, for Grandfather and Mother had their heads together over the desk in his study and were signing papers with ink and sprinkling fine sand on it, so I knew it was important.

Later, on the way to pick up Grandfather Fancler, my mother and I were at the bottom of the hill and waiting when we saw him coming. My mother was afraid to try to turn in his driveway, overloaded as we were, with canvas roped over the top. As we waited, my mother said, "Hughie, you just bought the farm."

I panicked. I could envision all the money in my boot going out. "No, I didn't. I didn't agree to pay anything."

"You're going to pay for it with a lifetime of effort, just as I am. Your grandfather Curtiss has deeded it to you and your heirs, which means you will never be able to sell it, and I'm your guardian until you're twenty-five."

Grandfather Fancler got in beside me, and I didn't know what to say. I must have looked perturbed, since he asked, "What's the matter?"

"Hughie has just learned that his grandfather Curtiss has deeded him the Curtiss farm."

"Didn't you think he would?"

"I don't like the part about not being able to sell it."

My mother said, "Hughie, you wouldn't."

"Yes, I would. When I'm sixteen, I might sell it and go to California and be a movie star, or go to Washington and be a crooked politician."

"I have never had a moment since I set eyes on that place that my every waking thought wasn't how to improve it."

"I'm afraid that's been your problem—every moment?" Grandfather sounded suddenly serious.

"Yes, every moment!"

"Even when you were making love to your husband?"

"I used to lie there and plan which field had been depleted by growing corn and would have to be planted in clover and turned over."

"No wonder your marriage failed."

We ate lunch while the boys were unloading the truck. The Dutch ladies kept making little extra treats and passing them first to Grandfather. My mother said she didn't think her father wanted any more fried chicken, and Rose looked so crestfallen that Grandfather said he could manage one more leg. He was saved only when she went to look at the antique chairs.

After lunch Grandfather got his bridle and saddle from the tack room and went down in the meadow to find his great black beauty. The horses were all down by the lower corral, where the timothy grass was ripe. When Black saw Grandfather, he separated from the herd and came running toward him. Hannah followed not far behind. Black nuzzled along Grandfather's neck, then pushed against his chest until he would have fallen if he hadn't grabbed the fence. Hannah whinnied for Black to move away, then turned her flank to Grandfather to be scratched. After Black was saddled, Grandfather mounted and pulled me up behind him. There was no one to ride Hannah, as my mother was busy figuring accounts—Grandfather Curtiss had given her an account book and switched the bank balances into her name so my father couldn't write checks from wherever he was—and Stanley had to drive the truck up to the sheep meadow with the Miller boys to deliver Uncle Billie's supplies and bring back the split-bottom rocking chairs he was making to sell at the Forest Festival.

I could ride around only twice and then got down, for I had a job to do. After I was off, Grandfather picked up his speed and gave Black a good workout, with Hannah galloping behind. I was headed down by the railroad tracks to pick muskmelons (called cantaloupes now). Boobie was going with me to help keep the basket from falling off my red wagon on the way back up over the meadows. Muskmelons won't grow just anywhere; they need loose, sandy loam and must be protected from the night cold. The only suitable plot we had was down where the railroad cut through our farm. Because the ground was soft, the track had been laid on a bed of stone at least two feet deep. There was a line of track going each way, and the rails would get so hot in the summer that you couldn't walk on them in your bare feet. That heat was transferred into the stone and warmed the earth around it through the night. So our muskmelons thought they were down in Georgia and prospered here.

By the time Boobie and I got down to the patch, it was three o'clock. I had my dollar Ingersoll watch in my pocket, and the train that was supposed to go by on the way to Marlington at two-thirty was sitting idly on the tracks. It had been here for some time, for the loud noise a good head of steam makes was reduced to a sigh, and the puffs that usually escape from the pistons were a mere wisp. I was not surprised to find the train parked here; it often was, and the engineer and the fireman would be off in our melon patch eating away. There wasn't any conductor, as there was only one passenger car, and people went by the engine and gave the engineer their ticket. Today there were three boxcars, a passenger car, and a caboose.

There were three people sitting on a stack of cross ties that served as seats when you were waiting. The woman among them was my aunt Sebe. I looked for Worthy and Harry and found them climbing on the top of the caboose. I knew there wasn't time to join them, as the three thieves in our melon patch were wiping their mouths, the two old men on red bandanas and Aunt Sebe on the hem of her dress.

The train and Aunt Sebe got up a head of steam and went their separate ways. I wondered if either of the three boxcars held the cookie salesman. I hoped not. If these two stopped at every melon patch they came to, he would never get to California.

Harry and Worthy stayed to help us pick melons and borrow five dollars each. Lloyd's birthday was coming up and no one had any money. School started the Tuesday after Labor Day, and everyone had to use what money they had for books. The textbooks could be bought used for fifty cents or so each. There was an advantage and a disadvantage to this: most of the answers were written in the books, but the average kid couldn't write so you could read it. The workbooks had to be new, and some kids went through the whole year with the teacher saying, "I'll give you just one more week to get your workbooks."

Lloyd's mother was going to buy him a new bicycle to ride to high school,

and Worthy and Harry were going to share his old one. Harry was going to buy
Lloyd a pair of roller skates for his birthday with the five dollars he would borrow from me.

"Lloyd is not going to want roller skates if he has a new bike," I said.

"I know. We can borrow them. When one of us is riding Lloyd's old bike,
the other can put on the skates and hold on to the back of the bike."

Worthy was more generous. He was going to buy his brother a yellow raincoat with a hood, so people would see him on his bicycle in the rain and not hit
him with a truck. Since Boobie and I had Harry and Worthy to help, we filled
the basket to the top. Boobie could eat a melon on the way back and not have
to push.

Worthy and Harry each had a canvas backpack filled with Cloverine salve.
They had become salesmen for this product because you could order it and send
back half the money when it was sold, at a clear profit of twenty-five cents per
can. The kicker was, you could have a beautiful color picture, big enough to
frame, of either *The Last Supper* or *Jesus in the Garden,* with each purchase. I let
them talk me into leaving six cans for me to sell. There were only two copies
left of *The Last Supper,* since all their buyers had preferred that one. Worthy told
me to say *The Last Supper* was just an old painting by Michael somebody, but
the Jesus picture was a genuine photograph made by God Himself with His
very own Kodak camera. I thought Worthy was dumb—all you had to do was
hide the others until you got rid of *The Last Supper.* I studied the picture of
Jesus, blue-eyed and fair with blond curls on his shoulders. It was no wonder
the Jews didn't think he was one of them.

My cousins could be especially helpful when they wanted to borrow money.
I was extremely careful to make sure they didn't see where I got it when I gave
them each five dollars. They promised to pay it back with the money they would
earn when my mother had the corn shucking.

Aunt Sebe had come to borrow twenty dollars. She had been able to save
only twelve dollars toward Lloyd's birthday bicycle. My mother suggested that
she buy Lloyd the bicycle, and Sebe could buy him something else with her
twelve dollars.

"Oh, yes, you'd like that, wouldn't you? Aunt Billy, Lady Bountiful."

"I just thought you wouldn't have to feel obligated."

"Obligated? Me? When I think of me working for nickel tips and most of
the time not getting them, and you dealing in your fancy horses for thousands
of dollars."

"I'll give you the money, and you don't have to pay it back."

"That makes you feel good, doesn't it?"

"It's true, twenty dollars one way or the other won't make much difference; I could use twenty thousand right now. What does bother me is this need you have to harp at me all the time."

Aunt Sebe sat down on a chair at the end of the table and drank the iced tea Tuba had put before her. "I guess I'm just naturally mean. But I see you here with everything you ever wanted, and I have three boys who want everything, and I can't give them anything."

"What makes you think this is all I ever wanted?"

"You had a choice as Miss Queen of the May. You could have Hugh and this farm or Lester Adams. You took the farm, and now you've driven Hugh away, and you get both the farm and Lester."

"I don't have Lester."

"Oh, you will. He was in to eat the other night, and he told me he was going to ask you to marry him again."

"And I'll say no again."

"Don't you love him?"

"You sound like a dime novel. Come on, let's go pick some vegetables for you to take home. Can you stay for dinner?"

"No, my ride will be here at four-thirty. I can just make it to the restaurant by five. Saturday night is a big night. I may make a dollar in tips, if I'm lucky."

Kirby Conway came at exactly four-thirty. He had a new black Chevrolet, and he looked different in a suit than he had in his motorcycle clothes. Aunt Sebe didn't seem to mind my mother being Lady Bountiful now. In fact, she showed off her rich sister. As he started to load the baskets of tomatoes and green beans and corn, Sebe said airily, "Oh, don't bother. Billy's butler will do that."

But Kirby ignored her and smiled as he loaded the vegetables. Aunt Sebe had to yell for Worthy and Harry, and they came carrying a burlap bag of apples between them. When they got in the car, they had to hold the bag of apples on their laps, as Kirby didn't want to stain his new carpet.

My mother was on Aunt Sebe's side of the car, and I heard her whisper, "He's handsome. Is it serious?"

"Enough so that I didn't want to endanger it by borrowing twenty from him—thank you, dear sister."

September 14, 1929

Leonadis Isaac came at exactly five-thirty in a dark green Ford pickup with a little gold monogram on the door. Grandfather had come in all sweaty and gone up for a shower, so my mother met Mr. Isaac at the door. He brought a basket with a strange assortment of gifts: a jar of rottenstone, denatured alcohol, beeswax, white shellac, some stain sticks to cover scratches, fine steel wool, all things to restore the antique chairs. When Rose saw the basket, she squealed with delight. It seemed she had restored furniture with her father in The Hague before the Germans came, and she was anxious to get started on the chairs but had not known what the supplies were called in English.

Mr. Isaac was looking at the dark old portraits in the hallway when Grandfather came downstairs wearing a bright blue linen shirt and the white pants to his Palm Beach suit. Mr. Isaac was also wearing light pants, with a green shirt. They were about the same size and coloring. They looked at each other strangely for a moment, then shook hands. I thought they might even hug each other. They laughed, and it was as though they had met after many years.

My mother said, "You two look like a couple of boys going to a party."

Almost in unison, they said, "We are."

"Dad, why don't you show Mr. Isaac through the house while I get us some wine. You do drink wine?"

"Oh, yes."

"We are having trout, I hope—I have a motto: 'When in doubt, serve trout.'"

"You mean because I'm Jewish? I don't really work at it. I'm like your father here—I think he is a Muslim Zen Buddhist from what he reads."

"Omar Khayyám has become my Bible."

And they went off down the hall reciting together:

> Life is a chequerboard of nights and days
> On which Fate with Man for pieces plays.

Mr. Miller served the wine out in the gazebo, but the clematis vines were in full bloom and the bees had ignored the setting sun, refusing to go back in their hives, so we had to be careful. We were really being fancy tonight. Mr. Miller was wearing one of my father's pleated white evening shirts and black silk pants and was acting like a butler. Mr. Isaac looked at the bowl that held the cheese crackers and said he would stake his reputation that it was made by Paul Revere. "You have a great many precious things."

"All stolen from the people of the South by my husband's great-grandfather."

"Oh, yes, I know about General Curtiss."

Grandfather volunteered, "Let's don't condemn the old boy. If it wasn't for greedy men like that, how would we keep civilization on the move?"

Mr. Isaac drank his wine from the Waterford goblet and agreed. "If it wasn't for the pogroms of Russia, I would still be there, a devout, uneducated little Jew with a beard, maybe even a rabbi, and missing this lovely evening."

There would have been eight of us at the table, but Miss Larkin stayed in her room. She said her feet hurt, but that wasn't it. She had found a complete coffee service in Rappasc Rosa and become fascinated with polishing it. She was digging in the crevices with cotton swabs, carefully restoring to luster each silver flower.

Stanley had not come down from the sheep meadow. His place sat empty, and my mother was worried that they couldn't see that pathway of a road after dark.

The Dutch ladies were wearing their blue dresses again, and each of them, when they thought they were not being seen, winked at Grandfather. As the evening progressed, it looked as if Grandfather was going to have competition. Mr. Isaac and the Dutch ladies were chatting away in three languages.

Mr. Miller was just going around the table with a tray of broiled trout when we heard a clamor from the kitchen. Stanley and the Miller boys were back, and from the sounds of their voices, they were angry about something.

My mother took over the trout tray and sent Mr. Miller to see. He was gone only a couple of minutes before Stanley came in, red-faced and angry.

"I'm sorry to disturb dinner, but I think I better tell you."

"Mr. Isaac, this is our cousin Stanley. What is it, Stanley?"

"Someone beat up Uncle Billie, tryin' to rob him, and took his dog."

"Who took his dog?"

"Joe Rhodes, you know, is the son of the John Rhodes nobody can find."

"Is Uncle Billie badly hurt? Did you bring him down in the truck?"

"He wouldn't come. We put some of the ice we took up there on his bruises, and he took aspirin. He wants to be there in case his dog comes back."

Stanley went to the kitchen to eat with the Miller boys. Mr. Miller was standing in the doorway, so angry that the coffeepot in his hand shook until the lid rattled.

My mother explained, "We have a bunch of bootleggers up Woolwine holler who have given us nothing but trouble."

"Wars come in all sizes," said Mr. Isaac.

Then someone pounded on our front door with his fist, ignoring the knocker. Mr. Miller went to see, and I followed. Near the door we had a hall tree on which a black coat hung all the time with a pistol in the pocket, and Mr. Miller put it on. He opened the door only a crack, but Joe Rhodes kicked it wide open and stood there, eyes blazing. His father had been tall and dirty and mean-looking, but this one looked like one of those loony hounds who ate too many locusts and went mad. "Where's my daddy?"

"Why should we know where your daddy is?"

"Don't give me no back talk, nigger. My daddy was comin' here that night, and I never seen him again."

"You mean old John Rhodes? I'm sorry, the people in this house do not associate with bootleggers."

"I'm gonna mash your black mouth!"

Mr. Miller stepped back. "Not if you hope to see your daddy, you're not."

A dog tied to our front gate began to howl.

"I knowed you knew where he was."

"Behave yourself and wait till I get a flashlight, and I'll take you to him."

They went down around the house toward the meadow, and I went out to the gate and untied Uncle Billie's dog, and he went running up over the hill. When I went into the dining room, I told my mother, "Somebody brought Uncle Billie's dog back."

Helga had made a giant chocolate torte with ten layers and a different filling between each layer. I was trying to decide whether I liked the raspberry jam or the walnut cream best when I heard the muffled crack of a pistol from outside somewhere. In a minute there was another, even more muffled sound, and I knew this time Mr. Miller had probably held the pistol against Joe's ear. The mint-cream layer was also delicious.

Everyone went in the front parlor for the brandy; I got only blackberry juice. Mr. Miller held my glance, and I nodded so he would know that if a secret wasn't mine to tell, I didn't tell it. His hands were damp, as though he had washed them. If I had just killed one of those dirty bootleggers, I'd wash my hands, too.

Mr. Isaac stayed the night and shared the room with the twin beds with my grandfather. They were still chattering away like two schoolboys when I went to sleep. I had tried to stay awake to see if Grandfather would take Mr. Isaac down the hall through the pink doors, but I couldn't. I must remember to ask Lloyd if interesting talk was as satisfying as fucking.

September 17, 1929

Aunt Lilly was not only very pretty, she was creative. She could make wooden tabletops look like marble by slapping them with paint, then using bunches of string and turkey feathers. She could antique things and put on thin sheets of Dutch gold until it looked like solid metal. What she really wanted to create was a baby, but she had not succeeded. There were all kinds of snide jokes in our family as to her effort in that direction. But the true reason poor Uncle Blake looked tired all the time was that he went to work in the tannery every morning at five and scraped acid-soaked cowhides with a hoe to remove the hair, then dragged home at three with that horrible stench still clinging to him.

Lilly always had a hot tub ready, perfumed with bath salts and coconut oil and shampoos from the Avon man. Sometimes she got in the big tub with him, and sometimes she waited until he got out and rubbed him vigorously with rough towels. Sometimes it brought the results she wanted, but most times it did not. He was just too tired. He would fall onto the bed and be asleep in three minutes, and Aunt Lilly would take off her black lace gown and put her old painting dress back on.

Within two months of living in Grandfather Fancler's house, she had painted every room and refinished almost every piece of furniture. In the living room, only the old pump organ had evaded her. Each time my grandfather passed the old organ, he loved to see if it had suffered a new incarnation. The mahogany parlor-set was now pale yellow, and he determined not to think about that. After all he had said, "This is now your home." He had not expected a rainbow metamorphosis.

Grandfather called a meeting of all his daughters, and everyone came except Aunt Russie, who lived in Washington, and Aunt Fannie, the eldest, who lived in Charlottesville and was busy helping to restore Monticello. Aunt Eva came, but she was white as a ghost and had to go lie down. Aunt Sebe whispered that she was sure Eva had TB. Everyone looked at the painted furniture without comment, but they exchanged glances with their eyebrows raised. Grandfather filled the glasses with his best elderberry wine, and Aunt Lilly served a new chiffon cake she had made with lime Jell-O that turned it green. The cake plate had gotten a recent coat of black enamel that was already beginning to peel around the edges. Aunt Sebe looked at it and said, "Lilly, this is really too much."

Aunt Lilly lifted her head on her long, patrician neck and said, "Too much of what?"

Sebe remembered her promise to her father to keep everything peaceful and quickly amended, "Too much cake, dear. It looks delicious, but I'm on a diet."

"Now let's get down to business," Grandfather began. "As you know, I'm seventy-seven." (There was a murmur of dissent.) "Let me go on. I don't see the hearse coming up the hill to get me, and my father did live to be ninety-one. Lilly may someday have nightmares about that. I think it wise to make plans. When I go, what savings are left will be divided equally among you, if I haven't blown it all on ladies of the evening by then."

Aunt Olie said, "If you're going to talk dirty, I'm going home." (It wasn't in levity; she meant it.)

"My old farm out on Craven's Run has a very good tenant. We sharecrop, and it's been bringing me about two thousand a year. This year there will be a little more. We are going to cut trees for telephone poles, and by the way, I wish you would each get a phone. I'm putting that money into a fund, as of now, to pay for schoolbooks for my grandchildren. I don't want to hear any excuses for them not to go through high school. Most of you have homes of your own, but when I give this one to Lilly, and I'm going to, that leaves Sebe and her boys without a home."

Sebe said, "I'm going to have to move soon. They're closing down the Bluebird Market, and Gertrude Gracey wants her house back."

My mother was surprised. "I didn't know Gertrude owned your house. How much does she want for it?"

"Thirty-five hundred dollars. It might as well be a million."

"She will take three thousand right now, as she can buy out the market for that much."

My grandfather was scornful. "Now, Billy-Pearl, would you leave her no operating capital? We will give her thirty-five hundred, if none of you object."

They all knew the only one who might object was Aunt Olie, and they looked accusingly at her until she mumbled, "It's all right with me."

"That's settled. I won't transfer the title on this house until after the first of the year, so Lilly and Blake won't have to pay taxes on it for another year. And I'll keep those up, as my share, as long as I live."

Just then Blake came through the door, and the scent of the tannery came with him. His eyes were red-rimmed, and he looked exhausted. He said hello to his sisters-in-law and went tiredly up the stairs. Lilly followed.

There were whispered remarks of "That boy's only twenty-five years old, and he looks forty." "Why doesn't he look for another job?" "Have you looked for a job lately?" "He's had no experience except scraping cowhides."

When the business was over, everyone went home. My mother and I were last, because I was sitting on the floor back in the hallway looking at Grandfather's archaeology books about Indian digs in Oklahoma. He wouldn't loan me these books, they were his favorites. Someday he was going on a dig.

It was a good solid old house, but the sounds of voices came down the stairs clearly.

"I want you to quit the tannery."

"And what?"

"And stay home. I'll get a job. I won't make as much, but we don't need much now that we don't pay rent."

"You want me to paint things all day, and you'll come home at night, and I'll rape you."

"Is that what you think I do when you come home, rape you?"

"Well, ain't it?"

At this my mother put down her glass of elderberry wine, and we went out the door, careful to close it quietly.

SEPTEMBER 19, 1929

The Tuesday after Labor Day, Stanley and I had started to school. The bus came at six-thirty, but if we didn't get out to the road in time, it didn't matter; it went about two miles up the road to pick up some other kids, then came

back. The first day we got on when it came back. I was anxious to go, but I
think Stanley was afraid somebody was going to recognize him and say, "You
ain't Stanley Fancler, you're Stanley Black." I didn't think they would, because
he looked, sounded, and acted very different than he did the day he came to us.
The one I felt badly for was Boobie. She stood behind the screen door and
watched. I knew how much she wanted to get on the bus. I knew Miss Larkin
and the Dutch ladies were going to have a surprise party back in the schoolroom
for her. I also knew it wouldn't help.

There were two new kids on the bus whom I had never seen up close before:
the Thorne twins. I had seen them out in the field at their farm, but up close,
they were a shock. Each of them filled two seats, with some rolls of fat lopping
over. The one nearer the front had his arms wrapped tightly around a very large
paper bag, obviously his lunch. His brother, farther back, had already lost control of his sack. The Marsteller boys had grabbed it and were looking inside.
Bob Marsteller was a nasty boy. "Let's see what you got in here that makes you
so fat," he said.

The front Thorne twin was twisting in his seat, unable to rise without something to hold on to. "Gimme that back."

Stanley was not as heavy as Bob Marsteller, but he was taller. "Give the boy
back his lunch."

"Who do you think you are?"

"I'm the guy that's about to slap you silly."

Stanley had his face very close to Bob's. Just then the fat boy made a grab for
the paper bag and the bottom came out of it, spewing the contents on the floor:
several apples and biscuit sandwiches wrapped in newspaper scattered in the
aisle. Bob grabbed up one of the biscuits and looked inside. It was filled with
brown beans. "Look, this fat kid eats rabbit-shit sandwiches!" The moon-faced
boy's eyes, almost buried by the fullness of his cheeks, now filled with tears.

The driver yelled, "You kids behave back there," but he didn't take his eyes
from the road. It took all his attention to control the rickety bus as he pulled to
the side to pick up the two Smith girls.

Stanley reached out and grasped Bob by the ear and twisted. "Get down
there and pick it up."

The pain in Bob's ear brought him to the floor, but it was too late; the Smith
girls tramped through on their way to the back, careful to step on everything
they could. As soon as Stanley let loose his ear, Bob went back, cursing and

threatening, and sat by the Smith girls. Stanley retrieved what he could and added it to the twin's sack.

We were lucky to not have to carry lunch. The grade school was only two blocks from the Curtiss house, and I ate with my grandmother. Some days, when Grandmother Curtiss was busy elsewhere, Aunt Almeda would have lunch served for just the two of us up on her little balcony, and those were the days I liked best. Across from the high school was a lunchroom where you could buy thick soup and a sandwich and a Nehi orange for twenty-five cents. Stanley ate there.

The only two at the high school who went to the end of the line on the bus were Stanley and Bob Marsteller.

Stanley usually tried to study on the bus, but it was hard to keep your eye on the lines with the bus jiggling. Bob Marsteller horsed around and threw things and teased the Smith girls, and sometimes Stanley would have to grab him by the shirt collar and twist until Bob's face was red.

The Thorne twins were going to be in the first grade, and it took them five minutes to lumber out of their seats and get down the steps of the bus. A circle of kids gathered around to see the new freak show. There was not a sound as the two, staring straight ahead, moved to the door, and the circle around them moved with them.

The principal was standing in the doorway, looking as though he would like to block their entrance. "Boys, are you registered here at Central?"

The boy carrying the surviving lunch bag answered, "Our mother says we have to go to school and learn how to read and write."

The second boy added, "We will be eight years old come November."

"Do you have a note from your mother?"

"Our mother ken't write no note, she don' know how."

"I'm Richie Thorne."

"I'm Lou Thorne. You kin tell us apart. Richie has his little finger off."

Richie held up his pudgy hand to show he truly was missing the end joint of his little finger. The children around them were beginning to giggle.

"Well, come in, come in. I will see if I can find a couple of chairs big enough for you," the principal said.

I was sorry I had passed the test to go into the third grade. I would have liked to be in the room with the Thorne boys. I wasn't even going to see that much of them on the bus, since they gave up by the end of the week.

It disturbed my mother when she found out the Thorne boys were not going to school. "At least it would get them out of that horrible place for the day." She did not really know that the Thorne farmhouse was a horrible place inside; she had never been there, and as far as we heard, neither had anyone else, but it certainly did look horrible on the outside. And then there was their father, Red Thorne. He was probably the biggest man in our county, not just fat but taller than anyone I had ever seen. The two older boys were very tall also but, unlike the twins, very skinny. No one knew what their mother looked like, for she seldom came out, and if she did and saw anyone coming, she ran back inside. You passed their house on the way to the Mount Zion church, and the Dutch ladies, the only ones in our house who went to church, said they had seen her peeking around the windows. But I didn't think you could, since the windows were all smudged over or boarded up where the glass was broken.

SEPTEMBER 26, 1929

WHEN LESTER ADAMS came to dinner at the end of the following week, my mother urged him to go up to the Thorne farm and tell them there was a compulsory school law. Lester had arrested Mr. Thorne twice for bootlegging, and after that experience, he was not anxious to face him again. He did promise to bring a couple of deputies out in the morning and call on Red.

My mother said, "Nonsense, I'll go with you. I would like to see what Mrs. Thorne looks like. No one I know has ever seen her."

Lester did not take my mother with him and he did not succeed. "Red Thorne told me those boys were his personal property, and he had decided not to send them to school. The whole thing was his stupid wife's idea, and the boys refused to ride on the bus. I guess that ends that."

"You're just going to let it go at that?"

"I saw those boys. They belong in a freak show. What difference does it make if they get an education?"

"Maybe an education would keep them out of a freak show. I'll go and see him."

"Billy-Pearl, when are you going to stop trying to run the world?"

"When I'm dead."

On Saturday morning my mother went to see Red Thorne. She took me with her, since I knew the boys from the bus. She had never seen the man up close before, and though she stood her ground, I knew she was intimidated. He towered over her, and with his red eyes and long yellow teeth, he seemed more like a wolf than a man. His four boys all stayed back, half hidden behind trees and broken doors.

"What you want?" was his greeting.

"I have come to make sure your boys attend school." Her voice quivered a little as she lied, "I'm from the board of education. You know there is a law you must send your children to school."

She backed away as his face flushed a darker shade of red. He spewed spittle as he yelled, "Them boys don't need to read an' write. I ken't read an' their maw ken't read an' we git along real good."

My mother surveyed the decrepit house and the old truck up on blocks, and she said, "Yes, I can see you do." Her sarcasm was lost on him. "The county will fine you ten dollars a day for each day you keep them out of school."

"I ain't got ten dollars. If'n I had ten dollars, I would buy some sugar and I'd be back in business."

"Then they will put you in jail."

Now he laughed, and it was an ugly laugh. "Who will put me in jail? You think da sheriff is gonna come an' git me?"

My mother held her ground. "Maybe not. What he can do, every time you get that still of yours in operation, is bring the federal revenue officers in to break it up, and you will be out of business."

He said, "I ain't makin' moonshine. I tol' you, I ain't got no sugar."

She looked down over their scant cornfields and at the potato patch up on the hillside behind the house. "Well, you certainly don't have enough crops out to feed your family until Christmas. Now, Mr. Thorne, you don't want a fight with the revenue officers. I tell you what I'll do. I have a certified teacher and a schoolroom in my house. If you send the boys there, I'm sure it will satisfy the board of education. It's not that far, they can walk from here. I'll expect them eight o'clock on Monday."

She turned and walked toward our car.

"I ain't sayin' I'll send 'em."

"There are twelve federal men in this county, all armed with guns. I will feed the boys their lunch, and they will start home by three." She started up the car and we drove away.

I said, "You told lies back there. How come you want me to tell the truth all the time?"

"There are lies, and then there are lies. Sometimes it's the only weapon we have."

"Are you gonna stand in the corner when you get home?"

"Maybe for a little while, until I stop fuming."

"What's Miss Larkin gonna think when she sees those two fat tubs?"

"She is going to think, as I do, that someone has to rescue those children from that mad dog of a father."

I had a feeling then that grew in me more each day: someone, but why does it always have to be you?

Monday was the first teachers' meeting of the year, and Stanley and I got to stay home. He was disappointed, since school had turned out a lot better for him than he expected. No one had recognized him as Stanley Black. I'm sure he was dressed better than most. He had fallen heir to the wardrobe my father had left behind. With very little adjustment, everything fitted. The linen shirts and silk neckties made him look like the gentleman my mother had professed him to be. Henry Harlin, the high school principal, had taken Stanley around and introduced him as a cousin from Kentucky, and he was off to a good beginning. He also discovered he was better prepared scholastically than he had expected. The French classes were going very well, with Erica helping him each night, and Miss Larkin had renewed her knowledge of algebra.

I didn't miss going to school on Monday, but I did miss having lunch with Aunt Almeda. I was finding it harder to go back to school each afternoon.

Around eight, the Thorne twins came walking slowly down the road. They were dressed in crudely made shirts from bleached flour sacks, on which some of the writing was still visible. I could tell by the way the Dutch ladies looked at them that they were mentally measuring them for new shirts. They seemed to have caught the disease called "fix up the world" from my mother. Mr. Miller had brought down from the attic two very big captain's chairs with broad arms and sawed six inches off the legs. These boys were wide but not tall.

They ate three muffins and drank two cups of cocoa each before Richie identified them with "I'm Richie and he's Lou." He held up his hand to show how they could be told apart.

Miss Larkin asked innocently, "How did you lose your finger, my dear?"

"My paw cut it off with a knife so he could tell us apart."

Miss Larkin turned quickly and wiped her eyes.

Stanley was spending his day in the paddock. He felt guilty being away from the horses because of school. My mother and I went to the upper meadow to take Uncle Billie his supplies. It was autumn, and it would not be long before we would sell off the rams and Uncle Billie would move to the lower meadow with the ewes, who would be the mothers of next year's flock. Uncle Billie was a loner and would not be comfortable living in our house. He wintered in an old log cabin down near the sheep shed that had been the original house on this farm, over a hundred years ago.

We did what we always did. We unloaded the supplies from the truck, and he came down to help us carry them across the meadow to his shack. In the bright clear light of morning, he looked very old, and some of the bruises he had suffered in his beating had not completely vanished from his wrinkled brown skin. We were ahead of him, and I whispered, "How old is Uncle Billie?"

"I don't know, ask him."

When we were sitting on the split-bottom chairs in front of his door and having the bowls of green tea he always brewed, I asked him, "How old are you, Uncle Billie?"

"Well, let's see." He sat with his mouth open and his eyes closed. The slight breeze stirred his wispy strands of white beard and the little hair that was left around his bald pate. I thought he had gone to sleep, but he said, "What year is this?"

"It's nineteen twenty-nine."

"An' what year did the railroad come through?"

My mother answered, "I think eighteen sixty-eight."

"Near as I can remember, I was forty then, when I thought to quit diggin' a path for that railroad and go and live in the woods."

I counted. "That can't be; that would make you one hundred and one years old."

"Way to go, boy, way to go. My grandfather lived to be one hundred ten. Over in China lots of men live to one hundred. I can't leave this old dog here." He fondled the shepherd at his knee. "He wouldn't know how to get on without me."

Flocks of sheep had gathered around us out of curiosity, but when we got up to leave, they scattered in every direction. The grass had yellowed, and this high meadow was beginning to look bare. The sumac along the fences was dark plum red, and the beech trees on the hills beyond were golden yellow. A flock of gray geese went flying over, and I hoped they would light down on our pond on their way south. You couldn't tell it by the warmth of the air, but winter was coming.

My mother and I made several trips to the truck, carrying the split-bottom hickory chairs that Uncle Billie had spent the summer carving and fitting together. My mother always sent them to the county fair, where they sold for five dollars each. We were careful not to let him carry any of them, since he had told us how old he was. On the way down the hill, I asked, "What does Uncle Billie do with his share of the sheep money and the money from his chairs?"

"I put it down in my safe for him."

"For what?"

"For his retirement, and I suppose he has a will. I don't want to ask him—when people start thinking about dying, they die."

"You know, he can't write. Next time I go up there, I'll write his will for him."

"And who will you write as the beneficiary?"

"I can't spell that. I'll just write, 'I leave everything to Hughie Curtiss,' and I'll get him to put his 'X.' "

"You wouldn't."

"Yes, I would. You want him to leave all his money to his dog?"

"Why not? That dog is his best friend."

STANLEY DID NOT WANT to interrupt his training routine for lunch, so he ate a ham sandwich in the saddle. I put the arm of the phonograph back at the beginning three times, then I went in to eat. He was playing a new record by a singer named Lily Pons. It was an opera called *La Bohème,* in French. I didn't know if he was teaching the horse or himself, for he sang along when he thought no one was listening, and I didn't know whether he was trying to learn singing or French.

I ate out in the gazebo with the twins and Boobie. On my way past the dining room table, I heard Miss Larkin say, "You know, if I can get through that wall of fear those boys have, I think they are capable of learning."

The Thorne boys had already emptied their soup bowls and were about through with their sandwiches and eyeing mine when I got to the table. Tuba had taken on the task of filling them up, and she made three trips to the kitchen. They even finished the pear dumplings from last night's supper before they seemed full. All the time they ate, they stared at Boobie across the table, and she didn't like it.

"Stop lookin' at me."

"I ain't never seen no nigger up close before."

"I ain't never seen no human hogs before, but I don't stare at you."

By the end of the week, the twins and Boobie were used to each other. Even Handsome, who had run crying at the sight of them, ventured closer but still kept behind a chair.

October 1, 1929

The first day of October was traditionally apple-butter day, unless it was raining, which would put out the fires under the kettles. Apple butter was probably my favorite food on our farm. It was good on griddle cakes, corn bread, biscuits, and it was at its best on a hot slice from the end of yeast bread, dripping in butter and slathered with apple butter, half an inch thick.

To make good apple butter, you need good apples, and some far-thinking ancestor fifty years ago had planted an orchard of thirty Northern Spy: a large green apple with muted red stripes and a sweet, tart flavor that cooked down into a thick dark red butter. Just in case the Northern Spy crop failed, that ancestor had planted thirty trees of Baldwin, bright red with a green blush. Years in which there was a bumper crop, like this one, we made a double supply of butter. This year we had twice as many people to feed, and my mother always gave away the butter with a lavish hand.

Everyone had been gathering apples for a week and stacking the full baskets in the canning shed. Mrs. Zucker and two brothers called Forrester, whom my mother had hired for the day, had already started at dawn. The hand-turned apple peelers were too slow, so my mother had borrowed two of the new electric peelers from the 4-H Club with a promise of several jars of apple butter for their booth at the Fall Festival.

Mr. Miller had built three tripods to hang the fifty-gallon copper kettles from, and enough oak and hickory wood had been cut to keep the fires going for at least twelve hours. Piles of the red ribbon peelings were caught in baskets and carried to the waiting hogs.

The apples were quartered and cored and dumped in the kettles until they were about two thirds full. A mixture of cider, pressed from the rough purple Winesaps the week before, was mixed with one cup of white sugar and one cup of brown for each gallon of apples; a half cup of cinnamon; a half cup of nutmeg; a quarter cup of oil of cloves; and a half cup of salt for each kettle. As the applesauce boiled down, more apples were added. Someone had to stir almost constantly with a very long paddle nailed to a stick to keep it out of the fire.

You could get up on the roof of the canning shed and look down to where the kettles stood in the yard, and see the thick bubbling cauldrons as the color darkened from gold to rust to brown. Each kettle boiled down to about twenty-five gallons and was emptied twice, for a total of about 150 gallons canned in half-gallon sterilized jars. The Dutch ladies were in charge of boiling the glass jars and ladling the boiling apple butter inside.

Grandfather Fancler and my grandmother Curtiss had come out for the day, as it was festive in spite of the work. We hadn't seen much of Grandmother Curtiss over the summer. Today she arrived in style in the brown limousine, with Alex in his brown uniform. She sat with stiff-backed dignity until Alex came around to open the door for her. He looked as if he had spent as much time polishing his boots as he had the car.

I had always thought it would have been better if these two grandparents had married. They always seemed to get along so well. Today they walked together over the farm, had tea on the porch, and talked constantly. Grandmother seemed to be sounding him out on many subjects. Each time I listened, it was something different: the fate of the world, your moral obligation to your husband and your children, and where did Billy-Pearl get all that energy? In the afternoon they played backgammon and drank cider. Mrs. Miller had put on a black uniform and a clean white apron before she served them. Grandmother Curtiss had that kind of influence on people. She had not seen the three Dutch ladies before and wondered how my mother could afford them until she explained that they had a small pension and worked here for room and board.

"Actually, we are all a kind of extended family. We all like each other and are concerned for each other's welfare."

Grandmother's voice had a bitter edge. "That is certainly more than you can say for most families."

"We are learning to depend on each other and to laugh together." (My mother didn't add "And kill together.")

Alex came back for Grandmother at six-thirty, and she went home with five gallons of apple butter. The wood ashes under the kettles were cooled and stored in barrels down by the barn. Later, they would be covered with water; the result was lye, used to make soap when we butchered the hogs.

Oᴄᴛᴏʙᴇʀ 4, 1929

Oɴ Fʀɪᴅᴀʏ, ᴀꜰᴛᴇʀ ʟᴜɴᴄʜ with Aunt Almeda, I skipped school and went with her to the park. Grandmother Curtiss was busy taking inventory of everything in the house Uncle Alvin had left her. I didn't understand why, she owned it all anyway, but she said she wanted to know what she had and declared it was a treasure trove. There was a lot of cash in the safe and in the safe-deposit boxes, and still Grandfather Curtiss seemed desperate to cover his obligations and was losing things to foreclosure right and left. But he would not ask her for money, and she was determined not to give him a nickel until he did. They had not spoken to each other for over a month.

Aunt Almeda wore one of those strange floating white garments that had belonged to Aunt Emma. With a white veil over her face, she looked like a ghost. We went over and sat on a cannon in the park where we could see the preparations for the senator's statue. They had just placed a bronze plaque on the stone pedestal that held the giant horse. I went over to see what it said and came back to tell Aunt Almeda: " 'He lived life as though he would die tomorrow. He died as though he would live forever. And now he belongs to the ages.' "

She wasn't so much angry that they had stolen the last line from Lincoln's eulogy as she was that "Now he belongs to me, his constituents are through with him. All that's left are memories, and they are all mine."

We went to the back of the park where no one would catch us, and broke off a big bunch of red leaves to take back to the house. Grandfather Curtiss was in the front hall talking on the phone when we came in.

"Mr. Martin, I just can't believe it has dropped that much . . . Yes, I know when everybody wants to sell and nobody wants to buy, the bottom drops out . . . I understood the Federal Reserve Bank was going to prop up the market . . . That forty million is gone? . . . I know, compared to that, my loss seems small, but it's no consolation. When you have lost everything, you're just as broke as if you had lost forty million . . ."

Aunt Almeda held her hand over my mouth and pushed me back out the door. When we came in again, Aunt Almeda was talking loudly, making noise. "We will press these leaves between wax paper, and I'll show you how to treat them with alum so they won't lose their color."

Grandfather Curtiss was slumped in his chair, looking like he had gained fifty pounds. Aunt Almeda chatted on, "It's hard to realize in the Indian summer, but in another month there will be snow, and we will be glad for any spot of color."

Grandfather's voice was hard to hear. He was making that sound you make when you are trying not to cry. He had hung up the phone and was talking to himself. "Not five people have paid their bills in the store in the last month. And the insurance business is gone."

Aunt Almeda put her hand on his shoulder. "Why don't you go and have a walk in the park? It's good for the soul."

He stood up with great effort, and I saw where a piece of fabric had been sewn into the back of his pants to accommodate his expanding girth. "How can you be so calm? I've lost your money, too."

"Huston, I gave you that money. If it's lost, it's lost. It was a long time ago, and I never really expected to get it back."

He wiped the perspiration from his face with a giant handkerchief. "You never expected to need it."

She removed her veil and patted her hair in place. "That's true. I thought the senator would always be there, taking care of me."

There was the sound of a car in our driveway, and I went to see. It was an old chauffeur-driven limousine, and I watched until the driver came around to open the door and help old Judge Brown to his feet. Grandfather waited at the door as the judge waddled up the steps. He was about as fat as Grandfather. Aunt Almeda found a chair and sat gracefully, with her skirts arranged around her ankles.

"Judge Brown, come in. I suppose you have heard the market news?" Grandfather said.

"I didn't realize you were that involved."

"If the store was the extent of my holdings, I'd be in a bad way. No one is paying their bills."

Almeda rose.

"Aunt Almeda, I think you have not met Judge Brown. This is my aunt Almeda."

She had extended her hand, and he had no choice but to take it, though he did so reluctantly. "I am aware of Madam's identity. You have been frequently about the town this last month."

His voice was as cold as he could make it, but she responded with a practiced charm. I am sure she had met many men in her life who didn't approve of her and didn't bother to hide their feelings. "This is, after all, my hometown. I was born here. I have been getting reacquainted."

He would not be charmed. "This is a small town. In a town this size, you know there is talk."

"I remember, well do I remember. Even in a town the size of Washington, there was talk. I've grown a hard shell."

"Well, my client has not."

Almeda was genuinely surprised. "And who is your client?"

He said it like beating a drum. "Senator Burton's widow."

She was more flustered than I'm sure she would have hoped. "I fancy thinking of myself as Senator Burton's widow."

Now he thumped his cane on the floor. "Well, you're not! You know very well what you were." He was losing control. "We all know."

Grandfather went and held the door open. "Now, that's enough. You can't come in here and insult my aunt."

Aunt Almeda took his arm. "It's all right, Huston. Nobody is insulted by the truth." And now she made her case as though she were in the judge's court. "For forty years I slept beside that man. I could reach out and touch him in the night, and he could reach out and touch me. That makes me more of a wife than that woman, who would not free him, will ever be."

The judge stared at her and blinked his old eyes like a turtle and realized he had lost a round. "Madam, I did not come here to argue your morality. I'm sorry, I've started my dance on the wrong foot. If you will forgive me, I will start over."

She found her chair and settled into it with grace. "If you will stop calling me 'madam.' My name is Almeda Curtiss, and you may call me Miss Curtiss."

He came to the chair opposite her. "Very well, Miss Curtiss, may I sit? I'm too heavy to stand more than ten minutes." She motioned to the chair opposite, and he settled in with a heavy sigh. "You know the market has gone to hell?"

"I knew in the spring that the Wall Street banks would not support the market; collapse was inevitable."

He learned forward. "How did you know that?"

"The senator said democracy is like a chicken coop where everybody crows."

"I don't understand that."

"Judge, you should know why they talked freely before me; you have the same attitude. I was beneath consideration, a thing owned. I passed drinks and cigars, and I smiled a lot, and I listened, and for forty years I wrote it all down."

"What are you going to do with it? Publish it? Blackmail your country?"

Grandfather had been quiet, "I can think of a title: 'Grease from the Inside Track.'"

"I was thinking of calling it 'View from the Catbird Seat.'"

The judge could deal with her no longer. "Or perhaps 'A Whore's-Eye View'?"

"That does it. Out you go." And Grandfather held the door wide.

Almeda quieted him. "It's all right, nephew. It's not the first time I've heard it."

The judge was not going yet. He didn't even try to rise from his chair. "Miss Curtiss, again I apologize. I came here for a point of information, since you are aware of the senator's affairs. The probate attorneys in Washington have not sent the contents of his safe-deposit boxes, and we have not seen his will."

"You know he secured his wife with trust funds long ago. She shouldn't expect anything else."

"She is his legal wife. I'm worried about his stock assets, with the market falling."

"I shouldn't tell you, but I will. There is no fear there. He got out of the market some time ago on the advice of the secretary of the Treasury, Andrew Mellon."

"He sold with the market still rising?"

Aunt Almeda's years in Washington had taught her well. "Mellon helped create the condition of the market. How would he not know what was to come? It was said in Washington that when Andrew Mellon and his daughter, Ailsa, sat down to trade, one or the other of them always won, and Uncle Sam always lost."

"Are you saying Andrew Mellon is a crook?"

"I'm saying Andrew Mellon has not supported the Wall Street banks, and the banks in turn are not supporting a falling market. With everybody selling and nobody buying, it's going to crash through the floor, and all this time Herbert Hoover is saying that business is fundamentally sound and prosperity has just ducked around the corner for a moment."

The judge managed to stand. He was fuming and sputtering. "If you weren't a woman, I would say you were a fascist."

She laughed in his face. "That's the most chauvinistic thing I ever heard. Do you think women incapable of fascism?"

Grandfather was holding the door wide, and Judge Brown was struggling out. "You with your red hair and your face paint!"

She followed him, laughing even more. "If I stopped wearing makeup and got a gray wig, would that open the door of fascism to me?"

Grandfather slammed the door before the judge got a chance to answer.

October 5, 1929

Saturday morning our stars must have been in all the wrong places, for it started off early and really bad. I awoke to the sound of my mother crying like her heart would break. She so seldom let her sadness show that I went running to the barn in my pajamas. She was standing in Hannah's stall, with her arms around the horse's neck. On the floor lay Hannah's newborn foal, shining black and dead.

Stanley came in his bathrobe and led Hannah into a clean stall and gave her fresh water and some hay and began to rub her down with a sponge and a towel, then wrapped her in a blanket. My mother was sitting on a stool in the stall, looking down at the little dead horse. She blew her nose. "I can't seem to stop crying. I know things die, everything on the farm dies sooner or later, but this little horse is so perfect, and I love Hannah so."

Stanley urged her to go to the house and have a cup of coffee. He would join her as soon as he had a shower.

"How will we get him buried? Mr. Miller is just getting over the flu, we can't ask him."

"Don't worry, we will figure it out."

I went up to Stanley's room with him and stood under the warm water with him.

We all ate in the little dining room. It was cool of a morning now, even with the Indian summer day, and Tuba had started a fire in the fireplace. Handsome had to be watched, because he was throwing little balls of paper into the fire.

Miss Larkin grabbed him back three or four times, and he squealed, and my mother said, "Let him squeal, I need to hear someone laugh."

The front doorbell rang, and Tuba went to answer it, mumbling, "Who could that be? It's only seven o'clock." She came back shortly with her eyes narrowed. "Miz Billy, you better come."

I followed my mother to the hall and saw the Thorne twins standing there. I had begun to call them Tweedledum and Tweedledee, but they didn't look like the characters in a nursery rhyme this morning. They looked awful: dirty, tear-stained faces, with their clothes disheveled. They seemed unable to look directly at my mother.

"Our ma says will you drive up behind the church? She wants to tell you somethin'." And as Lou wiped his face with his sleeve, my mother saw the back of his shirt.

"Oh my God!"

She walked behind them as they stood, heads down. The blood had soaked through their shirts in wide streaks, now turning black. She didn't need to ask who had done this, she knew; but she didn't know how to deal with it. "Hughie, go and see if Mr. Miller is well enough to come down here."

He was getting dressed when I got up to his room and just needed his shoes. He, too, said, "Oh my God," when he saw the boys. He and my mother took the twins into the kitchen and soaked the shirts loose from their backs with warm wet towels and viewed the damage.

My mother was seldom at a loss, but she was now. "What will we do?"

"Well, down south, when my people were beaten, they used to put suet and marigold leaves on the wounds."

"Some kind of salve, I think, so the bandages won't stick to their skin. Hughie, that Cloverine salve, did you sell it?"

"Only one jar to Tuba."

"Go get it."

It took the other five jars to cover their fat backs. They didn't cry out much, although it looked like it really hurt. Maybe they were used to pain. Rose came in with her bottle of laudanum and gave them each a spoonful. After they were bandaged and had drunk several cups of cocoa, they lay down on the couches in the hall and were almost immediately asleep. But not before they had declared, "We ain't never gonna go home agin. We're goin' up on the hill an' hide in a cave!"

My mother put off calling Lester until she went to meet with the twins' mother. Mr. Miller wanted to go with my mother, as he was afraid it might be some kind of trick. "That devil is capable of anything."

She went and put on her old canvas hunting jacket, the one with a pocket that would hold a pistol. "I don't want to call the sheriff if I can deal with this myself."

"I'd be obliged if you would say if *we* can deal with this."

"No, I'm all right. If there was only some way we could lure him down here." And even I knew what she had in mind.

Mrs. Thorne was hiding behind a tombstone when we drove up behind the cemetery. When she finally decided it was safe to come out, she held one hand over the side of her face, which was bruised. I moved to the backseat, and after a little urging, she got into the car. She apologized because her bare feet were muddy. She was sorry for everything; sorry to send the boys to us. I thought she was sorry to be alive, and she didn't look like she would be for long. There was a bald place on the side of her head where the hair had been pulled out.

"Please, ma'am, could you have the revenuers come an' git him? He's gonna kill all of us. He says he is, an' he will. He does terrible things to the boys, I ken't say it."

"Is he up at his still?"

"No, he don't have sugar to set a new mess of mash. He's up in the barn."

"I'll see he is put in jail."

"They won't keep 'im. He's too mean', an' when he gits out, he'll kill us!"

"All right, I'll take care of it."

"You won't tell that I talked to you?"

"No, and you won't tell that I talked to you. Now, stay up here until afternoon. Where are your other boys?"

"They're hidin' out. I think he broke John's arm."

She got back out and cowered behind a stone that said "Rest in Peace."

We stopped at the curve before we got to the Thorne house, and Mother got out and spread an old horse blanket over the backseat, and I knew she was going to get that scary old son of a bitch into our car. I hoped she knew what she was doing. She did it by promising him two hundred pounds of sugar if he would come and dig a grave and bury the dead colt. We opened all the windows in the car, but I still had to hold my handkerchief over my nose.

He was truly a giant. He lifted the colt to his shoulder and carried him down over the meadow as though the dead animal weighed nothing. My mother pointed out a spot very close to where Joe Rhodes was buried and requested a deep grave that the dogs would not dig out. It was in a sheltered place that you could not see from the house, and about half of us were down in the field anyway. Mr. Miller, Stanley, and Rose all stood behind my mother as though they were going to conduct a funeral, but what they held behind their backs were not hymnbooks. Thorne stood in the hole and threw dirt out until he was shoulder-deep.

From where I stood on the knoll above them—my mother had forbidden me to come any closer—I could see things that Red Thorne could not. My mother and Stanley each held a pistol behind their backs, Mr. Miller had a deer rifle, and Rose had a double-barreled shotgun.

He grumbled, "This is deep enough," and started to climb out—when my mother's first shot hit him in the shoulder. The second pierced his chest, but still he climbed, until his red wolf face began to splatter away. I don't know whose shot got him in the eyes, for Mr. Miller, Stanley, and Rose were all pointing guns at his head and firing away. Even then he held on to the edge of the sod and pulled it loose with him when he fell back.

They all came and looked down into the hole and fired their last shots, just to make sure.

They pushed the dead colt down on top of him and said it was a shame to bury a dear little animal like that with Red Thorne. Stanley went and got the tractor to push the dirt into the grave and roll it firm. Mr. Miller said he felt much better, but my mother insisted he go back to bed nevertheless.

Rose and my mother packed several baskets of food into the car and went to tell Mrs. Thorne that she was safe now. I called Worthy to tell him I had sold all six jars of his Cloverine salve, and I didn't even have to give away any of the pictures of Jesus.

IT WAS THE KIND of scene of which nightmares are made. For years to come, in my dreams, I saw that giant clawing his way up out of his grave, the top of his head gone and his bloody brains spilling down over his demonic face. All that time, the five of them were firing at him, but still he came. Sometimes, in my dreams, the four of them would back away and leave me standing there with only a toy gun. I must ask my psychiatrist what that means.

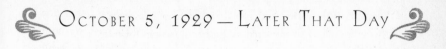

LLOYD'S BIRTHDAY WAS on the third of October. Saturday wasn't a good day for a party. The early autumn rains had started, and it had been raining off and on all day, but Aunt Sebe had a party for Lloyd anyway. Although it was a Saturday, business was slow enough at the inn that Sylvia Tingler could manage it all, and it would have been just as easy to have his party there except my mother would not be in the same room with Sylvia Tingler. Too, there would have been trouble if the owners had come around, because Aunt Sebe had stolen almost everything she served.

This was a kind of double party, since it was the first time Aunt Sebe had had a group in since Grandfather had given her the deed and she owned her house free and clear. It was also the first party to include her new boyfriend, Kirby Conway, and he was a good addition. He laughed a lot and told jokes, and he brought Lloyd a leather motorcycle jacket like his.

Worthy was mad because Lloyd put it right on instead of the yellow raincoat. Lloyd strutted around and said, "Now if I just had me a motorcycle." So when Aunt Sebe brought out his new bicycle, some of the bloom was off it. He got a lot of presents, for there were about twenty-five people there, if you count cousins.

Grandfather gave him a whole lot of books, including several by H. G. Wells that I knew I could get away from him later. Grandfather was always hoping Lloyd would begin to enjoy reading, but I knew he never would. The kinds of books he enjoyed were sold secretly by the Greek man who also sold popcorn.

Lloyd had whispered to me, "You wanna see what Popeye did to Olive Oyl after he ate the spinach?"

"I don't like spinach."

"You will after you see this."

My mother gave him a wallet with twenty dollars in it, and I thought that was too much, since she always seemed to be counting the cost of things these days. Tuba had sent the cake, and it was big enough for thirty people. I took a piece home to Boobie. I had wanted to bring her, but my mother had said, "Better not, since we don't know who all will be there."

The boys took turns going out on the front porch and looking at the motorcycle, where Kirby had parked it out of the rain. Stanley said he had lessons to do and stayed home, but I knew that wasn't it. Some of the older boys at school had called him Pretty Boy, and Lloyd had stopped talking to him in the hall, even though Stanley still answered his history questions for him.

I guess it was a pretty good party. Everybody seemed to like Kirby. He invited everyone up to see his coal mine. He had two tunnels into the hill and five men working. Since it was autumn, people were filling their coal cellars for winter. Most were more interested in buying coal wholesale, for less than five dollars a ton, than they were in seeing where it was mined.

Grandfather went back home with my mother and me. The rain was turning to sleet, and it would take every hand to get in the peppers and tomatoes and all the vine crops before they were damaged by the cold. Mr. Isaac was coming out in the morning, and I knew there would be lively conversation in the bean patch.

We had not been asleep long when the phone in the upstairs hall began to ring. Somebody was really twisting the crank on it, for it rang steadily until my mother came out in her old blue flannel nightgown, with her braid hanging down her back.

"Oh, no! Lester, are you sure it's him? . . . Have you called Sebe? Don't, I'll go and tell her. Did they take him to the hospital? No, I suppose not. Thank you, Lester, for calling me . . . No, I can drive myself in."

She turned her face up to Grandfather and me. "It's Lloyd. He's been killed. He drove a motorcycle into the end of the cement bridge."

Grandfather, behind me, was already pulling on his pants.

The rain had stopped by Monday morning, but it was still cold. Because my cousin had died, I didn't go to school, but the rest of the world continued pretty much on schedule.

Lloyd's body was in Runner's Funeral Home. They didn't have to do much work on him, because his face had gotten pretty battered on the end of the bridge and the casket would stay closed. Kirby Conway was paying for the funeral, but Aunt Sebe wasn't speaking to him because he had left the key to that "death-dealing machine" in his jacket pocket when he went upstairs to bed with her.

Worthy and Harry had gone off to school. They didn't know what else to do, since they were being ignored. My mother wanted Stanley to go to school, but he didn't; not because of Lloyd but because of the threat of early snow in the high meadow. We took the tractor with a trailer hooked on the back. The heavier truck might mire down in the mud on the way to get Uncle Billie.

My mother sat on the seat beside Mr. Miller, and she looked messy, which she almost never did. Her neat braids were usually pinned to a high crown; today they were just wrapped around her head and tied with a ribbon, and strands hung loosely down her neck.

When she cried in the night, I heard Grandfather get up and go to her room. I knew she would need to be held and hugged, but I didn't think he hugged anyone. Maybe he would just pat her on the shoulder, that would have to do, and maybe it was all she knew how to receive. The only one I knew who could hold you and hug you and make you feel better was Stanley, and that was his secret.

The Miller boys and Boobie and Stanley and I and one of the Forrester men sat in the trailer. Uncle Billie was ready. He said the birds told him we were coming. His shack was all nailed up, and all his belongings were in an oak box at least six feet long that he had made over the summer. For a storage box, it had a very nice, smooth finish and had been rubbed with an old woolen fleece until it had a soft glow. He and his box were loaded into the trailer, and we began our job. His old black shepherd knew his job better than we did, and was already trotting back and forth behind the flock, yapping and nipping at their heels, guiding them toward the gate in the meadow. My mother drove down behind the sheep, with Mr. Miller riding guard to catch any strays. Boobie and I each had a long switch and were yelling at the top of our voices to keep the dumb sheep from straying into the blackberry briers.

There were two hundred sheep to sell, besides the ewes and the rams who would be the parents of next year's crops. We ran them through a chute as they went into the sheep sheds, and marked the ones to sell with a dab of red paint on their sides. My mother did not know to whom she would sell the sheep, since Grandfather Curtiss had closed his butchering business and the store had been let.

The cabin had been winterized for Uncle Billie, with a surplus of everything and extra kerosene heaters. The fireplace roared, and his wood-box was full. In the past, he had pretty much taken care of himself, but now that my mother had discovered he was over a hundred years old, she felt compelled to look out for him. She also believed in planning ahead, and somehow or another, things worked out.

A market for the sheep did work out. Mr. Isaac had a cousin in Pittsburgh who had a kosher meat-processing plant, and he came with two trucks and bought them all at twenty-three dollars each. It wasn't a bad price. Mr. Isaac said, "What, did you think you're going to get rich, dealing with Jews?"

Uncle Billie didn't seem particularly interested in his share of the money, so I volunteered to keep it for him, but my mother put it in the safe.

OCTOBER 8, 1929

LLOYD'S FUNERAL WAS on Tuesday, and though it was still cold, thin yellow sunshine came through the amber Gothic windows of the church. The church wasn't as full as it had been for Grandmother Fancler, but there were quite a few people, considering it was a weekday. Several of Lloyd's friends stayed out of school. I saw his sweetheart, Sarah Simmons. She was wearing a black dress, which seemed strange on a fourteen-year-old girl. Most everyone was wearing the clothes they reserved for funerals.

Lloyd's casket was up in front, covered with the last roses of summer. The preacher gave his standard "cut down in the springtime of life" sermon. And everyone sang the hymns, and Aunt Sebe paid no attention whatsoever to any of it. She sat with a big Bible in her lap and a notebook and a pencil, leafing through the pages, taking notes of chapter and verse. Only at the end of the service when they sang "Shall We Gather at the River," and Stanley's voice soared full and round among the rafters, did Aunt Sebe look around to see who it was. Stanley didn't seem to know how to sing little and low, so he stopped singing.

Eight of our cousins were pallbearers, and they lowered Lloyd into the grave at the Oddfellows cemetery beside his father, who had been a member of the Oddfellows Lodge. Kirby Conway was there, and a couple of times he tried to take hold of Aunt Sebe's arm, but she pulled away. Grandfather let Mr. Isaac take his elbow as if he had always been doing it. Sylvia Tingler was there, but she stayed behind the only tomb in the cemetery, which looked like a marble doghouse.

Graveside service was over with "Ashes to ashes and dust to dust, dear Lord we commend this boy to Thy eternal mercy," and people threw rose petals down in the grave and began to move toward the gate. Aunt Sebe didn't want to go. She said she just wanted to sit there quietly by herself. My mother reminded her that people had brought food and would be coming back to the house, and all her sisters would be there. But Sebe said, "You all go ahead. I'll walk down in a little while."

It was only down over the hill four or five blocks, and they couldn't drag her, so they left her marking passages in the Bible. Grandfather and Mr. Isaac were riding in our car, and we took Worthy and Harry, and the "family" car from Runner's Funeral Home went back empty. We got in, but before we could drive away, Sylvia Tingler came up to my mother's car window.

"There were a great many before me. I didn't take him away from you, I don't want you to be mad."

My mother touched the hand Sylvia lay on the door frame. "I know you; that's not what I'm so mad about."

Sylvia let a faint little smile color her round moon face as she turned away. In the car, Worthy said, "Kirby wanted my mother and us to go home with him over the weekend. He said to her, 'You know I didn't kill him,' and she said something funny. She said, 'If the dead can rise from their grave, then he isn't dead, and you didn't kill him.'"

Harry added, "Them's her exact words."

And my mother said, "Oh, poor Sebe!," like her sister had gone mad and there was nothing we could do about it.

Jews have the long view, and Mr. Isaac said, "It will look different tomorrow."

Aunt Lilly said she would stay down at Aunt Sebe's house to get dinner for Worthy and Harry, but no one believed her. She had been acting strange lately, staying out late and coming home with no explanation. We dropped Mr. Isaac off at his store, and I went home with Grandfather Fancler. My mother told me to cheer him up, and she went on home.

I went upstairs to see if Uncle Blake was up there sound asleep. Aunt Lilly's black gown was thrown over the foot of the bed, and Uncle Blake smelled like he had skipped his perfumed bath.

I liked to eat with Grandpa. He sliced the salt-rising bread thick and added chunks of ham and cheese until you couldn't get your mouth around it. We washed it down with the new cider. Aunt Lilly had left an applesauce cake, colored blue. It tasted pretty good if you closed your eyes.

Grandfather made a big oak fire in the living room fireplace, and we each got a book. I got one about Egypt, with pictures of King Tut's tomb. I was afraid I would talk about Lloyd's death, but I didn't. I would miss Lloyd, but it didn't make me afraid of dying, I would just stay off motorcycles. I was having trouble keeping my eyes open, so I moved to the couch and was getting a cover when someone rang the doorbell. It was Mr. Isaac.

"I got to thinking about you and thought maybe you would like some company." He was wearing his old green velvet jacket. "If you're not sick of me."

Grandfather said, "No, no, I'm glad for an excuse to go and open a bottle of peach brandy. Hughie doesn't hold his liquor very well."

Mr. Isaac had brought a long brass telescope and a tripod, and he set it up in the doorway going out to the porch. It was the perfect night for looking at stars: there was no moon, and the great black dome of sky was cloudless. I couldn't remember ever seeing the stars so bright.

Mr. Isaac aimed the telescope into the south skies, on a group of sparkling gems he called Pleiades. "Most people call them the Seven Sisters. There's a cluster there of about five hundred, but you can only see the seven with the naked eye." He was adjusting the telescope. "Now look." There was a brilliant scattering around the seven big ones, more than anyone could count. "The Chinese wrote about that star cluster at least four thousand years ago. Astrologists tell us those stars were born in a great explosion fifty million years ago."

Grandfather wanted to get his two cents in on Mr. Isaac's lecture. "That's just about the time the last dinosaur died here on earth."

Mr. Isaac added, "And maybe about the time the first flower opened."

My grandfather laughed for the first time today. "Leon, you constantly amaze me."

"And Peter, you me."

I was swinging the telescope from side to side and looking at the whole sweep of the heavens. Grandfather was afraid of compliments, and he always covered up. "In the Book of Job, there is a famous line from God's speech out of the whirlwind: 'Canst thou bind the sweet influence of the Pleiades, or loose the bands of Orion?' The Pleiades are hundreds of light-years away and may already have burned themselves out before that light reached us."

That was beyond my boyish concept. "Grandpa, you can't really see heaven with this telescope, can you?"

Mr. Isaac looked at him and must have wondered how near to the truth he would dare. He went the whole way. "You can't see heaven there, because it is not there. Heaven is an idea in your brain; each of us has to give it shape for ourselves. Some people have made a pretty strange business out of it. The more primitive the people, the stranger it gets."

I was getting cold, so I went back under my blanket on the couch. Mr. Isaac brought his telescope back in.

"Peter, I hope this won't embarrass you, but I think heaven is finding a friend."

"Well, certainly, being lonely is about as bad as I expect hell to be."

"Do you know this is our anniversary? We met three months ago today."

"You're keeping track of the time?"

"It's been twenty years since I've had someone to talk to, do you blame me? I'll have a glass of your brandy now, and a slice of your cake, because I'm also celebrating my birthday."

"Happy birthday, friend. Why didn't you tell me?"

"I was afraid you would give me another book."

"What do you want?"

"I would just like you to put your arms around me and hug me. It's been such a long time."

"You know I'm Scotch, and we're not good at that."

"Well, I'm Russian and we are, we learned it from the bears. Just stand still and I'll hug you."

I peeked out from under the blanket and watched them. Grandfather's face seemed to glow in the firelight. Mr. Isaac went up and put his arms around him and held him close. At first Grandfather didn't move, and then he slowly brought his arms up and clasped Mr. Isaac against him. The last thing I remember was Grandfather looking over Mr. Isaac's shoulder, his cheek against Mr. Isaac's cheek, but I may have been dreaming by then.

OCTOBER 9, 1929

WE WERE ALL AWAKENED EARLY. It wasn't more than six o'clock, it was still dark outside. Aunt Lilly had called my mother from Aunt Sebe's to come at once, as Aunt Sebe was getting ready to do some crazy thing, and everyone had to gather 'round and stop her. Within an hour, my mother pulled into the lane at the bottom of the hill, where Grandfather and I were waiting. I had been allowed to go because there was no one left at home for me to stay with.

When we got there, the house looked dark and deserted. The window blinds were pulled down, and Aunt Lilly was back in the kitchen making a new pot of coffee. Just as we came in the front, someone was trying the kitchen door. Aunt Lilly peeked around the blind. Aunt Sebe was yelling, "Open the door!"

Aunt Lilly's voice had an edge to it close to panic. "Are you by yourself?" She slid the latch and let Aunt Sebe in.

"Are you afraid he would be with me?"

Aunt Lilly said, "I don't know. I've been up all night, and I've drunk twenty cups of coffee, and I'm getting as crazy as you are. Dad's here, and I'm going home." She grabbed her coat from the back of a chair and hurried to the front door.

Grandfather guided Aunt Sebe to a chair at the kitchen table and sat down opposite her. My mother found cups and gave everyone coffee. Aunt Sebe grasped her father's hand and squeezed it tight. Her eyes were wide and red, and the pins had come out of her hair, letting it fall down over her face. "Oh, Dad, I tried. But it's just not enough. I can't do it alone, I've got to have help. I yelled until I thought my lungs would burst. I yelled, 'In the name of God, come home.' But I couldn't speak for God, I was a lone voice. I've heard you preach a hundred times: 'Where two or three are gathered in His name, there also am I.' That was the trouble; I was just one."

Grandfather pulled away from her hand. "It's just a ploy to get people to come to church. Sebe, this is a damn fool idea you have. Drink your coffee and stop this."

"Why is it such a damn fool idea for a mother who loved her son to want him back home?"

"He is dead and buried over there in the cemetery. He sleeps under six feet of dirt."

"That's it. He sleeps. I'm going to wake him, but I need your help, all of you."

My mother stirred sugar into Aunt Sebe's cup. "Here, drink your coffee. You are just going to have to accept Lloyd's death, or you'll end up over in Weston."

"One person alone does not have the Lord with them. But when the three of us gather in His name, the kids, too—Hughie, go up and wake Harry and Worthy—all together, we will speak with the voice of angels."

Grandfather was now annoyed. "Sebe, the neighbors are going to call the police."

"Daddy, I failed because I was alone. I had a dream. I went up to the fence in my dream. I knew I couldn't go over the fence, and I didn't. I called him from there, and he came, all smiles. You know what a pretty smile Lloyd has."

Grandfather was losing patience. "Daughter, it does not work like that."

"Just because it hasn't doesn't mean it can't. It did in the past; Jesus rose on the third day."

"If He did, it was because He was the son of God. But he didn't; that's a fantasy, a tale told to hold people to a faith."

"Oh ye of little faith. I dreamed I was combing his hair, combing bloody meat out of his hair. That means there is no time to lose, we have to get Lloyd home quickly." She started for the door.

My mother grabbed her by the arm. "You're not going back up there?"

Just then there was the sound of a motorcycle pulling up to the back porch, and everyone in the room froze in place. The motor died, and Aunt Sebe's voice sounded like a prayer. "Oh, dear Jesus, forgive me . . . I should have known you wouldn't fail me. That motorcycle took him away, and the motorcycle has brought him back home. Quick, Billy, look out the window."

My mother started to raise the blind in spite of herself, then stopped. "I can't."

Grandfather was furious. "Enough of this nonsense," he said, and he flung the door wide open.

Kirby Conway was standing there. "Sebe, have you gone clean off your rocker? Lilly called me."

"How dare you bring that thing that killed my boy back to this house?"

"It was the quickest way to get here. I'm going to sell it now."

Kirby tried to put his arms around Aunt Sebe, but she shrugged him off. "You killed him with that thing."

"He killed himself because he was fifteen and full of piss and vinegar. I forgot what that was like. Do you think I would kill a boy who I hoped would become my son?"

Aunt Sebe looked down at his shoes. They were splashed with red. She backed away from him and pressed herself against the wall. "There's blood on your shoes."

"Sebe." He grabbed her by the shoulders and shook her. "It's paint, paint, Sebe. I was changing the sign on my shop and my mines so it said 'And Sons' — it was a surprise for after our wedding."

The noise had awakened Worthy and Harry, and they peered sleepy-eyed from the dining room doorway. They looked like they had slept in their clothes.

"All right, if you want him as your son, come and help me call him up from the grave."

Kirby looked from my grandfather to my mother for an explanation. My mother gave it. "Sebe believes that we as a group can call Lloyd up from the dead."

Sebe gathered up her Bible and her notes with trembling hands. "All of you doubters, sit down here at the table and just listen." Everyone did, because it seemed to calm her. She read: "Here it is in Corinthians. Christ preached that He could rise from the dead. 'How say some among you that there is no resurrection of the dead? But if there be no resurrection of the dead, then is Christ not risen.' You do believe Christ is risen, don't you, Kirby?" I noticed she did not ask my grandfather or my mother.

"If Christ is not risen, then faith is vain and preaching is vain, do you hear that, Father? Verse sixteen." She found where she had marked it. " 'If the dead rise not, Christ is not risen and ye are in sin. Since by man came death' — he means the sins of Adam — 'by man also comes the resurrection of the dead.' " Aunt Sebe closed the Bible with a bang and looked from one to the other. We stared at her blankly. She went on, "A door has closed; we have to open it with faith."

My mother tried. "Sebe, you have two other sons. What would I do if I lost Hughie?"

"What would you do?"

"I think a door to loneliness would appear, and that's the door to hell."

"You would have to open it. I would help you, just as you must help me."

Grandfather tried again. "All you could possibly call up would be a ghost, and there is no chance of that. And who would want a ghost? A live, breathing, joking Lloyd was our laughter. I may not laugh quite that much again."

Kirby got up and got himself a cup of coffee. "This is crazy."

Sebe grabbed on to that. "All right, what if I am crazy? What's the best thing to do with crazies? Humor them. Come with me up to the fence and help me holler his name just a few times, and if he doesn't come home with us, I'll never say his name again."

They all looked at one another, and you could see in their faces, they had agreed to it. It was the easy way out. Kirby objected. "The people around there are going to call the sheriff, and he will put us in jail for disturbing the peace."

My mother said, "I don't think so."

And my grandfather added (whether he meant it or no), "We will be gathered in His name, and He will be with us, and who will put the Lord God in jail?"

I guess a lifetime of preaching got the better of him. And so we all walked up to the fence that went around the Oddfellows cemetery.

You could see Lloyd's grave from there. It was covered with wilted flowers. And we all yelled, "Lloyd, in the name of God, come home!"

We yelled five times, and Grandfather said, "That's enough."

Aunt Sebe agreed in a dry, hollow voice, "Yes, I guess that's enough."

We waited a little while in silence, and Harry said, "I'm cold." All of us had our eyes on that grave and, in our hearts, a mumbling fear that the scheme of things had been altered and his grave would open and Lloyd would climb out; but he didn't. I didn't really believe Lloyd could get up out of the grave and come home, even though I wanted him to, almost as bad as Aunt Sebe.

Lloyd was my best cousin. How could I learn to deal with girls without him? I had given up believing in God, but I resurrected Him just for the moment so I could go around back of the house and cry, "God, you're a stupid son of a bitch, why did you have to take Lloyd?"

OCTOBER 10, 1929

ON THURSDAY MORNING Boobie was washing peanut butter off the wood panels in the hall. She had let Handsome out of her sight, and he had smeared the wall all the way to the end. She wasn't smiling. "When I grown up, I'm not going to clean up other people's dirt. I'm going to be a schoolteacher."

It would appear that I would never grow up to be a gentleman, for I said, "No, you won't. You can't be a teacher, you're a nigger!"

She looked up slowly and held my eye. Her hand was on the rim of the bucket, and I thought she was going to throw the soapy water on me. She didn't get a chance. I was yanked up by the back of my collar and propelled into the back parlor, and the door slammed behind us. I could hear my mother breathing through her teeth. The drapes were pulled, but there was enough light to see that her eyes were blazing as she slapped me across the mouth over and over, until my face was numb.

"Hughie, how could you? Could I be so wrong? Is this the kind of person

I'm raising? Don't you realize how little hope that poor child stands for a decent life? She will have to work so hard and be so determined to have any kind of life at all, and you want to help destroy what little hope she has?"

With each explosive line, she slapped me until I cried, "Enough! Stop! All right, I was a dumb shit. I'll go and tell her if you don't knock my mouth clear off my face."

She stopped and looked at her hand as though surprised at what it had done. She sank into an old green velvet chair. "Maybe I'm wrong; maybe you have the right to grow up to be a cruel dumb shit, but I don't think so. I think that's the reason I'm here, to teach you a standard of decency that you can carry on." She got up and put her arms around me and squeezed me too tight. "You know, Hughie, if you grow up to be a cruel, unfeeling man, it will be my obligation to shoot you in the head."

When I went down to apologize, Boobie was scrubbing like a machine. She was already halfway down the hall.

"It don't matter. Nothing you say is gonna make any difference."

OCTOBER 11, 1929

AUNT OPAL HAD BEEN making an effort to establish some kind of an income for herself. Since Grandfather deeded her the theater, she had tried unsuccessfully to become an impresario of sorts. After Sir Harry Lauder, she had run some ads for Galli-Curci but hadn't received one order for an advance ticket. She would not believe, just because we lived in the hills of West Virginia, that we had no culture whatsoever, but it seemed to be true.

She booked a minstrel show that turned out to be white people in exaggerated blackface. White people came and said, "Ain't niggers funny?" Aunt Opal did not think so, and even though she made two hundred dollars, she never did it again. The only good result was that when the minstrels left, they took the two high-kicking girls from the Bluebird Market with them.

She had rented it on Sunday to a group of religious revivalists from Tennessee, and when she came in on Monday to show the hall to a square-dance group for a Saturday rental, a large diamondback rattlesnake, used in the preacher's test of faith, came slithering toward them. That was the end of cult religions. Now, with the Fall Festival approaching, the folk-dance group would rent the hall every night for two weeks at fifty dollars a night, after a careful search for more snakes.

It didn't satisfy Aunt Opal; she wanted an ongoing business. She suggested to her father that they turn their house into an inn during the Fall Festival, as there was always a shortage of rooms. Several thousand people converged on the town, and if her mother added Uncle Alvin's house, which had now become "her" house, they could rent a total of thirty rooms. Between them, they had five in help who were doing very little.

Grandmother said, "Absolutely not. I don't want a bunch of dirty farmers on my linen sheets. It's an interesting idea, if one could be selective." She had become quite snobbish since she now had the setting and the money to play rich bitch. She had given several small dinner parties to which none of her family were invited, except my mother to one. Grandmother had instructed her to wear a long black dress and white gloves and loaned her a strand of opera-length pearls from her safe. When I asked my mother why she didn't take me, and if she would go again, she said, "It was charming and dull, and I don't have time for that sort of thing."

Still, she played the game by the book and sent a bunch of white roses with her thank-you note. I could tell she wanted to keep the pearls; she wore them to breakfast, but she took them back.

Aunt Opal decided to start a bakery. After all, she had her newly painted delivery truck and three women in the kitchen who were very good pie makers. She canvassed the restaurants and the two hotels, and they all agreed to try some free samples. She started baking various kinds of pies, figuring out the cost of the ingredients, seeing which would be profitable. Of course, apple was the obvious choice, since they lived in front of an orchard.

Grandfather was the official taster. He ate all day between naps, and he hadn't had his shoes on all week. He said he wanted nothing to go to waste, and Aunt Opal said, "That's exactly where everything is going, to your waist."

Grandmother was indignant about the pie business, but she didn't really care, as she seldom came over to the Worth Street house. When she did, she was like an aloof visitor. She and Grandfather were still not speaking, each waiting for the other to go first. Occasionally she came to borrow the maids and Matthew; she felt free to do so, since she was paying their salaries. She went to the White Sulphur Springs Hotel for a day or two almost every week, she said to study the operation, but we all suspected it was to meet the people who occasionally came for the weekend.

The only one who met them was Grandfather Fancler. She would draft him as host at the end of her table, and he found he liked playing social games. He even bought a dinner suit. When there were dinners with a predominance of women, which there were often (mainly rich widows who could afford to lull their days away at resort hotels), he suggested Mr. Isaac.

"But he's a Jew."

"He's a very erudite gentleman, and he does not wear his Star of David or his yarmulke."

Grandfather brought him, and Mr. Isaac was a professional charmer. He could talk knowledgeably about the many artifacts in the house. As a gift, he brought Grandmother a bookmark that had belonged to Thomas Jefferson, who had sketched on it a Palladian window and a doorway and scribbled some instructions for building.

"Mr. Isaac, this is charming. It is, I am sure, quite valuable. I can't take it."

"If you had said it was valuable first and then charming, I would have taken it back, but I insist."

Alex drove them home at midnight, and they sat in the back of the limousine and laughed at their social success like two college boys. "Peter, I do believe you and I could be gigolos!"

At the beginning of October there were always three days of heavy frost to color the leaves for the Forest Festival the following week. The cold sweetened the wild grapes and withered the pumpkin vines that seemed to melt from the field of pumpkins. They lay exposed like giant golden plants in a dark sea.

Every year at the festival, there was an award for the largest pumpkin, and my mother had tried again this year, but already the rumor had gone down the road that Tuck Marsteller had a pumpkin that weighed around eight hundred pounds. He had won last year and every year for four years. It was a well-kept secret how he did it. It wasn't the seeds, because at the end of the three-day festival, the winning pumpkin was cut open, the meat sent to the orphanage, and the seeds sold for a dollar each. There are always at least two hundred seeds in a big pumpkin, and that's the real prize, not that silly ribbon and your picture in the paper.

Last year my mother had bought five seeds from Tuck. Four of them sprouted in the middle of the patch. They were twelve feet apart and had a fence around them. The talk was that Tuck poured milk around his plants, though someone else thought it was buttermilk. My mother tried buttermilk around two, chicken manure and lime in water around another, and tobacco leaves around all of them to keep the insects away.

The pumpkin has both male and female blossoms, and the female has to be fertilized with the stamen early in the morning, when the female first opens — before some errant bee brings the wrong pollen — and then the blossom is closed up with a rubber band. When they bloomed, they were thinned to a couple of blossoms on each vine. Nothing went to waste, the fat pumpkin blooms were dipped in beaten egg and fried for lunch; with some celery salt and a little tomato sauce, they weren't bad. The male pumpkin blooms the day before the female. If she bloomed first, she might get fertilized by a squash, which is in the same family, and reduce the prospects of her size by half. Nature is very organized; when she brings the female along, the male is ready and waiting.

When the pumpkins were the size of oranges, we left only one to a vine. That year our biggest pumpkin measured only twelve feet around and probably didn't weigh over five hundred pounds. We all climbed up on it one at a time and got our picture made, but it was not a winner. There had not been as much hot weather this autumn, and my mother suspected Tuck had somehow kept his pumpkin warmer, as they could gain fifteen pounds a day in warm weather.

Lester had spent Saturday night in my mother's room, for I heard them quarreling on Sunday morning. I had set the alarm to get out to the mailbox and get the Washington *Herald*'s funny papers first, so Stanley could hold me on his lap in the rocking chair and read them to me. But I couldn't go down because my mother was sitting on the top step in her nightgown, braiding her hair, and Lester was about halfway down tying his shoes. It was one of those kinds of arguments where you could keep your voice down but your tone was still sharp.

"Why should I get a divorce. You give me one reason."

"I thought you just might want to get married again."

"What, to some man I see once every two weeks? I don't want that kind of marriage."

"Well, you're not exactly sittin' around waiting for me."

"I have a life. I thought you didn't like passive women."

"Did I say that?"

"You said you liked aggression."

"You know what I meant. I meant I'd like it if you made a pass at me once in a while."

She stood up, and her braid hung down to her knees. Her voice raised in spite of herself. "You want me to grab you by the crotch and drag you into bed?"

There was a smile in his voice. "That would be nice." He buttoned his top button and turned to go.

"Wait, I'll make you some coffee."

"Can't. We're raiding Virgil Johnson's still this morning."

She came to the doorway. "Take care."

He came back and held her tightly in his arms and kissed her, breathing hard, lifting her off the floor. "Remember me!"

She sat on the porch step and watched him drive away. I went past her to get the paper, and she didn't even say good morning.

OCTOBER 12, 1929

TUESDAY WAS HANDSOME'S first birthday, but we were going to have his birthday party on Monday night so his sisters who worked in town could be there. He was big for his age and already had a lot of teeth. He could walk now, and Tuba said he could dance, but I never saw him do it. He was a spoiled brat; he didn't even have the sense to know his own mother. He would smile and show his new white teeth and hold up his arms, and Rose would take him and dance him around in a circle and swing him to Erica and on to Helga, and even Miss Larkin would hold him if she was sitting down. Tuba, who rocked him, said he was the grandchild she never had. I would have been the grandchild she never had, in spite of the difference in color, if she had rocked me.

My mother bought him a kiddie car and a little red wagon to hook on the back. He got drums, and a big stuffed rabbit you could sit on, and a stick horse Uncle Billie had carved with a mane made out of sheep's wool, and all kinds of things; not more than I used to get, but a lot of things for a black boy. After the cake and ice cream, Rose gave him a gingerbread boy before even I got one, and he promptly bit its head off, and everybody laughed. Even the Thorne twins held out their hands before I did and got one to eat and two to take home. I had been an only child for seven years, and it was hard to give that up.

Miss Larkin didn't want Boobie to feel left out, so she announced that starting tomorrow, the child would be doing second-grade work and would get an A for first grade. She took a gold star and licked the back of it and stuck it in the middle of Boobie's forehead. One of the Dutch ladies had made Boobie a bright red dress with a full white petticoat, and the other two had each knitted a bright blue sweater for the Thorne twins. I didn't get anything. On the way up the stairs, my mother said it was because I already had everything I needed. Need and want were whole different things, and I was beginning to make my list for Christmas.

October 13, 1929

The week before the festival was mostly rehearsal for the parade and pageant that would be performed before the queen of the festival. Kids who rode the bus and couldn't practice after school weren't in anything, so I didn't bother going to school the week before, which let me be home for Uncle Billie's funeral.

We would not have known he died until late in the afternoon—someone always took him his supper—except for his old sheepdog. He was howling at our back door before daylight, and Mr. Miller took a flashlight and followed him out to the cabin. By the time he got back to the house for my mother, it was just breaking light. The Miller boys and I went with her in rubber galoshes, for the grass was wet.

The box that Uncle Billie had used to pack his things from the cabin held his body, with a candle burning at each end. He was stretched out in it with his hands folded over his chest. He looked dead, but my mother had to make sure. She held a light over his eyes and felt his pulse and announced, "He's gone."

It was obvious that Uncle Billie's box had been intended as his casket all along. It was lined with red Christmas paper, and the lid was fitted with screws to fasten it on. The box was in the middle of the floor, and his dog kept walking around it and looking in and whining as though he wanted to jump in, too.

Mr. Miller asked, "What religion was he?"

"I have no idea. Certainly nothing we would recognize."

"I'll dig a grave up on the hill, if you don't mind. I don't feel like putting him down here with all that trash."

"We will have to say something—do something. We can't just stick him in the ground. He was a dear old man."

Mr. Milller put the lid on, and the dog jumped up on it and lay down. Mr. Miller and my mother stood there and stared down at him.

"Let us have breakfast, and we will think about it," my mother said.

Halfway through breakfast, my mother must have thought about it, for she was out the door, in her car, and on the way to town, leaving me halfway through my bowl of cornmeal mush with prunes.

Mr. Miller dug a grave up on the hillside under the aspen trees whose leaves quivered with the slightest breeze. The whole tree seemed in constant motion; just now they were golden yellow. All the adults came and helped carry his casket up the hill. It didn't really weigh very much, for he was a fragile little old man with hollow bones.

We were all sitting up there on the dry yellow grass when my mother returned with a surprise: Mr. Chang and the gold-dust twins.

Mr. Chang wore a long red gown, and the gold-dust twins had on their purple stockings and sequined dresses from the carnival. He was carrying a gong the size of a dinner plate and a wooden hammer to hit it with. Each of the girls had a blue and white bowl, one filled with rice and the other with what seemed to be apricots. They also had some long strips of paper that the two girls set on fire and let drift down into the grave as Mr. Chang pounded on his gong. All three of them chanted with an ear-splitting cadence, and the poor dog howled. I looked at Stanley's face; he was listening intently and trying to copy the sounds. He couldn't seem to let any new sound escape him.

Then the three Orientals sat down cross-legged and silent a little way from the grave, waiting for the grave to be filled in so they could complete the ceremony. Only the dog was crying; everybody else knew "there comes a time."

Mr. Miller was wearing the black coat from the front hall. He reached in the pocket and handed the pistol to my mother. "I thought you would want this."

"You do read my mind."

She held the gun down close to the dog's head and fired, and old Shep went with Uncle Billie wherever he had gone.

Mr. Chang beat on the gong as we all filled in the grave, and then the gold-dust twins embedded the two bowls in the fresh mound. My mother gave them each twenty dollars and took them home.

I announced at dinner that Uncle Billie had designated me his rightful heir. My mother asked, "What will you do if some nice old Chinese lady comes down the road and says, 'Hello, I'm Mrs. Uncle Billie'?"

"I know what you will do, you'll run out and say, 'Come on in. Live with us. We have lots of room.' "

"I'll tell you what I'll do. I'll lock the door."

Miss Larkin had determined that the Thorne twins had something she called manual dexterity. Mrs. Miller wove willow baskets with the long supple branches that Mr. Miller cut from the trees growing down by the river. One day the twins saw her at it and picked up some of the scraps, and while they were eating their lunch, each of them wove a little basket.

Mrs. Miller could not believe her eyes, and the twins sat there and grinned like Halloween pumpkins. She gave them some long strands with the bark peeled off, and showed them how to begin larger, more difficult baskets. They took the willows back to the classroom and wove while Miss Larkin practiced the sounds of the alphabet. She discovered that when their hands were busy, their minds seemed to work better. During the afternoon, they each wove a basket big enough to gather eggs, and they could say all twenty-six letters of the alphabet. Their fingers were so sure, they seemed not to even look down.

The next day at noon, they were more interested in starting another basket than they were in eating. This was an improvement, for it seemed that up to now, their main interest in life was gluttony. I had loaned them my red wagon. The truth was, I was outgrowing it, but I didn't want to just give it to them. Every afternoon when they went home, they took something: milk, buttermilk, butter, bags of potatoes, tomatoes, and onions. It was usually more than they could carry, so they needed the wagon. I had warned them they were too fat to ride in it, but they didn't listen. They both got in to ride down the hill that led to their house, and they bent the axle. They were afraid to come back the next morning, so their brother John came with them.

Half the kids who rode our bus got the mumps and stayed home. Since the bus made fewer stops, it was early, and Stanley and I missed it. My mother was getting ready to drive us in to town when John came carrying my wagon. My mother was glad to see him, since he was overdue to get the cast off his broken arm. John had watched his house from the hill above for a week after his father was gone, to be sure it was safe to come down. By then his arm had started to knit, and when my mother took him in to see Dr. Owens, his arm had to be rebroken. John and his brother were nice boys, shy, and as thin as Richie and Lou were fat.

My mother thought while we were at the doctor's office, Stanley and I should get educated about the mumps. The doctor explained how dangerous they were, how they leave a boy sterile, and then my mother saw the look on Stanley's face and reached over and patted his hand. I was riding in the backseat with John, but I heard her whisper, "I'm sorry."

The whole thing in Dr. Owens's office took only about five minutes. We drove to the high school and let Stanley out. John hadn't said five words the whole time. Now he stared in awe at the new brick high school, half a block long.

"I ain't never even seen the outside of a school before. I guess that makes me pretty dumb."

My mother looked around. "No, it doesn't. You just haven't had a chance."

I thought, Oh, dear Jesus, she's going to give him a chance!

When we got to my school, I pointed out to John that I was already in the third grade, with all A's, and I wouldn't be eight until March. I had to lord it over somebody. Boobie was already learning carols to sing at Christmas in English, French, and German. I was planning to put lumps of coal and chicken feet in her Christmas stocking to even the score.

The two Forrester men had moved into the old log cabin where Uncle Billie had died. My mother was glad. She said it left us a manned outpost in the lower meadows. I thought if those two were part of our army, we were going to lose the war. My mother sent me down there with the Sears & Roebuck catalogue for them to pick out winter coats and boots, and I discovered they could not read or even write their own names. They had a kind of blank look on their faces, and they laughed a lot.

One thing I noticed: smart people didn't seem to find as much to laugh about.

OCTOBER 14, 1929

WE NOW HAD FOUR horses that my mother thought were trained well enough to sell. She ran ads in some rich-people magazines. Usually she waited until spring, but this year, with the bottom falling out of the economy, she was afraid no one would have any money by then. So far she had only two inquiries, and she mailed them the brochure she'd had printed.

There was a bank robber in Pittsburgh who robbed five banks in five days and, when caught, said he had speeded up his schedule, as he feared the banks would fail. Mr. Miller wondered why he hadn't quit with four banks, as he had stolen $110,000 by then, and that was all anyone would need. My mother was asking $25,000 for each of the horses, figuring that would carry her through for a while, but no one knew what bad times were coming.

When Grandmother Curtiss called to invite us to lunch on Sunday, my mother was not sure, at first, if it was her. She had changed her tone and said, "Billy, my dear! Please lunch with me on Sunday." She had always called my mother Pearl before. Now she was "Billy, my dear."

When we pulled in the iron gates, there was a new brass plaque that said:

ORCHARD HOUSE
1908

I forgot each time what a massive pile of gray rock the house was. We went around to the front door and rang the bell. Even though this was now Grandmother's house, it was not the kind of place where you just opened the door and ran in.

Alex opened the door and said, "Good day, Mrs. Curtiss and Master Hughie." I didn't know when I had become Master Hughie, but I liked it. Alex had a new black uniform. The black marble floor in the entry was polished to a mirror shine, until it reflected the round gold-leaf table in the middle and its enormous arrangement of lilies. The flowers looked like they had come from a greenhouse, which we never used except in winter. Grandmother came smiling toward us, and I hardly recognized her. Her face was a white mask with black upswept brows, and her hair was blue-black with the sides lacquered into raven's wings. She wore what my mother called a housecoat at home, but when it got this fancy, it became a hostess gown. It was brown lace with matching jewelry. Grandmother seemed to have matching jewelry for everything these days.

She kissed my mother lightly on the cheek and said, "Billy, my dear, I have a strand of pink tourmaline that will be perfect with that suit." I obviously wasn't welcome, for she patted my cheek with "Hughie, I didn't really expect you. This is just going to be girl talk, why don't you run through the orchard and have lunch with your grandpa?"

I looked up into her face. Her lips looked like those wax kind you can chew later. "What's the matter with you, Grandma?"

Grandmother bent down close to my ear. "I have a very important guest who is going to teach me how to be a *genuine* snob. It's something I always wanted to be but could never afford until now."

My mother was pushing me toward the kitchen. "It's a good idea, Hughie. I'll tell you everything that happens here, and you can tell me everything that happens over at Grandfather's; that way we will cover everything."

Before I could pass the bottom of the stairs, Grandmother's guest teacher was coming down. I hung back and Grandmother had to introduce me.

"Mrs. Maugham, I would like you to meet my grandson, Hughie, and my daughter-in-law, Billy. Syrie Maugham."

There was something about her, like she and Grandmother had bought their faces at the same place, except her hair was brown. I put out my hand as I had been taught, but my mother was pushing me out of the way.

"You're not Somerset Maugham's wife?"

"Well, not anymore, and I would like to be known for something else now."

Grandmother said, "Mrs. Maugham is one of the most renowned interior decorators in the world."

My mother meant to apologize but didn't help much. She said, "I was just reading his *The Constant Wife* last night, and I still had it in my mind."

"He wasn't writing about me. If he had been as good a husband as he was a writer, I wouldn't have been reading *The Well of Loneliness* last night."

I could see the subject needed changing, so I said, "What color are you going to paint Grandmother's house?"

They all smiled. "And what color would you suggest?"

"I like red."

"Well, at least you have an opinion. Most of the men I deal with seem to recognize no color but brown, except for the Duke of Windsor, and he only likes blue."

I could tell by my grandmother's face what she liked about this woman: she could talk about dukes. I was going through the kitchen when I heard my mother ask, "You're not really going to do this house over, are you?"

Grandmother scolded, "Billy, you're as bad as Hughie."

Mrs. Maugham said, "Oh, dear no, except that bedroom Virginia is sleeping in. It's a morgue, but everything else is a monument to William Morris."

The kitchen was a surprise. There was a new cook in there, a dark little man who wore a big white hat to make him taller, but it didn't fool anyone. Mrs. Kessner was grating cheese, and I knew by the way she was looking at the new cook that he was going to make her wash the pan he was cooking lamb chops in. I was glad I wasn't eating with them. All those limp little lambs at home, who had to be bottle-fed when their mothers disowned them, had turned me against eating it. Also this cook obviously didn't like boys.

You didn't have to knock at Grandfather Curtiss's house. I went through the orchard and in the French doors to the dining room. Aunt Opal was setting the table, and she held her finger to her mouth to signal that Aunt Almeda was on the phone. She went to get a plate for me, and I stood in the door to the hall and listened.

"Is that you, Helen? . . . Yes, I can hear very well. How nice to hear from you . . . You tracked Vera down? Is she happy in her new job? . . . Yes, I miss you, too, and I miss Washington. Vera told you, I suppose, I was locked out of the house? . . . I haven't heard what's in the will yet. I have to hope so, it's the only thing I have left to hold on to . . . You're all out? . . . Well, you shouldn't give it away. Of course I will, but Vera knows how to grind the kohl and mix it in the mineral oil . . . Oh, that rouge is my secret formula. I'll make you some and send it to you . . . Me in the cosmetic business? Do you think any business would succeed now that everyone seems to be broke? I guess I'm judging it by the people here, but of course . . . I know. No, I haven't become bitter; well, yes I have, a little. I like to call it realistic . . . Thank you. You are a dear . . . Good-bye."

"You miss it, don't you?" Opal asked Almeda.

"I'd lie if I said no. It's a wonderful town. There are so many levels of activity, currents flowing in every direction."

"Not everything just flowing down the drain the way it is here. Was that *the* Mrs. Mitchell?"

"Her husband is the attorney general."

"You have friends like that?"

"I wasn't sure I had any friends at all. I was afraid without the senator, I would move into purdah."

"What was this about makeup?" I asked, then said, "Hello, Aunt Almeda."

Aunt Almeda saw me in the doorway. "Hughie—how nice! Come and give your old aunt a hug."

I was almost as tall as she was, and she felt good and she smelled good, but up close her face was thick with paint.

"Do all the women in Washington paint their faces?"

"Yes, but they don't wear as much as I do. I don't know why I feel such a compulsion to layer it on." She laughed a laugh with no fun in it. "I'm getting eccentric in my old age."

Grandfather was eating in the kitchen, where no one would restrict him, and we three sat at the dining room table. Aunt Opal made tuna-salad sandwiches at the table to go with steaming bowls of tomato soup. She said, "If you get out of this town, you won't get old, and neither will I. I have a hundred and eleven dollars saved. Let's you and me sneak out of here tonight and take the train to Washington."

"Oh, wouldn't I like to. But we couldn't make it long on one hundred and eleven dollars."

I was thinking I would go home and get the money out of my boot and join them, but Aunt Almeda wasn't ready to go yet.

"As soon as the will is probated, I'll have money. Are you sure you want to go to Washington?"

I answered "yes" with Aunt Opal, but she had a better reason to go than I did.

"If I stay here, God knows what I'll become."

"If you go, you might turn into another me."

"At least you know what's going on in the world."

Aunt Almeda washed her sandwich down with iced tea. "Oh yes, I was the woman in the catbird seat."

"I could sew for a living."

"You certainly could. This dress you made me"—it was a lavender wool—"is as well made as anything I've ever owned."

They went on with girl talk and forgot me, so I went into the kitchen for another bowl of tomato soup and to say hello to Grandfather Curtiss. He had already eaten so much that the kitchen maids were giggling as they refilled his plate with rare roast beef. He offered me some, but I took my soup and went, though not before I offered to go get his shoes and lace them for free. He said he wasn't going anywhere.

Aunt Almeda was talking about her house in Washington as though she might not ever see it again. She told about keeping every dress she ever owned packed away on the third floor of her house, maybe five hundred ball gowns over forty years. "I could start a museum."

"Or a rental business. Ball gowns don't really go out of style, and I could alter them."

Aunt Almeda reflected Opal's enthusiasm. "And I could go into the cosmetic business."

Now Aunt Opal was rolling. "I could bleach my hair and say I'm eighteen and find a rich man. I'll say you're my mother and have to live with us."

Aunt Almeda was brought up short. "You mean live the life I lived?"

"Do you want me to live the life possible here? I want to go to Europe every year and have five hundred ball gowns."

Aunt Almeda put down her glass and sat back in her chair. "Oh yes, my trips to Europe that coincided with his wife's visits to Washington."

And then she told us why she saved all her old clothes: because at any time, he might find someone younger and more attractive, and she would have to make do for the rest of her life. Now it was even worse than that, since she couldn't even get in the house to get them. Aunt Opal was really disappointed. Now she thought she would never get out of this town. Aunt Almeda wanted Opal to wait until some man came along who would put a ring on her finger. Aunt Opal wanted a ring on every finger. But Aunt Almeda said to get that, you also had to have a ring through your nose. I didn't get that explained, because there was a big old car coming up the drive.

It was Judge Brown again. Aunt Opal and Aunt Almeda went to hide in the parlor and told me to get Grandfather to open the door. Grandfather still had his napkin tucked in his collar and didn't bother to remove it. He settled into a big chair in the hall and told me to open the door.

The judge didn't wait to be asked before he came storming through. He looked like he was dressed for business, with his derby hat and a briefcase. In a mocking voice, Grandfather said, "Won't you come in?" and made no effort to rise.

The shutters were closed in the hall, and the judge blinked through his thick glasses to see. "I want to talk to you, Huston, then I want to see that aunt of yours."

Grandfather stared at him with his eyes half closed and said nothing. I didn't know if he had given up the race entirely or if this was another way of winning. The judge knew from his years on the bench that the man seated can dominate, so he found a chair and pulled it up before Grandfather and settled his considerable girth into it.

"I don't mind telling you, Huston, that I'm worried about Friday. The dedication of that memorial is the most important thing this town has known in a good many years."

"Important to who?"

"To the whole town. The monument will be the centerpiece of our lives."

Grandfather stared at him blankly. The judge began to sputter, "We can sell postcards of it to every tourist who comes through here."

"If the market keeps dropping, there won't be any more tourists."

The judge got up and paced. "All right, you are not going to make this easy, are you?"

"No."

"Here it is! I will not have that woman showing up at the unveiling, embarrassing everyone. When that flag comes off, every eye in the state will be on the heroic horse and rider."

"And you don't think this is important to my aunt? She loved the man."

Now the judge's face got red. I would have gone to get him a glass of water, but I didn't want to miss anything.

" 'Love' ? You dirty the word. That kind of love has to be swept under the carpet and kept there. We are not going to have the whole town embarrassed by that woman's presence."

"My aunt is an adult who knows her own mind."

Now the judge got Machiavellian. He pulled his chair up to Grandfather's face. "I'm beginning to wonder just how sound that mind is." He reached out and took Grandfather's hand, "I want you to give me your pledge, as a thirty-second-degree Mason and a member of the Fraternal Order of Elks, that she will not be in that audience."

Grandfather jerked his hand back. "I can't lock her up!"

The judge stood now, and the effort made him huff. "Well, I can. Standing around behind trees in the park like some old cat. She ought to be committed! I can sign the order that will send her to Weston."

Grandfather stood with such an effort that his chair fell backward. "My aunt is not crazy."

"Are you a doctor? I don't believe you can make that judgment."

"And you can?"

"I am a judge elected by the good people of this county."

Grandfather's voice was getting louder, and his face was getting redder, and the judge backed away as Grandfather moved toward him. "The whole world is not your courtroom! My aunt does not stand in judgment."

The judge was trying to be as loud as my grandfather and failing. "Your aunt has stood in judgment before the decent people of this town and been condemned."

"By a majority of two: you and that vindictive woman, the senator's widow. I understand the woman scorned, but where do you come in?"

Judge Brown may have been wondering if he could get out the door safely. "Easy, Hugh, easy. Remember, we are moving into a troubled economy. I can make a difference."

"It would make a difference if you would pay your grocery bill."

Aunt Almeda was watching from behind the door. The two fat men had waltzed each other over in front of the hall tree, and Aunt Almeda must have feared Grandfather might take one of the canes and beat the old bastard.

"I will not be insulted. Summon your aunt. I have a copy of the will."

Aunt Almeda hurried out, extending her hand to separate them. Her voice was oil on water. "Well, if it isn't the eminent judge."

Grandfather was backing into his chair, wiping his face with the big white square of his napkin.

"You're looking well, madam."

She was all charm. "If I had known you were coming, I would have run up and put on my strait-jacket."

The judge was holding on to the back of his chair to stand. "Madam, I never apologize. I move with the expediency of the moment. I make judgments that seem right at the time and move on. I do not berate myself for mistakes, and I do not look back."

Aunt Almeda was walking, moving easily on her feet like a dancer. "Well, it seems we do have something in common after all. I, too, have lived a life for which I do not berate myself."

The judge got oily. "I did not come here to compare reminiscences; I see that you are a woman of some charm, and I can understand the senator's preference, though his good wife is my client."

Aunt Almeda wasn't buying it. "Since we are not going to exchange compliments, perhaps we can get on with the reading of the will."

The judge, flustered, shuffled papers from his briefcase on the hall table before he sat down. He put on his judicial voice. "I shall read only that part applicable to you." He was turning pages. Aunt Almeda was settling apprehensively into the chair opposite. "This is contained in one of the many codicils in which he provided for his help."

Aunt Almeda was close to screaming. "Help?"

He ignored her. "And subtracted the names of retainers who died."

She couldn't sit down now. "Since I was 'retained' for over forty years, that would make me one of the more enduring ones."

"And you have been suitably rewarded." He found his place with his finger and read: " 'Herein, herein, and et cetera, and to my faithful . . .' " He was enjoying this. He looked at her stricken face. "In common parlance, he left you two thousand dollars as a burial fund."

She was trying to adjust her glasses and read over his shoulder. "I don't believe it! He wouldn't be such an old Judas. He never wanted to clip my wings." She tried to pull the legal folder away from him, but he held on. "Let me see the exact words."

"Here it is, dated May 1924. 'And to my faithful secretary, Almeda Curtiss, who I am sure will grant she had been adequately rewarded for services, the sum of two thousand dollars to provide for her burial.' "

Almeda was looking over his shoulder. "That is not part of the body of the will, and it's only initialed. I was not incidental to his life. I was a partner for forty years."

He was assembling his papers with an air of finality. "I think you have an exaggerated notion of your position, madam. Such women always do. You see, when it comes down to stating your value in black and white, it is 'secretary who had been adequately rewarded.' " He snapped his briefcase shut. "A will is recorded in the court records of the land; you don't think he would record in stone, so to speak, his shameful relationship with you?"

Aunt Almeda went and leaned against the knoll post and dabbed at her eyes. "I don't believe it. I don't believe it for a moment." She sat on the bottom step and held her head in her hands. "I was his partner, so many times he told me so. I listened in places where he couldn't be seen. I drew out from politicians' wives information their husbands would never have divulged. It was I who told the senator that Mellon, secretary of the Treasury, was selling his stocks last February, at the time when Hoover was telling the country"—she looked up and deepened her voice—" 'the temporary upset has run its course, prosperity is about to return.' "

The judge was getting ready to go now, but he had listened with greater interest. "Your rambling changes nothing." He patted his briefcase. "It's all legal. Just as soon as we get this statue thing out of the way, I will file for probate."

She jumped up and faced him, her head high. "I will get William Randolph Hearst to print in his papers that it's dishonest, a fraud."

Now he was scornful. "Why would he listen to you?"

"He sat in my parlor and plotted the defeat of the League of Nations against Wilson. After all, Marion Davies is in the same position I was. He will be sympathetic to me."

The judge said it slowly as one speaks to a child. "No one is going to listen to the ramblings of an emotionally unstable radical. If you weren't a woman, I would brand you a Bolshevik."

Now it was a duel. They went back and forth at each other.

"Another Huey P. Long!"

"You sully the name of the great of our nation. I know how women like you live; you spend your life in back bedrooms."

Now Almeda sounded very clipped and proper. "I sat in a parlor with mahogany paneling on French gilt chairs. My maids served bootleg brandy in Irish crystal to the great and near great of this nation. I have a journal with enough destructive truths in it to bring this nation down, if I choose to publish it, going all the way back to Grover Cleveland."

Grandfather was hoisting his weight from the chair. He had had enough. The judge was yelling, "I defy you. Name me one recent incident in which a member of our government contributed to the market debacle!"

If it was a debate, Aunt Almeda pulled ahead, because she had become calm and level-voiced. "Start at the top. Hoover knew early on that the New York banks would not support the call fund. It is only a matter of days now until the market crashes."

The judge turned back to Grandfather, who only smiled. "That kind of talk is dangerous. This woman is a fascist."

Grandfather was now laughing. "I thought you said she was a Bolshevik. Which is she?"

The judge couldn't deal with laughter. "She's half and half, and that's the worst kind."

Now Grandfather was incredulous. "My little aunt is going to overthrow the government?"

"Harriet Beecher Stowe was a little woman, and she destroyed the fabric of this nation with a book. You can never tell, when a bad seed is planted, where it will grow." The judge put his hand on my head. "Even in the mind of this innocent child."

"Now my grandson is going to overthrow the government?"

I thought this was a chance for a little money. "What will you give me not to overthrow the government?"

The judge yanked his hand back and was almost to the front door, but then, thinking of another thrust, he pointed his pudgy finger at Aunt Almeda. "I can have you committed for maligning Andrew Mellon. The man is worth two hundred million dollars, why would he need to sell his country short?"

Aunt Almeda explained as she would to a child. "He will buy his stock back for a few cents on the dollar, and then he will be worth five hundred million. I have kept a journal on that man. He has used the office of the secretary of the Treasury to spread rumors and skillfully manipulate the stock exchange for his own gain. I have recorded all the transgressions of our officials, their secret sins, all these years. It looks like I will have to take my two-thousand-dollar burial fund and get my journals published. The sale of such a book should make me quite secure."

The judge played his trump card. "Your two thousand dollars will be paid upon your death to your nephew to bury you."

"It did not say that."

He put on his derby hat. "I say it. I am the executor of the will."

She couldn't hold back the tears any longer, and she went crying up the stairs. "You're a fraud, a forger, a pompous ass! I have friends. I'm not going to let you get away with this."

The judge was relieved. "I think we had better proceed with the commitment right away." He was fishing for a paper in his briefcase.

Grandfather snapped the judge's briefcase shut, almost on his hand. "Nobody is going to rush into anything."

The judge stood in the open door and made his curtain speech: "You are a thirty-second-degree Mason, and as such, it is your sworn duty to guard the security of your nation. The book that woman proposes to publish could shake us all to our very foundation. The little men of our country cannot know that their leaders have feet of clay. Even I have small chinks in my armor of respectability. We have to commit."

Grandfather held the door, impatient to close it behind this guest. "Would one of those small chinks be a crazy seventy-year-old wife who is going around town telling people she is pregnant? If you want to commit somebody, Judge, start at home."

Grandfather shoved the judge through the door and slammed it behind him. He smiled and put his arm around my shoulders. "Hughie, I think I'll go out in the kitchen and have another piece of pie, maybe two. Would you care to join me?"

OCTOBER 15, 1929

THE WEEK OF THE FESTIVAL, there was no school. It was clear and bright and cold. There were none of our usual forest fires yet, so the skies were blue. There had been enough frost to turn the leaves, and the hillsides were gold and red. Everyone was up and out early this day. It was that kind of a morning. I awakened to the sound of music from the training ring and went to the window. Stanley was up on the most beautiful of our sorrel colts, Fanny, and in this clear morning light, she looked almost pink.

She moved in the patterns of dressage to Lily Pons singing "The Bell Song" from *Lakmé*. There was a second voice singing with her that had to be Stanley. Stanley's appearance was the perfect complement, as his red hair gleamed in the sun. It had grown out long enough to show how golden red it really was, and he wore his favorite orange shirt. Boobie had my job of manning the phonograph. I wondered how she could get up so early and where she got her yellow dress that was the color of linden leaves. I saw my mother and Mr. Miller going toward the lower meadow carrying bridles, and I knew they were going to ride.

Tuba pounded on the door and yelled, "Git up, lazy, your oatmeal gonna be cold."

When I got to the kitchen, only Handsome and Miss Larkin were there. Miss Larkin was heating water for her teapot, and Handsome was eating. When he saw me, he turned on his smile that showed two new teeth, and his eyes sparkled, and oatmeal dribbled down over his chin. He couldn't say my name yet, he could only say "Who." I had to remember to give him a good smack in the mouth before he learned to talk well enough to tattle.

Miss Larkin was singing a song about a bluebird, "A flash of blue in the meadow, a flash of green in the rain," to Handsome, and he was beating time on his high chair with his tin cup. Miss Larkin had a pretty voice, and she seemed to sing more lately than she used to. She was also walking better.

I didn't know why I was feeling so left out. I knew a song that fit, "Nobody loves me, everybody hates me, I'm going out and eat worms," but there was nobody who wanted to hear me sing it.

The Miller boys came in with butter and buttermilk and put it in the refrigerator. They told Miss Larkin they were going to work on her old Model T today. But she said, "Boys, you have to stop saying 'my' car. I'm so glad you

bought her from me and gave her a new lease on life. You have painted and polished her until I hardly know her."

Raymond was getting down two blue teacups. "She's a beautiful car, and as
soon as the sheriff brings us our license so we can go out on the road, we will
take you for a ride."

I took a piece of bread and apple butter and went and sat on the front steps.

The Thorne twins were just coming in our gate, and they had brought their
two older brothers. The twins looked like they had grown six inches these last
two months; they even looked thinner. Although I don't know how they could,
since they still ate like hogs. Maybe it was all those willow baskets they kept
making.

Before they could get halfway up the lane, my mother and Mr. Miller came
around the house. Mr. Miller was up on Grandfather's Black, and my mother
was riding Hannah.

"Can I go with you? I could ride behind Mr. Miller," I said.

"No, we're going to the upper meadow to give the horses a good workout."

When Mr. Miller saw my crestfallen face, he said, "There may be a stray
sheep or so up there. If there is, I will have to tie it on behind me."

My mother dismissed me and turned her attention to the Thornes. "Boys, I
don't think Miss Larkin planned class today."

The Thorne brothers acted like they had rehearsed their speech. John was
first. "We have come to work, ma'am. Our mother says we can't jes' take an'
take and give nothin' back."

One of the twins piped up. "Our mother says thank you for the split-
bottom chairs."

The oldest brother's voice was considerably darker; I don't remember his
name. "Our mother says thank you for our lives. I don't know what she means,
but we aim to pay our debts."

My mother looked for a minute like she might cry; she didn't, she seldom
did. "Well, we are cutting cabbage today. You can go down in the field and help
the Forrester men after you have had some breakfast."

"We et at home, ma'am."

"I know, but it was a long walk down here."

The two fat boys were already on the way to the kitchen.

I sat on the step with nothing to do. At nine o'clock, the mailman would be
here with yesterday's Washington *Herald,* I would wait and read the funnies. I

certainly wasn't going to carry in cabbage heads. After all, I was Huston Curtiss III, and I owned this farm.

The first frost had wilted the weeds, and the cabbages stood high on their stalks. The Forrester men were whacking them off with sharp machetes, and the three Dutch ladies were sorting the best of the heads to go to the root cellars and the rest to the canning room for kraut. We had an old dray horse named Kelly who had a blank kind of dumb look about him—very much like the two Forrester men—and he was used to pull the wagon or sled from one field or garden plot to another. The older Thorne boys led him to the cellars and the canning shed with the loads of cabbages. When there was a large pile, the boys cut away the dry outer leaves, and the Dutch ladies began the process of making sauerkraut.

The big forty-gallon stone crocks were lined up along the wall. They had to be in place; filled with cabbage, they would be too heavy to move. The Dutch ladies cut the heads into long, lacy slivers using cutters that looked like washboards, with blades instead of ridges. When there was a layer three or four inches thick, they sprinkled in a layer of salt, then took a mallet and pounded until the juices began to flow—layers of cabbage, layers of salt, and pound away. And as they worked, they laughed and sang and reminisced about the same chore at home in Holland when they were girls.

When the crocks were almost full and a salty brine covered the cabbage, a round board was placed on top with a big, clean rock weighing it down. A round piece of cloth was tied over the top so the cabbage could breathe and ferment, and big bubbles of gas would come to the surface with a small moaning sound as though the process of transforming into kraut was painful. It took about a month until the crocks were quiet and the kraut could be tonged out and washed under the faucet until enough salt was out to lay it in an iron skillet and enhance the flavor of pork ribs, or sausages, or ham, or to be eaten raw if you had a taste for it.

Eight crocks of kraut joined the two crocks where elderberries fermented into wine, and two empty crocks waited for the wild grapes that would become wine after a good freeze brought out the sugar in them, and we would all take to the woods to gather them. There were many jars and crocks and tin cans that would feed, over the winter, the fifteen people who lived in this house.

❦

MY MOTHER AND I took our lunch trays to the little latticed porch on the north wing and ate at one of the round marble-topped tables. The day was so bright and clear that the inside of the house seemed gloomy. This porch was one of my mother's favorite places. The back wall and the floor were old brick that molded into a soft green, and when there wasn't enough mold to suit her, she sponged it down with buttermilk.

There was a circle of lawn in front of the porch, with a hedge of yellow chrysanthemums. It was hard to realize that any day now, a wind would come down from the north and coat everything with inches of frozen sleet. We couldn't say we hadn't been warned: for the past three weeks, migrating birds had passed over going south. A gaggle of gray Canada geese had gone over just this morning, in their precise arrow formation, and settled down on our lower pond to feed before continuing south. When it was migrating season, my mother posted our lands to keep hunters out, and each evening we spread a bushel of shelled corn on the ponds, which kept the birds from diving for our trout.

From our table, we could see Miss Larkin having lunch in the gazebo with the fat boys and Boobie, and we could hear their laughter. The older Thorne boys seemed to have made friends with the Forrester men, they were all talking at once in the kitchen. I thought they suited one another fine; they all seemed dumb. I didn't know where Stanley was eating. He took turns having his meals with each one of the Dutch ladies at a time, to perfect the French and German he was studying. They had a rule to speak no English through the whole meal.

I was planning to ask my mother what she and Mr. Miller had talked about. It seemed she wanted to tell me so I could help explain to Boobie. She was unhappy about it. Mr. Miller was going away. He was going to Detroit, Michigan, to stay with his brother and get a job in the Ford motor plant. Eventually he would send for the rest of his family.

"Don't the Millers like living with us?"

"The Millers are very grateful for the life they have here, and I don't know how I will get along without them, but he wants his sons to have an education. The boys want to go to high school and even college, if they can. Raymond wants to be a veterinarian, and Donald wants to be an attorney. When they are not even allowed to ride on the school bus, there are no opportunities here."

"When is he going?"

"After we have our butchering done and all the crops are in. He wants to be fair to us. Don't talk to Boobie about it yet. He hasn't told his family."

She didn't say any more, for Stanley came around the end of the house riding Fanny into the circle of flowers. All at once, it became a circus ring.

Stanley had showered and changed his shirt. He was wearing yellow now, with a red silk scarf at his throat, and his hair was still shining from the water. Horse and rider stopped in the center of the circle. Stanley sat elegantly tall and communicated to his mount the dressage message with his knees, and she arched her beautiful head and high-held tail in a burnished curve and bowed toward us. Stanley's voice was high-pitched but clear and resonate. "Ladies and gentlemen, may I present Miss Fanny, the world's most beautiful horse." Fanny held her head up and whinnied as close to gay laughter as a horse can. Stanley looked around, confused. "Boobie is supposed to be here with the phonograph cart."

I looked over at the gazebo and heard her laughter and knew she had forgotten, and I called out, "Sing to her." For a moment fear passed over his face, and then he turned his magic mount into a light-footed trot around the circle and began to sing, accompanied only by the beat of the horse's hoofs, "The Bell Song" from *Lakmé* in French, with a note-for-note imitation of Lily Pons. Soft and subdued at first, but when he got into the intricate pattern of the horse's movements, he forgot himself and sang out full-voiced and strong. The sound filled the space between our house and the hill on the other side of the road. And when he got to the bell tones, his voice soared as though there were a symphony orchestra supporting him. The grass circle had become a ballroom, and the horse and rider had become dancing partners; extending, prancing in diagonal steps, this way and that, partners in love with the dance.

The object of dressage is for the horse to balance her weight perfectly on all four feet, and to bend equally well on both sides of her body, and to learn to accept and follow the rider's signals with leg, seat, and hands. It's as though the bones of your seat extend down through the horse's legs. The trick is to get the horse to carry itself so well that almost before the rider knows which movement he wants to do, the horse does it. Fanny wanted to be beautiful, you could see it in her every move. She danced through a sequence of equine ballet steps that the nobles of the court of Versailles, where this training had been brought to its zenith, would have envied. You could not watch without being aware of the love that passed between horse and rider. You do not train this kind of horse with a whip and a spur any more than you would whip a ballet dancer.

When Fanny did the piaffe, trotting in place, and a pirouette, a pivot on the hind quarters, followed by ballotade, an aerial leap, I heard my mother whisper, "Any judge in the world would give those two a ten." When he had reached the last clear, ringing note and held it until it seemed to crystallize against the glass window behind us, and Fanny took her last bow, my mother applauded through her tears; the Dutch women and the Forrester men standing in the doorway applauded; and the children and Miss Larkin applauded. I knew something had changed, I didn't know what, but I did know that our lives had changed. I could see it in my mother's face. She hugged the horse, and she hugged Stanley, and she told him that there were kings in Europe who would have built gilt and mirrored theaters to show off a performance like that.

Stanley stood back, still unsure. "You are pleased with me?"

"Yes, yes, my dear child, you two are wonderful."

"And you're a wonderful teacher. I just wanted you to know that all the time you spent on me wasn't wasted."

He jumped into the saddle. Fanny backed off doing a piaffe and center pirouette and danced away.

My mother called after him, "You sing like an angel."

OCTOBER 16, 1929

ON MONDAY THE TOWNSPEOPLE had started putting up the decorations for the festival. Preparations had been going on for months. This was the one chance in the year to draw crowds of tourists who would spend a lot of money. Our town had eight thousand people, and during the festival it doubled, and this year everyone hoped for even more. They needed the money. In half the houses in town, people rented out rooms. The festival committee had chosen this time of year so it would be too cold for people to sleep in their cars or in tents. Nevertheless, some people did. This was the first year Grandmother Curtiss had been on the hospitality committee. She didn't know whether it was because word was out about all the money she had come into, or because she had that big house with all those bedrooms. Anyway, she ended up volunteering to house six of the princesses, and they didn't pay.

Each one had to pay five hundred dollars for the privilege of being a princess, and even then she had to be appointed by a United States senator, plus buy a velvet dress with a long train in the colors of autumn leaves, so I guess it would have been too much to ask her to pay for her room, even if most of the girls were daughters of the rich. My grandmother had wanted to house the queen, but Senator Burton's widow got her. She had to be really rich, since her fee was a thousand dollars, and she had to be appointed by the governor and buy a rust-red velvet gown with a train twenty feet long.

It was a great honor to be Sylvia, queen of the forest. Already, there were tales going around about this year's queen. She was supposed to be a hot little number. People said she was doing this only to attract attention so she could get in the movies. Supposedly the paper in Wheeling had interviewed her—she said they just made it up—but the reporter had asked her if she was a virgin queen, and she said the festival committee had fucked her good when she had to pay a thousand dollars for the privilege! When my grandmother read that, she said old Mrs. Burton could have her. Of course, they didn't say the "F" word in the newspaper. They said "deflowered," to confuse the people, but I knew what that meant. Lloyd had told me. I missed Lloyd.

Aunt Sebe called my mother on Wednesday morning and wanted her to come into town right away.

"Sebe, what is it? Is something wrong with the boys?"

It had nothing to do with Worthy or Harry, and Sebe couldn't say what it was with everybody listening on the party line. Some of the people listening got their feelings hurt, and you could hear the click as they hung up.

"All right, I'll come, but I've just gotten through working the horses, and I have to take a bath."

Aunt Sebe said she couldn't smell any worse than what was going on there, but my mother got in the tub with foaming essence of roses.

I wanted to go see Aunt Almeda and cheer her up. I took her a big bunch of yellow chrysanthemums. We passed the senator's statue. The road in front of it was down to one lane now, for a giant wooden platform had been built around it that extended at least two hundred feet in every direction. You couldn't see the statue at all now, as the flag completely hid it. It was going to be a big surprise for the tourists when they yanked that flag off. That was the first item on the program. Workmen were busy building benches around back for the band, and others were unloading folding chairs, borrowed from the lodge halls and funeral homes.

Aunt Sebe was waiting at the curb in front of her house, and she got in front with my mother with no explanation except to direct her down First Street. My mother did so slowly, because people were tying corn shocks around the base of all the light poles, and hanging bunting on the wires over the streets. When we got past the Randolph Hotel, Aunt Sebe said to stop. We were in front of Eddie Horner's studio. Aunt Sebe got out, and we followed.

In Eddie Horner's window was a full-length portrait that looked very much like my mother, if my mother stood around in the woods in a flimsy nightgown with one side open clear up her thigh. When we got to the glass, we realized it was Aunt Lilly. Maybe she looked the way my mother did before I knew her; Aunt Lilly was only twenty-two. There was a brass plate at the bottom of the frame that said "Queen of the Forest."

Aunt Sebe's voice was deep and level, which meant she was mad. "Well, what do you think of that?"

My mother was standing back, looking carefully at it. "I think it's beautiful."

"Billy-Pearl, for God's sake, that painter's a nigger! How could Lilly do this? Our own sister! When?"

"Well, let's go in and ask him." My mother was already half through the door.

"I'm not going in there," Sebe said. But she did.

A woman's voice sang out, "I'll be with you in just a moment." Aunt Lilly turned toward us. She was wearing a purple smock with spots of paint on it, and she was tacking canvas to a stretcher. Her silver hair was loose around her face and down her back, and she looked about fifteen.

"Billy, Sebe, did you see my portrait?" She stood up and laughed. "Of course you did. Isn't it wonderful? Eddie says I'll hang in a museum someday, if not that one, another of me."

My mother agreed, "It is very beautiful."

For once Aunt Sebe didn't say anything. She was circling the room looking at the walls. Aunt Lilly's likeness was everywhere. She was sketched in charcoal and pencil and red crayon. She was painted in oil in profile, three-quarter-length, and full-faced. Aunt Sebe realized that these had been done over a period of time. "How long have you been coming here?"

"Oh, over the summer. Look around, I've got to keep at this. Eddie may get some commissions during the festival. I prepare the canvases and paint in the backgrounds."

There were several canvases the right size to paint heads on, set against the wall to dry. They were painted in cloudy gradations of green or brown or blue-gray.

"What does Blake say about this?"

"He said to stay home or he would leave me, and last week he did. He went back to Pennsylvania."

"Why hasn't Dad told us about this?"

"Because he thinks as I do, that it's none of your business."

Aunt Sebe was losing control and sputtering, "But he's—he's—"

My mother was standing where she could see the door. Aunt Sebe could not. Eddie Horner was coming in, and my mother finished her sentence: "He's an extremely talented painter."

Eddie Horner looked from one to the other. He was wearing a green velvet jacket with a yellow scarf at his throat and looked younger than I had thought last time. He was carrying a large canvas folder.

"Eddie, these are my sisters, Billy and Luceba," Lilly said.

"Ladies! You couldn't be anything but sisters. You must be the three most beautiful women in this town."

He didn't need to shake hands, for Aunt Lilly came toward him and took the folder impatiently. "Well, tell me."

He was smiling, and his eyes shone, and his dark face gleamed, and I thought, There are times when Handsome has that very look.

"Yes, yes. We got it."

I thought Aunt Lilly was going to kiss him, but she didn't.

"Did you hold out for two thousand dollars and two hundred for the frame?"

"I forgot about the frame. She wants it to look just exactly like your portrait, only with her face."

We three might just as well have been forgotten. "Well, there you are. Just paint her face right over mine. You won't even have to change the hair much, she's a yellow blonde. Did you get a deposit?"

"Yes, three hundred dollars. But Lilly, that's your portrait."

"You can paint me again. You know my face so well, you could paint me in your sleep."

Aunt Sebe's eyes narrowed, and she looked from one to the other. I knew she wanted to ask if they were sleeping together, but she didn't.

"Well, it would only take a couple of sittings that way."

"You see? And did you ask about referrals?"

My mother laughed. "I see! Just who is running this studio?"

He smiled and loosened the yellow scarf. "I couldn't get along without her."

Aunt Lilly went back to tacking canvas to its frame. "I'm his apprentice. I'm going to learn to paint."

"I couldn't do without her," he repeated. "White women are at ease coming in here now."

Aunt Lilly remembered I was there. "This is my nephew, Hughie."

His voice thinned to an edge. "I think the young man and I have met."

I decided to prove to myself I could be generous, too; maybe he would paint me. "That must have been some other kid. I would remember."

"You're probably right, so would I." He looked from one sister to the other. "Turner did the *White Sisters*. I could paint you three in a beautiful ocher-yellow haze as the 'Golden Sisters.' "

Aunt Sebe spoke up now, but she didn't sound really pleasant. "There are ten of us."

"All beautiful? I don't believe it. Lilly, why didn't you tell me?"

Aunt Lilly took the tacks out of her mouth. "Remember, we said nothing personal, strictly business."

Aunt Sebe said, "Well, that's a relief."

He laughed. "I thought you meant the fact that I'm a faggot and a nigger. Everyone in town knows about me since Alvin Channell's death, and my face gives my color away, though I did think I might be able to pass for an Indian if I could straighten my hair. I really am three-quarters Egyptian."

My mother was looking closely at the portraits of Aunt Lilly on the wall. "You don't have to pass for anything but what you are, a very able artist. When I get a little more flush, I would like my portrait done."

Aunt Lilly stood up. "We will give you a discount if you let us show it in Washington."

"Are you moving to Washington?"

He answered, "Lilly says we have to eventually, there is no future here."

"There is no future here for anyone," Lilly rejoined.

My mother was moving toward the door. "Gotta get home. I just remembered, we are moving the beehives today."

As we went out, Eddie shook each hand. Aunt Sebe hesitated only a moment. My mother said, "My husband has a great-aunt who once had influence in Washington. It's a shame she is not still there."

I didn't know if she was saying something nice about Aunt Almeda or if she wished she was still there so I couldn't like her as well as I did.

When we got to the sidewalk, Aunt Lilly came to stand in the doorway. "Remember, you two, when you're talking about me, this is my ticket out of the damn hills."

Coming out of Eddie Horner's studio was very much like the last time, because Lester Adams was standing there looking at the painting. When he saw us, he didn't even say hello. He said to my mother, "Is that nigger gonna take your picture out of the window?"

"This is not a painting of me."

"Well, half the town thinks it is."

"That's their problem, not mine."

"You look naked. You can see right through that dress."

"Lester, Sebe just drug me in here to stick my nose in something that is none of my business. I am having beehives moved today, and they may very well swarm in the attic if I don't get home."

He obviously didn't know what she was talking about, and she didn't care. We were getting into the car. "What if my mother comes by here?" he asked.

"Just tell her it isn't me."

"You know I can't tell my mother anything."

"Lester, I don't care." She was starting the car.

"You have to care. She is yelling at me now for planning to marry a divorced woman."

"Who?"

"You, dammit, you."

He leaned in the car window. She was letting out the clutch, and the car was beginning to move forward, though he still had his head in the window.

"You can relieve her mind. I'm not going to get a divorce, and I am not going to marry you." The car was moving faster, and he was running faster. His face was getting very red, and people on the sidewalk were laughing.

"Then why do you sleep with me?"

"For the same reason you sleep with me. I enjoy it. Now, get out of the road before I run over you."

When we got to the corner, I looked through the back window, and Lester was still standing in the middle of the road, looking mad.

OCTOBER 17, 1929

THERE ARE LOTS OF kinds of bugs on the farm, some good, some bad. My favorites are fireflies. If you can catch a glass jar full of them, you can hold it down under the covers and they make enough light to read by. But the insects we could not do without were the bees. Every plant on a farm has to be cross-fertilized to bear fruit. Mr. Hansford came in the spring and fall to take care of our bees. He told me a lot about bees that I really didn't want to know. Mr. Hansford liked to talk dirty, and he told me every blossom has to be fucked or it just dries up and dies; of course the bee doesn't know what he's doing. He's just busy gathering nectar, and the pollen just happens to stick to his legs and gets carried to the next flower. Mr. Hansford said that proved if you want to get fucked a lot, you have to be real sweet, then he said his old lady kept forgetting that.*

This year we got about a hundred pounds of honey, which was a lot, to see us through the winter. But with Boobie's sweet tooth, it didn't seem enough. My mother wasn't afraid of many things, but she was very fearful of bees. She closed all the doors and windows and stayed inside when Mr. Hansford was here. Last year one of the colonies that had two queen bees divided, and one of the queens took half the colony and swarmed away. She went into our attic and established her hive in the space between the floors. We could hear them humming away, and my mother was afraid to go in the attic. Finally Mr. Hansford came and wound a lot of old greasy rags around brooms and set them on fire and smoked out the bees. For a long time honey dripped out around the chandelier in my bedroom whenever the house was hot.

Thursday afternoon my mother dropped me off at Aunt Sebe's, so I could go with Worthy and Harry to watch the final preparations for the next day's festival. There were hundreds of yards of glazed chintz in the bright color of autumn leaves, decorating storefronts and draped around light poles. Last year I had gone with my cousins the last evening of the festival and gathered up a hundred yards or so of the stuff. This year we were going to do the same. We didn't

---

* We must have had about sixty hives. That's as many as one farm can support. There are about fifty thousand bees in a colony. The hives are boxes about a yard square, made like a chest of drawers. In the spring, you put them in empty, and the bees, whose job it is to make wax combs, get busy and build the perfect squares of wax. Each cell is octagon-shaped and just big enough to hold an egg that will hatch into a bee. There is only one female, the queen, in each box, and all the rest are male. The jobs are all divided up, and everybody knows exactly what his job is. The queen lays about a dozen eggs every minute. The drones squirt a little semen on each egg, and the young workers put the egg down in a wax cell; then a bee who makes royal jelly out of a gland in the top of his head comes along and puts in a little under each egg. Then they add honey and seal up the top. When the bee hatches and eats his way out, he already knows exactly what his job is. I always thought the world would go around a lot faster if people could do that. Our hives were scattered around over

have Lloyd, but we were all a year bigger, so we could do without his help, but it was hard to do without his laughter. Aunt Sebe would make Halloween costumes from the chintz and sell them for five dollars each.

We went by Mr. Isaac's store, where Grandfather Fancler was helping him clear all the old junk out of his storeroom that he hoped to sell to tourists. There were coffee grinders and spinning wheels and handmade cradles, piles of stuff you couldn't give away at any other time. They looked like they could use some help, so we hurried away before they could draft us.

The main streets had been blocked off, and there were tents and booths set up, and down by the train station, a merry-go-round and a thing that whirled you around until you hung upside down for about a minute before you swung down again. It was already going, and Worthy and Harry wanted to stand and wait in case money fell out of someone's pocket when they were hanging upside down. We waited around about a half hour, but only a couple of nickels fell out, and the man who ran the loop beat us to them.

Down at the agricultural display was a row of giant pumpkins. Tuck Marsteller was just pulling his truck in and getting ready to unload his pumpkin. He pulled off the canvas, and some of his competitors came to see and compare. It was big, all right, but it would be close. Tuck put up two big boards for a ramp and began to roll his pumpkin to the ground. It must have weighed eight hundred pounds, and the ramp was unsteady, so he gave a loud "Watch out!" as the great round orange sphere got away from him and rolled toward a telephone pole, where it crashed with a cracking, crunching sound and fell into at least a dozen pieces.

His competitors, standing by their pumpkins, which now stood a chance, tried to look sorry for his tragedy, but most could not contain their glee and

---

the farm where they were needed, in the alfalfa fields, among the clover, the corn, and the potatoes, everywhere. They were up on sawhorses so the skunks couldn't get at them. Skunks and dragonflies eat bees. Every bee goes back to his own colony, and there are guards at the entrance to make sure he is in the right hive.

Mr. Hansford came and put on his big-brimmed hat with the netting sewn all around like a window curtain, and a long coat, and gloves with the fingers cut off. He moved very slowly, as the bees attack if you swat at them. Hansford's job was to remove some of the drawers of honey, leaving enough to feed the bees over the winter. They do not hibernate, and when they get very cold, they cluster in a big ball and buzz to keep warm, all except the drones. They are thrown out in the cold to freeze, and a new bunch hatches when spring comes. In winter, the hives had to be moved to sheltered areas with bales of hay stacked around them.

began laughing. They could not forget how Tuck had gloated last year when he won. A crowd gathered quickly to gather up pieces of the pumpkin to take home. Tuck stood on the back of his truck and looked as though he was crying, and his competitors began to hoot and cry with him. Then he began to laugh, and he went to the front of his truck and pulled off another canvas, and there was the largest pumpkin any of them had ever seen. And now it was their turn to cry. If I could sell two hundred pumpkin seeds for a dollar each and lost the chance, I would cry, too.

I went to the house on Worth Avenue when the light began to fade. There were a lot of strange faces in town, and I wasn't taking any chances. Everyone there had eaten early, because Aunt Almeda wanted to go and walk in the park. She had spent her life in Washington and was used to strangers in the street, so she was not afraid. I had my dinner in the kitchen, and Grandfather Curtiss joined me for a second dessert.

Aunt Almeda wanted me to walk with her. She always talked to me as though I was grown, and I liked that. Aunt Opal loaned me a sweater, and Aunt Almeda wore her riding habit because it was the warmest thing she had. She let me wear her derby hat.

When Aunt Almeda left Washington, she could not get into the house, but she had a little writing room out over the stables that the court had failed to lock. Her journals were there, and several books of poetry and history. She had given the poetry books to me, and now she wanted to talk about them as we walked under the dark trees that overhung the sidewalks. The autumn leaves blanketed the ground, and I went along kicking them in the air, so she wouldn't ask me if I had read the books. But she did anyway.

"My mother said I'm too young for those books."

"Of course you are too young now for most of the great English poets, but you put them on your shelf, and when you're older, take them down and get to know them, and you will always have friends. Chaucer, Shakespeare, Spenser, Milton, Browning, and Tennyson are the six great poets of the English language. I think you could start on Browning now, he's the most approachable. He has the curiosity of a young boy." She stopped under a streetlight to quote him with her arms held wide: " 'Whate'er he looked upon, and his looks go everywhere.' He is a companion who walks beside the reader, thinking aloud. It may be a little too soon, but I do hope you will take Browning down from your shelf by the time you're ten."

"Will you read him to me?"

We had reached the park and went over and stood behind the bandstand and watched.

"I doubt that I will be here. I have already overstayed my welcome."

We could see the final preparations around the statue. There was a string of bare lightbulbs, and the bunting here was all red, white, and blue stripes.

"Where will you be?"

"You do know, Hughie, that nobody lives forever, and one day I shall be with the senator."

I couldn't accept that, so I said, "You mean riding up there on the back of his horse?"

She was still for a moment, then she stooped down and grasped me by the shoulders. Her voice sang out with laughter. "You're right. Oh, you are a wise child. It's where I intended to be all along."

Just then the workers turned off the lights and began climbing in their trucks to drive away.

"I'm going to climb up there under the flag and sit behind him on the horse, and when they pull the flag down in the morning, there I'll be, and they will know how I loved him, and he loved me. Let's hurry home. I will have to get a pillow and a ladder and put on some more rouge so I will look bright in the morning sunlight."

I wanted to hurry home so I could tell Grandfather Curtiss. I thought he ought to know.

 October 18, 1929

THE NEXT MORNING Aunt Opal and I were in the park by eight o'clock, and already most of the good places to sit were occupied. We had each brought a cushion and were able to climb up on the barrels of the Civil War cannons, where we had a good view. I couldn't tell whether Aunt Almeda was up under the flag or not, and I couldn't tell Aunt Opal, since it wasn't my secret.

The band from the Virginia Military Institute was already in place, and the red plumes on their hats seemed to bloom in the sun. There was a passage left for the governor's car to pull up, and a red carpet to the podium where he would make his speech. Most of the reserved chairs were already filled, and latecomers were quarreling about their positions. People behind the chairs had to stand, and there was a mass of them, clear down to the middle of the next block. I recognized my mother from her gold crown of braided hair. The Dutch ladies and Stanley were with her. I wondered where the Millers were. Black people had to move to the back. If I could find Boobie, she could sit up here on the cannon in front of me, but I didn't dare get down to look for her. Then I saw Grandfather Curtiss. He was back behind the statue where all the news reporters' trucks were parked, and I knew he couldn't see anything from there. I thought maybe he was embarrassed to go out front and let people see how fat he had become.

By eight-thirty the band began to play all the rah-rah songs, the Sousa marches, and "America the Beautiful." All the folding chairs for dignitaries were full, the mayor, the council, the festival committee, all except Grandmother Curtiss's, who had stayed home to see to her guests, and later she thanked God for that. There were reporters with big cameras crouched around everywhere. Four men with trumpets stood up and blared away as the governor's open car drove up. He had a state policeman for a chauffeur, and another one to get out and open the door. Beside him was a fat lady in a big black hat and a long veil that hung down as far as the beekeepers' hats. Opal said it was Mrs. Burton, the senator's widow.

Judge Brown was in the front row with his wife, Daisy, and he jumped up to greet the governor. Daisy jumped up, too, in spite of the fact that the pillow under her dress had grown larger. The judge pushed her back in her seat and went to glad-hand the governor, who looked just the way a politician should: silver hair, a ruddy face, and a potbelly. The judge beat him to the microphone and said, "Ladies and gentlemen, I give you the governor of West Virginia."

The mayor, who was scheduled to make the introduction, seated Mrs. Burton in a big gold chair provided for her, and the governor took the mike.

"Thank you, Mr. Green—no-no, I'm sorry, Mr. Brown. Judge Brown, isn't it?"

The judge mumbled as he took his seat, "Judge Brown, judge of the circuit court for thirty-seven years."

The judge knew very well the governor knew him. But what could you expect from a Democrat? He had told the whole town that if the Democrats got into the White House, the country would go to hell in a breadbasket. Now it looked like that breadbasket was going to be empty before the Democrats got to it.

The governor began a long rambling speech, pointing out the lifetime of service to our fair nation that Senator Burton had unselfishly rendered. He told about his forty years in Washington, in which his office and home were a mecca for the great and near great, seeking fair and honest regulation of this great nation, and never a breath of scandal attached to his name. All this and a whole lot more, and not a word about Aunt Almeda.

"You will know how difficult it is to replace this man when I tell you it is my duty to appoint his successor for the four years left in his term, and I have not been able to fill that vacancy."

At this, the judge rose from his seat to be seen, but the governor ignored him and plowed on. "Behind a great man there is always a great woman, reassuring him and keeping the home fires burning. I give you the senator's widow, Gertrude Burton, who will unveil the statue of the great politician riding into history."

Mrs. Burton stood and grasped the gold rope. If she said anything, a fit of wheezing and coughing and a drum roll from the band covered it. She yanked away, and the huge flag hiding the statue fell to the ground. And there she was, Almeda Curtiss, sitting on the great iron horse behind her iron man.

There was a gasp of surprise from the audience, and then a roar of laughter and applause. The reporters all stood up and flashed and snapped their cameras and cried out, "Look here—look this way."

The widow's legs gave way, and the governor's quick action, easing her into her chair, kept her from falling on her face. Aunt Almeda smiled and waved to the crowd, which was registering loud hoots of approval. She looked bright and at ease in her red riding jacket, with her derby hat sitting jauntily on her mass of hennaed hair. The officials in the front row were waving frantically and demanding she come down, but the governor was laughing. Grandfather Curtiss hurried up with his ladder and held it so she could climb down, and by that time Aunt Opal was climbing up on the platform with me right behind her. I heard the governor say as he took Almeda's hand, "Well, if it isn't my old poker partner. I see you have decided to show your hand."

"Jokers, all jokers, I'm afraid."

Some smart kid in the band began to play "The Lady in Red" on his trumpet, and the rest of the band joined in. They gave it a kind of burlesque swing as the governor took Aunt Almeda by the arm and guided her to his waiting car.

The judge was running up behind the governor, disavowing any knowledge of the criminal act, and Daisy was waltzing along behind him, holding her hands on either side of her pillow to keep it from falling out. Aunt Opal took the other end of the ladder and gathered up the blanket Aunt Almeda had been sitting on and started around behind the statue to escape for home when she suddenly dropped the ladder and ran to the front of the platform. Before Daisy knew what was happening, Aunt Opal reached up under her dress and yanked out the pillow. She thrust it into the judge's arms, yelling loudly, "There, Judge Brown, you have just become the father of a lovely green velvet sofa pillow!"

I didn't try to find my mother. I was sure she was running for her car. She had been embarrassed by Aunt Almeda before, and this would really ice the cake. I went with Aunt Opal and Grandfather to help carry the ladder. Grandfather was walking pretty well for a fat old man who had forgotten to put on his shoes.

When we were in the front hall at Worth Avenue, Aunt Opal started in on him. "Why, Dad? Just tell me why."

He collapsed on the couch, and his voice was wheezy. "Because she wanted it. I'm not able to give anyone what they want anymore, and I owed Aunt Almeda. She was there all night, and I had to protect her."

"You better get to bed, you're liable to get pneumonia."

He got to his feet with great effort and started toward the stairs. "I suppose we will all have to leave town now."

Aunt Almeda was coming down. She had washed her face until she looked pale, and put on her lavender dress. "No, dear nephew, you will not. I am sure Judge Brown is at this moment filling out my commitment papers. That should satisfy everyone. A nice, quiet asylum may be just the thing. I can write my great exposé of the last forty years of government and make you all rich."

Aunt Opal went and hugged her. "How did you come to know the governor?"

We all moved toward the kitchen, where Aunt Opal made cocoa to go with her mincemeat cookies.

"The governor used to come to the Washington house about once a month, bringing the bribes from the railroads to get their bills through, hundreds and thousands of dollars."

"In cash?"

"Of course. Everything was in cash, so it couldn't be traced."

"Is there any left?"

Now Grandfather was interested, though he was about asleep in his chair. "The senator wouldn't risk putting that in a bank. What did he do with it?"

"There is a safe in the basement of the Washington house."

"And who knows the combination?"

"The senator, of course. But the old dear is dead."

"Who else?"

"Well, I do, and I'm the only one."

Aunt Opal waltzed around laughing until she spilled cocoa down the front of her apron. "Then our problem is solved. We can live on that money."

I was going to have to eat fast if I was going to get any more cookies. Grandfather was eating those big fat cookies one a minute.

Aunt Almeda looked at herself appraisingly in the kitchen mirror. "Well, aren't I a pastel-tinted remnant of the old order? Sitting on an iron horse all night does not improve one's appearance. I'm not going to say I'm sorry; that would imply I had some control over my behavior. I felt compelled to make a gesture, I had to stick my tongue out at them for the last time. Maybe I really am mad."

Grandfather talked with his mouth full. "You sure shot them pompous sons of bitches full of holes. There was a minute when every mouth was hangin' open. It's a shame Herbert Hoover wasn't there."

The front doorbell rang, and since Grandmother Curtiss had taken all the help over to her house, Aunt Opal went to see who was there. Aunt Almeda was twisting her hair in a little knot in the back, preparing to be taken away.

Aunt Opal came running back. "It's Judge Brown, and there is someone with him."

"He didn't waste much time, did he? Is it the sheriff?"

"You won't believe it. Come and see."

Grandfather didn't care who it was. He went back to eating cookies, and I went to watch through the crack in the parlor door. Aunt Almeda looked through the lace curtain. "Oh my God, it's Gertrude. What can she want from me? I am not going to say I'm sorry." She went running up the steps.

Aunt Opal opened the door, and huffing and puffing behind yards of black veil was the senator's widow. The judge was trying to push reporters back to keep them from coming in.

"No pictures. No statements."

One reporter had his foot in the door. The judge held the door and yelled out, "The grieving widow has seen fit, in her generosity, to come and console her dead husband's secretary."

The reporter hooted, "Come off it, Judge. You mean his tootsy, don't you?"

At that, the judge stomped on the reporter's foot and got the door shut and locked. He turned to face a furious Opal, who said, "I am not aware that either of you were asked into this house."

The judge pushed a chair under the fat lady in black. You could hear her breathing clear across the room. She was fanning air up under her veil with her purse. The judge sounded like he needed to sit down, too. "Don't get on your high horse with me, young woman, after what your aunt did to this dear lady today." He found a chair.

Aunt Opal did get on her high horse, and she lied through her teeth. "There is already a move afoot to put a statue of my aunt up there on the horse behind the senator. It isn't really necessary; no one will ever look at it without remembering how right she looked up there waving."

Mrs. Burton was moaning, "Water, please."

Aunt Opal called to me to bring two glasses of ice water, but I heard the judge say, "I hope you're not giving out statements to the press."

When I got back, the phone was ringing for the tenth time. Aunt Opal was mad. "Hazel, I told you, no calls . . . No, my aunt can't come to the phone just now . . . Washington?" The judge leaned forward. "A Mrs. Mitchell? Let me talk to her." To the judge and Mrs. Burton, she said, "It's the wife of the attorney general." It was necessary with long-distance to raise your voice, and she did. "Yes, yes, Mrs. Mitchell, I'm her niece. It's already being talked about there? . . . Yes, yes, it's true." Opal said to the judge, "It's all over Washington." My aunt listened, then said, "She was desperate. The senator left her nothing." This time she listened even longer, then turned to the judge. "Who owns the house in Washington?"

The judge was pompous. "That property was not part of the estate. The senator has been paying rent for years. I got a bill just yesterday from something called the Medford Trust. I sent them six thousand from the estate and told them we give the house up."

Aunt Opal called in the phone, "Could you hear him? Yes, yes, are you sure? . . . I know your husband is the attorney general, and he doesn't make mistakes." Now she was laughing and crying at the same time. "I know, I love her, too . . . Oh, thank you! I'll have her call you when things calm down around here." She hung up and sat down on the steps and wiped her eyes on her apron. She had forgotten she had it on, and she rolled it in a knot and threw it up the steps, as though she would never wear an apron again.

The judge wasn't sure this wasn't all an act. "Was that really the attorney general's wife?"

"Oh yes, you will be getting a letter tomorrow."

It was all the explanation there was time for, for Aunt Almeda stood on the stair landing like an actress on a little stage. She had changed back into her riding outfit, rouged her cheeks, and carried her riding crop, which she snapped smartly against her palm.

"Well, well, Judge. How nice of you to come to see me off. I'm going into the asylum voluntarily, you know. I need a nice long rest." She strode down, clicking the heels of her boots. "Being the observer of humanity that I am, I am thoroughly convinced I am on the wrong side of the wall."

Mrs. Burton was holding up her veil and spraying an atomizer into her nose with the other hand. The judge stood behind the widow and patted her shoulder.

Almeda asked, "What's the matter with her?" She had forgotten to pull the pins that bound her hair. She did it now and fluffed it around her face as she walked back and forth like a bird on a wire. "I used to have asthma occasionally, when it served my purpose. One day the senator said to me, 'My dear one' — he always called me his dear one — 'I don't want you to have asthma anymore. It's all mental.' So of course I never did. Perhaps the lady would like to tell me the purpose of this visit."

The judge said, "It's hard for her to speak above a whisper."

"Then perhaps she would like to whisper what she wants, although I'm left with nothing but the outfit I'm standing in, and I am afraid neither of you could get into it."

The judge started again, "The senator's widow —"

Aunt Almeda cut him short. "I prefer to think of myself as the senator's widow."

Now he was getting mad. "You were never the senator's wife; you were nothing but his fancy woman!"

Almeda turned on her heels and cracked the whip against her boot. "I'm still pretty fancy. All right, she can be his widow in fact, I will be his widow in fancy." Almeda was staring at the woman in black, trying to see through her veil. "The senator always said to me, 'My dear, you have the kind of face that should never be veiled.'"

There was silence in the room except for the widow's breathing. Aunt

Almeda seemed to have suddenly run down as the woman in black slowly raised her heavy arms and lifted her veil. She pulled the covering back over her hat until it fell down her back and left her face exposed.

It was a ruin of a face, round and blank and seeming without structure; fold on fold of white flesh in a network of fine lines, only the watery gray eyes seeming alive. She had the same look that fat white hogs get in the last days, when it always seemed to me they knew butchering time was near. Her labored breath forced out words between wheezing. The black silk expanse of her ample chest rose and fell.

Aunt Almeda was not often at a loss for words, but now her arms fell limply to her sides, and she just stared. Mrs. Burton was whispering something, and Almeda found a little velvet bench and pulled it up and sat astraddle of it so she could hear. "They told—me—you—were—pretty, and—you—are. Even that would not have held August—all these years—you must be smart—too." She broke into a fit of coughing.

I could see Aunt Almeda's face. For a moment she looked as though she felt sorry for this woman, then she thrust out her sharp chin. She was going to have none of that. She wanted answers faster than the widow could respond. She snapped at the judge, "Why did you come here?"

"The senator's widow would like you to tell her how it was at the end. You owe her that. You usurped her place in the senator's life. She would like to know if, in his last moments, he thought of her."

Aunt Almeda stood up so quickly the bench almost fell over. "I'm sure he had barely given her a thought in years." Now she stared at the old woman with real hatred in her eyes. This was the woman who stood between her and marriage to the man she loved. But she did bend to listen to the whispered "His last words? You—were—there—when—August—died?"

My aunt began to stride back and forth, clicking her booted heels on the polished floors. "Of course I was there. I was always by his side."

Aunt Opal and I moved back into the dining room. We recognized an actress was about to take center stage for a calculated performance.

"Well, August called to me. He was lying there on the big black bearskin rug in front of the fire in the library, naked as a jaybird. I knew when he called me in that honeyed, gruff tone what was on his mind. I had heard it often enough. I was wearing this very riding outfit—of course, I dropped the skirt. 'Mead, sweetheart,' he said, 'you're a comely wench, and the river of lust is running through me.' He talked in poetry when he had the hots. He didn't have to draw me a picture, I could see for myself."

She grabbed the bench and straddled it as though it were the senator, lashing out with her riding crop, one side and then the other. "He was so horny, I must have worn out a dozen riding crops over the years." She was riding away now, bouncing up and down, and both the widow and the judge were staring open-mouthed. The widow forgot to wheeze.

"Tallyho! Tallyho! I would have blown a bugle if I had one." She slowed her motions and settled down on the stool. Her head dropped forward in fake melodrama. "I would have blown taps. That was the end of him. His life's juices just squirted right out of him."

She rose, then, all energized, held the whip above her head. "He went in a moment of exultation, with me in the saddle the way he always said he wanted to go. The only sound out of him was a moan of satisfaction." She held the crop under the widow's nose. "And not a last word for a vindictive wife."

Almeda turned her back to them and stood with her feet apart while the widow lowered her veil and slowly lumbered toward the door. The judge went out before her to clear the reporters away. Aunt Opal was staring at Aunt Almeda as though she didn't recognize her.

"Oh God! Wasn't I awful?"

Aunt Opal didn't hesitate. "Yes, you were."

Almeda turned quickly. The judge was just pulling the door shut. She ran quickly and yanked it open. Cameras flashed, and a dozen voices started yelling questions. They quieted when Aunt Almeda called, "Mrs. Burton . . . I forgot to tell you, his last words were for you. He was dictating a letter, proclaiming his love and devotion."

She closed the door and locked it against the intruding reporters. The energy that the interview had cost her had thinned her voice.

"He really died in his sleep, you know. I rolled over in the night and put my arm around him, and he was as cold and stiff as a stuck pig." She lay down on the couch and seemed to be asleep instantly.

Aunt Opal pulled Almeda's boots off and covered her with a blanket. She then sat down beside her and asked, "What is the Medford Trust Foundation?"

Almeda answered as though being called in a dream. "It's a dummy corporation set up to funnel political bribes."

"Who owns it?"

"It's in my name, but it's worthless. There haven't been any assets in it for years."

"You're wrong. The deed to the Washington house is in it, and six thousand a month for the last five years."

Aunt Almeda was jarred fully awake. She sat upright. "How do you know that?"

"The attorney general's wife told me just now. With the safe in your basement, you're rich."

It took a minute for it all to register. Aunt Almeda blinked the tears from her eyes and hugged Aunt Opal. "We're rich. Oh, he took care of me after all. He must have really loved me."

"You will take me to Washington?" Aunt Opal still did not seem sure of the sudden turn of events.

"Of course. You're the only one with any money to buy the tickets." Aunt Almeda was busy pulling her boots on again, thoughts of tiredness forgotten.

They were a closed circle, busy planning their escape on the four o'clock train. Grandfather and I sat at the dining room table and ate pie. I ate lemon, and he ate raisin. I never ate raisin. Too often raisins are full of little white worms, and once they're baked, you can't see them. Aunt Almeda came in to tell us good-bye.

Grandfather said, "I've been listening. I'll be sorry to see you go."

"I could take you with me."

"I remember I wanted to go with you when you went to Washington the first time, and you said, 'I'm not in the driver's seat.' "

"I am now; I have money."

He put his arms around his ample girth. "Are you sure you have enough to feed me? No, I'd better stay here, where I know my way to the kitchen."

She kissed him on his forehead, and then she kissed me. "Hughie, maybe your mother will let you come and see us next summer."

The only luggage Aunt Almeda had brought was the little trunk with her journals, and she gave that to me. She told me that maybe when I was grown, it would be the right time to expose those crooked politicians. This was a bad time, with the coming recession. She added, "Who am I to throw the first stone? It seems I have profited mightily from dishonest politics."

They got one of the reporters to drive them to the station in exchange for the story they would tell him. Grandfather wanted Aunt Opal to go and say good-bye to her mother, but she said she would write a letter from Washington just as soon as she had some stationery engraved.

Aunt Opal left her two cars way back in the corner of the carriage barn and never went near them again. Eventually my mother took the Nabisco flatbed truck and drove it out to the farm. But the little red sports car that had belonged to Alvin sat there, covered with an old canvas tent, for almost thirty years.

October 19, 1929

By the time the festival queen was crowned at two in the afternoon, there was no one who did not know about Aunt Almeda on the senator's horse. The gossip mills had been busy, and the story had grown to bizarre proportions via the people who were not witnesses. One version had the senator's widow taking a gun from her purse and shooting the nasty whore on the back of the horse. Another story went that the widow fainted dead away, and brazen Almeda Curtiss, as she was led away by the governor, stepped squarely on her stomach. By now, they said, Almeda was locked in the insane asylum and would remain there to her dying day.

Aunt Almeda had worn a veil to the train station, and no one knew the truth—that by this time, she was halfway to Washington. That wouldn't have made as good a story.

Each evening of the three-day festival, there was a ball. The first night was the Queen's Ball, and that was the big one and the most glamorous. The second night was the Princess's Ball, for the younger people, and Saturday night the festival closed with the Governor's Ball, which usually ended with a drunken brawl. An old apple-packing warehouse had been transformed into a ballroom, thanks to hundreds of yards of bunting and crepe paper and mirrored balls.

My mother had two tickets from Grandmother Curtiss, and she had invited Lester, but now she decided not to go. She said Aunt Almeda had blackened the Curtiss name until none of us could be seen in town again. Grandmother Curtiss called and said for that very reason, we had to put a bold face on and show up like rich bitches. She planned to be there on Grandfather Fancler's arm, wearing her ruby bib. She had never worn it before. It was a necklace that old General Curtiss had brought back as part of his war booty. She had it cleaned and polished and had a brown velvet gown made with a neckline designed to show off the jewels. Syrie Maugham came back for the festival and was escorted by Mr. Isaac.

The ball didn't start until nine o'clock, and my mother had changed her mind about going three times between an early dinner and time to dress. Her black velvet dress hung in the laundry room, where Mrs. Miller had steamed it for her. She had Grandmother's opera pearls in her safe. She had borrowed them so many times Grandmother had given up and said she could keep them.

The decision was out of her hands. Two of the Dutch ladies arrived in her room to unbraid her hair and brush and polish it into a more formal style for the evening. When it was all let loose, my mother had a great lot of hair. The Dutch ladies were expert at this sort of thing, and they knew the patterns of generations of hair braiders. They drew her hair back tightly except for a tendril, which they curled in front of each ear, and then braided a crown that sat elegantly on top of her head, six inches high. They filled it with coils and twists, each perfectly formed and pinned securely in place with every pin hidden.

My mother was afraid people would think she was trying to be the queen of the festival, and the ladies said, "Why not? You will be the most beautiful woman there!"

When my mother was ready to dress, Rose appeared not with the black velvet but a green watered-silk taffeta ball gown in the grand manner. She pushed it through the door, still on its dress form, and I heard my mother yell, "Oh, my God!" I ran over to see what it was. The three ladies were grinning like Cheshire cats, and my mother was walking around the dress, unable to believe it. The dark green silk gleamed like a wet laurel leaf, and there was a spiderweb over the bodice of black jet beads.

Rose volunteered, "We found a whole bolt of this silk in your attic." Erica added, "We took the jet beads from an old dress we found in a trunk."

"I'll feel like Cinderella at the ball."

"Then we will have to be the three wicked stepsisters," said Rose, still grinning.

"Oh, dear ladies, not wicked. You three are the sweetest stepsisters a girl ever had." My mother kissed each of them on the cheek. But she was looking at the cut of the bodice, which was very low, with no back at all. There was only a jet-fringed drape over each arm.

"What can I wear under it?"

They smiled. "Nothing. You have a perfectly good figure."

"Well, whatever I've got is going to show in this dress."

Rose said, "We have a saying in Holland that translates 'Them that's got 'em is glad, and them that ain't is mad.' You will be the envy of every woman there."

My mother dropped her robe, and they began dressing her. First a voluminous red taffeta petticoat to hold the full green skirt in place. Then they carefully lowered the gown over her head. When it was in place with the waist laced
and hooked, my mother swept over to the pier glass and looked at herself. She
turned and smoothed the tight waist and the bodice that barely covered her
breasts. "Ladies, it is beautiful!" She put her hand to her throat. "There is so
much of me exposed, what will I wear?"

Erica drew a green jewel on a gold chain from her pocket and held it to the
light. It was pear-shaped and as large as her thumb, and in its heart there seemed
to be a tiny red flame. "My father gave it to my mother when they married. It's
been in our family for a very long time. I don't know what it is; we always called
it a dragon's tear."

When it was clasped around my mother's neck and fell between her breasts,
she knew it was the perfect complement to the dress. As it warmed between her
breasts, the flame at its heart seemed to grow brighter.

The dress now needed the right shoes, even though you would probably
never see them. The ladies had dyed my mother's white satin pumps green and
sewed black jet beads around the edge.

Everyone in the house was assembled in the lower hall when my mother
swept down the stairs. Lester stood at the bottom in his tuxedo with a spray of
white orchids in his hand. "Well, you will certainly be the belle of the ball!"

Stanley had a new recording of Grace Moore singing "One Night of Love,"
and he put the needle down on it. I had never thought Lester was romantic or
charming, but he was that night. He was polished to a shine, barbered and
smelling of bay-rum astringent. He took my mother by the hand and swept her
the length of the hall to the rhythm of the waltz. There is a moment in the life
of every flower when it is at its zenith, the absolute peak of its perfection, and
I think this was my mother's moment. Everyone in the hall seemed to recognize
it, and they began to applaud. One by one, my mother whirled a circle with
each of them, even the two Forrester men, who were strangely graceful.

Mr. Miller was wearing what looked like a black chauffeur's cap and had polished our old limousine until it gleamed. One of the Miller boys went along to
open the door. When they were gone and the record was finished, we all stood
and looked at one another and wondered where the joy of the moment had
gone. We knew how the poor sister felt who didn't get to go to the ball. So we
did what most people do when they feel left out: we went into the kitchen and
ate. Tuba had made a very thick blackberry cobbler with a sweet crust, flavored

with black walnuts, and we drank cider that had a nip to it and was beginning to harden.

I went with Stanley back to his room and waited in his blue rocking chair while he showered. He came out smelling like Lifebuoy soap and dried himself slowly in front of the mirror. In the months since he had come, he had changed. I studied his body as he did. His waist was as small as ever, but his hips and thighs were fuller, and his chest looked softer, as though he was developing breasts. He reached down and pushed his cock between his legs until you couldn't see it at all, and he asked me, "Do you think I could look like a girl?"

"Why would you want to be a girl?"

"I want more than anything to look the way your mother did tonight. If I could look like that, and really learn to sing, I could go into opera and become rich and famous."

"You mean sing the women's parts?"

"I'm going to be seventeen my next birthday, and my voice hasn't changed. Since they cut my balls off, I don't think it's going to. I want to be a singer, and I'm a soprano, so I have to sing women's parts. If I could just get my cock cut off."

As he talked, he squeezed my cock and balls until I had an erection.

"If you get your cock cut off, what are you gonna pee through?"

"The same as women do. I'll have to sit down to do it."

"Will you let me fuck you?"

"Sure, when yours gets a little longer."

I thought I was doing pretty good. It seemed to be getting bigger since Stanley had sucked on it so much this summer.

"You can't be named Stanley if you're going to be a woman."

"No, I thought maybe — Stella."

The next morning I looked out the window at seven o'clock, and Lester's car was in our drive, so I figured he'd stayed all night. But when I went by my mother's room, the door was open and she was sleeping in the bed, and Lester wasn't there. She had put her green ball gown back on the dress form, and it stood like a beheaded queen in the corner.

Mr. Miller had already slopped the hogs and was back for his second cup of coffee. He'd had a short night, for he and his son had waited in the car until two o'clock, when my mother came out. Lester had stayed in town to find a place to jail all the extra drunks on the street. It had not been a total loss, as Mr. Miller had shot craps with some of the other drivers and won thirty-one dollars. He gave his boy ten dollars and let him sleep in. Mr. Miller was a good man.

At eleven Tuba made a waffle and some coffee and a glass of tomato juice with Tabasco in it, and I took the tray up to my mother. She was still lying crossways on the bed and was half awake. Rose was sitting on the floor, taking the pins and the braids out of my mother's hair.

My mother told us all about the ball. Her dress had been a sensation, thanks to the ladies. The man who manned the spotlight had singled her out over and over on the dance floor. Grandmother Curtiss had her share of attention. She and Grandfather Fancler had danced in a conga line, showing off what they had learned. I was really surprised to hear that two of my grandparents had been taking lessons together for the last month. I didn't understand what had happened to Grandfather Fancler, he had completely changed. I was sure it was somehow Mr. Isaac's fault.

There had been only one little problem that Mother knew of, and that was Aunt Lilly, who had shown up at the door with Eddie Horner. They had tickets, but black people did not go to white dances. Still, they were a strangely elegant couple. Aunt Lilly wore the Grecian gauze gown she had worn to pose in for her portrait, only she had dyed it a pale gold, almost the color of her hair, which was combed down loose to her waist. Eddie Horner had looked like a drawing in an Egyptian tomb when I saw him the first time at Grandmother's, and at the ball he looked even more so; my mother said he looked exactly like King Tut. He could not straighten his black hair, so he had shaved it all off, and his head was as polished as a piece of granite.

The committee at the door did not know quite how to handle it. Aunt Lilly had made the reservations in the name of the Honorable Abdul Kabal. The rope had not been lowered for them to enter when my mother and Lester glided up. Aunt Lilly called, "Hello, darling! Sheriff Adams, you remember the ambassador from Egypt?" Lester had had two drinks, which made him colorblind for the moment, and he shook Eddie's hand and unhooked the barring rope, and Eddie and Aunt Lilly glided into the spotlight.

Rose didn't want to hear about that. "Tell us about you. Did everyone tell you how beautiful you were?"

My mother sat up and drank her coffee. "I had the strangest feeling, like this was my last dance, my last season to be beautiful. I can get old now."

Rose lathered egg whites into Mother's hair. "That's silly. You will be beautiful every day of your life, if you live to a hundred." My mother patted her on the cheek and went to stand under the shower.

The last night of the festival, the whole town seemed to be one big glorious drunk. Grandmother told us later how the princesses were running up and down her steps in their teddies and the boys from West Point were chasing them, and someone had gotten sick and vomited down over the balcony onto the arrangement of white lilies in the hall.

People sat on the curbs and sang. There were two houses set on fire and two false alarms. Lester arrested so many people, he had ten in each cell where there were only beds for four, and they all got in fights. Aunt Sebe got off work at ten-thirty and left Sylvia Tingler to hold down the fort, so she could go with Worthy and Harry to pull down as much of the decorative fabrics as they could. Most of the customers at the Dew-Drop Inn were drinkers, not eaters, anyway. By midnight, there were only five men left in the bar, and Sylvia said, "Time to close up."

One of the men said, "You wrong, honey." He went and locked the door. "Time to open up. Me and my buddies want a good fuck."

Sylvia said, "No!" But it didn't do her any good. She couldn't get to the door before they caught her and began tearing her clothes off. They threw her on the floor, and each held an arm and a leg while the fifth one climbed on her. They took turns until they all came at least once, some twice. When she screamed, they slapped her across the mouth, and when she said she would tell the sheriff, they told her if she did, the Klan would tar and feather her. They hit her fat breasts and blackened her eyes. Her teeth were loosened, and her mouth was so swollen she could no longer speak.

Birdie Bender was the last, and he couldn't keep his erection up, and he screamed, "You call yourself a whore? My eight-year-old Mary can do betterin' that." And he kicked her in the side.

She gave up and lay quiet, and the men thought she was dead. They pulled on their pants, turned off the lights, and went out, leaving her lying there, silent and cold on the floor.

It was morning before she could crawl over to the counter and drag herself to her feet. She found a pint of moonshine whiskey and drank most of it. She was on the floor behind the counter when Aunt Sebe came in about ten o'clock to clean up. Since it was Sunday, they would not be open for business, and it was dark before she could revive Sylvia enough to wrap her in old tablecloths and take her home, pulling her in Harry's wagon by way of the alleys.

OCTOBER 20, 1929

MY GRANDMOTHER CURTISS had left the brochures about my mother's horses on her library tables, and the father of one of the princesses came out to our farm to see them. At the festival, each of the princesses had had a mother or father, sometimes both, to chaperon her and stand by the aisle and say "That's my daughter" as they came down the hill in their velvet gowns to surround the queen. Ernestine Benson's father accompanied her. Grandmother said from the look of Ernestine, her mother was probably too ugly to be let out of their house. She must have been very rich for Mr. Benson to have married her. He wasn't bad-looking, a little too fat, maybe, and he chewed tobacco and spit indiscriminately everywhere. Alex had found him a spittoon, but he didn't always hit it.

Alex drove him out to our farm on Sunday morning after the festival. There was something about the way he got out of the car and looked around, as though he was going to spit on us all. He announced that he had come out to have a look at our horseflesh, and if he liked what he saw, and the price was right, he just might buy one, maybe two or three. My mother extended her hand and introduced herself, and when he said he preferred to deal with the trainer, who might be a little more apt to tell him what the flaws were, she withdrew her hand and rested it on the pistol she was wearing from target practice. She took the smile from her face and told him she trained her own horses with the help of her cousin. She led him down to the paddock, where Stanley was up on Fanny. He was practicing forward and backward and side steps to a humming sound he was making.

Mr. Benson leaned against the rail and spit out a stream of tobacco juice and said, "She's good-lookin', damn good-lookin'."

"Fanny is one of the smartest two-year-olds I have ever bred."

"I don't mean the horse, I mean that little gal that's ridin' her."

My mother looked up at Stanley; you could make that mistake. His bright copper hair had dried and was blowing loosely around his face. He wore a blue scarf that was hiding the fact his Adam's apple didn't show.

"That's my cousin Stanley—he's a boy."

"Well, I'd take bets he won't ever turn into a man."

"He's only fourteen."

"I'd sure put him up against that daughter of mine, ugly as a mud fence."

"I met Ernestine. She was—quite mannerly."

"Did you know them crooks charged me five hundred dollars to be in the hillbilly circus?"

"The princesses each paid five hundred dollars. It defrays expenses."

"I thought they had seen her picture."

"I do hope you don't say that sort of thing in front of your daughter."

"My daughter can look in the mirror, she knows very well I'm going to have to pay some man to marry her. I didn't come out here to talk about my daughter. I came to buy a horse. Let's see that filly run."

"I'm afraid there has been a misunderstanding, Mr. Benson, my horses are trained for dressage."

"That's sissy business. Tell that nellie kid to put the whip to her, and let's see what that filly can do. I got to build a new stable of racers. I put mine all up in claiming races last month and sold them while I could. The way the market's goin', there won't be enough money in the country in a month to buy a mule."

"I'm sorry, I have just decided not to sell Fanny. I'm withdrawing her from the market." She called to Stanley to put Fanny out in the meadow and saddle Trojan.

Mr. Benson splattered a mouthful of tobacco spit against the white railing. "I'm not interested in some Trojan horse. I know that game, lady. You're trying to bargain me up in price."

"I haven't started training Trojan yet. He has good Arabian bloodlines and is a bargain at one hundred thousand."

"Lady, I didn't just fall off the turnip truck. I'll give you twenty-five thousand for the filly without even seeing her run." He smiled a sly smile and winked. There was tobacco juice in the corners of his mouth. "I might even make you a price for the pretty boy to go along as a trainer."

"Mr. Benson, would you please leave?"

"Come on, lady. There ain't that much money floatin' around these days that you can get on your high horse."

"Mr. Benson, I'm the champion shot of West Virginia. Don't make me prove it."

"You gonna do my old lady a favor and shoot me?"

"I daresay she might send me the hundred thousand and I could keep my horse."

He stared at her, and she didn't flinch. She had that half smile around her lips, and I thought maybe she really was going to shoot him. But he said he was wastin' his time, and if he could find that kraut driver, he'd get on his way back to Pittsburgh. My mother said she thought that was a very good idea.

After he was gone, Stanley came over to the fence and said he had heard what the man said.

"He's an idiot."

"No, he's right, you know. I'm never going to grow up to look like a man."

"If Mr. Benson is an example of manhood, then I hope you don't. You're just going to be a beautiful man, that's all."

I knew something she didn't, but it wasn't my secret to tell. Not many men are named Stella.

Mr. Benson took a crying Ernestine, who did not want to go, and started back to Pittsburgh by the noon train. To make up for him, Grandmother Curtiss brought another potential horse buyer, a friend of Syrie Maugham, out to our farm in the afternoon. It looked like a parade coming up our drive. Alex was driving Grandmother's limo in front, the middle car was a long black one with two uniformed men in the front seat, and bringing up the rear was a small closed truck pulling an elegant white horse trailer.

My mother had just climbed up an apple tree to shake down the last of the russets. When she saw how polished Grandmother and Mrs. Maugham and the new woman, a tall blonde about twenty, were, she began tucking in her shirttail and picking the leaves out of her hair.

I ran to Grandmother, and she bent down and gave me one of those kisses on the forehead that don't really touch you; she had practiced since she started painting her lips. She whispered, "Be a good boy. This lady is the richest woman in the world."

I took a good look at our guest. She certainly didn't look rich. She looked like she didn't get enough to eat. Her gray dress was silk but plain, a shirt and a pleated skirt like a schoolgirl's. She had on only one little piece of jewelry, a small gold pin on her lapel. My mother, standing there with a brown leaf in her hair and holding a basket of apples, was richer-looking by far.

Grandmother said, "Billy my dear, may I present Miss Doris Duke."

My mother held out her free hand. "If I had known you were coming—"

Mrs. Maugham chattered, "I told Virginia not to call. So many people, when they know Doris is coming, think they have to roll out the red carpet."

Miss Duke had a nice voice. "Syrie told me about your beautiful horses, and I had to come."

My mother shook the lady's hand. "I'm fresh out of red carpets, but I would have gotten down out of the apple tree a little sooner."

Miss Duke said, "If I could look like that climbing an apple tree, I would climb every tree in your orchard. May I?" She took an apple and bit into it. The juice ran down her chin. It was not a particularly pretty chin, too sharp, but a nice gesture.

Between them, they explained that Doris Duke was on her way to Winterwood, Virginia, to buy a dressage horse, when she stopped by to visit her friend Syrie at Grandmother's house. Syrie had told her about our beautiful pink horse, and so here they were.

The two men in the big black car drove it back to our gate and parked it across our drive so no one could get out or in. I found out later that they were bodyguards to keep anyone from kidnapping Miss Duke.

My mother took the women up to the brick porch and told me to go and tell Stanley to saddle Fanny and bring her to the flowered circle. I went down to the paddock, where Stanley and the two Forrester men were working on Trojan. Trojan was the biggest horse on our farm, sixteen and a half hands high and at least two thousand pounds. He was out of a white Morgan mare, sired by Grandfather's big Arabian stallion, Black. But Trojan was a throwback, a recessive gene from somewhere, and he looked like the ancient Greek horses carved on the Parthenon. He was a dappled gray with a heavy coat, heavier still now with winter coming, and long feathery hair on the backs of his great legs. But it was the head on that heavy, arched neck that set him apart. His profile was straight, and his big black eyes were set high in his head. Grandfather had named him and given Stanley the pictures of the marble bas-reliefs. Stanley had cut his mane into a brush to match the carvings.

They were all brushing vigorously with the currycombs, but Trojan was never going to have the kind of mirror polish that Fanny had. He had gotten so big that his cinch had to be pieced to go around him, and all his tack was tight. The thing that was going to defeat Trojan was not his size; it was his personality. He was a joker. In the meadow, he could jump raising all four feet at once, two feet in the air. When you went to bridle him, Trojan would run to you as though to knock you down, then stop a foot in front of you to look you in the face with his big black eyes and whinny. If you turned away, he would nudge you in the seat of your pants and lift you off your feet. Nevertheless, Stanley was pushing his training, and we all knew why. He wanted Trojan to be the next horse sold, not Fanny.

When I told Stanley the prospective buyer was the richest woman in the world, Stanley said, "Then she probably has a whole barn full of horses. Why does she need Fanny?"

"She may not need Fanny, but we need the money."

Reluctantly he said, "All right." He yelled at the Forresters to saddle Fanny while he got on a clean shirt. He didn't put on his orange or his pink shirt; he wore white with a thin black necktie. I think he was planning to go into mourning if Fanny sold.

Boobie had gone to church with her family, so I got the phonograph cart, and Stanley gave me a Strauss waltz. The ladies were having tea from our best silver service, and Mrs. Miller had quickly changed into a black uniform with a starched white apron. It was apparent we were putting our best foot forward. I put the needle down on the record, and Stanley swept Fanny into the circle just as the sun broke through the morning mist. Even God was cooperating to put on a good show, and Stanley on Fanny certainly did.

They came forward and did a piaffe, marking time in place, and bowed. Miss Duke extended her hand and bowed her head as though accepting an invitation to dance, and the waltz began.

Even I knew that if Doris Duke wanted to buy, it was bad business to seem so pleased. My mother was watching her closely, and I am sure she was adjusting the price upward. Miss Duke whispered to my mother, "She's beautiful, and so is the rider—that is a boy?"

"Yes, he is my cousin. He's fourteen."

"Who trained him? I spent a year in a Spanish riding school, learning to shift my center of gravity for those turns and pivots; he does it effortlessly."

"He's a natural. I'm his trainer."

"I wish I had known about you. I thought this business was completely in the hands of men."

My mother wanted to keep the attention on the horse. "Fanny is three-quarters Arabian and one-quarter Appaloosa."

"You know, there was a famous Arabian who looked like that, that pink splashed down over the shoulders. Lord Oxford brought him into England and gave him the horrible name of Blood Shoulders."

"I've never seen a picture."

"Oh, that was seventeen seventeen. But he is in a famous portrait."

If Doris Duke was playing one-upmanship, she seemed awfully guileless. My mother wasn't sure. "You know more about bloodlines than I do. You must own several horses now."

"Yes, I have six Arabians, each of whom is a direct descendant of one of the first six stallions imported by Archduke Charles."

"With such a stable, why are you looking at Fanny?"

Miss Duke's eyes never left Fanny and Stanley. "Those are my stable: a commodity, the kinds of things you buy when you have access to unlimited money, like paintings and houses. But I want a horse who responds to my heart and I to hers, the way Fanny does to your cousin. Do you think she could learn to love me like that?"

The music was moving to the last full measure, and horse and rider danced. A swing to the right, and then the left, and then a final extension toward us, her neck extended, his face forward, pressed against her. It was the final dip, and the quick kiss when the lips barely brush each other, and Stanley slid to the ground. I heard him whisper, "You were wonderful."

Doris Duke heard him, too, and came forward quickly. "You were both wonderful." She hugged Stanley around the shoulder with one arm and, with the other, caressed Fanny. "Do you have a lump of sugar for her?" Stanley brought it out from his pocket, and Miss Duke said, "May I?" She took it and held it up to Fanny's muzzle. Fanny hesitated at the strange scent only a moment, then licked the woman's hand.

"She's the most wonderful horse in the world. Are you going to buy her?" Stanley asked.

"You don't want me to, do you?"

Stanley looked at my mother and knew what he had to say. "We are in the business of training and selling horses."

"Could I get up just a minute, please?"

Stanley went to cup his hand to help her mount, but she pulled her full skirt up over her knees, put her foot in the stirrup, and swung aboard easily. I put the needle down on the record. She rode around the circle twice, with Stanley standing in the middle. Miss Duke tried the slight shifting of weight that is called ballasting, the only signal you can see in dressage, and Fanny shifted the weight of her body to compensate so she was free to dance right or left as her rider asked. It was asked, not commanded, a gentle nudge from the ankle, a pressure from the thigh. Miss Duke moved her up to Stanley and dropped the reins in his hands and slid easily to the ground.

"Someone is going to buy this darling animal. Wouldn't you rather it would be someone who would love her? You do see that I will, don't you?"

I am sure Stanley could not help but compare her to that bastard from Pittsburgh. "Yes," he said. I saw him blinking his eyes to keep from crying. "I have to go rub her down now." He led her away quickly.

When she came back to the porch, Grandmother said to Mrs. Maugham, "Let's leave the horse traders to their business and let me show you the attic. You won't believe what is going on up there. Billy has three Dutch gnomes she keeps up there who weave the most beautiful things with wool they dye themselves." They went.

Miss Duke sat at the table with my mother and took a checkbook from her purse. "You will let me buy Fanny?"

"She is for sale."

Miss Duke was writing, and she handed the check to my mother. I looked over her shoulder. I wasn't sure what that many zeros meant, but I could read one hundred thousand dollars.

My mother looked at it, and her voice was thin. I knew the hundred-thousand-dollar horse sale in her brochure was for all four horses.

"Help yourself to tea, please, and I will just run and get the bill of sale."

She hurried out, but it was to catch up with Mrs. Maugham on the stairs and show her the check. "Is she of age? Can she write checks in this amount?"

"My dear, she can write a check for a million if she wants to."

When my mother came back to the porch, she had the papers for the transfer, but she stood at the table and looked at Miss Duke, who was eating a watercress sandwich.

"Miss Duke, there is something I must tell you. That flyer of mine you see, the price of one hundred thousand was not for just one horse."

"But Fanny was the prize, right? Mrs. Curtiss, I believe in paying what a thing is worth, but if it will make you feel any better, throw something else in on the deal."

"What?"

"Stanley."

My mother couldn't believe what she had just heard, and her faint voice showed it. "You want to buy Stanley?"

Miss Duke was pouring more tea. "No, no, I just want to rent him for a week. I want him to go with Fanny and help ease her into her new surroundings, and I thought if he saw where she is going to live, he might not be so brokenhearted."

My mother sat down. "You know, I have read a lot of things about you. Jealous, mean, nasty things; all lies, I'm sure now."

"Being called the richest girl in the world is like living in a glass house, and everybody has a license to throw rocks. That's why animals are so wonderful. They learn to love you, and they've never heard of your bank balance. I think I can earn Fanny's love."

My mother filled in the bill of sale. "Let me go and talk to Stanley. I think he will want to go, but he may be afraid. He's never really been out of this county."

All at once *I* was afraid. What if Stanley liked all those rich people and never came back? Who would put their arms around me and rock me in the blue chair?

My mother got down a good Gladstone bag and showed Stanley how to pack. He had a very good wardrobe of all the clothes my father had left behind and indulgences of Uncle Alvin's that Grandmother Curtiss had given him and the Dutch ladies had altered to fit. Stanley took his French book to study on the way and got in the back of a limousine with the "richest girl in the world," and he was gone.

OCTOBER 21, 1929

ON MONDAY I HAD to get on the bus by myself, and since there was no one to tell on me, I skipped school and went up to Grandfather Fancler's house.

I still had my visits with him, but I didn't like them as well because the emphasis was no longer just on me. Often Mr. Isaac was with us. I walked between them, each holding a hand, and often they jumped me over ditches and rocks. It should have been like having two grandfathers, but they spoke now in areas that were over my head, and they seemed to have as much interest in each other as they did in me.

We were living in one of the backwashes of the world, but they somehow seemed unaware, constantly probing what was going on at the center of our government. They read all the news, and my aunt Russie, in Washington, sent Grandfather pounds and pounds of pamphlets from the U.S. Printing Office. Her husband, my uncle Ryan, was president of the Railway Express in Washington, and she could ship things for nothing. Grandfather got a daily account of what was said in Congress, and these two old men were of an opinion that the world was fast going to hell in a wheelbarrow.

The only thing they were not so sure of was whether Herbert Hoover was riding or pushing. They were afraid that this time the industrial complex, which had always manipulated the economy to its own benefit, would not be able to get it back on track. They thought our national house was on fire, and those who always let it burn just enough to collect the insurance had gone too far. Was Herbert Hoover a fireman, was he the man caught with the can of kerosene in his hands, or was he just a dumb fat pig, bought and paid for and about to get roasted? I didn't understand all that, but I remembered it.

We sat on top of a hill in a warm autumn breeze, the last reprise from winter, and looked out over the hazy hills. People in the town were burning leaves in the streets, and spirals of smoke dotted the landscape. Most of the leaves were on the ground by now, except for the oak, whose leaves just turned brown and hung on until spring, when the new buds pushed them off. We sat under an apple tree of Winter Nellies. If you rustled around in the leaves under the tree, you could find the hard, round, rust-colored globes, and the three of us bit into them. They wouldn't really be soft until around Christmas, but the bittersweet juice took the place of a drink of water, as the hillside springs were dry.

As we sat, Mr. Isaac told us something I hadn't known. He had a daughter, and she was studying music in Heidelberg, Germany. He had written, urging her to come to New York and study at Juilliard, as he had an old friend who taught there. He feared from the tone of *Mein Kampf* that Germany would soon be unsafe for Jews. He had in his jacket pocket the last letter he had gotten from her. It looked like he had read it and refolded it many times, but he read it to us again. She was refusing every suggestion he had made. She was going to marry a German man and live in Munich. She said her father was wrong about his analysis of the Third Reich. After all, he was a Jew in the United States and could not help but have a biased viewpoint, whereas she was in the very center, about to marry a man who was one of the prime movers. It would not do to align yourself with people who were sucking the lifeblood from the German culture, and henceforth she was not Jewish and she had no father.

He folded the paper slowly and put it back in his pocket. The tears were creeping down his cheeks. "She was my only child."

I wondered how many times he would read it and refold it before it fell apart.

Aunt Lilly had been gone since the night of the festival ball. She said she was going to Washington to help Eddie Horner find a studio because he had no future in this little one-horse town. Grandfather had called Aunt Russie to see if Aunt Lilly was staying with her, but she had not seen her. My aunt Russie was one of the Daughters of the American Revolution who, ten years later, kept Marian Anderson from singing in Constitution Hall, so she sang instead from the steps of the Lincoln Memorial to hundreds of thousands. So Grandfather didn't really think it likely that Aunt Lilly would show up at her sister's with a black painter with his head shaved, even if he was the son of the Egyptian ambassador; obviously his mother had been a nigger. His family must have been pretty black, too, for there was an article in the Washington *Herald* about a movie theater in Washington that had turned the Egyptian ambassador away because they thought he was a Negro. President Hoover apologized to the ambassador.

GRANDFATHER COULDN'T FIND any dishes for our lunch. They were all dirty in the sink, and he had used up all the paper plates. He refused to wash dishes and had not yet found a woman to come in and do them. Mr. Isaac stacked them on the draining board, filled the sink with hot suds, and began. He said he didn't mind, it was a chance to get some of the dirt off his hands where he had been staining old furniture. I stood on a stool and dried. Grandfather liked to cook, so he sliced tomatoes and made ham and scrambled eggs.

While we ate, I told them about Stanley going away with Doris Duke. My grandfather put his fork down and laughed. I didn't see anything funny, but Grandfather said it was one of life's little jokes. Here was a boy who last year was living in a miserable orphanage where they made him fire the furnace instead of going to school and then threatened to throw him out on the street. And now here he was, a new name, a new life, and off to spend a week in a sixty-room mansion with the richest girl in the world.

"Hughie, don't you see what that says? Anything is possible. The most impossible dream can come true!"

"My mother helped him. It wasn't just luck."

"But that's what luck is all about, finding the right fairy godmother."

"Can I tell you something about Stanley?"

"Is it a secret?"

"Well, sort of, only he didn't swear me. No, it's just—I think he needs another fairy godmother. My mother can't do this."

"All right, Hughie. As long as it's true and does not harm."

"Stanley wants to get his dick cut off and be a woman who sings in the opera."

The two older men exchanged looks. Mr. Isaac didn't ask what was wrong with Stanley's dick, but he did say, "Can he sing?"

"Yes, he sings with phonograph records, and he sounds like Lily Pons and Grace Moore."

Mr. Isaac had a second cup of coffee and thought about it.

Grandfather said, "I suppose that operation those bastards gave him has kept his voice from changing."

Mr. Isaac said, "That takes a great deal of study, and he would have to go somewhere like Juilliard."

Then Grandfather said, "He would need a fairy godmother for that."

Mr. Isaac cleared the table and answered, "Or a godfather." He was a good cleaner-upper and wiped the table and put everything away. Grandfather had said he didn't mind cooking, but he hated to clean up. "You and I make a good pair. We ought to get married."

Mr. Isaac laughed and said, "You have only to ask."

I laughed, too, but the way they looked at each other, I didn't think it was a joke.

My mother gave me five smacks with a board for each day I skipped school. I could take five but not twenty-five, so I went to school the rest of the week. I missed Stanley on the bus because Bob Marsteller acted up and kept everybody in an uproar. I had decided if Stanley didn't come back by Saturday, I would take the money out of my boot and buy a bus ticket and go and find him.

Tuba was beginning to act funny, and I thought it wouldn't be long until she had to go over to Weston. She had always gone around complaining under her breath, half the time about me, but now she said it out loud as she swept the kitchen for the third time in an hour.

"We got too many nigger trash round here. I jes' don't understan' why Miz Billy don't throw them all out in the road."

I reminded her if she threw out the Millers, they would take Handsome with them, and then she was as close to panic as I had ever seen.

"They ken't do that. He's my gran'son. I'll call the sheriff. Ever'body knows that little baby's mine."

"Well, you better be nice to his mama if you want to keep him."

"Hughie, you're a bad boy, jes' like your daddy."

My mother was in her room braiding her hair. When I told her, she said most people get a little strange as they get older. Nobody knew how old Tuba really was. Sometimes, when she was throwing it up to me that my great-grandfather had killed Abraham Lincoln, she acted like she was there, but everyone knew niggers were not allowed to go to the theater. My mother said they were lucky. "They were probably the only ones in Washington that night who didn't get blamed for the murder."

I reminded her that Grandfather Fancler was old and he wasn't acting funny. My mother did not agree, she thought he was acting very funny. "Buying a new tuxedo at seventy-seven and going to dances with your grandmother Curtiss, no less. Speaking of funny—look what all that money has done to your grandmother, the way she flaunts all that jewelry."

"She gave you a pearl necklace. You're just mad because she didn't give you her ruby choker."

She was pinning her braids in place, and her hands moved quicker. "Well, it would look better on me than it does on her." She rammed a big hairpin in her scalp and yelled, "Ouch!"

I got over by her door and sang one of those nonsense rope-jumping songs:

> Little jealous Mary
> In a jealous snit,
> Gonna shit her pants
> And fall right-in-it!

She threw her hairbrush at me, as I ran.

For the last month Mr. Miller had done less and less of the routine chores around the farm. He was trying to make sure everything could run smoothly without him when the time came for him to leave for Detroit. The Miller boys had been teaching the two Forresters how to care for the cows and the milking machines and the churns, so when their father found a job and a house in Detroit, they could go and start high school. They had been coached an hour a night all summer by Miss Larkin, and she thought they were in pretty good shape. The Forrester men were something quite different. They sat in the back of the room and listened, but they didn't seem to have absorbed much. They couldn't remember the alphabet from day to day, even enough to spell their own names. It turned out they, too, were twins. Not identical like the Thorne boys, but they were both born at the same time.

They said there were so many legs and arms all trying to come out that each had the cord of the other tangled around his neck. They didn't breathe for a long time, and they turned blue and a part of their brains died. It was that part where the alphabet is learned, but the part about numbers they knew as well as an adding machine. They could add and divide and multiply faster than you could on paper. Miss Larkin said there was a name for that kind of a brain, but she couldn't remember what it was.

The two older Thorne boys worked part-time here and part-time on their own farm, and when the Millers left, they would work full-time here. They had taken some of the money they earned and ordered new clothes for their mother from Sears & Roebuck. She walked by here on Sunday on her way to church, and she didn't look bad. I guess that was because she hadn't been beaten up for a while. The Forrester men would wait for her, and the three of them walked together.

When Mr. Miller told Mrs. Miller he was planning to leave by the end of the month, she put together a whole list of reasons why he shouldn't go. His best answer was "We have intelligent children. Do you want them to grow up with no education at all? Raymond wants to be a veterinarian, and Donald wants to go into law. And Handsome can probably put the world in his pocket." He did not mention Boobie's ambition, for no one knew what she really wanted beyond getting on the school bus Monday morning with white kids. "They got to have an education."

Mrs. Miller had one condition, and then she would let him go. He was not baptized, and she wanted him safe in the arms of the Lord in case something horrible happened to him in Detroit and she wouldn't be able to meet him in heaven. He agreed.

Mrs. Miller called the preacher at the black Baptist church in town and arranged for Mr. Miller to be baptized next Sunday. The black church did not have a little metal tub in the floor after you pushed the altar over, like the white churches did; they just took their people down to the river that ran right in front of the church and waded out to where it was deep enough and ducked them under. Mrs. Miller said she thought since it was the twentieth of October next Sunday, the river might be too cold, and she would settle for just a little sprinkle on the head the way the Catholics did it. After all, it was the talk that let the Lord in.

But the preacher said they were Baptists, they got their name from baptizing, that meant total immersion, and hot or cold, if she wanted Mr. Miller's sins washed away, he would have to be dunked under. She agreed reluctantly.

The intake for the pumping station that filled the town reservoir was just below the Baptist church. I always wondered how many of those sins that washed off the blacks and came out in all those white people's faucets had found a new home.

While Stanley was gone, it seemed a good time to go and snoop through his room. I didn't find anything I didn't know about already, except a box of clippings under his bed that he had cut from old magazines my mother threw away. They were all pictures of women, not undressed, the way the pictures that Lloyd had were, but with every kind of clothes: hats and scarves and coats. He had written things along the side: "This would look better green" or "I could wear this hat or belt or scarf." Advice about makeup and how to bleach freckles. All women talk. I believed Stanley really was planning to be a girl. He was certainly studying the directions.

I put it all carefully back in the box and was getting ready to leave when I heard someone in the tack room. I peeked down the stair opening and saw my mother filling the coffeepot and putting it on the electric burner. She came here often to bring her books up to date and to think. There was no escape for me now, so I figured I might as well take a nap. I climbed into Stanley's bed.

The sound of the outside barn door closing shook me awake, and when I heard Mr. Miller knock on the tack room and ask, "May I come in?," I moved over to lie on the orange carpet and listen at the stair opening.

"I just made some coffee, would you like a cup?"

"Yes, please. I just had a letter from my brother."

"How do things look in Detroit?"

"I don't really know, he didn't answer any of my questions. He just says come as soon as you can and bring your truck, I need you. I never said I had a truck, and he doesn't say what he needs it for."

"If you need a truck, my sister-in-law left one here, as you know."

"I can't take anything else from you."

"The man who gave it to her stole it from the Nabisco people, so there is a risk there, although she repainted it."

"I have learned a certain amount of risk taking from you. Among your other gifts, I prize that most."

"Mr. Miller, I lie awake and think, What did I do to that man? I've turned him into a murderer."

"Mrs. Curtiss, do you realize what you did for me? When you gave me that gun and taught me how to use it, you gave me the first power I ever had in my life. I grew up where, if a white man slapped you, you turned your face and let him hit you again. We had to stand and watch our wives or daughters be raped, and we couldn't do anything. Move away, maybe; keep moving. When you took me and my family in, this was the first safe place we have ever been."

"Mr. Miller, why don't you stay?"

"You have also shown my children what is possible, what an education might do for them, and they can't get it here."

"Mr. Miller, do you believe in hell?"

"I did in Alabama and when we moved to Tennessee, but not here. I started to when the Klan found our house, but then you arrived."

"I think of murdering Red Thorne."

"Mrs. Curtiss, you didn't murder Red Thorne. We together killed a mad dog, that's all. There are a lot of mad dogs out there. Nobody else had guts enough to do anything about it. We could make a list. We could pick off the Klan one by one and that bastard who runs the orphans' home."

"In a Gilbert and Sullivan opera, a character sings, 'I've got a little list of folks who won't be missed.' Judge Brown does come to mind."

"Shall I take care of him for you before I leave? A sort of thank-you!"

"Have another cup of coffee, Mr. Miller. I'll grant you it should be done, but I couldn't take care of all their dependents."

"Do you have to?"

"I feel obligated to take care of the Thornes, and I just can't look out for the whole world."

"I haven't had a chance to meet any other women like you in all my life. You're a caretaker, but I can't let you take care of mine anymore. I'll send for them as soon as I can."

"I will miss you, Mr. Miller. I can't tell you how reassuring it has been to have you here."

I peeked down the stairs and saw her reach out and touch his hand. He stood up so quickly that he upset his coffee cup.

"I better go. I have to be sure the Forrester men know how to handle the electric generators."

She followed him to the door. "Next year they are going to run the electric through here, and I won't need the generators. Things get simpler all the time, they really do, Mr. Miller."

And he was gone.

I watched her go out to the barn and into the stall with Hannah. She took down the curry brushes and began rubbing her down and singing softly. I used to call it the "Whata" song when I was small and she was still rocking me.

"What will I do when I am all alone and missing you, what'll I do?"

OCTOBER 26, 1929

SOMEWHERE IN TROJAN'S racial memory was a racehorse, and the genes of that horse now shaped his behavior. Unfortunately, those same genes had not shaped him physically. That great stature, with his strong legs and big feet, would be just right to carry a knight in full armor into battle, but it would never win the day at Lexington. They didn't deal with misfit clowns; they would have been too embarrassed to have this clod win over all their sleek and delicate steeds.

Daily, sometimes two or three times, he would race around and around the perimeter of the meadow until his dappled gray coat foamed with sweat. Then he would come to the barn to be rubbed down and blanketed as a proper race-horse should, so he wouldn't chill.

The other horses would gather and watch him from the middle of the meadow so they wouldn't get run down. A few times Black ran beside him and even reached out and nipped him on the neck. But Trojan quickly outran him by half the length of the meadow. Black gave up and joined the group of onlookers.

One day my mother and grandfather sat on the top rail with a stopwatch and timed Trojan two laps around the meadow. They judged the meadow to be a half mile around, so Trojan was running a two-and-a-half-minute mile. Grand-father pointed out this was bareback, and the weight of a rider would pull him down considerably, but my mother said, "Training might bring him back up again."

"Billy, he's a misfit. Look at him. Even if he could run the mile in a minute and a half, what would you do with him?"

"I might just get up on him and run away."

"Of all my daughters, I thought you were the girl who had caught the golden apple."

"Dad, it's just not as sweet as I thought it would be."

Stanley came home on Saturday night. He came in on the six o'clock train that had its connection in Pittsburgh. He did not call out to our farm for a ride home; he took a taxi, the first one in his life. In his week away he had experienced a great many firsts, and he seemed to have taken a big step over that bridge from childhood toward being an adult. He was full of smiles and so wound up he hardly knew where to begin. Only twenty-four hours before, he had been in New York City, sitting with the richest woman in the world, listening to Lily Pons sing and he had the program to prove it. Not only that but Miss Duke had taken him backstage, and he had Lily Pons's autograph on his program and a glossy picture of her. He had pictures of himself with Doris Duke and several other celebrated people, including a Russian grand duchess. He had pictures of Fanny in her new mahogany and brass horse barn, which looked more like a fairy-tale palace. She even had a large window where she could look at the meadows when it was too bad to go out. Music was piped in, and her private handler was a very nice German woman. Doris Duke had been up on Fanny all week, and Fanny seemed to like her. For Stanley, the hurt of parting was still there, for when he talked of Fanny, he turned his face away so we wouldn't see him wipe away a tear.

The Duke house had sixty-four rooms, at least twenty in help, plus guards everywhere. Stanley went on and on. The Miller boys finally walked away mumbling that they would probably never get out of this town. Boobie stayed close and listened to every word. He had brought her a red velvet bonnet with a plume on it. She put it right on and moved over to the mirror. He brought Handsome a pair of patent-leather shoes with taps on them. He brought me a Swiss knife with sixteen blades. My mother got a long green silk chiffon scarf exactly the color of her ball gown. She was surprised that Stanley could carry that color of green in his mind so well. For everyone else, he brought a ten-pound box of chocolate-covered macadamia nuts from Miss Duke's ranch in Hawaii. He could afford gifts, as Miss Duke had paid him five hundred dollars for the week, taken him into New York on Friday evening, given him a choice of entertainment, and put him on the train home at midnight. She had left him with the promise of a visit to see Fanny next summer.

He'd had an hour between trains in Pittsburgh, so he walked around and looked at the downtown. He had wished for nerve enough to get on a street-car but hadn't been brave enough for that.

By the time he ate his supper, it was nine o'clock, and he was almost asleep in his chair. As he got up to go, my mother asked, "What's the most important thing you learned this week?"

Stanley didn't have to think about it. "When I watched Lily Pons come out on that stage and the orchestra began and her voice soared clear to the last balcony, I said to myself, I can do that, and I will."

Even my mother, who believed if you wanted the moon you should go after it, was taken aback. "Well, that's quite an ambition."

"When you brought me from the orphanage last spring, could you possibly have guessed that before Halloween I would be sitting with Doris Duke listening to Lily Pons?"

"Not in a million years, my dear, so anything *is* possible."

As he went out the door to his room, he said sleepily, "You know, I thought I was just coming out here to keep your horse stalls shoveled out."

The phone was ringing two shorts and a long, and my mother hurried to answer. Handsome had on his new dance shoes, and his daddy was holding him up by the elbows so he could try them out. My mother came back with her coat on and carrying her car keys, announcing that it was another of those mysterious summonses from Sebe that she could not discuss over the party line, but she needed my mother and five gallons of kerosene.

"God knows what for. She has electric lights; maybe she wants to burn down her house for the insurance. I had better go and see."

Mr. Miller handed his little dancing son to his wife and said, "I'd better go with you. It's starting to rain, I'll get my coat from the hall."

Even I knew what that meant: the jacket with the gun in the pocket. He was more afraid for her than she was for herself that somewhere the Klan lay in wait.

They didn't get back until three o'clock, and I was asleep long before that. My mother slept in later, and so did Mr. Miller. Stanley managed to get up and dressed and made me get on the school bus with him. I could hardly wait to get there and ask Worthy and Harry what had gone on. I found them at recess and gave them each a handful of chocolate-covered nuts to tell me.

Sylvia Tingler had been tarred and feathered by the Klan, or the part of the Klan who had raped her two weeks before. The five of them dragged her out of the restaurant and took her in their old truck out to the fairground. There they had torn off her clothes and, with a mop, covered her all over with tar. Then they had emptied a pillowful of feathers over her and left her there in the dark. They had yelled at her, "That will teach you to pass your syphilis on to decent men." Birdie Bender had added, "My poor little eight-year-old girl has probably got it." Mary Bender hadn't been in school for about a month, so my cousins and I couldn't ask her about fuckin' her daddy.

Sylvia had dragged herself down dark roadways and up alleys to Aunt Sebe's house. When my mother got there, she found Sylvia Tingler sitting in a washtub in the middle of Aunt Sebe's kitchen. When she saw what the problem was, she asked, "Sebe, why did you call me? I felt like tar-and-feathering her myself."

Aunt Sebe said, "I have you to call when I need help; you have me to call. This woman has nobody. A little charity, Billy."

Sylvia was crying at the top of her voice, and that probably helped soften my mother up. She put on a pair of rubber gloves and began with a pile of rags and the kerosene to scrub the tar off. Sometimes Sylvia cried, "Do you have to rub so hard?"

I guess my mother did. They couldn't get it all off. She was still sticky and black in spots, especially in her hair. She got in a tub of hot water with Octagon soap powder, which helped a little, but she still screamed.

Mr. Miller had gone to find Lester Adams to tell him, and Lester came, but he wasn't any more inclined to do anything than he had been when Aunt Sebe told him about the rape. After all, Sylvia was nothing but a dirty little whore. He had heard that there was a meeting of the Klan tonight at Martins' pool hall, which was a barn on the edge of town. He pointed out that since they had caught syphilis, they were already being punished. My mother pulled off her rubber gloves and threw them in the trash and said, "I'm getting disenchanted with you, Lester."

Worthy had remembered the exact words, but he wasn't sure of the meaning. I explained it was like in the fairy tale, when the princess finds out the prince isn't a prince at all but a blue monkey.

I had promised my mother that I would have lunch all this week with Grandfather Curtiss, because he was so lonely. It was a lonely house, empty and quiet except for the crackling sound of the radio from his study. He had become as much a fixture of this room as his mounted grizzly bear. He ate here and he slept here and he kept his radio going constantly, tuned to the market reports. He had bought an electric battery charger to keep his power source up, and the acid spots on the blue Chinese rug were as big as dinner plates.

There was one kitchen maid left, and only Matthew came over to bring Grandfather's meals. Grandmother Curtiss said when he was ready to treat her on equal terms, she would come over. I guess he wasn't ready.

Grandfather greeted me with "General Electric has fallen forty dollars since nine o'clock this morning." Another ten points and it would be below his margin, and there would be another stock shot to hell. He wondered which property the bank would foreclose on this time. Thank God he had not mortgaged our farm or this house and had transferred ownership safely out of his hands.

I did not share his taste for kidney pie, and I doubt if he tasted it. He seemed to move the spoon back and forth automatically, and he kept his eye on the speaker as though that made the static-muffled voice more discernible. The maid gave me a peanut-butter-and-jelly sandwich and a glass of milk. Everything tasted funny in this room, since he kept a pile of some powdered herb smoking from a tray on his desk for his asthma. The whole room stank. When Matthew came to help Grandfather into a clean shirt, I was glad to escape back to school.

Stanley had told his teachers he was absent for a week because he had delivered a horse to Doris Duke, but not many people believed him. They did when the newspaper came out on Tuesday. My mother had come in on Monday with pictures of Stanley and Doris Duke and a flattering write-up she had carefully composed and typed. It also flattered her and our horse farm and pointed out that the richest woman in the world had been the guest of her mother-in-law, Mrs. Huston Curtiss, of this city. The young man at the front desk did not seem too interested in this information until his editor pointed out that this was the same Mrs. Huston Curtiss who held a two-hundred-thousand-dollar mortgage on this newspaper.

Lester Adams came out to our house on Monday night. He came right at dinnertime, but he acted stiff-necked and wouldn't sit down, even though we were having stuffed pork chops. The Forresters had butchered the first of the hogs today, and we were feasting. We went on eating; if he wouldn't sit down, that was his problem. He stood in the doorway and my mother asked, "Lester, is this official business?"

"I don't know whether it is or not. I have to ask you that. I suppose you know Slim Middleton and Birdie Bender were killed last night, shot back behind that old barn where the Klan was meeting?"

"Why would I know that? If they killed each other, well, that's two more snakes gone."

She was busy cutting up her pork chop, but Mr. Miller, who had brought Lester a plate, seemed frozen in place.

"There were no guns found."

"Isn't it possible the other Klansmen took the guns away?"

"That's the way I'm reporting it: Klansmen shoot each other in argument over control."

"Well, then, it's all settled. Why don't you have a pork chop, Lester, they are very good."

"Witnesses say someone turned on headlights as these two came out the door, shots were fired from two different guns, and then they drove away. There are very few people in this county who can shoot like that, it was a hundred feet away, and one of the shots to Slim went right through his eye."

"Did anyone see the car?"

"No. Whoever it was was lucky this time."

"There must be five or six people who could shoot a man through the eye at one hundred feet. Are you going to harass them, too?"

"No."

"Lester, did you know Birdie was molesting his eight-year-old daughter? Somebody probably thought they had to do something to protect women and children, since the law won't."

"And why do you suppose Slim Middleton was shot?"

"I expect that was just a lucky accident. Surely, Lester, you could think of several reasons to shoot Slim Middleton."

Lester eased into the place Mr. Miller had set without being aware he was doing it and began filling his plate. Mr. Miller hurried back from the kitchen with hot biscuits so he wouldn't miss anything.

"But people can't just go around shooting other people." Lester filled his mouth with mashed potatoes.

"Mr. Miller and I were just laughing the other day about the Gilbert and Sullivan character who sings, 'I've got a little list of folks who won't be missed.' "

Lester sputtered, and mashed potatoes rained out of his mouth. "Billy, you don't have a list?"

"Oh, I'm sure everyone has a list in their minds. The world is full of dirty, rotten sons of bitches we would all be better off without. If I had such a list, would you help me? You're in a very good position to get away with it."

Lester looked down the table at the Dutch ladies and Miss Larkin, at Stanley and me, and we were all studying his face, waiting expectantly for his answer.

"No, goddammit, no! I'm here to protect life."

"Then I suggest you do it. Mr. Miller, what are we having for dessert?"

"Wild fox-grape pie."

"I do hope it's not too sour. I didn't think we'd had enough frost yet to sweeten the grapes."

IN SPITE OF a slight rally in the market on Tuesday, there was no assurance that William Randolph Hearst's people would come up with the money to pay Grandmother's mortgage. She might end up owning the paper. So by Wednesday, Stanley Fancler was a minor celebrity, and stocks had dropped again dangerously close to collapse. U.S. Steel had fallen to a hundred and thirty dollars from a high of eight hundred.

We had dinner with Grandmother Curtiss on Tuesday night, and she didn't seem the least worried over the economy, and we found out why. She had not liked Aunt Almeda, but she knew she wasn't stupid and she had been in a position to learn the facts. Grandmother had taken her advice and sold every share of stock and converted it into cash. There were several boxes of hundred-dollar bills in her safe and enough gold coins for a trip to Europe. The only mortgages she held were the newspaper, and she had gotten half the cash on that, and a clothing factory down in Virginia that she had never seen. She was in great shape financially, unless the government itself went under.

My mother asked when she was going to help Grandfather out of his plight, and Grandmother answered, "When he asks me. I have been oppressed by men all my life, and now I am free—and so are you, Billy-Pearl. Let us celebrate." She offered a toast with French wine in a Waterford wineglass. Even I was given half a glass. I did not know what I was toasting, for I intended to grow up to be a man if these women would let me.

We took home twenty copies of the newspaper, and Stanley just sat and stared at it in numbed silence.

On Wednesday the market broke again. The voice on Grandfather's radio said the market was on a toboggan ride from which it would not recover. When Grandfather heard Westinghouse was down to a hundred dollars, I think he was crying, but I'm not sure, he was wheezing so from his asthma. (If he had lived to 1933, he would have seen it drop to twenty cents.)

The kitchen maid believed in economy. She prepared our entire lunch in the oven while it was hot, roast chicken, baked potatoes, and baked apple for dessert. She wasted her time. Grandfather stared at it without seeing and didn't touch it. I took his tray back to the kitchen to look for a hungry cat when a bum knocked on the door, and I gave it to him. There would be a lot more hungry men at our doors in the days to come.

Grandfather dumped his asthma vapor burner in the wastebasket; he didn't seem to care whether he could breathe anymore. My mother tried to get him to come out to the farm, but he wouldn't. He said he would come next week when we butchered, and he added, "May Herbert Hoover roast in hell!"

Aunt Almeda called from Washington to tell Grandfather she had a large cash reserve and ask what did he need? He got very red in the face and said, "Nothing, nothing at all," and slammed down the receiver. "Why does it always have to be some damn woman who thinks she can save you?"

Grandfather was red-eyed and huffing. I thought if he was getting ready to die, I wanted to be sure he willed me his grizzly bear; it was all he had left, or maybe he was just going crazy. Either way, I wanted that big bear.

I did walk over the hills with Grandfather Fancler on Saturday, when he went to help Mr. Isaac put away all the things he didn't sell during the festival. There was a lot of junk to return to the basement under the store, and it looked to me like he hadn't sold anything, but Mr. Isaac put a good face on it and said he had done as well as he expected. He was inclined to put a good face on everything. I swept out the store and the sidewalk in front, and he gave me a quarter.

Mr. Isaac's living quarters were on the second floor over the store, and when lunchtime came, he went upstairs and made us what he called latke, a potato pancake served with sour cream and applesauce. They were crisp and good and we drank hot tea out of glasses. Grandfather always had that same silly joke, "Leon, you will make some man a good wife." Mr. Isaac always answered, "Peter, I'm just waiting for you to ask me."

We ate on a little gilt table with a marble top. Mr. Isaac said it had belonged to Marie Antoinette. I didn't see how that enhanced its value. Since she was dumb enough to get her head cut off, I thought this might be a bad-luck table. I didn't tell my mother that, since she thought "we all make our own luck."

When she came for me, we went by Woolworth's to buy Halloween costumes. I wanted to spend my quarter. My mother would not let me buy candy unless I bought some for the Miller kids. Since I was an only child, she was constantly looking for ways to teach me lessons in sharing. What this taught me was that I should spend my money when she wasn't with me so I could go off somewhere and eat it all by myself. I suppose there was a lesson in that, since I usually got sick and threw up.

I bought some "nigger toes." They were cones of fondant covered in bitter chocolate. I had to eat them before I got home; if Boobie saw them, she got mad. I bought her five little wax babies filled with fruit juice. They were a good buy, for you could bite off the heads, drink the juice, and then chew the wax bodies. I always bought Handsome three long black licorice whips, because it took him a long time to chew them. If you bought him anything that went down fast, he would gobble it and then scream for yours.

For Stanley I bought a big red jawbreaker. It was really a three-way treat; you licked the bright red coating off the outside first, which colored your tongue and lips, then you sucked away the sugar coating, and when that was gone, there was a big gob of bubble gum that would last half a day. Stanley would look in the mirror at the bright red stain on his lips and say, "I really do look like a girl, don't I?" A jawbreaker cost two cents, but I was getting to like Stanley better all the time, and he was worth it.

OCTOBER 27, 1929

WE HAD ALWAYS butchered on the last Sunday in October. It was cold enough by then to preserve the meats, and the butchers who came to help were free from their regular jobs on Sunday. This year the butchers didn't have another job, since Grandfather Curtiss had lost his butchering business to the bank. We butchered on Sunday out of habit.

The butchers came with the equipment, their knives as sharp as razors, their gun, and their mallet for hitting the hogs in the head. My mother could shoot a man if she had provocation, but she could not shoot a cow. We were butchering two cows and two hogs, fifteen hundred pounds of beef and twelve hundred pounds of pork, and we would do it again in December. We were feeding fifteen people three meals a day plus guests and the Thorne family.

Stanley and my mother had taken two Arabian two-year-olds down to the lower meadow to break them to bridle and saddle. They didn't fool anyone. They wanted to get out of earshot so they wouldn't hear the screams and squeals of the hogs and cows. It was true, though, there were potential buyers coming up from the Lexington stables next month to look for likely prospects as racers. Stanley was not quite ready to start on another horse for dressage, even though my mother had warned him this time to "just use your mind, not your heart." He had hesitated taking the five-thousand-dollar bonus, 5 percent of the sale, which was his share for training Fanny. He said he felt like Judas with his thirty pieces of silver. My mother opened a bank account for him to save toward his college tuition. I had decided I would really push and get through two or three grades each year, and I would go to college with Stanley when he left.

I was surprised to see Grandfather Curtiss's car coming up the driveway. Matthew pulled as near the barn as he could and gave Grandfather his arm as he struggled out of the car. He had a cane in his other hand. The butchers had told him they were coming today, and I knew what he had come for. He wanted to drink the warm beef blood. He thought warm blood was a cure for all his ills and had drunk it daily when he still owned a butcher shop.

The Forrester men brought the two cows designated for slaughter from the meadow. The others stood and watched complacently, their big brown eyes unblinking. If they understood what was in store for two of their number, there was no indication. They munched away at the last of the summer grass, filling their two stomachs to regurgitate and chew later.

Miss Larkin was on the back porch trying to see if her cow was one of the two. It was not. My mother understood that when you have nothing living to love but a cow, you love a cow. I could certainly understand that, since I had once given my heart to an ungrateful hound pup.

The cow was shot in the head, and her legs folded under her, and she collapsed. A rope was tied around her hind legs, and she was hoisted up by a pulley and a set of big wooden gears that allowed one man to lift fifteen hundred pounds. Her throat was quickly cut and the jugular severed and a bucket held under it to catch the gushing blood. I don't think the cow was really dead yet, since the heart was still pumping and the blood pouring into the bucket in spurts. There were about two gallons per cow.

Rose had brought down a cup for Grandfather, and before she poured it full, she rolled up her sleeve and thrust her hand into the hot blood. She stirred around and around, and when she withdrew her hand, it was covered in long white tendrils that looked like spiderwebs or hairs, called fibrinogen. It was necessary to remove it to keep the blood from congealing. I asked Rose if this blood didn't turn her stomach, and she said she was in Holland when Bismarck's army came through on the way to Paris. After what she saw out of the Germans, nothing would faze her. Grandfather Curtiss drank three cups of blood and got in his car and went back home. He didn't even bother to wipe off his bloody mustache. Rose watched him closely, for she wanted enough blood left to make pudding. I didn't eat any.

The butchers cut the skin loose at the tail and began ripping the hide from the cow, careful not to tear it, as we got them tanned for rugs and upholstery. This one would look pretty, as she had red-brown spots on a cream-colored coat. I thought it looked better on the cow. The carcass was quickly cut in half down the middle with saw and knife, then into quarters. There was a long table covered with wax butcher paper, and the parts were laid out on it to be wrapped and labeled and put down in the freezer, when the body heat had cooled. A mist now rose from it. Rose watched so closely that nothing went to waste. The tail bones were cut into lengths for soup. The suet or fat had many uses, first for the mincemeat, the other ingredients of which were already boiling in three big kettles on the back of the stove.

The other cow finally got it through her head what was going on. She rolled her eyes, pulled back on her rope harness, and mooed as close to a scream of panic as a cow can get. I ran in the house, away from the sound. My mother had had the old piano from the theater in town moved out here to the back hallway, and Erica was teaching Boobie to play. I went and played "Chopsticks" with her for a while to get the sound of the cow out of my ears.

By noon both cows had been slaughtered and parceled out. Now it was the hogs' turn. When the two big porkers were goaded out of the pen, I went down and looked at the remaining hogs. It was said that hogs were smarter than horses, smarter than dogs, and I knew dogs thought and planned and connived and, in the case of Uncle Billie's shepherd, had their hearts broken; so what did the hogs feel now? They all seemed busily unaware; gnawing, mauling dry corn off the cob, except for one sow who had dumped the water trough into the mud and was tramping it and rolling in it until she was covered. Perhaps she was the widow, and this was her way of showing grief. Maybe they were all just keeping busy to keep from thinking about it.

"Don't do it, Hughie." My mother's voice was close behind me. "You can't let yourself have feelings for farm animals; if you do, you will never be able to be a farmer."

Just then we heard the mallet strike with a dull thud, and the hog gave one last squeal. I couldn't help it, I ran and hid my face against my mother's blouse, and she put her arms around me and held me close for at least a whole minute.

"I don't want to be a farmer. As soon as I save enough money, I'm going to leave here."

My mother stiffened and pushed me away.

Pork is easier to preserve than beef because whole sections of it can be smoked: the sides of bacon, the hams. Already the air was pungent with the hickory-wood smoke from our smokehouse. Most of the hog meat has the skin still attached after the carcass has been dipped in boiling water and the bristly hair scraped away. Rose took the two hogs' heads to the house to remove the brains and mix them with her stuffing and put back in the head to be slow-roasted for dinner. I intended to eat a peanut-butter sandwich.

I ended up having a toasted cheese sandwich and a bowl of potato soup, as did Stanley. After dinner, Handsome went running up and down the hall with a hog's bladder on a string that his father had blown up for him, like a balloon. Aunt Sebe called and began her conversation the way she usually did, with "Something real terrible has happened." She never wanted to say what the dire tidings were, but my mother insisted she was too tired to drive into town, and Aunt Sebe should tell her, regardless of who was listening on the line. Just then a very distraught-looking Lester Adams came through the driveway door.

When my mother said, "Lester just came through the door," Aunt Sebe answered, "Let him tell you," and she hung up. There was a chorus of disappointed sighs on the party line.

Lester came in and shut the door and just stood there. I didn't know the meaning of the word "distraught" then, but it fitted Lester. He was white-faced and red-eyed, and his clothes looked like they were about to fall off of him. His gun belt and his holster were gone, and his sheriff's badge was hanging on his torn pocket like he had tried to yank it off. "I killed a man!"

"Lester, come on in here." Mother pulled him by the arm to a chair in front of the fireplace. "You're the sheriff. I'm sure if you killed someone, it was in the line of duty to protect someone else." She pushed him down into the chair and pulled up a stool so she could look him in the face.

"Yes, me! I never killed anyone before," he whispered.

"Who did you kill?"

"Zeke."

"Zeke McCoy? I thought he was long gone."

"He came back to get Sylvia Tingler."

"Did he—hurt her?"

"He killed her. Sebe was in the back, she heard it all and called me."

My mother looked around and saw me standing in the doorway listening. "Let me get you a drink," she said to Lester, and went to the sideboard in the dining room and filled a water glass with brandy. As she passed me, she said, "Hughie, you promised to hold the book for Stanley. Get to it."

She went back to Lester and held the glass to his lips like he was a baby. I went around the door frame, out of sight.

He choked and sputtered. "He wanted to punish her, to make her die slow. He said she doped him and dumped him in a boxcar full of ants."

"Yes, Sebe told me about that."

"Why didn't you tell me?"

"You didn't need to know. Besides, Sylvia did it for me."

"He sure as hell made her pay; he took twenty minutes to kill her. He held her down and took his knife and sliced her up slowly, starting with her knees so she couldn't run. He ended up cutting her throat. He had a gun, but he didn't use it. By the time I got there, he was coming out the back door. He raised his gun at me, and I shot him twice in the face. Once right through the eye." His voice was a whine now. "How did I know his gun was empty?"

My mother put her hand on each side of his head and turned his face toward her. "Why did you try for his face, Lester? I thought you were supposed to shoot the legs."

Now his voice was level. "I promised myself if I got a chance to shoot a man, I would shoot him through the eyes so people wouldn't say you were the only person in the county could do it. You know you're on the Klan's list for that shooting behind the barn."

"I'll bet you haven't had any dinner. Come on in the kitchen. It won't take a minute to heat up something. Then I'll draw you a good hot bath." She was pulling him up out of the chair.

He stood, but he refused to move. "Billy-Pearl, didn't you hear me? I just killed a man."

"In self-defense."

"His gun was empty."

"You didn't know that."

"I do now."

"All right, Lester. This is your baptism into manhood, a little late. You just killed a low-down rotten snake. If I had been there, I'd have done it."

"I suppose you would have, and just smiled and walked away."

"It will be easier the next time. Come on in the kitchen."

He walked like a sleepwalker as she led him through the dining room. He was still reciting his little piece. "He just lay there in the alley—like a dead dog. The blood running out of his mouth. I never get used to the blood."

"It's easier for women. We see our own blood every month. And if Zeke had still been working for me, he would have been cutting the throats of hogs today."

They went through the swinging door.

I went on out to Stanley's room. He was trying to learn "The Rime of the Ancient Mariner," and I had promised to hold the book for him. I hated the ancient mariner, even though my mother had explained that the albatross around his neck was just a symbol of all the things we are saddled with.

I didn't say it, but I thought it: This farm.

OCTOBER 31, 1929

HALLOWEEN DAWNED BRIGHT, clear, and warm, a perfect day for a cornhusking. Traditionally it was the day when all the neighboring farmers from clear up and down the road to town came and helped us husk, in exchange for the use of our equipment. We had a gasoline-powered corn sheller and a grinder for making cornmeal. And, of course, no one wanted to miss the square dance in our barn on Halloween night. Girls came at dusk and joined the men and danced until midnight to the music of fiddlers and banjos and guitars. We had a bumper crop of corn, and all our cribs were full to the top. The equipment from the biggest barn had been moved outside, and the corn would be brought a wagonload at a time and dumped in the middle of the floor. The men would attack it from all sides, pulling the dry husks back from the corn, breaking it off at the bottom, and throwing the clean, dry ears of corn into the wagon, where they would be loaded back into the cribs. Five hundred bushels would be shelled off the cobs and sewn into muslin sacks to be ground later into cornmeal.

I wanted to stay home from school, but my mother wouldn't let me. Stanley always seemed anxious to get to school. He studied on the bus going and coming. He worked even harder now that he thought he might go to college.

As the school bus pulled away, a deputy from the sheriff's office pulled into our driveway. Lester was afraid of this day. Recently the city council had passed a law that no one could wear a mask except on Halloween. The newspaper had headlined THE INVISIBLE EMPIRE WILL NOW BE VISIBLE. Lester was afraid the Klan would use this day to show up and do us harm, though my mother didn't think any of them would be dumb enough to show up here in their robes. The Klan was known for drawing its members from the illiterate and the slow-witted.

I was glad I had gone to school, since the teacher moved me into the fourth grade for half of each day, something they called their enrichment program. Harry was mad, as he was in the second grade for the second year. Harry said I got moved up only because my grandmother Curtiss was on the board of education, but I knew it was all the extra help I got from Grandfather Fancler, especially in history. I felt a little guilty about that; Harry was his grandson, too. Grandfather's sidelights certainly made the people in the history books a lot more real. I tried to share what I learned with Harry, but that didn't work out very well.

The bus didn't get us back home until almost five o'clock, and it was getting dark. Our farm looked like a circus. There were cars, trucks, and wagons parked all over the place. The corral was full of other people's horses. The outside lights were all on, and the husking was over, for we could see men sweeping out the barn for the square dancing.

When we got to the back, there was a big fire in the barbecue pit, and tables and benches were set up for an outdoor dinner. A full moon was already halfway up the sky. The sweethearts and wives were coming in to join the men. Some of them already had on costumes, and some were carrying them to change here.

Stanley and I went across the summer porch toward the kitchen. We always had a quick snack to hold us until dinner. Mr. and Mrs. Miller were in the kitchen quarreling. Stanley grabbed my arm to hold me back. Grown-ups have a habit of changing the subject when you come in the room, and you miss all the good parts. It seemed the black preacher who had baptized Mr. Miller had slipped on the slick rocks of the river bottom the day he dunked Mr. Miller. Mr. Miller had pulled him out, but not before he had swallowed a lot of cold, dirty water, and now he was dead. Mrs. Miller thought it was an omen.

Mr. Miller laughed. "Do you think God looked down from heaven and said, 'I'm gonna kill this good ol' preacher to keep Miller from going to Detroit'?" You could tell she was beginning to cry and he was putting his arms around her.

"Raymond read to me out of the paper how bad the Klan was in Ohio and Indiana, and if they saw a nigger drivin' down the road in a big blue truck, they were like as not to shoot him."

"I'll go upstairs and get them Klan hoods, and when I get to Ohio, I'll put one on. You know I have to go before the winter is on us and the roads are bad."

She must have pulled away from him, for her voice got louder. "We are safe and happy here, for the first time in our lives."

"Honey, we're not all happy here. The boys are smart, they're ambitious. They want to go to school. So does Boobie."

Mrs. Miller sounded suddenly angry. "That Boobie wants the moon, but that don't mean she's gonna get it!"

Mr. Miller agreed to wait and leave on Friday, but Mrs. Miller said Friday was bad luck and he should wait until Saturday.

I couldn't wait outside any longer, I had to go to the bathroom. Mrs. Miller set out gingerbread and buttermilk, and Mr. Miller went upstairs to look for Zeke's hood.

Tuba came down the back steps from her nap, with Handsome over her shoulder still half asleep. She said she just lay down beside him to get him to sleep, but that was a lie; she was old and tired and wouldn't admit it. I said she was a hundred years old, and she said I was a bad boy, worse than my father ever was; it was true she did not know how old she was, but she was sure she wasn't a hundred. I said I counted the folds in her neck when she was asleep, each fold was ten years, and she had ten folds. She said I was going to hell for sure. I looked down the hall to be sure my mother wasn't coming before I yelled, "There's no room in hell for me; hell is reserved for fat old nigger women!"

My mother was closer than I had thought. When I started to run down the hall, there she was carrying a stack of mail she had just gotten out of the box. She was reading from a sheaf of reprints she had received from the Emporia, Kansas, *Gazette*. She knew the people of Kansas had pretty much cleared out the Klan, and she had written to the editor, William Allen White, to see how they did it. She spread it out on the table, saying, "I'm going to read through all this, but right now I've got to go up to the attic and find something to wear tonight. Come on, Stanley, we will find you a costume."

I went with them to escape Tuba boxing my ears.

The trunks in our attic held clothes that went back to the Civil War. There was even a box of hairpieces and wigs. Many of my forebears had needed their hair augmented. It was mostly blond and red, but my mother found a short black wig that seemed to be what she was looking for. She was going to dress as Charlie Chaplin's little tramp. She cut a hole in the top of the wig and pulled her crown of braids through it and fitted a plug hat over all.

"Now, let's see what we can find for you," she said to Stanley.

She was holding up a uniform from the Spanish-American War, but Stanley had found a purple dress with a bustle and leg-of-mutton sleeves that could have belonged to Lillian Russell.

"Could I?"

"Why not? Try it on."

Stanley took off his shirt and pulled the dress over his head. My mother buttoned it up the back. He was as thin around the middle as the owner of the dress had been, but he needed a lot of padding in the front. They found some red curls and some black lace gloves. There was no mirror, so Stanley looked at me. "How do I look?"

"If the kids on the bus could see you now, they really would call you a sissy!"

My mother seemed to be having fun dressing Stanley; she found him a black lace fan and showed him how to flirt with it, with just his eyes showing. She said she hadn't realized what beautiful eyes he had, all he needed was a little mascara and some eyebrow pencil. He had trouble walking in high heels downstairs to my mother's room.

I had to put on my Hansel costume. I was mad that Stanley could be whatever he wanted, but I had to be Hansel, and even worse, Boobie was going to be Gretel. My mother said I could trade with Boobie, but no thanks. I had wanted to be a clown or maybe a devil, but never a girl.

When I was dressed, I studied myself in the mirror. It wasn't as silly as I had thought. The yellow wig was a little longer, but the color wasn't far from my own hair. There were short leather pants, held up by flowered suspenders, a pale green shirt, and a red velvet vest. I carried my wooden shoes and the funny pink-cheeked false face down the steps.

Boobie was before the big mirror. Her yellow wig had two long braids that came to her waist. She wore a full red skirt with a lot of ruffled lace petticoats sticking out. There was a white apron and a bib over her yellow blouse and a funny winged hat on her head. She had her wooden shoes on. I watched as she held her pink-cheeked false face over hers and peered into the glass, then took it away and looked again.

I wanted to make up for some of the nasty things I had said in the past. Besides, I wanted her to dance with me, so I stood behind her and said, "You look better without it."

"That's easy enough for you to say. You already have a pink face."

I stood beside her, and we both stared in the mirror with our false faces on and then off. I looked into the mirrored reflection of her eyes. They were shining wet, and I realized how very much she hated her black skin. We had been intent on the mirror and hadn't heard Mr. Miller coming up behind us until we saw his face in the glass.

"Well, that's a pairing I don't think the Klan would approve."

WE HAD A VERY large kitchen with a double stove and four ovens, but just now it seemed full of cooks. My mother had hired Mr. Marino from Marino's Italian restaurant in town to come out and make his Italian spaghetti, and all the women from our household were watching to see how he did it. It was no mystery how to put several big pots of water on and boil forty-eight pounds of spaghetti, and his sauce was no longer a mystery, either, as the ladies had made note of everything that went in the pots and bubbled on the back of the stove. Marino did not seem to mind. He was laughing and speaking in Italian to women who laughed and spoke back in French, German, and English.

Lester was at the end of the table, having a cup of coffee. He had driven Mr. Marino out. Only last week the Klan had written with red paint on the front of his restaurant WOP — GO HOME. Lester wanted to be sure he got here safely. When you hired Mr. Marino, you got two for one, as he also played the accordion.

The outdoor tables were all set up, and the outside lights were all on. A row of small jack-o'-lanterns went down each table. All the floodlights on the barns were lighted, and there was a full moon. The air was warm and stirring just enough to make the burning logs in the fire pits sparkle. The perfect night for Halloween. More of the girlfriends and wives of the huskers descended upon us and had to be provided with places to change into their costumes.

The fiddlers and the banjo players came, and a couple of old ladies with zithers. Even Petey Leonard came and brought his whole set of drums. He had been in New York, playing in a theater band, for years. Now his father was dead, and he had to take care of his mother's farm. When I heard about it, I thought he ought to set it on fire and go back to New York.

By the time Grandfather Fancler and Mr. Isaac came, everyone was sitting around eating spaghetti with hot garlic bread like they were starved. The Dutch ladies hurried to get them plates. Grandfather stood up and banged on the dinner gong for attention.

"Ladies and gentlemen, I want to remind you that the delicious spaghetti you are all enjoying was made by Mr. Marino, the owner of Marino's Italian restaurant at Third and South Avenue in town. Don't forget, when you're in town, that that's the place to eat. Come on out, Mr. Marino, and let these good people meet you."

Mr. Marino came down the steps from the kitchen with his accordion strapped in place. Everyone applauded loudly, and there was even more applause when he ran his hand over his keyboard and began to play a whole medley of Italian songs as he walked around the tables. He smiled broadly, and everyone smiled back as they wiped his wonderful spaghetti sauce off their chins.

Grandfather whispered to Mr. Isaac, "I don't think any of these people will be putting hate messages on his glass."

The dancing began with a Virginia reel, as it always did. "Form around in a shoestring line, ladies in front and the gents behind." The caller had a microphone, and speakers were mounted on the outside. Mr. and Mrs. Miller and their two boys were dancing in the driveway. They would not dare go inside. My mother had made her attitude perfectly clear about Jim Crow, but there were still rednecks inside who would cause trouble.

Two of the young mares who were in training for dressage began to move to the music, and Trojan, who could be set off with a handclap, was racing around the meadow in the moonlight.

Boobie fastened on her white face and went with me into the barn. Up in the loft, we joined some of the other kids who were imitating the movements of their parents below. You could see all the costumes better looking down than you could on the floor. Most everyone had dressed up in something because they all wanted to win the prize of a twenty-dollar gold piece. Grandfather, Mr. Isaac, Mr. Marino, and Lester were the judges. I knew they wouldn't give it to me, though I should have had it just for wearing these dumb wooden shoes that belonged to Rose. They hurt even with wool batting stuffed in the toes.

They had already danced about six sets, and their initial energy was worn down a little, and men were wiping their necks with red bandanas, when my mother and Stanley arrived. Petey gave them a drum roll when they came on the floor, and I heard a round of whispers, mostly "Who is that?," because you could not tell. Stanley had become just about the prettiest girl I had ever seen in my whole life, and my mother was Charlie Chaplin the way he looked in *The Gold Rush* — the last Chaplin film to show at Grandfather Curtiss's silent theater — complete with the walk.

If Stanley was embarrassed by the sudden silence, he did not show it. He stepped forward and raised his head, crowned with a mass of red curls. This wasn't just some pretty country girl, this was an elegant young woman, the kind of face from Mother's *Harper's Bazaar* or *Vogue*. Every freckle was hidden and the face molded with shading until all you saw were those beautiful high cheekbones and the flash of amber eyes under long, sweeping black lashes. My mother took the mike from the caller's hand.

"Ladies and gentlemen, may I present my cousin . . . Stella."

Stella folded the fan she had been holding before her so that people saw the tightly wrapped waist and the swell of her breasts. My mother couldn't let well enough alone, and she added, "Stella has just returned from New York, where she is studying singing."

Several of the young men had pushed forward to get a better look, and their women weren't far behind them. One of the boys asked, "Are you gonna sing for us?"

Stella looked surprised when my mother said, "Do, Stella. You know 'One Night of Love,' I've heard you singing it with Grace Moore's record."

"Oh, I couldn't."

Mr. Marino said, "I know that." And he began the opening strains.

My mother called to Mr. Marino, "Stella is a soprano." Mr. Marino moved his hands up an octave, and Stella began. In years to come, the greatest orchestras in the world would support that voice and lift it through the glittering space of the world's opera halls.

The first notes were tentative, and then she realized that she had a great, soaring roomful of people listening, and she filled it with a soaring sound. There was a flute, an oboe, and a bank of violins in every note she sang. No one in that room had ever heard such a sound before. They stared blank-faced, wide-eyed, openmouthed. When Stella saw them, she smiled with her eyes and with her voice, and she began to move. She held her skirt in one hand and her fan in the other, and she floated about the open circle in an elegant waltz. Petey had added a soft drumming, and old Mrs. Dunlap, who recognized a waltz rhythm when she heard it, strummed her zither.

Later in life, Stella was to remember this moment and prize it: this first time when she held a roomful of people in the palm of her hand. It was like a first lovemaking, when nothing would ever be the same again.

On the last note, her voice caressed each man in the room until he felt he had been kissed. She covered her face with her fan and would have backed away, but they clapped and stomped their feet and whistled. She looked around for my mother and found her smiling as broadly as one can behind a fake mustache.

Stella began the song from the other side of the record, "A Kiss," and hoped the musicians would follow; they did. I wondered what she could do after that. I knew her other records were too operatic for these musicians, or for this audience.

When Stella talked, it was in the same magic voice she sang with. In church, people speak of a rebirth, a transformation that a belief in God brings; here we had such a transformation. I wondered if Stanley was completely lost, for he certainly had completely transformed into Stella.

Now she smiled in complete command, knew the exact encore to close with. "There is an old song my mother used to sing to me as she rocked me to sleep. I think you all know 'Pretty Red Wing.' "

Petey began an Indian tom-tom beat on his drums, and the musicians joined in. Now hers was a voice brought down to a common dimension as she sang:

> *There once was an Indian maid,*
> *A shy little prairie maid.*

She went on to tell the story of a girl's love for a young brave who was killed, then dropped down a whole octave, and the fiddlers made their instruments cry:

> *Oh, the moon shines tonight on pretty Redwing,*
> *The breezes sighing, the night birds flying*
> *While Redwing's crying her heart away.*

Petey brought the drums to a loud staccato ending.

"Thank you for letting me sing for you. I loved it. Go on with your dance. I'm going to find some dinner."

There were a dozen young men who would have gone with her. Petey dropped his drumsticks and ran to take her elbow, but my mother said harshly in his ear, "Petey, she's only fourteen."

"Dear Jesus — I want to be around when she's twenty!"

Mr. Isaac waved the rest of them away and took her arm.

The caller began the next set. Grandfather Fancler took her other arm. Mr. Isaac was saying, "Yours is the most amazing voice I have ever heard." And Grandfather wanted to know, "Where did you come from?"

Stella stopped under a hanging light. Her voice was like a tinkling Chinese chime. "Why, Uncle Peter, you still don't recognize me? I'm your adopted nephew Stanley Fancler, and I have decided to become your niece Stella. I'm going to sing in the opera and make you proud of me."

Both Mr. Isaac and Grandfather said at the same time, "Oh, my God—it is!" They laughed and put their arms around her.

Stella reached down and took off her shoes. "I may have a little trouble wearing these heels."

Slowly the moon dropped to the far side of the sky, the ash from the fires turned gray, and the last of the guests went reluctantly home. Only my mother and Lester still stood in the middle of the dance floor, and Mr. Marino played a tune that moved as slowly as they did.

The loft was empty except for Boobie and me. We had lain on our stomachs where we could look over, and I was hesitant to move, for Boobie had been asleep on my arm long enough to make it numb.

They were an odd-looking couple: Charlie Chaplin dancing with the sheriff.

"Lester, do you love me?" my mother asked him.

"Yes. I always have."

"Are you afraid for me?"

"Yes. You have angered the Klan, and they are madmen."

"How many are there?"

"There were thirty-three. Four are gone. I killed one of them—I suspect you killed two. I don't know what happened to Hannibal."

"That leaves twenty-nine; none of us will be safe until they are gone. If you truly love me, Lester, you will kill them."

"That's crazy. You can't just go around killing people."

"We have been doing it. I'll help you."

"Billy-Pearl—"

"Those sons of bitches have made me afraid of the dark. I never was before. They have taken that away from me, and I want it back."

"I think we may all be afraid of the dark from now on."

My mother did not cry easily, and I'm not sure now if her tears were real, but she turned and pressed her face against his neck and sobbed.

I AWOKE THE NEXT morning with Tuba shaking me. It had been a very short night.

"Git up, you lazy thing, you're gonna be late for the school bus."

"I'm not goin'."

"Oh, yes, you are. It's only Friday."

"Stanley's not goin'."

"Oh, yes, he is. He's down in the kitchen eatin' his oatmeal, an' you better git down there if'n you want any breakfast."

"He's Stella now."

"Stella las' night, Stanley this mornin'—jes' like puttin' on a clean shirt, which you better do."

Mr. Marino had stayed all night, since his accordion was outside the door of our guest room. I wondered if Lester was in my mother's room, but I was too sleepy to care.

Stanley was at the table looking like he just got out of the shower, his face shining clean and his hair brushed. He gave me a Stanley smile and a Stanley good morning, and I wondered where Stella had gone and if I would ever see her again.

I was still only half awake when I climbed in the bus and sat down. The driver was reaching for the door handle when a girl's voice called, "Wait, wait for me!" and I looked out to see a strange apparition running across our front lawn. It was Gretel, her yellow pigtails flying and her white face with its bright red cheeks in place, redder still in the morning light. A little black hand grabbed the railing and was pulling herself up the steps.

"Nigger, git off this bus!"

"I'm white now, see my white face." Boobie was more defiant than tearful.

Stanley ran forward, for it looked as if the driver might hit her. Stanley loosened her grip on the door and handed her into the arms of her father, who was right behind her. The bus pulled away. I could see Boobie still kicking and screaming, even after Mrs. Miller had run out to them.

Mrs. Miller said later that Mr. Miller had said to her, "Now do you understand why we have to leave here?"

And Mrs. Miller understood.

November 3, 1929

THE SIGNS OF WINTER were everywhere, though the days still had some warmth. The sky wasn't as high as it had been. There were autumn fires set by lightning, bootleggers who let their still fires spread, and hunters who used the fires to drive the deer before the wall of flame so they could shoot them, that left a pall of smoke over everything.

The windows had all been washed and the storm windows attached. Long strips of rags had been wedged into all the cracks. The snow fencing had been unrolled and placed where the winter winds would drift the snow. The gullies and ditches had to be fenced off, because when they were full of snow, they looked like level ground and the livestock would fall in and smother. The small tractor had been fitted with a blade for plowing snow out of our driveway and to make paths to the barn and chicken houses. Bales of hay had been stacked on the north side of all the sheds and against the north side of our house, up to the first-story windows. The *Farmer's Almanac* and all the signs predicted a heavy winter. All the animals had grown particularly heavy coats, and the woolly worms were brown clear down to their ends.

One of the best parts of winter was our third-floor attic. It was a wonderful big space. One of my ancestors had decided to build a ballroom up there and had laid a polished maple floor before he changed his mind and decided to build a mansion in town. It was light and bright from big fan-shaped windows on either side, at the ends, and the eight dormers that went across the front of our house. There were four big stone chimneys that pierced the space and warmed the room and still left a large open area, perfect for roller skating or tricycle riding.*

Handsome brought his kiddie car up here and rode by the hour, now that the Dutch ladies had adopted this as their work area. Rose was still working on the eighteen Chippendale chairs. She was trying to get them finished by Christmas

---

* The wing of the attic that went to the east was quite a different story. It was partitioned off from the main hall and was one big glorious clutter. It was dark and dusty, and the history of our family could be read in the boxes and round-topped trunks that had been squirreled away there. Picture frames and bottomless chairs hung from the rafters. There were rolls of carpet and mysterious cardboard boxes that had darkened until you could no longer read the list of contents written on the outside. One thing that could be said for the Curtisses, they seldom threw anything away.

as a surprise for my mother, though I had already told her. Under the worn blue brocade on the seat covers, Rose found a covering of needlepoint in a very nice pattern, a wreath of bees favored by Napoléon Bonaparte. The fabric had been carefully washed and lined and repaired and put back, and Rose declared them a treasure.

At the end of the space under the north windows was an old loom that hadn't been used for years. Now it had been restrung with linen cord, and the shuttle was being thrown back and forth between the warp and the woof, with its tail of tightly dyed and twisted woolen strands, to produce shawls and blankets and scarves in rainbow hues. There was something about the motion of the foot pedals and the motion of the shuttle that seemed to dictate that the weaver sing. It didn't matter whether it was Rose, or Erica, or Helga. They all seemed to sing to the same rhythm, the German lowland songs. But on Mondays, when the Miller girls took a turn at it, they sang the old church songs of the South. When my mother and Aunt Sebe wove, they sang the old Scotch and English minstrel songs that their ancestors had brought into these hills in the sixteenth century.

The attic was also used for drying fruits and vegetables. There were racks and racks of screened frames that held walnuts and the seeds for next year's crops. Sweet apples had been peeled, quartered, and threaded on twine until there were ropes of them the length of the space: the pies of February and March. It gave the attic a delicious aroma.

In one of the dormers, there were several dress dummies standing near the two sewing machines, waiting for their half-made garments to be completed. There was even a new little short one the size of Boobie. I was going to make a funny blackface and pin it on, but I didn't. I remembered too well the last time my mother had slapped me across the mouth.

Mr. Miller finally left for Detroit on Sunday morning. Dark clouds were piling up in the north, and he wouldn't be put off any longer. The blue Nabisco truck had been painted black with gold lettering on the door: RANDOLPH COUNTY SHERIFF'S DEPT. Lester had given him a letter saying he was driving to Detroit to bring back auto parts for the sheriff, and he had a sheriff's cap to wear. Inside the truck were cans of gasoline, extra tires, and a battery, plus a bed and food for a week.

He and my mother had talked in her office the night before with the door shut. I knew she was giving him money, because when I went in, the door to her safe was still open. When he actually left, everyone stayed inside but his family so they could tell him good-bye. We all waved from the porch, and at the last minute, my mother grabbed up the black coat from the hallway and ran and thrust it in the window to him.

"You better take this, you may need it."

I didn't understand why Mr. Miller would need a gun to go to work in an automobile factory, but it turned out that he did.

Mrs. Miller held a wet washcloth over her eyes and went back to bed. She wanted Handsome to go with her, but he wanted to play with his older sisters. He saw them only once a week. They had changed their day off so they could say farewell to their father. They spent the day telling Handsome how cute he was, how smart he was; I didn't think he was so smart. He was almost thirteen months old and still shit in his pants.

All week Mrs. Miller jumped when the phone rang, and ran to overhear if Mr. Miller was all right. She had read some dark foreboding things in the bottom of her coffee cup when she turned it three times and stared into the grounds. My mother had explained to me that the coffee grounds said nothing. It was just that staring at the bottom of the cup helped you to focus your own thoughts. I didn't understand how Mrs. Miller could read things in a dirty cup when she couldn't even read a letter. I had overheard Mr. Miller telling my mother he would write her just how things were in Detroit, but he wanted my mother to read Mrs. Miller only the good parts.

Most of the calls this week were from Aunt Sebe, about Sylvia Tingler's funeral; she hadn't had one yet and wasn't going to until someone came along and paid for it. Aunt Sebe thought my mother should. Runner's Funeral Home had Sylvia in the refrigerator, and they were hoping some relative would show up and claim her. When Aunt Sebe spoke of her, she called her Miss T. I'm sure everyone on the party line knew who Miss T. was. Even the Wheeling papers had headlines that read ELKINS CROWNS SYLVIA, TARS AND FEATHERS HER, AND THEN STABS HER DEAD.

Aunt Sebe wrote my mother a letter near the end of November, and my mother left it on her desk top. It said:

Dear Billy,

I'm writing you instead of calling, because this is too private for the party line, and I don't have time to come out on the train. Since Sylvia is gone, I work double shifts. Christmas is next month, and I'm glad for the extra money. Of course, you don't have to think about things like that, but here is something you might think about. You know them five kluckers that raped Sylvia was in here at the restaurant. As soon as I saw them, I called out the back to them big boys that are always pitchin' horseshoes in the alley. I said come on, free games of pool on the house.

I don't guess they would want to rape an old woman like me, but they were gettin' drunk and loud-mouthed. I heard them talkin' about goin' over to South Elkins and burnin' out the gold-dust twins. They got themselves a little house over there now, right below the cement bridge, and they're open for business. As soon as the Klan went out of here I tried to call the sheriff's office, but nobody was in. Then I called the police, but they don't care. I think one or two of them are in the Klan. I was tryin' your ring for about the third time to see if Lester was at your house, instead of tendin' to business, when a wild-lookin' boy came in the back carryin' that Wheeling newspaper that said Sylvia was crowned, raped, and killed.

He slammed it down on the table and said, "What do you know about this? I know Syl worked here. I'm her brother Estel." He was a tall, gangly, snot-nosed kid but he looked a little crazy, and I wanted him out of here. So I told him if he had come in five minutes before, he would have seen the five men who did it. And he asked me where he could find 'em and I told him. I did tell him, you're just a kid and them are five mean bastards—they're liable to do you worse than they did your sister. He said he had him a deer rifle out in his truck and "I'm a pretty good shot." He had them cold blue eyes like you do, so I figured maybe he'd do it. I guess he did. He was back before closing, and I gave him some coffee and three pieces of pie. All I ask was, did ye? And he said, "Yep." He told me how he stood on the bridge and picked them off as they ran around and around that kerosene-soaked cross. Them two Chinese whores came out and dragged the bodies all in a pile and pushed their cross over on them, and it made a real good fire.

I thank you for the Thanksgiving invites and Worthy and Harry want to come; could you keep them till Sunday? I'm just so tired, I just want to lay around with Kirby and do nothin', well almost nothin'.

I almost forgot. Estel ask me where his sister was buried, and I couldn't tell him. I'm a believer that no good deed should go unpunished. Burn this letter.

Your sister Sebe

November 10, 1929

SATURDAY MORNING DAWNED very warm for November, and it seemed like a good day to make soap. Mrs. Miller was down behind the barns with the Dutch ladies, loading the copper kettles with hog fat and our homemade lye, when Mr. Miller called. There were crackling noises on the line, and he and my mother were yelling at each other.

"Yes, yes . . . Well, I'm glad you got there safely. How do things look? . . . Oh. Oh, I am sorry—your brother didn't really have a job for you? . . . Yes, you had better put that in a letter. They won't let you in the union at all? . . . That damn race thing! I wonder if we will live long enough to see it pass. If you have to come back, I know you'll be sorry. But I'm selfish, I shall be glad . . . I'll tell her there is hope . . . yes. Good-bye, Mr. Miller."

The barrels of ashes we had saved all summer were wheeled around and boiling water run through them and collected from the bungholes in the bottom. It was almost pure lye. The grit was strained out and dumped into the kettles. All six of the kettles hung on tripods with hot oak fires going under them. There were three different kinds of soap. The first was made from the fat saved from cooking, and that had salt in it, so it was just used for scrubbing floors and rough cleaning where it didn't touch your skin, for it also had the most lye in it and a shovelful of borax and a scoop of lime. Then there was the soap that was used for washing clothes, which also had a little borax in it. Last was the soap for your hands and face, and it smelled good in the bathtub. It contained the best of the fats and less lye and several kinds of barks and leaves, mostly sassafras bark, which gave it a very nice smell and a lavender color. When it had all boiled for hours and the lye had changed the nature of the fat and the fat had rendered the lye harmless, it was all strained and poured out into wooden trays about three inches deep. When it began to cool and firm up, you took a big knife and cut the soap into usable sizes, about the way you cut chocolate fudge. The face soap made enough lather when you brushed it that all the men on our farm used it to shave with. All except Stanley, who didn't have any beard.

The dyeing of wool had become the province of the Dutch ladies. My mother, who was determined to be the world's biggest know-it-all, watched them closely. She pressured me to do the same. Years later, when I decided to be a writer, I was amazed at how much I remembered.

The Dutch ladies had already spent weeks washing and cleaning the dirt and burrs out of the fleeces of wool sheared from our sheep in the late spring. Our wool room in one of the barns was filled to the top. There had not been a good market for wool for two years, nor would there be again for years to come.

Before the wool could be dyed, it had to be carded; that is, combed with boards driven full of long nails that separated the fibers. At this point, it stands in great fluffy piles, and each fleece is five times its final size until it is twisted, a handful at a time, on the spinning wheel into long, loosely intertwined strands and tied into hanks of yarn, enough to roll into a ball. Each hank is thrown into the boiling dye pot and held under until it reaches the desired shade. Onion peelings, saved all year, make bright yellow; pokeberries make purple; fresh walnut hulls make green, and the dried ones make brown. Chestnut burrs and marigolds together make orange. There wasn't a color in the rainbow that couldn't be duplicated with something you gathered from the land, except bright sky blue and scarlet red. Those we had to buy. A great deal of salt was used to set the color and make it permanent. When the hanks of wool were dipped out with a wooden rake, rinsed in cold water until it ran clear, and then hung on lines and over the railings of the paddocks to dry, the whole back area looked like a rainbow.

Trojan came down to the fence and looked over the display as though choosing his racing colors. I could have told him they would be blue with yellow fringes. After the wool was thoroughly dry, which took days, it had to be run through the spinning wheel again and twisted tighter before it could be knitted or woven on the loom.

That week my mother had a private telephone line run out from town. She had said we had to watch the money now—with the market gone, we might never sell another horse—nevertheless, she spent two hundred dollars and made our party-line neighbors mad. I think she did it because of the calls from Mr. Miller, but she could have saved her money. He never called again. Besides, you couldn't get a really private phone call, since Aunt Olie's oldest girl, Betty, worked on the switchboard and listened in on everything. She had a longer nose than Aunt Sebe.

It seemed Mr. Miller was not to escape the Klan even as far north as Michigan. The papers all week were full of reports of a "daring daytime robbery of a Brinks truck by two hooded members of the Klan." They had gotten away with the whole payroll intended for the Ford Motor Company at Dearborn. Only two shots had been fired, each through the hand of a guard holding a gun. Lester laughed and said, "Billy, that sounds like your kind of shooting." My mother said nothing.

At the end of the week, a letter came from Mr. Miller. Actually two letters, one for my mother telling the truth and one for Mrs. Miller with soft lies. To my mother, he said there was no work in Detroit. He had gone to the Ford plant in Dearborn, and they were laying men off. The unions were closed shops, with no way for a black man to get in as long as there was a white man unemployed, and there were long lines of white men waiting. The business his brother had was theft. His wife would go into furniture stores that displayed their wares outside on the sidewalk, and while she distracted the manager, he would load up and steal the sidewalk display. That's why he wanted a bigger truck. Even that wasn't possible, since in winter, merchants no longer put their wares on the sidewalks. Mr. Miller said he wouldn't do that anyway. If he was going to risk going to jail, it would have to be for more than the value of a mattress or a rocking chair.

By the next week, we had our first real snow. The ground had cooled off enough that the snow didn't just melt and run off. It wasn't deep enough yet for the snowplow or slick enough for tire chains, but my mother kept the car's wheels in the established tracks when we went into town on Saturday morning.

In the cold weather, eggs got scarce. Only half the hens tended to business, while the others sat hunched down in warm nests with their heads under their wings. The price had gone up in spite of the depressed economy, and we brought two cases into the Bluebird Market, now owned by Gertrude Gracey.

The Railway Express office at the train station had called, saying there was a package there for my mother and it might be a couple of weeks before the truck could come out our way. My mother was surprised when she saw what it was: the big old brown leather suitcase that she had given Mr. Miller, tied together with several lengths of rope. She certainly had not expected to get it back. The man put it on our backseat, and I got in beside it. On the way home, I untied each knot and worked each rope loose with my Swiss army knife. I sprung the lock and opened the lid. There was an old sheet and some Detroit newspapers, and under the papers, packed tight, were a great many packages wrapped in waxed paper. I tore one of them open, reached over the seat, and held a bundle of fifty-dollar bills under my mother's nose.

When we got home, she drove the car into the barn. We wrapped the sheet around the suitcase, and together we carried it into her office and locked the door. We unwrapped it all. There were a few packages of ones, but it was mostly tens and twenties and fifties. There were ten packages of hundreds, with five hundred in each package. My mother counted one of them, not believing the markings. There was a note that said "I know I can trust you to care for this until I can get back." There wasn't even a signature.

NOVEMBER 26, 1929

MY MOTHER AND I went into town to have Thanksgiving dinner with Grandmother Curtiss. I would much rather have stayed home, as it looked like dinner there was going to be a lot of fun. By eleven o'clock, the two roasting turkeys smelled wonderful. My mother had won both turkeys at a shooting match. We didn't raise turkeys on our farm because they were so dumb. Because of the two turkeys, extra people had been invited. The whole Thorne family came. Mrs. Thorne had turned into a different person, and even my mother didn't know her. She had gained twenty pounds and smiled all the time like a silly Kewpie doll, and both of the Forrester men kept looking at her like she was the prettiest thing they ever saw.

Worthy and Harry had both gotten the mumps two days before Thanksgiving, so they stayed home. Kirby had stayed away because he never had the mumps and they could make a grown man sterile. My mother said to Aunt Sebe, "What do you care?" But apparently she did.

Rose was playing the piano in the back hall, and Boobie was singing her Christmas carols too soon. We were going to have to listen to them for a whole month. Mother and I had to go, because Grandfather Curtiss was coming to dinner and Grandmother said this was probably his last Thanksgiving. Grandmother seemed to have buried the hatchet since she saw he was failing fast.

My mother seemed nervous, since another of the packages from Mr. Miller had arrived the day before, and she asked Stanley to go with us and to drive. We'd had a clue that more money might be arriving, as Lowell Thomas said in his evening news broadcast that the daring Klan robbers had struck again. This time it was a Detroit bank, just as the Brinks truck was unloading money. The box was smaller this time, but there were no ones or fives, so the total amount may have been as much. My mother didn't count it, she just opened her big old safe and dumped it in.

Matthew had brought Grandfather around to Grandmother's house in a wheelchair and wheeled him up to the end of the table. There were ten guests, including us. Four were people from Washington whom we had never seen before. Grandmother was chatty, playing social hostess, and Grandfather might have stayed home. He hardly ate and seemed half asleep. Even before the plum pudding flambé, Matthew had to wheel him into the drawing room and give him oxygen. I'm sure the turkey at our farm looked better. Grandmother's French chef had removed all the bones and reassembled it into something that looked like a sausage roll. With it were Brussels sprouts arranged to look like a bouquet. I didn't blame Grandfather for not eating much; when I got home, I filled up on leftover sweet potatoes and cranberry sauce.

On Sunday morning my mother stood out by the road in her long fox coat, waiting for the newspaper. She had heard the radio report, but she wanted to read the account before she spoke to Mrs. Miller. I was trying to be nicer to my mother these days. She seemed distracted and upset much of the time; besides, Christmas was coming, so later, I brought her a cup of hot coffee into the living room where she was reading the papers.

She looked up at me, genuinely distressed. I took the paper from her and read the account: KLAN ROBBERS — STOPPED BY FIERY DEATH!

There had been a police chase after another Klan attempt to rob Brinks. This time the cops had been waiting for them. The chase on the icy roads had ended with the truck going over an embankment and bursting into flames. It was thought that there were cans of gasoline in the back, as the fire was intense. The two robbers had been burned beyond recognition. The license plates on the truck had been traced back to a truck stolen earlier in the summer by a disgruntled worker of the Nabisco Bakery. The governor of Michigan had declared the Ku Klux Klan disbanded in Michigan.

My mother sat awhile and stared into the fire, which blazed up as she fed the Sunday papers into it. Then she sent me to get Mrs. Miller.

Mrs. Miller wasn't in the kitchen, but Tuba was. She was just putting a big pan of hot cocoa on the tea cart. She told me Mrs. Miller was back in the schoolroom, and since I was going there, I could push the cart. The blue and Willowware cups were on the bottom tray, so I pushed it carefully back through the hallway. Before I got there, I could hear the chatter. It sounded like all the women in the house were back there, and they were.

They were all seated around the big wooden table that had been the billiard table until it got a wooden top for schoolwork, and they were all working on what looked like a big green comforter. When they saw me, they went suddenly silent and tried to cover their work with their arms. Miss Larkin was nearest and said, "Hughie, you won't tell your mother, please. It's a surprise for Christmas, a new horse blanket for her Hannah."

I went over and looked; it was very pretty. It was dark green wool padded an inch thick and bound with yellow edges. There were the letters C/F, for Curtiss Farm, in a circle of yellow leaves on the side.

"No, I won't tell. Trojan needs a new blanket, too. He would like a blue one with gold fringe, he told me. And my mother would like Mrs. Miller to come to the front parlor—she wants to tell her something."

Mrs. Miller looked up from her sewing. "What is it, Hughie? Is it something bad?"

I lied. "I don't know." It was all right, this was a day for lying. I wondered what Mother would tell Mrs. Miller. I didn't get to hear. My mother was standing at the parlor door, and she closed it in my face when Mrs. Miller went in.

I stood for a minute with my ear against the door, but it was too thick to hear through. I ran to get Tuba. It seemed to me Mrs. Miller was going to need someone of her own kind when she came out. I told Tuba that Mr. Miller was dead, but I didn't tell her how. I didn't know how yet. We stood out in the hall a long time, and I was just about to do one of my Christmas good deeds and go and get Tuba a chair when Mrs. Miller came out. Her eyes were wide and wet, but she wasn't really crying, just staring forward like a blind woman.

Tuba said, "Honey, has you got a mama somewhere?"

Mrs. Miller's voice was thin and small. She sounded more like Boobie. "My mother jes' dropped me down in the tobacco field. I never knew who she was."

Tuba put her big fat arms around Mrs. Miller and patted her head down to her big shoulder. "I'm gonna be your long-lost mama. Now, you jes' cry all you want to; jes' cry it all out, honey."

And she did. I heard through the sobs, "He'd been on his new job one day— when this accident happened."

I went into the parlor and shut the door. My mother looked tired, like she had just been racing one of the horses. I knew she hadn't, but she would now. She always did after a bad time.

"You told her a big lie, didn't you?"

"It was a necessary lie. It's terrible enough to know he is dead. I grieve for him, and he wasn't my husband."

"What are you going to do when she wants to bury him?"

"I told her several men were burned in the accident, and they couldn't identify his body. I also told her there was insurance to take care of her and her children."

"You got enough in the safe for that?"

"I haven't counted it yet, but I'm sure there is. Tonight after supper I'll lock the door, and you and I will count it."

I stirred the fire and looked at her sitting there beside it. She was vulnerable. She didn't think so, but she was.

"What would happen if you got killed? Who would take care of all these people?"

"Why, you would, of course. You will be older by then, I hope, and it will be your responsibility."

I put a big oak log on the embers and thought to myself, Like hell I would. I would throw them all out and take the money and go to California.

NOVEMBER 30, 1929

WHEN I GOT HOME from school on Monday, there was a postcard from my father postmarked Buffalo, New York. It was the first message since he had left. On the front was a picture of Niagara Falls frozen over. He had very nice handwriting; I always wondered how he could do that, since he was half drunk all the time. The card said:

> Dear Son—
>
> I am living with your aunt Bea and her husband in Buffalo, New York. It is very cold here. I think of you, and I miss you, and maybe sometime in the summer you can come and visit me.
>
> Your dad

I looked at the picture for a long time and wondered how long it would take for that much ice to thaw. I tore the card into little pieces, then I chewed it into spitballs; some of them stuck to the ceiling, but most fell off.

By Tuesday evening Mrs. Miller still hadn't come down from her room. Tuba was carrying food up and spooning it into her like a baby.

The Miller boys waited for my mother down in the barn. "Mrs. Curtiss, you didn't get any more telephone calls, did you, 'bout our daddy?"

"No, boys, I'm sorry, I didn't. I will put a call through to the newspaper in Detroit and see if they know any more. I'll call the morgue there and see if they have identified his body. You know, there is money enough in his insurance for you two to go to a good black college."

"But there is no high school for us."

"You can study here with Miss Larkin. She says you are making real progress, and you're bright boys. I will bring in another tutor if you need it. I will force the board of education to give you a proficiency test and a high school diploma."

One of the Millers wanted to know if there would be enough money for them to go to New Jersey and live with their father's sister and attend school there, and my mother assured them there would be.

After the boys had gone down to the meadow to bring the cows up, I said to my mother, "You know that money really belongs to the Ford Motor Company?" She answered, "Mr. Miller went to Detroit to secure his children's future, and he has paid with his life."

"That's a lot of money for a nigger." I was never going to learn to keep my mouth shut, even if my lip was swollen for a week where she slapped me. "If you don't quit hittin' me, I'm going to Buffalo, New York, and live with my father."

"If you don't watch your nasty mouth, I'll pack your suitcase and put you on the bus."

Grandfather Fancler had explained to me the skill necessary to construct a house of lies. Like a house of cards, each layer must be laid on with skill. One false move and the whole thing collapses. On Tuesday evening, when my mother announced that she was going upstairs to talk with Mrs. Miller, I wondered what lie she was going to add now. Mrs. Miller had not been down since Sunday, and her trays were coming back mostly uneaten. My mother got a pot of tea and a bowl of bread pudding covered with cream. I carried the cup and saucer and the sugar bowl and followed her. I didn't want to miss this.

Mrs. Miller looked like she hadn't slept at all in the last three days. Her eyes were solid red, and her hair stood out in rags and tags. When she saw my mother, she tried to pat it down and smooth her messy bed.

"Oh, Miz Curtiss, I thought for a little there that you might be him."

"No, you have got to accept, he is never coming through that door again."

"I keep thinkin' if they can't identify his body, how do they know it's him?"

"You know I have been calling Detroit, trying to find out what they have discovered. If you will eat some of Tuba's delicious bread pudding, I will tell you what I have just learned." She put the tray on Mrs. Miller's lap and the spoon in her hand. "Hughie, pour Mrs. Miller a nice cup of hot tea." She pulled a chair up to the bed. "Now, eat or I won't tell you." She waited until Mrs. Miller had swallowed two bites reluctantly.

"Mrs. Miller, your children can't lose both of their parents."

"Are you tellin' me he really is dead?"

"Yes. The morgue identified his body today."

"Till I see 'im buried, I won't believe it."

"I have asked that his body be shipped back here for burial."

Mrs. Miller held the spoon halfway to her mouth and stared at it. "Handsome needs his daddy. The boys need their daddy."

"Right now they need their mother. You are going to have to be both mother and father to your children, just as I am to Hughie."

I thought, Boy, that will be the day! There isn't another woman in the county with as much guts as she has, or one who lied as well—on her feet.

"You eat your food and have a nice warm bath. We have to make plans for his burial."

Mrs. Miller had let her full spoon drop back into the bowl. "When I kin look at his grave, I'll know it's really true."

"You know they won't let us bury him in any of the white cemeteries, even the private ones."

Mrs. Miller got practical and ate a couple of bites. She had heard that the black cemetery down by the river had so much groundwater, the graves were half full before they even dropped the casket down in. My mother suggested they bury him up on the hill beside Uncle Billie, as if she had just thought of it. Mrs. Miller smiled and ate faster, like she was really hungry.

"That way I could go up and talk to him every day. Oh, thank you." She embarrassed my mother by trying to kiss her hand. My mother patted her on top of her shaggy head; she wasn't a good hugger, she wasn't even a good patter.

On our way downstairs I asked her, "Where are you gonna get a dead body?"

"I just might have to go out and shoot somebody."

"I wouldn't put it past you."

DECEMBER 5, 1929

ON SATURDAY MORNING the three sets of brothers went up on the hill inside the ring of aspen trees, now bare, and dug a grave beside Uncle Billie's. The ground had not frozen deeply yet, so it was not too difficult.

My mother had coordinated her lie perfectly. She said Mr. Miller's body would be coming in on the two o'clock train, and the men from Runner's Funeral Home would meet the train and bring him out here. It was all on schedule. My mother followed the hearse, which held the casket, out from town. Grandfather Fancler was in the car with her. She would have preferred a black minister, but the old man had died recently and had not been replaced, and Grandfather could be relied on to say the right thing.

I thought she was just burying an empty casket until I saw the effort it took all our young men to hold it over the grave and hold on to the ropes that lowered it into the earth.

Grandfather looked into Mrs. Miller's eyes and said what he knew she wanted to hear. "Oh Lord, this was a good man who loved his family and gave his life trying to provide for them. Lord, that's all you really need to know about a man, so I ask you to take him into the kingdom of heaven and let him sit at your right hand. Amen." All the women standing by the grave said "Amen," and Stanley began to sing "In the Sweet By and By."

My mother and the others added their voices, and even Mrs. Miller sang, and they kept time by clapping their hands. (Each time I heard Stanley sing, his voice grew stronger and more assured.) And the other women guided Mrs. Miller back down the hill as though she were a sleepwalker.

The Forrester men and the Thorne boys stayed behind to shovel the pile of dirt into the grave. But Grandfather told them to go on. He would like to do it, he said, he needed the exercise. I stayed behind and watched him. He hung his coat and tie on a tree limb and didn't seem to notice I was there. The grave was half full before I asked him, "Who's in the box, Grandpa?"

He didn't look up. "Sylvia Tingler." He went on shoveling. Now it was full enough to start tramping it down. "Your mother needed a body. Sylvia needed a grave. You see, Hughie, everything comes out even, with just a little effort."

A canopy of dark clouds was moving down over the hills toward us by the time he had placed the last shovelful of dirt and tramped it into place. His shirt was wet from the effort. I held his coat for him and said, "Just in time," as the first big wet flakes of snow began falling.

"You see, the Lord is very obliging when you work with Him."

"How can you say that? You don't believe in the Lord."

"That doesn't keep me from working within the framework of belief. Did you see Mrs. Miller's face when I told her her husband was with God?"

"That's being a hypocrite."

"I know." He put his arm around my shoulder as we walked down the hill. It was the first time I could remember him doing that. "I may be God's very own hypocrite and not know it."

We had to take off our muddy shoes at the door and go to the back porch to clean them. We all ate together at the big table in the kitchen: pigs in the blanket, with sauerkraut and navy bean soup. Mrs. Miller ate like she was really hungry.

The roads quickly got too slick to drive Grandfather home. His muscles ached from the unusual exercise, so after supper he soaked in a hot tub with Epsom salts. There was a question that bothered me, so I went in and asked it.

"What if you're wrong and there really is a God?"

"That's possible but, my reasoning mind tells me, not very likely."

"But if there is, shouldn't you have told Him that was Sylvia Tingler in that casket and not Mr. Miller?"

"Well, if there really is a God, He would know without being told that it is Sylvia. He might even welcome her into heaven; after all, she wasn't too far removed from Mary Magdalene. She, too, was a woman of the streets and a friend to Jesus."

"Good night, Grandfather." I was going out the door when his voice caught me.

"Hughie, today was a secret. The book is closed, never to be talked about again."

I went to bed, but I still had questions I wouldn't be able to ask: such as, did Mary Magdalene give Jesus syphilis?

It was that kind of night when everyone disappears right after supper with a hot-water bottle and something to read. It must not have been Christmas week, for none of the decorations were up yet. There was a foot of snow on the ground, deeper in the windblown drifts, a couple inches of hard ice on top, and temperatures cold enough to keep it that way for days to come.

You had to be very careful of horses with this kind of ice. Only the ones with cleats on new shoes could walk without falling and breaking a leg and having to be put down. Ours were all safely in their heated stalls, wrapped in wool blankets.

Stanley and my mother and I were in the parlor with just the bright light from the fireplace. My mother was playing the scales for Stanley to sing. He was practicing over and over how to breathe in the middle of a note. I was heating three pokers in the fireplace grate to stir the three pewter mugs of cider that sat on the hearth. The odor was wonderful, mostly of the cinnamon bark that floated on the top. They each boiled, and I put the pokers back in the fire for a second round.

I had just put two mugs on the piano when the bell on our front gate sounded. We wouldn't have heard it, except that Stanley had stopped to drink. After the Klan incidents, you couldn't open or close the gate without a clang from the attached bell. I went and peeked through the drape. "Somebody in a little old truck."

"How many?"

"Just one."

"Then it's not the Klan. Those cowards come in groups. I'll go see."

"No, I'll go. Even the Klan wouldn't shoot a kid," I said.

"I wouldn't bet on it. There have been times when I could have shot you myself, and I'm your mother."

I opened the door, which squeaked from the cold, with my mother right behind me. A tall, skinny boy-man stood there, looking like half the young men in this county. Blond hair sticking out of a stocking cap and pale blue eyes. Right now his nose was very red and needed blowing.

"Yes?"

"I'm lookin' for Mrs. Billy Curtiss."

He didn't look like he had a gun under that long ragged overcoat, so my mother said, "I'm Billy Curtiss."

"I hear tell yer the sheriff's woman. He ain't here, is he?" He stuck his head around the door frame and looked into our hallway.

Now my mother's apprehension was growing. "Who sent you? What do you want?"

"I'm Estel Tingler. Your sister told me what you done for Syl."

My mother stared at his face. "Sylvia Tingler's brother? Is there no end?" She grasped him by his lapels and pulled him through the door. I slammed it shut. "Come on in here before we all freeze."

She pushed him toward the parlor. Stanley stopped singing, and his eyes narrowed. I think his first response where my mother's safety was concerned was to run and get a gun.

"Your sister, at the restaurant, tole me what you done."

My mother pulled the parlor door shut behind her. "Stanley, keep on singing. I don't want anyone to hear. My sister Sebe should mind her own business."

"I want to say, what kin I do for you?" He couldn't resist moving toward the fire. He held his hands out to the flames. He had on knit gloves, but the fingers were all out.

"Estel, you shouldn't be here. The sheriff thinks you killed those five Klansmen."

"I did, ma'am. Them's the ones that raped my sister."

"Then you have already done something for me. They were also my enemies."

"So I heered tell."

I gave him my mug of hot cider, and he gulped it down. "Ma'am, I didn't even git to say good-bye to ole Syl; I wondered, could I look at her grave?"

"Estel, it's dark. She's buried up against the hill on the other side of the road, the ground is covered with ice."

He put down his mug and just stood there and said nothing. He reminded me of a scarecrow in the middle of winter after the crows have all gone south. Stanley had gone up and down the scale four times. Now he just played the piano and watched. My mother looked at Estel for a long time, then she breathed a deep sigh.

"Wait till I get my boots on." I knew she was going up on that icy hillside. Stanley and I went to get our coats and flashlights when she stopped us. "There is no need for all of us freezing to death."

She took both our flashlights and gave my new big light with the seven batteries to Estel. Through the hall window, we watched the two circles of light on the bright ice cross the road and make their way up the hillside. We could just see them through the naked trees as they crossed over the sty into the little circle where Uncle Billie and Sylvia were buried.

It was lucky Mr. Miller's little marble marker wasn't up yet. (It was ordered but couldn't be put up until the ground thawed.) That would have been too much for even my mother to explain.

When they came back down, Estel was saying, "I expect that's a real purty place in the summertime. Syl should ought to have a nice place, she wuz a good girl. She wouldn't do nothin' with nobody, not even me, and I wuz her own brother."

As they came in to the fire, my mother said, "Why don't you take your coat off?"

"Thank you, ma'am, but I got to go. What if the sheriff comes?"

"I don't think he is going to work very hard at catching you. He knows how relieved I am that those men are gone."

"There's a lot more of 'em."

"Yes, there were thirty-two, I believe. You shot five, the sheriff one, and Estel—" she touched his hand—"this is our secret: I killed three."

"That's nine. How many does 'at leave?" He was trying to subtract in his head, but he couldn't. I said, "That's twenty-three."

"Thata many. 'Course I couldn't kill 'em all at once, but I could maybe pick 'em off one ata time."

"Estel, you can't do a thing like that."

"Why not? Yer sister tole me they wuz all your enemy, an' you're a nice lady." He smiled with his head down. "An' you sure are purty."

"I won't say don't do it, since I will be glad when every last one of those bastards are dead. I'll do it myself if I get the chance."

"I'm a purty good shot, but I couldn't shoot 'em through the eyes the way you kin."

"I won't do that anymore. When will that sister of mine learn to keep her mouth shut?"

"I won't tell 'er nothin'. I gotta go 'fore the radiator in my ole truck freezes."

When he went toward the door, my mother gave him my new flashlight. He didn't want to take it, but she insisted, "It's dark out there, Estel."

He stood in the doorway one minute more, as though he owed us an explanation for his visit. He gave it. "You know, ma'am, today woulda been Syl's birthday. She was fifteen."

He pulled the door shut behind him.

December 16, 1929

ON FRIDAY NIGHT, about two weeks before Christmas, Grandmother Curtiss called and said she thought my mother ought to bring me to see Grandfather the next morning, because he was failing fast and she thought it might be my last chance. I had seen him the week before and wasn't anxious to go back. He just lay there and wheezed. There were a lot of smells in that room, excluding fresh air: liniment, and oxygen, and something I thought was fat old man dying. He stared at me with watery eyes buried in the heavy folds of his face, and I couldn't tell whether he knew me or not. After a while, his old horse-faced nurse said, "You better go now, boy," so I went.

Now I was going to have to go again. As we drove out, the Thorne twins were coming up the driveway. They didn't have sense enough to know you didn't have to go to school on Saturday. They looked a foot taller, and even bigger around, in the new long black coats their brothers had bought them. Miss Larkin said she didn't mind their coming, since they were making real break-throughs. I thought the only breakthroughs they were going to make, the way they ate, was through the floorboards. They had stopped making baskets; there wasn't room for even one more basket anywhere, and no one left to give any to. Now they were making angels out of cornhusks. They ironed and trimmed and wired and painted until plain old cornhusks became angels in bright red and blue robes with white wings. They had round pink faces and yellow hair and halos made out of tinsel, and they hung on a string as if they were flying. As the twins worked, they recited the presidents all in a row, from Washington right down to Herbert Hoover. Even I couldn't do that, and sometimes they did the capitals of each state, and all the time their fingers kept busy, four angels an hour.

We stopped by the bakery to get Grandfather a big cream puff. They were his favorite. His doctor said he couldn't have anything like that, but my mother said if he was dying, what difference would it make.

Most of the town's storekeepers were busy decorating the store windows with red and green crepe-paper streamers and paper bells. They piled goods against the glass that they hoped somebody would come in and buy. The newspaper said everyone was afraid to spend what little money they had. We parked in front of Mr. Isaac's store and went to look in his window. He had just a big blue curtain and, in front of it, a crèche. There were a lot of figures around the manger, shepherds, and sheep, and the Wise Men. It all looked very old and carved out of wood, with some of the gilt worn away from years of touching. The baby Jesus looked awful big, like a two-year-old, with blue eyes and yellow hair, and one of the three Wise Men had a black face. There was a glass star hanging over it all with a lightbulb in it.

My mother ran in and told Mr. Isaac how pretty she thought it was.

"I just had a visitor who didn't think so."

"Who on earth could object?"

"The Baptist minister. First off, he said nowhere in the Bible does it say one of the three Wise Men was a nigger."

"But Balthazar came from Egypt."

"I think the good minister's real objection is me. What is a Jew doing with a Christian symbol? He said the Klan would take care of me."

"He certainly has the Christmas spirit. I'll call Lester and see that he talks to the good minister. Don't forget, you're coming out to dinner Sunday night."

When we got to Grandfather's, I thought maybe he was already dead. The whole house seemed to be in mourning. The blinds were down, and the hall was dark. My mother said to the horse-faced nurse, "Why don't you go down and have a cup of coffee? I'll call you if you're needed." My mother said it like "Get out of here." The nurse didn't want to, but she went.

Grandfather was propped up to a sitting position so he could breathe. It felt like he had already breathed up all the air in the room. He whispered, "Could you open a window? That witch won't let me have any air."

My mother did. I really liked the big old brass bed he was in. It had fat polished posts with glass balls on top, and rings between the bars that you could spin. I thought, As soon as he is out of it, I'm going to ask Grandmother for it—that and the grizzly bear.

My mother found a spoon on his tray and spooned the custard out of the cream puff into his mouth. The effort of eating tired him. He settled back on his pillows; I thought he was asleep. My mother went outside and sat in the hall.

His voice cracked. "Hughie, did they tell you I'm dying?"

"Yeah. Grandmother said you're sinkin' fast."

"I suppose it can't be fast enough for her. You're my heir, Hughie. You're supposed to carry on for me. I don't find much comfort in that. You're the last of the Curtisses."

"I want to ask you something." I got close to his ear so my mother in the hallway couldn't hear. "Some people say Curtiss ain't even our name."

"Oh, it's our legal name. My grandfather the old general adopted me and gave me his name."

"Tuba says you're a bastard and your father killed Lincoln."

He seemed to get stronger, like he wanted to set the record straight. "I don't really know the truth of that. It's haunted me all my life. I know that a man who called himself John Ferris was my father, but whether he was Booth or not—who knows?"

"Tuba said you killed him."

"That old black bitch talks too much."

He had a fit of coughing and spit blood into his napkin. My mother came to see to him, but he motioned her back to the hall. Now he whispered, "You got a right to know what I know. My mother was Aunt Almeda's sister. They were in Washington when Lincoln was killed. And when my mother came back here, John Ferris was with her. They lived over at Meyer's Lake till I was born. My mother went a little crazy, and she came back here to this house with me, to live with the old general. I only saw John Ferris a couple of times as I grew up. The whole town seemed to know more about it than I did. Old people were always sayin' to me, 'Your daddy killed ole Abe!' Finally I couldn't take it anymore, and old Doc Butt—he was my best friend—and I went out to the lake to learn the truth. Ferris laughed at me, and I hit him with a log chain. We couldn't tell if he was dead or not, so to be sure, we wrapped that big chain around him and dumped him in the lake. He wasn't done haunting me. After a couple of weeks, enough gas formed in his rotting body to bring him to the top. We dragged him out and buried him up here in the family cemetery. I didn't know any more in the end than I did in the beginning."

He was silent for a long time except for his heavy breathing, and then his breath got less and less, and I thought he was dead. I called my mother, and she heard him say, "That was my deathbed confession, Hughie. I'm sorry, I don't know the truth about anything. I never did." He tried again. "I'm supposed to tell you great truths, something meaningful. I never experienced anything really meaningful."

I thought I'd make it easy. "Do you want me to tell you a truth?"

"Yes, if you know any."

"I never loved you, even when you gave me five dollars."

"I knew that. We Curtiss men don't know what love is. Not me—not your father—not you." He giggled until tears rolled down. I thought maybe his brain was coming apart and the water was leaking out. "See if you can figure it out." His voice got slower, and the last words popped out of the bubbles on his lips.

Now he really was dead. His chest stopped going up and down, and a couple of bloody bubbles came out of his nose. I think he peed in the bed; there was a big wet spot on the counterpane. I didn't care. When I got the bed home, I would get a new mattress anyway.

When the nurse came back and felt for Grandfather's pulse, she began to yell, "I knew it, I knew it would happen—five minutes out of the room—just five minutes!" My mother gave her a good sharp smack across the mouth.

We went over to tell Grandmother Curtiss he was gone. She wasn't home. She had gone to the beauty shop to get her hair marcelled.

Mr. Isaac didn't come to dinner on Sunday night because he was in the hospital. On Saturday night, just after Mr. Isaac had turned on his Star of Bethlehem and gone up to his apartment, some of the Klan were standing on a truck bed out in the street yelling their usual rhetoric: "Christ killer . . . dirty Jew . . . nigger lover."

One of them wrapped a brick in kerosene-soaked rags and set a fire by throwing it through Mr. Isaac's upper window. It landed on his Marie Antoinette dining table, and the kerosene ran a flaming stream down over the gilt legs and onto his Aubusson carpet.

He said that without even thinking, he had grabbed up the flaming mess and thrown it back out through the broken window down onto their truck. It caught the bucket of kerosene on fire, and flame spewed out everywhere as they drove away. One of them fell off the fender and broke his leg. By the time they got to the next corner, the fire in the back had spread until they had to jump out of the truck and leave it to burn. Mr. Isaac did not realize how badly he was burned until the fire department came and took him to the hospital.

Dr. Butt called our house on Sunday afternoon and told my mother to come and get Grandfather Fancler. He had been at Mr. Isaac's bedside since the night before, and he wouldn't go home.

It was six o'clock and dark by the time we got there. Mr. Isaac was doped up and looked dead, but he was just sleeping. Both hands were bandaged to the elbow. Each finger was spread out on what looked like a Ping-Pong paddle, and his chest was covered in gauze.

Grandfather was in the chair beside his bed, fast asleep. He didn't want to go home with us, he wanted to be there when Mr. Isaac woke up so he would know he had a friend.

"He will have a sick friend if you don't go home and get some sleep," my mother said.

Grandfather agreed. "Yes, I'd better. Leon is going to need me now."

On the way home, he said, "I'll have to learn to drive Leon's truck. I have always resisted learning; I really don't know why now. If Leon's hands don't heal right, he may never be able to drive again. You can start teaching me in the morning."

My mother looked straight ahead and said nothing.

Grandfather Curtiss was buried on the twentieth of December. Grandmother said that was just like him to spoil the holidays. He was not buried in the old Curtiss cemetery. Grandmother had been expecting this for some time and was all ready. She had bought a big plot in the new Maplewood cemetery, just up the knoll from Senator Burton. She had a large block of polished gray granite placed in the middle, with CURTISS in big bold letters, and twelve headstones around it where everyone else would be eventually. I didn't tell her, but I resolved that no "eventually" was going to stretch far enough to put me under one of those little gray stones.

My father came in on the morning train and went back on the five o'clock to Buffalo. My mother drove him to the station. She said, "Do you have to go back so soon?"

"Do you want me to stay?"

"No, I just thought Hughie has hardly seen you."

I said, "I've seen him."

He said, "I have someone waiting."

She said, "I'm sure you do. Hughie, say good-bye to your father."

"Good-bye, Father."

He got out, and we didn't wait for his train to pull away. He had shrunk, he was much smaller.

Aunt Bea did not come because she was pregnant and had to stay in bed for fear the baby would drop out. Aunt Opal came with a new boyfriend who wore plus fours and looked like the Prince of Wales and worked as a private secretary for Herbert Hoover. He took her all over the White House when no one was home and even let her lie down in Lincoln's bed. I was going to ask her in private how it felt to know maybe, just maybe, your grandfather killed him, but I didn't get the chance.

Aunt Almeda came in a long black sealskin coat and a black hat with a veil.
She seemed to be the only one really crying. I heard her all through the church
service and the quick graveside service. The sleet was falling like a rain of ice,
and therefore the service got short shrift.

My mother invited Grandmother for Christmas, but she said she was of two
minds about Grandfather. She didn't know whether to grieve for him or celebrate. She didn't want to spoil the holidays for us. She would go to one of the
Sea Island hotels off the coast of the Carolinas, where people got paid for having their holidays spoiled. She left us all very large packages wrapped in silver
paper and tied with red velvet.

Just three days before Christmas, Mr. Isaac was released from the hospital.
Grandfather Fancler was planning to take him home and take care of him.
When I asked him why, he said he was his newfound brother and he had a
responsibility. Mr. Isaac couldn't go back to his apartment, since Grandfather
and the Forrester men had nailed it up tight, boards over all the doors and windows, so everything he owned wouldn't be stolen. Some people thought you
could steal from a Jew and it wasn't like regular stealing.

Mr. Isaac couldn't do much for himself, since both his hands were bandaged
up like big white mittens. Every day the bandages had to come off, and his hands
were soaked in hot water and exercised and wrapped back up again. Rose knew
all about that sort of thing, since she had worked in a hospital for soldiers with
burns during the war—that was where she had met her husband—so my
mother brought Mr. Isaac and Grandfather to our house. Grandfather gave him
the bed in his room, and he slept in the trundle that pulled out from underneath. Mr. Isaac was like a baby: he had to have the water glass held for him and
the food spooned into his mouth. And when he went to the bathroom, somebody had to help him. Sometimes it was Rose and sometimes it was Grandfather. I made it clear it was never going to be me.

I got a Christmas card from Aunt Almeda with a hundred-dollar bill in it.
It was one of those old-fashioned bills that were bigger but still good money. I
figured she had been digging into her safe in the basement. She wrote me a
strange note. It said, "Hughie, don't forget your promise to me. When I am
buried up in the old cemetery, you will come and sit on my grave and talk
to me."

My mother got a card from Aunt Opal that made Aunt Almeda sound even
stranger. She told us that Aunt Almeda talked to the senator all the time and
even set a place at the table for him. Aunt Opal said she would soon be out of

there, as she was going to marry the fellow she brought to Grandfather's funeral. His name was Elwood Harrington III, and he had social entrée. (Whatever that was.) My mother said she didn't know Aunt Opal had social ambitions.

I said, "There are a lot of things you don't know."

She said, "I know it doesn't pay to have a smart mouth only three days before Christmas," but I knew anything I was going to get was already bought and she wouldn't take it back.

Aunt Russie wrote a letter instead of a card, mostly about Aunt Lilly. Her nose was out of joint because Aunt Lilly hadn't called her. Lilly had her picture in the paper as hostess for a gallery opening sponsored by the Egyptian embassy. Aunt Russie said the man beside her was as black as the ace of spades. "I suppose that is why she hasn't called, she knows how I feel about those people. I will say, she is cutting a very broad swath."

Aunt Lilly hadn't written to us, either, or to anyone else, even Grandfather. I guessed cutting a broad swath took up all your time.

My father sent me a pair of high-tops with a pocket in the side that held another of those Swiss knives with sixteen blades. That made three I had amassed in a very short lifetime. The shoes were too small, I couldn't even get them on. We'd have to find someone to give them to.

We had a big Christmas tree in the front hall, and a second one in the rear dining room so the Millers could have a private Christmas, since this was their first without Mr. Miller. My mother told another of her big lies; she said Mr. Miller ordered a lot of things for them before he left. I was with her at Montgomery Ward when she bought Handsome a fire truck he could ride. The gold wedding band she said Mr. Miller bought because Mrs. Miller never had one she bought at Thompson's.

She paid the Thorne twins ten cents each for all the dozens of angels we hung on the trees. The twins bought their mother a big pink glass punch bowl with eighteen cups. She said it was the prettiest thing she ever had in her whole life.

I got a big Lionel electric train with twenty-one cars and enough track to go around the base of the Christmas tree two times, but I had to share it with everyone, even Grandfather Fancler.

Mr. Isaac gave me his telescope and a big chart of the night sky I planned to paste on the ceiling over my bed. He gave it to me because he didn't have any grandchildren, and Grandfather was sharing everything else with him.

New Year's 1930

On New Year's Eve, my mother dressed Handsome like the New Year and wrote "1930" on a ribbon across his diaper. He wore a gold paper crown and carried a long red horn. Some of the people at our party didn't like it and whispered behind my mother's back, "The New Year looks black enough without that." Nevertheless, they ate the food and danced in our hallway to records of "Star Dust" and "Tiptoe Through the Tulips," "Singin' in the Rain" and "Moaning Low." And at twelve o'clock, they drank toasts with seventy-five-year-old brandy from our wine cellar.

There were maybe eighty guests in our house, so it was hard to tell who did it, but someone stuck a piece of paper on the mirror in our powder room that said "Nigger Lover."

January and February 1930

Not much happened in the first months of the year. The snow stayed on the ground, three feet thick with a crust on top. People stayed in, mostly, and studied seed catalogues. They let their potbellied stoves get too hot, and two houses on the road to town burned down. (My mother didn't take those people in. We don't have any more room.) One old woman burned up because she had gotten too fat to get down their narrow enclosed stairway. A bootlegger had been sent to prison, and his wife hid behind a road repair shack trying to steal enough dynamite to blow up the prison and get him out. She froze to death. It did get very cold. Most of the hound dogs had come into the house. I slept with three under my feather tick, one at each side of me and one at my feet. When the snow finally melted, you could see where the sheep had been gnawing on the bark of trees some four feet from the ground.

Stanley and I missed only three days of school, and they weren't our fault. The school bus broke down because the radiator froze and burst. The driver had put moonshine whiskey in it to keep it from freezing. I guess the bootlegger put too much water in it. When times get bad, people seem to cheat all up and down the line.

Grandmother Curtiss's library tables were all covered with floor plans and drawings. She had hired an architect full-time. She was planning to build a two-story addition of thirty bedrooms between her two houses. She was going to build a hotel. She had realized that she could not afford to entertain and associate with the level of people she so admired, people with millions of dollars. I don't know how much money she had now, but it wasn't millions. She had figured a way she could still be a hostess in the grand manner and be paid for it. Just when it seemed everyone else in the country was cutting back, she was surging forward. She planned for the Orchard House Inn to be selective, expensive, and as stylish as she could figure out how to make it.

While her architect worked on the plans, she went from one exclusive hotel to another, studying them, meeting everyone she could. She hired a little fat woman named Elsa Maxwell to introduce her around New York, and when she got the hotel finished, Miss Maxwell was going to invite her friends to the opening party, all for a price.

By February Mr. Isaac's hands were healed well enough that the bandages were off, and he was anxious to do something about his store. He moved it into the hall that had been Aunt Opal's theater, which was a lot bigger. He was going to expand into restoring antiques, refinishing, and upholstering. Now he had no apartment, so he moved in with Grandfather Fancler.

Rose had done such a good job on the eighteen chairs that Mr. Isaac put her in charge of refinishing. She couldn't go back and forth, so she, too, moved in with Grandfather. I think she and Mr. Isaac were sweet on each other. If someone had held on to my dick while I peed, I guess I would get sweet on her, too.

MARCH 1930

BY THE END OF the first week in March, a sudden warming had melted the snow, and the river was out of its banks. It rained and kept on raining. My mother said that was a good thing. The grand wizard of the Ku Klux Klan was in town on a recruitment drive, and at least there would not be any burning crosses. There had been threats. I don't know how many were in our mailbox, because my mother would crumple them quickly and put them in her pocket. She had moved a gun rack to the front hall, near the front door. It had become clear that the law wasn't going to do anything about the Klan. Judge Brown had refused to issue warrants for arson or attempted murder after their attack on Mr. Isaac. He said you could not prosecute a whole group for the actions of a few men, and you couldn't even see their faces. Lester had hired two extra deputies without the permission of the county commissioners.

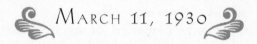

MARCH 11, 1930

IT WAS MY BIRTHDAY, and I wanted to go to the movies. The Grand Theatre was showing *Hell's Angels.* I would have gone by myself, and my mother would have picked me up, but now she was afraid for me to be loose in town without her. Lester felt the same way about her, so all three of us went to the movie. Lester and I liked it. The week before we had all three sat through a movie with a Swede named Greta Garbo being *Anna Christie,* and only Mother liked that one.

When we came out, Lester went to get the car while we waited under the portico. A voice behind my mother said, "Miss Curtiss, could you let me have ten dollars?"

We turned to see Sylvia Tingler's brother, Estel. He was wearing a cowboy hat dripping rain from the brim, and carrying an old straw suitcase. My mother reached in her purse. "Estel, are you going out of town?"

"No, ma'am. I'm gittin' inducted in the Klan t'night, and it costs ten dollars."

"Estel, why on earth would you?" She was holding on to the ten-dollar bill.

He put his mouth close to her ear, but I could hear. "The only way I kin git 'em is frum the inside. I got me ten sticks-a-dynamite here. It's what my daddy uses to blow fish out of the river. I'm gonna blow them bastards all to hell."

"Estel, you're going to get yourself killed."

"No, I ain't. I got me a long fuse. They're meetin' out at Martin's barn."

She gave him the ten dollars, and he went.

Because it was my birthday, we stopped at Stanaker's drugstore and had hot fudge over ice cream. I ate mine and my mother's. She said she was watching her weight, but she kept turning her head to the side like she was listening, and she seemed distracted and didn't answer when Lester said something to her.

We drove slowly toward home, because the water was up to the hubcaps in the dips in the road. We had gotten about to the Smith place when we heard the explosion. It was like the loud noises in *Hell's Angels* when James Hall and Ben Lyon dropped a bomb on a German munitions center, and a couple of booms followed. The sound was distant, but you could hear it rumble up the road even through the falling rain. Lester said, "What the hell?" and stopped the car and rolled down the glass. My mother didn't say anything, but she knew. She looked quickly into the backseat at me, which meant "Keep your mouth shut."

When we got back to the edge of town, we saw the fire truck and four or five other cars going toward Martin's barn, and people running in that direction. Only one person was coming this way. Estel had lost his hat, and the rain made his face shiny in the headlights, and he looked a little crazy because he was laughing.

The barn had completely collapsed, and the old tin roof and the big square beams stood at odd angles. If there was any fire, the rain had put it out and settled the dust. The firemen pulled up their truck so the bright beam of the spotlights lighted the destruction. They jumped out and began pulling debris off the assembled Klansmen.

Lester said to my mother, "You better stay in the car."

Mother got out anyway and put up her umbrella. She said to me, "You better stay in the car." I got out and took the lap robe with me for over my head.

Very quickly, there must have been at least forty people there. Someone hooked a tractor to a long chain and began dragging away the fallen timbers. Lester tried to take charge, but no one listened. Someone said, "If they ain't dead, they soon will be when they get through draggin' that stuff over them."

They were dead, all of them. Whether from the explosion or the falling building or the actions of their rescuers, not one was alive. People began pulling them out and laying them faceup in the rain. Some still had their hoods on, and some of the robes were in tatters, and you could see their bloody bodies underneath. My mother walked between the rows, shining her flashlight into their faces. A beam had cut across the Baptist minister's neck, and his head hung to his neck only by a bloody cord.

When my mother got to the end of the row, she called to Lester to come and see. Near the end was the grand wizard from Louisiana. You could tell by

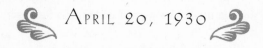

what was left of his red satin and gold robes, and beside him was a purple-robed pulpy mass of flesh that had once been Judge Brown. On the front of his robe you could still see a big red satin letter "D."

I said, "What do you think that stands for?"

My mother looked at the "D." "In his case, I should think 'damnation.'"

"I thought you didn't believe in hell."

"I have reevaluated my beliefs and my thinking this last year. I'm basing my belief in hell on a case-to-case basis, and in Judge Brown's case, I think he may very well be suffering the torments of fire and brimstone."

I studied his face. His lips were pulled back in a silent scream, and his eyes looked like they might be staring into the fiery pit.

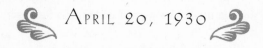

APRIL 20, 1930

THE GROUNDHOG DID NOT see his shadow that February, so spring came early. By the first week in April, a warm wind had awakened the flowering cherry trees, a gift from Japan around the tidal basin in Washington, D.C. My mother thought the trip would be fun, so she took Stanley and me to see them.

The Western Maryland railroad ran an excursion train arriving early Sunday morning in Washington and leaving Sunday night, round-trip for three dollars. Even in the new depression, most people could still afford that if they took food in a basket. The train was packed. The railway added two extra cars.

Grandmother Curtiss was going, too, but not on that cattle car, as she called it. Matthew drove her in her limousine. She got there the day before and stayed in the Senate Hotel. Just to prove she wasn't a complete snob, she took Miss Larkin, who was good company on a long trip. To help Miss Larkin in and out of her bath and push her wheelchair, Grandmother had requested that Mrs. Miller accompany them. She could stay in an adjoining room and go up and down the elevator as long as she wore her black uniform. There was no car on the train for black people. Mrs. Miller had two nieces in Washington, and she wanted to see what the schools were like now that my mother assured her there was money to educate her children. In 1930 Washington was 25 percent black.

Grandmother went to Washington because Aunt Opal was getting married. She had received a formal invitation on White House stationery, and all it said was what, who, and where. Opal was marrying that funny-looking fellow who was a private secretary to Herbert Hoover, and the president had invited them to use the East Room. There had been no note from Opal on Grandmother's invitation that said "Come and stay with us." She wouldn't have anyway, in Aunt Almeda's house.

We got the same kind of invitation, except ours said "To Mrs. Huston C. Curtiss and Son." My mother just inked in a neat little "S" to make "son" plural, so she could take Stanley. We each took a blanket with us on the train, and when they turned out the lights, we all rolled up and went to sleep to the music of the train rattling along over an uneven track that cut its way through the Allegheny Mountains.

We arrived at Washington's Union Station at six in the morning and took a taxi to Aunt Russie's house. Aunt Russie's nose was out of joint because we were going to the White House, and she had never been there in her twenty years in Washington, except on tours. Her daughter Helen had married recently, but no one nearly as important as the president's secretary. Her husband, my uncle Ryan, was helping to set up the Pan-American Airways, and he was hardly ever home. Also, she said, the blacks were taking over the city. It wasn't safe for a decent white woman to get on a bus, so Uncle Ryan had given her a chauffeur-driven limousine that he was probably going to charge up to his new company. Now here she was alone, with a car and a driver and no place to go.

After we ate breakfast, my mother put on her new outfit and her Easter hat. Stanley and I had new linen jackets. (Again she was dressing him like he was my brother.) We borrowed Aunt Russie's car and driver and left her in bed with a headache and got to the White House at ten-thirty. Grandmother's car was already in the parking lot, with Matthew sitting at the wheel like a statue, and Mrs. Miller and Miss Larkin were wandering around the grounds.

A uniformed man checked our invitation at the door and guided us to the East Room. The wedding wasn't going to be very big. There were maybe twenty little gilt bamboo chairs and a young woman playing the largest, most elegant piano I had ever seen.

We were barely seated beside Grandmother Curtiss when an attendant came and got my mother. Whatever he whispered, she smiled and followed him, so I knew they weren't throwing her out. There was a fat woman with a hat that had about a bushel of flowers on top. I guessed she was the groom's mother. I'll bet when Grandmother saw that, she was sorry she had only two white gardenias on the lapel of her brown silk suit, but hers were real, I could smell them.

Aunt Almeda wasn't here, and I was sorry. Aunt Opal said she had stayed home to get lunch for Senator Burton's ghost.

Some of the people looked like they worked here in the White House. The groom, Elwood Harrington, came in wearing a gray morning coat and a stiff white collar. He stood in front of the fireplace with an old man who I thought must be Charles Evans Hughes, head of the Supreme Court. Grandmother whispered that he was going to read the service. I wanted to see the president, but he had gone down the Potomac River in his yacht, leaving the vice president and his sister to host the annual Easter egg hunt on the lawn. You could hear the kids yelling through the open French doors.

We heard "Believe Me, if All Those Endearing Young Charms," and I thought they ought to play the march and get them in here. Elwood was shifting from foot to foot like he needed to go to the bathroom or his underwear was too tight. Stanley had sung all the songs under his breath, and when she played the intro to "I Love You Truly," he couldn't sit still any longer. He said to my grandmother, "May I?"

Grandmother said, "Why not?" And a voice filled that grand old room, every bit as elegant as the gilded plaster and the hanging crystal and the portrait of Dolley Madison. Stanley stood as he sang, and he walked up to the piano. He faced the room full of surprised guests, with that innocent glow of his gold-speckled face and the full soaring sounds, as though another instrument of great resonance and power had been added to the piano. Even I knew there should have been masses of violins, and someday there would be.

Charles Evans Hughes wiped his eyes as Stanley found his seat and the pianist began the wedding march from *Lohengrin*. Grandmother grasped Stanley's wrist and whispered over me, "Now you can say you have sung in the White House."

First my mother marched in, and I knew what Aunt Opal had wanted. She didn't even have a matron of honor, so my mother was it. Her white leghorn hat had a high crown to accommodate her hair. I wouldn't tell her, but I thought she looked really beautiful, and I felt sorry for poor Aunt Opal. I need not have. She came smiling through the door, looking much taller and prettier than I remembered. The Kewpie-doll curls around her face had been swept back into deep, smooth waves, and her big yellow hat sat on the back of her head like a halo. She wore a long white silk coat open down the front over a yellow lace dress. I saw Grandmother leaning forward, looking at her strangely, no doubt wondering if this was truly her daughter Opal and who had wrought the change.

After the ceremony was over, Grandmother asked her. Aunt Opal said in her commanding voice, "It's called getting away from home and growing up at last." I think Grandmother was more amazed than miffed. She didn't think it would ever happen.

I looked around to see if there was something I could steal to prove to Boobie that I had really been in the White House. I was considering the plate the staff served the cake on, but they came around with a little piece of cake in a box, with the presidential seal, to take home, and that would do it.

Mrs. Harrington kept on gushing, "My boy, my boy," and dabbing tears from her eyes. Aunt Opal smiled, but she had her teeth pressed together when she said, "Mother Harrington, if you don't remember that your boy is now my man, this marriage doesn't stand a chance." She took her man by the arm and hurried him out the door. They were going to the Bahamas for their honeymoon, and I guessed she didn't want to miss the boat.*

Grandmother went out on the terrace to be sure Miss Larkin and Mrs. Miller got cake and champagne; after all, she was their hostess. The woman who had played the piano came up to Stanley and said she could get him work singing at weddings, but Stanley said, "No thank you, I'm a horse trainer, and I have to go back to West Virginia."

When we came out the French doors from the East Room, we found that Mrs. Miller had pushed Miss Larkin up to where she could see the Easter eggs rolling on the east lawn. Vice-President Charles Curtis and his sister, Mrs. Gann, were hosting this annual tradition for the poor and underprivileged. My mother and grandmother both went down on the lawn to meet Vice-President Curtis. When my mother came back to the portico, Miss Larkin was sitting there wiping her eyes.

"Miss Larkin, are you all right?"

"Yes, my dear. I was just thinking that here I am sitting on the portico of the White House, and just a year ago I thought I would be sitting the rest of my life on the front porch of the poorhouse." She grasped my mother's hand. "You do have a way of putting everyone's life in order."

I don't know if my mother was embarrassed, but she bent and whispered, "That's my mission." I knew even then that she was going to think it was her mission to order my life, too, and I would have to start planning pretty soon how to get away.

---

* It was hardly worth the trip; they were married only two years. When Hoover left office, Elwood went home to his mother, and Aunt Opal found herself a Democrat.

Grandmother took her guests to lunch somewhere, and we went back to eat with Aunt Russie and drive around until train time. We saw Ford's Theatre, where Lincoln was shot, and the room across the street where he died the next morning. I was glad no one started that old tale of how the assassin might have been my great-grandfather. I was getting pretty tired of that old story.

Aunt Russie did fight the Civil War over again at every opportunity, and when we got up to Arlington she pointed out how dear General Lee's plantation had been turned into a northern graveyard, and then she really let go. She said all the problems of the country started when the Negroes left the plantations, and if they could be driven back again, our lives would all be restored. My mother reminded her that they had not come from an old plantation and were only the daughters of a simple country preacher. Aunt Russie frowned and motioned to the driver's back. She didn't want him to hear things like that. He was white, of course. Three or four times when we stopped, my mother found a phone and left messages for Aunt Lilly.

We were in Union Station at eight. They hadn't opened the gate yet, Aunt Russie was waiting with us when Stanley said, "Will you look at that!" and we did. A figure was coming toward us out of a movie magazine or a Russian fairy tale. She was tall and thin and white and silver. All capes and towering hat, she held a leash in each hand attached to two huge white Russian borzois pulling her forward.

Aunt Russie breathed, "Dear God, I think it's Lillian." You couldn't be sure, even when she came closer; her face was painted like a porcelain mask. Aunt Russie was glued to her seat, but my mother rose to greet her. When I saw the man walking ten feet behind her in a long black robe, a red turban, and a face copied from the wall of an Egyptian tomb, I knew he used to be Eddie Horner, and this had to be Aunt Lilly.

People in the station had gathered around in a wide circle to look at them. My mother said, "Lilly, I'm so glad you could come." Aunt Lilly extended one gloved hand. We were not kissers in our family; you wouldn't have kissed her anyway, she looked like she might break. She waved one hand airily behind her and said, "You know Abdul Kabal, my associate."

Aunt Russie looked at him and narrowed her eyes and lips. "You make me want to go somewhere and hide."

Aunt Lilly smiled with her mouth but not her lavender-lidded eyes and said, "Why don't you?"

The big white dogs sniffed at Stanley and me. I could see Stanley was memorizing Aunt Lilly in case he wanted to look like that someday. The dogs were about five feet long, with the sharpest noses I had ever seen, and only about six inches wide.

"Those dogs sure look like they belong to you."

"Well, thank you, Hughie."

"I sure wish they belonged to me."

My mother shook the Egyptian's hand. He didn't say anything; Stanley and I wondered later if Aunt Lilly had had his tongue cut out. My mother said, "That's quite a show you put on."

Aunt Lilly smiled that smile again without cracking her face. She was good at it. "That's all there is to life, you know, show. I just wanted to come down and tell you good-bye. We are going to Paris soon, and then on to Egypt."

"Will you write?"

"No, probably not."

The big iron gates rolled back, and the loudspeaker announced our train.

"Please just tell Dad I said good-bye."

There wasn't anything else to say. The show turned around and went back the way it came. We moved toward the train. Aunt Russie was left sitting like a scarecrow out in the cornfield after all the crops were in.

Around midnight the hawker came through the train, and Stanley and I each bought a hot dog. My mother was curled up on the seat opposite us, her knees drawn up under her chin, sound asleep. Stanley sat and stared at her as he ate.

"I've seen a lot of pretty women today, but you know something, Hughie, I'll bet your mother is the most beautiful woman in the world." He licked the mustard off his fingers. "I've got to learn how to look just like her."

Grandmother's car did not get back until Wednesday night, and Miss Larkin and Mrs. Miller were both so wound up, they didn't even seem tired. On Monday they had driven to Fredricksburg, Virginia, where Grandmother owned a factory for making military uniforms, part of her inheritance she had never seen. She was aghast at the enormity of the sewing factory and the storage warehouse. It had been shuttered just after the Great War, when it seemed the need for uniforms was at an end. Mrs. Miller told about the hundreds and hundreds of new coats packed away, and what a shame it was when so many people in these hills were cold. Grandmother must have felt the same way, for the shipments started arriving very soon. Miss Larkin was more interested in the bolts and bolts of new cloth: white cotton duck, navy wool, khaki-colored serges, and the power sewing machines to stitch them.

Miss Larkin told my mother, "Your mother-in-law is a wonderful woman, and as soon as she figures out how to do it, she is going to move that stuff out of there."

On Tuesday they drove on to Charlottesville, where my mother's older sister, Fannie, was busy helping to restore Monticello. Aunt Fannie knew my grandmother, since they had been schoolgirls together. After the restoration began, the committee sent out pleas for people who had the original furnishings to return them. Everybody in Virginia seemed to think they had an original Thomas Jefferson piece, so a dozen times more stuff had piled up in the barns than would ever go back in the house. That was why Grandmother stopped over. She wanted to see about buying some of the excess, since she had decided to furnish her new inn with early-American antiques. The money Grandmother paid could be used to refinish floors and paint brick, so they had made a deal.

Miss Larkin repeated before she went to bed, "Your mother-in-law is absolutely wonderful."

She didn't even limp very much as she went down the hall.

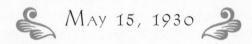

MAY 15, 1930

ON THE LAST DAY of school, you could tell by looking at the kids' faces as they got on the bus to go home that nobody had flunked. The year before, there had been five. Everybody knew the improvement was because of Stanley, but not one kid said thank you. Every evening all year, Stanley had gone up and down the aisle of the bus saying to each one, "What's your assignment for tomorrow? If you don't know what you're supposed to do, you sure as hell can't do it." In the morning, he checked to see if it was done. Instead of screaming and yelling and throwing things, we spent the time saying the multiplication tables and having spelling bees, and sometimes we sang. Stanley had to shake Bob Marsteller only about once a month. I guess it worked; Bob was one of the kids who had failed last year, and this year he didn't even get one D.

Stanley kept his report card in his pocket, and as he got off the bus, the driver didn't even say thank you for making his job easier. He just said, "And how did our little teacher do?"

Stanley just said, "Fine, thank you," and kept his card in his inside coat pocket.

I knew when I followed him, looking for my mother, that he probably got straight A's, as usual. He found her down in the exercise ring, currying Black, trying to brush the last of his winter coat off him. I saw him hold out the card; she looked at it and hugged him, she who seldom hugged anybody. She saw me going toward the kitchen and yelled, "Hughie, come and let me see your report card." I pretended I hadn't heard and went on into the kitchen.

I got promoted all right into the fifth grade, but I got a D in deportment, and all because of a drawing on the blackboard that I did of the teacher when she was out of the room. The only way she could know I did it was that I could draw better than most kids in the room (I got an A in drawing). She was just mad because I drew her butt so big. She did have a big butt. Anyway, we wouldn't see her anymore; she was going to get married, so she had to quit teaching.

Aunt Sebe got married because she was pregnant. She and Kirby went up to Maryland where you could get married without notice and it wouldn't be in the paper, so when the baby was born, people couldn't count back nine months and say it was a bastard. Being a bastard in our town was a terrible thing that stayed with you until the older generation who remembered died. My new uncle Kirby paid the clerk five dollars to move the date on the marriage certificate back three months. Of course Worthy and Harry told me. They were glad to have a daddy. Their father had been dead before they could remember. Aunt Sebe said if they didn't behave themselves, they would have to go to work in their stepfather's coal mines. I was glad I wasn't a part of that. The worst my mother could threaten me was to send me out to shovel horse shit.

The Irish Catholics got their church done and dedicated early in June. They had been building it since the year I was born. Many of the European cathedrals took three hundred years, so I guess eight wasn't so bad. They built it stone by stone as they raised the money. Part of the delay was caused by Grandmother Curtiss's father, Joseph Channell. He had drawn the original designs and trained a group of young Irishmen to cut the sandstone into usable shapes. He had also carved the figure of Saint Michael the Archangel that was to stand over the entrance and to whom the church was dedicated. It was a mammoth figure, twice life size, and with spreading wings that covered the whole width of the bell tower. He held up the flaming sword with which he had driven Lucifer out of heaven. He was naked except for a little wisp of cloud that drifted across his middle, and it was the shape of that little cloud that caused a lot of trouble. It bulged too much for Catholic taste, and some people thought they ought to bring in a stonecutter and trim the cloud to a respectable jockstrap, but no one had risked it. Saint Michael was very beautiful, and with good reason. Great-grandfather Channell had used his nineteen-year-old son, Alvin, as his model.

JUNE 1, 1930

THE CHURCH OFFICIALLY OPENED the first of June, and the paper was full of it, including pictures of the nave and the altar, the pipe organ and the new priest. They got three for one in him, because he had been a choral director in Italy and was an accomplished musician who could play their complicated pipe organ, which had cost twenty thousand dollars.

Mr. Marino told us the parishioners, who were mostly Irish, wanted an Irish priest, but the diocese was fresh out of Irishmen, so an Italian was sent. Mr. Marino said the trouble was, the priest was too smart for this bunch of dumb Irishmen. He was determined to teach some of them to sing. When Stanley heard that, he said, "Hughie, let's you and me go in on Friday and see if he will teach me to sing."

Stanley had his license now, since he was officially fifteen, and Grandmother Curtiss wanted milk and butter and eggs and some of our eight new kinds of lettuce, so we took the truck. Lettuce was about the only thing from the garden this early, except green onions and rhubarb. We had all those different packs of lettuce seeds left from the Burpee rack in the closed store, and most of them grew.

It was still early. No one seemed to be going out or in, and the door to the church was half open. When we passed under the statue of Michael, I looked up and saw that he really did have a big bulge in front, especially when viewed from right underneath. I thought, No wonder Saint Michael is the number one angel in the Catholic heaven.

The church was empty. The stained glass colored the air with nice streaks of red and blue, and it smelled interesting, like new wood and paint and incense. A few candles burned near the door, but we saw no priest. We could hear mumbling, and after a while a little door opened on a side wall and a fat girl came out. She lighted a candle and left, and we decided the priest must be behind that door, but no one was there. There was just a kind of grillework you could see a shadow through. Stanley said, "Hello."

The voice said, "Come on in, sit down, shut the door. Don't you people know anything? First you cross yourself, then you say in the name of the Father, and the Son, and the Holy Ghost, then confession."

"I have nothing to confess, sir."

"Not even a sin of omission?"

"I don't believe in sin."

"What kind of Catholic are you?"

"I'm not Catholic at all."

"You are obviously in the wrong church, and you are holding up my confessions."

"There is no one here but me and Hughie. I came to learn to sing; I read about you in the paper."

"Choir practice is Wednesday night in the choir loft, but it's restricted to members of this parish."

"Are you going to just turn me away? How do you know I don't have the best voice you ever heard?"

"Young lady, I doubt it."

"I'm not a young lady."

Then Stanley did an extraordinary thing. He took a deep breath and sent a sound soaring like a crystal bird into that shadowy space: "Ave Maria, gratia plena, Maria."

He turned as though to escape and went quickly toward the door. I followed, knowing he was timing his footsteps. I heard the confessional door behind us open. We were in front of the bank of contrition candles when the priest's voice caught us. "You there, boy, wait."

Stanley stopped and turned slowly. The priest was tall and thin, and his black wool cassock rustled as he hurried up the aisle. We looked at each other.

"Who taught you to sing like that?" the priest asked.

"I taught myself from records, but I need help now."

"How old are you?"

"I'm fifteen—no, that's a useful lie. I'm really seventeen."

"You don't look seventeen."

It seemed that in spite of himself, he was staring at Stanley's beautiful face. "You won't have that soprano voice for long. I'm surprised it's stayed this long."

"It's because I was castrated when I was ten. I think it may not ever change."

The priest's black eyes widened in anger. He had a very full head of dark, curly hair, and he ran his hands through it and made it stand on end. "So, it starts already. Who sent you? I know you Irishmen didn't want me, but I didn't think you would sink to this."

"I don't know what you're talking about."

"You all know about my Vienna choir days—you think because I was there, I'm not completely a man." Now he was cynical. "And you want a man for a priest, preferably an Irishman. Young lady, take your tricks and get out of my church."

I said, "You're wrong. Stanley has a dick, it's not very big, but he's got one."

In spite of himself, the priest's eyes went to Stanley's crotch. There was nothing else to do. Stanley quickly unbuttoned his pants and shorts and pushed them to his knees and stood so it was evident that what he said was true. "I'm going to sing in the opera."

"There are no soprano roles for men. A few concert pieces, castrati musicos, they're called, but no operas."

"I'm going to pretend I'm a woman and sing women's roles. They're the best roles, anyway. The article in the paper said you had directed operas."

"Yes, yes, but I've enough to do as it is. I've got to build a choir, and I haven't heard a trained voice since I came. I've got to build up this church."

I thought for a minute Stanley was just going to leave, so I said, "I'm Hughie, and Stanley's my cousin, and if it wasn't for Great-grandfather Channell, there wouldn't be a church here. He designed it and built about half of it before he went off to cheat the Indians. He made that statue in front of the angel Michael who is really Uncle Alvin, naked as a jaybird."

The priest sat down at the end of the last pew and looked blankly at us. "I can see I need to be brought up on the local history. This beautiful Uncle Alvin, is he a member of my parish?"

"Uncle Alvin hanged himself last year. I bet you wouldn't want all the people in your church to know that."

"How old are you, Hughie?"

"I was eight in April."

"God help us when you're ten."

Stanley wasn't sure whether we had gained an advantage or not. I knew the advantages of blackmail, since I had practiced it on my father when I was six.

Stanley said, "I can sing if you will help me. I have a sound like Gladys Swarthout or Grace Moore or Lily Pons—I'll come and sing in your choir every Sunday morning."

The priest gave us a look and went to the front of the church. Stanley didn't know whether to follow or not, but I pulled him along. In the choir loft was the organ that fed the sound into the whole mass of brass pipes covering the rear walls. The priest switched on the pumps and sat down. He pulled out all the stops and leaned forward and sent a burst of sound through that tall thin space like a round of cannon fire, and the reverberation of sound that followed shook the aisle. He was showing off. He looked around innocently and said, "Let's see what kind of a voice you really have."

Stanley matched each note exactly until they reached an upper registry of ear-splitting intensity. The priest held the note to see how long Stanley could sustain the sound, and I could tell by his expression that he was amazed.

"Who taught you to breathe in the middle of a note like that?"

"I've been practicing. I have some records of vocal instruction, but I need someone to tell me if I'm doing it right. The instructions say not to listen to your own voice. How am I going to tell?"

"I'll tell you." Father Giovanni rose and carefully looked Stanley over. "You have great strength in the upper register, and it's a lot easier to build a voice downward than it is to move upward. You've got a good rib cage, a wide mouth, an open throat. When you have learned to sing like a diva, what good is it going to do you?"

"I'm going to put on a dress and pretend to be a woman named Stella. I can be quite pretty, with a little help." Stanley was holding the priest's eyes with his own, willing him to like him.

The priest whispered, "Yes, you are very pretty." Then he said loudly, "All right, I'll try teaching you for a month. Then if you can sing my Sunday morning service, the Ave Maria, et cetera, I'll take you on as a student. You will wear a robe." He stood up and spread his arms so we could see the falling sleeves. "You will go out and in the side door, and as you can see, you will be quite sexless in your robe."

Thus Stanley found his first teacher.

On the way to Grandmother Curtiss's Orchard House, we talked about the priest, and I wondered if, when he was a Vienna choir boy, he had had his balls cut off. Stanley didn't think so because you could see a shadow of black beard on his face, and Stanley had read that when you were castrated, your beard didn't grow. We hoped that was true. I was planning to grow a long black beard when I ran away from home so my mother wouldn't recognize me when she came running after me.

When we got to Orchard House, I wondered if there was any orchard left. It all seemed to be out in the street. There were sawed-off limbs and the trunks of apple trees from one end of the block to the other. Some late bloomers were covered in red blossoms, and some early varieties had already set apples as big as walnuts. There was a crew of men with handsaws and crosscuts and axes, converting the limbs into fireplace lengths and hauling it back against the carriage barn to dry out. Apple-wood smoke has a marvelous, pungent odor.

We parked across the street and climbed over the debris, carrying Grandmother's food to the kitchen. A strip of trees five or six wide had been cut out between the two houses, and the gazebo now stood in the middle of a bare swath. There was still a row eight or ten trees wide on both sides, so you still could call it Orchard House.

Stakes in the ground with ropes stretched between them told us where the new rooms were going to be. There was activity everywhere. Grandmother had recently purchased the remaining strip of land on the far west side, so she now owned the whole block. That parcel was being scraped and rolled into four tennis courts end to end, each 120 by 55 feet running north and south. She had explained that you couldn't have a first-class establishment without tennis courts and a reviewing stand. We were to hear that phrase, "first-class establishment," many times. Right now it applied to the group of ten young people in the dining room. Grandmother had taken the full crop thrown out by the orphanage this year and was already training them to be polished hotel help, though she wasn't planning to open until the first of the year. They were balancing trays and saying, "Serve from the left, take away from the right." And diction and manners: "I just must say 'just.' " "I will not say 'git.' If I say 'git,' she'll throw a fit!" I heard a gangly kid on the end say under his breath as we passed, "I will not say 'shit,' even if I fall in it!"

OVER THIS LAST WINTER, Trojan looked as though he had gained another two hundred pounds and stood twenty-two hands high. All that was strange and different about him seemed to have been drawn into sharper relief: his straight profile, his eyes set high, his ears forward. Stanley had again trimmed his mane into a brush. His summer coat was darker and shinier, like an old piece of tarnished silver, and his platinum tail almost swept the ground. He looked even more like a throwback to ancient times, like no horse anyone in our valley had ever seen before. He was still determined to be a racehorse, ill fitted as that was to his appearance. Trojan had run around the perimeter of the meadow until he had worn a track, and my mother finally gave in and had a track scraped and rolled. We estimated twice around was a mile, and he sometimes ran it six times before he came to the barn tossing his head, flicking the foam off his neck, and expecting to be immediately sponged down and dried. There was something imperial about him. He seemed to know his position in life, and it was as a winner. Grandfather had clocked him several times, and he was running the mile in under three minutes, but of course that was without a bridle or saddle or a rider on his back urging him onward.

Old Mr. McKenney from the saddle shop came out and fitted Trojan with tack. The saddle and bridle were blue leather with silver trim. This tack had a history: Mr. McKenney's father had made it for General Robert E. Lee's horse, Traveler, but when Union soldiers occupied our area, he had been unable to deliver it to the Confederate leader, so he put it down in a barrel and covered it with oil until the day when the South would rise again. That dream was dead. Even the use of horses was rapidly declining. Mr. McKenney recognized in Trojan a lost cause and a fitting recipient of this blue saddle.

Rose had made bright yellow tassels to fasten on the sides of the bridle, and added a golden-yellow fringe to the dark wine saddle blanket. He was elegant-looking and knew it, like a horse in the circus. Now what he needed was a rider, light of weight and wiry. My mother looked at me, and I backed away. Even Stanley was afraid to risk it. My mother laughed at us. "All right, you two, out of my way. I'll show you how it's done." Before Trojan knew what she was about, she swung into the saddle.

He had practiced with the bit in his mouth for the past week, and the saddle for three days, but a rider on his back was something else. Whether his racial memory, which seemed to shape his days, would include a rider, no one knew. My mother held tightly to the reins and leaned against his neck, and they were off.

Grandfather and Mr. Isaac came up to the railing, where everyone had gathered to watch, just as she was making the second round. She was sitting tall in the saddle now, and Trojan was holding his head high.

"I have heard that expression all my life, 'woman on a high horse,' but I have never seen it so exemplified before," Grandfather said.

Mr. Isaac added, "All she needs is a lance; maybe a helmet with a plume."

Three times around the meadow track and she was still firmly in the saddle, though her hair had lost its pins and the braid had loosened. She could have played Lady Godiva if she was naked. Trojan was shining wet, and his eyes were wide with excitement. He tossed his head from side to side and snorted. My mother looked as exhilarated as he as she pulled him to a halt and sprang down. She threw the reins to one of the Forrester men to walk him around the training ring until he cooled off. But before she let him go, she hugged him around the neck and rubbed his muzzle. "He's not for sale; he's mine." She twisted her hair back into a knot. "If I'm going to ride Trojan, I'm going to have to cut this hair."

Stanley, who was trying to grow his own hair as long as he could, said, "Oh, no!"

Erica was best with the scissors, and when my mother came down to lunch, her hair just touched her shoulders. She wore a red velvet ribbon as a headband and looked like a schoolgirl. Stanley's eyes were wet when he saw what she had done. Both Grandfather and Mr. Isaac applauded as she tossed her loose mane very much the way Trojan swung his tail.

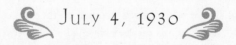

JULY 4, 1930

My MOTHER DID NOT ride Trojan in the Fourth of July parade. She was afraid to take him into a noisy crowd until he was better conditioned. There was always the idiot who thought it was smart to throw a firecracker under a horse's hoof. She rode Hannah. Stanley rode in his first parade on a roan mare named Lark Song. Though he had promised not to learn to love her—she was the next dressage horse to be sold—he lied. Grandfather rode Big Black. He said since he was now seventy-eight, this would probably be his last parade. Rose said, "Nonsense, you're as good a man as ever," and she winked. The next time Grandfather and I played truth, I was going to ask him what that wink meant. So I wouldn't feel too left out, Lester let me ride on the back of his motorcycle as he patrolled the curbs. Mr. McKenney was standing in front of his saddlery waving a Confederate flag, disappointed that he did not see his blue tack go by.

When the parade was over, we all went to Grandmother Curtiss's for lunch. It looked like much of the town had the same idea. The frame of the new addition was up, and the contractor wanted to get the roof on before it rained. He had put out the word that he would double the usual five dollars a day for men who would work on the holiday. This was about the only construction job left in town, and a lot of people needed money. There were at least thirty men on the roof hammering away. The glass-domed roof over the central hall and the big dome over the gazebo had been finished the week before by a crew from Pittsburgh, and all the copper water pipes that were going to heat the floors were in place, and men were pouring cement and smoothing over the pipes. They were uncrating the bathroom fixtures. Each suite would have a half bath downstairs, tucked under the stairway, and the bedroom upstairs would have a full bath. Since there were thirty-two suites, sixteen on each side of the central hall, that made a lot of fixtures to unpack. They were shiny new American Standard: pale green, lavender, and caramel. Later the chocolate-brown ones would come to replace all the fixtures in the old Curtiss house, which was going to be a kind of men's club at the far end of the new hall. When I heard that, I knew I was not going to get the grizzly bear. It would be just the thing for a men's club, and when I complained to my mother, she said, "Hallelujah!"

The tennis courts had already been cemented and painted green, and men were fastening up the high wire around them. Hot dogs, potato salad, lemonade, and coffee were being served in the gazebo. There was an awful lot of everything in copper boilers, and mustard, relish, and chili in crocks. One fat bricklayer bragged that he ate ten hot dogs. Grandmother said she didn't care if he ate thirty, as long as he built the fireplaces so they drew the smoke up the chimney. The beamed ceilings were exposed and painted white, and she didn't want them darkened by smoke. Each suite had a fireplace down in the living room and another up in the bedroom.

The Curtisses had always been the subject of gossip in this town, all the way back to the old general and the tales of John Wilkes Booth. Now, with

Grandmother building this expensive inn in the midst of a great depression, she really got talked about. They said she was crazy, but no one wanted to have her committed because they needed the jobs. Besides, at three o'clock every afternoon, she served homemade ice cream and root beer. Today there were three dips, strawberry, blueberry, and vanilla in honor of the Fourth of July.

Grandmother had hoped to have the inn finished by festival time the first week in October, and it looked like she might make it. It also looked like she had beaten the impending rain. The last of the roof was on before sundown, and the piles of black clouds to the north no longer were a threat. Matthew stood at the curb and gave each man his ten-dollar bill. As a bonus, Grandmother had bought a truckload of watermelons from Georgia, and each man took one on his way out.

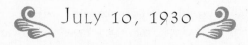

JULY 10, 1930

ON SATURDAY MY MOTHER and I went in town to sort through Grandfather's new books. His friend in Pittsburgh had died and left him the library from her printing company, and ten thousand dollars to build a room for them. There were boxes stacked to the ceiling in what had been Aunt Opal's theater but was now Mr. Isaac's shop. He needed the room for all the furniture Grandmother and Mr. Isaac were buying at auctions as far away as Baltimore.

Grandfather and Rose were already there, laughing like two kids at Christmas. They were sitting on the floor with piles of books all around them. My mother quickly joined in and began to assemble a pile to take home. There were at least a thousand boxes with twenty to thirty books each. Some of the printings went back fifty years. Some were duplicates of six or eight, and others were single, rare first editions. I hadn't found very many boy books yet, just a Tom Swift series, but I had already read that. There were about twenty books for Boobie, including her favorite, *Toad in Toad Hall,* and some reference books that would interest Miss Larkin, like *The Psychology of Learning.* There were encyclopedias by the dozen, and how-to books on everything from growing orchids to making a kiln and firing ceramics. My mother took that one. Also how to build a greenhouse, which had been in her plans for a long time.

They were all on their third cup of tea and their fourth or fifth carton of books when my mother said, "Dad, where are you going to build your library?"

"I've been thinking about that. These books really ought to go to a college. The library here is part of the YMCA and not very well administered. The books really get mistreated."

"If you were going to build a college here in Elkins, where would you put it?"

Grandfather took only a minute, but I knew from the look on his face that he was surveying the town in his head. "Why, Senator Burton's estate. I guess that hill his mansion is on is the best location in town, and there must be at least fifty acres in the meadows behind it."

Rose said she had heard gossip in the market from one of Mrs. Burton's maids that the old lady had gone completely off her rocker at the news of Judge Brown's death in Klan robes. My mother and grandfather looked at each other and smiled and said as one voice, "So much the better."

August 1, 1930

THE MILLER BOYS went down to Howard University in Washington, D.C., to take an equivalency test for admission in September. Thanks to Miss Larkin's coaching, they were accepted, Donald in prelaw and Raymond in premed. It looked as if they were on their way to being the attorney and the veterinarian that they dreamed of.

The older Thorne boys had been trying to learn the Millers' chores, and now the training intensified. They were not nearly as bright, so it took longer for them to understand the complexities of the milking machines and the handling of the milk and butter. Something was going on between the Forrester men and Mrs. Thorne. We were not quite sure what or even who. She seemed flirtatious with both of them. She was trying to turn herself into Clara Bow; she put her hair up in kid curlers and rouged her face and painted her mouth so it looked like she was whistling all the time, but to whom?

Her boys were worried, and one Saturday night they stayed late and came into my mother's office. They couldn't seem to get started with the conversation, so my mother tried to help. "I'm very pleased with your progress.

By the time the Miller boys go to school, I think you can take over the milk business."

"Yes, ma'am, we are tryin'."

"You know that will mean extra money, because you will share in the profits from the milk and butter."

"What we wanta ask you, ma'am, are you gonna learn us everything the Miller boys learned?"

"Yes, I think you can. It may take a little time."

"We know they're smarter 'an us, even if they are niggers."

My mother flinched but let it pass. Lou picked up the line. "Maw says we're dumb 'cause our daddy beat us in the head so much." Richie added, "An' we hardly ever had enough to eat."

"Well, that's all behind you now, and you're going to catch up."

"You gonna teach us everything, includin' the shootin'?"

"You want to learn to use a gun?"

"We got to." Now they both talked at once, and the words piled out. "Ifin he comes back, we got to kill 'im."

"Ifin he finds out how good we're doin', he'll kill us all for sure."

"And our mommy, soon's he sees her, he'll tear her apart!"

Their voices had risen high above the harsh whisper they came in with. She took each boy by the hand and looked into their eyes. "I'm going to tell you something, and you're not to repeat it—your father isn't ever coming back. I guarantee it."

"Did the Klan git him? We kept hopin' they did. Ifin it was the revenuers, he'll be gittin' out pretty soon."

"No, it was not the Klan, and he won't ever be getting free. He's—he's dead. I can't tell you how I know this, but he is."

"We know you're friends to the sheriff, did he tell you?"

"I can only assure you that he is dead and will never return."

"We been waitin' every day, wonderin' how we could kill him when he comes."

Once again she put out her arms and hugged both of them, like she didn't hug me, and her eyes were wet. "Oh dear God, and to think I wanted you to learn how to measure the butterfat when you were carrying this fear around inside you—I didn't think. Forgive me, boys, I'm so sorry. I absolutely guarantee he is dead and buried."

"Kin we tell our maw?"

"Yes, you can tell your mother and your little brothers, but no one else."

"No one else gives a damn."

Lou said, "I'd still like to learn to shoot squirrels."

"And so you shall."

We knew that the boys had given their mother the good news, because she turned into a real floozy. She wore high heels when she walked down the road to meet the Forrester men, even if the gravel did cut the red kidskin off of the heels. She even carried an old umbrella to keep the sun off her face. We still didn't know which of the Forrester men she was sweet on. When she met them, she would smile that simpy smile of hers to both. My mother said, "Let her have them. Even two nice young men couldn't make up for the terrible life she has lived."

THE BURTON ESTATE had a gatehouse that was empty now. The iron gates stood open, so Matthew drove right through them and up the winding road to the top of the hill. The house was red brick with big white columns and even bigger than Grandmother's house, although not as big as hers would be when she got it all added onto.

My mother and grandmother were in the backseat, and I was up front with Matthew because I didn't like the jump seat in Grandmother's limousine. I thought this whole trip was silly and we wouldn't even get in the front door because we weren't invited. Mrs. Burton's housekeeper, Gretchen Hogarth, who was Rose's friend, said she would fix it, since Mrs. Burton wouldn't remember whether she had invited us or not, and we should come to tea.

We got out under the portico, and Grandmother said, "Somebody is in charge here, just look at this." The rows of flowers looked artificial and the grass as perfectly trimmed as though it had been done with scissors. Up both sides of the wide stone steps were pots of blue hydrangeas. I wondered how many iron shavings it took to do that; ours were still half pink, and there was a pound of nails around every root.

The big doors swung open before we got to them. The woman at the door said, "I'm Mrs. Hogarth, do come in." No wonder she and Rose were friends: they looked enough alike that this woman could have been Rose's mother, with the same apple-red cheeks and bachelor's-button blue eyes, except her yellow hair was mostly white now and she was much fatter, even in her black silk uniform. Grandmother extended her hand, and the housekeeper looked surprised.

Grandmother whispered like a conspirator, "We are very grateful you arranged our visit."

"If nothing else, it will break the monotony. There has not been one person through this door since that terrible old judge died."

She led the way into a blue brocade sitting room as big as our fourth-grade schoolroom, and Mrs. Burton was sitting there behind a silver teapot and some blue cups. The last time I had seen her, she was covered in black veils, and I thought that had been better. She had a lot of chins and a kind of blank look like she wasn't quite sure, and with good reason, because everything Grandmother said was a lie. "My dear Mrs. Burton, so kind of you to see us. I had met with Judge Brown the very day of his death, and I was afraid your plans for the college might get sidetracked. I'm so glad you are going ahead."

Mrs. Burton really did look confused now. "Did I call you? My memory is so—so—unsure now."

"You wrote me a note, since I'm on your committee. Don't worry about forgetting, it comes to us all. And this is Billy-Pearl and her son, Hughie."

My mother tried to help. "I'm Billy-Pearl Curtiss," she said, and held out her hand, but Mrs. Burton had her hands over her face.

"I knew it. I lived in fear all those years that that woman would give him a child, as I never could, and now here you are—and I suppose this is his grandchild?" She was in real despair now, with eyes almost buried in fat and tears running out.

My mother sat beside her and took both her hands. "No, no, my dear, I'm not Almeda's daughter, she never had a child. I'm no relation to her; I don't even like her."

Mrs. Burton found a handkerchief. "Are you sure?"

Grandmother added, "We're absolutely sure." She sat across the table from her. "Now, why don't you pour us some tea and we will talk about the college."

"What college?"

"Why, the college you are planning to build here on this hill, Burton College, as a memorial to the good senator."

My mother added, "As only a true wife could. Here, let me pour for you." They chatted away as though the plans for the college were already under way, all the time watching the poor woman's face, judging just how far they could go, like two cats with a fat old robin. They promised her a seat on the college board and as much involvement as her asthma would allow. She informed them that she no longer had asthma, she had it only in the presence of the senator or Judge Brown or some other overbearing man.

Grandmother said she was glad to hear that, because she had been thinking maybe they ought to have all women on the board. She told Mrs. Burton all about the wonderful architect who was designing her hotel, and how her workers would be finished in a couple of months, and they could just move up here and get started. When she got to the part about this house becoming the administration hall, with wings going off each way for classrooms, Mrs. Burton's teacup shook on her saucer and she panicked. "My home, I can't give up my home!"

"But don't you remember? It was your idea. With all this space, we can start a school as soon as we can assemble a teaching staff and funds to support it."

"But this is my home. Where will I live?"

The two conspirators exchanged glances. Surely they did not plan to put this poor old woman out on the street if their mad scheme worked. Each was signaling the other with her eyes to pick up the ball. Grandmother's voice was faint in the beginning but strengthened with her do-right resolve. "You are going to come and live in my inn. That's been the plan from the very beginning. You will love it; there will be loads of activities, charming people coming and going all the time, and you can bring Mrs. Hogarth and your maid and your gardener. We will be just one big happy family."

Mrs. Burton put down her cup and stood and looked at the two of them. "I want you to know something, understand it right now." I thought, Oh, oh, she's not as far gone as they thought. But they were safe. "If that woman, that Almeda, is going to be there, I will not."

My mother threw her a bone. "Oh, no. Haven't you heard? That evil woman has completely cracked up. I think she was always a little mad. She will have to go into an asylum soon."

Mrs. Burton sat back down and refilled her cup. The room was silent for a long moment. She seemed deep in thought, and fear that she might pull down their house of cards at any moment kept the others silent. Perhaps Mrs. Burton recognized that it might not be long until she, too, passed that way, for she said, "Poor dear."

My mother and grandmother were so proud of their accomplishments as conwomen that they went to call on poor Daisy Brown. She looked even sillier than she had last summer, for she had an even bigger pillow pinned under her dress.

Daisy was surprised to see us, but she quickly made coffee for the ladies, and she and I had milk, because it was good for the baby. Her hired girl had left the week before, Daisy said, because she didn't want to care for the coming baby, but in fact the girl had told one of Grandmother's maids that she was afraid of loonies.

When my mother told Daisy about the judge's dying words, I was as surprised as Daisy. My mother gave me a look. Daisy said, "I thought my dear husband was killed instantly." (I was going to say "mashed flat" but didn't dare.)

"He lived long enough to send you a message with his last breath."

The poor old thing patted her pillow and leaned forward in complete trust. "What? Oh dear, was it about our child?"

My mother picked up the cue. "Yes, yes, it was about your son's future, his college education. He wants you to put the money he has hidden away into the fund to build a college right here in Elkins, so that my son and yours can get an education without leaving the protection of their mothers' love."

I think even Grandmother thought that was a little thick. She smiled behind her coffee cup. But Daisy took the bait. "You mean that money he had hidden in the grandfather clock?"

"Yes, that and the other."

There had to be other and lots of it. The bribe to keep the governor's daughter from being sent to prison when she ran over a child must have been fifty thousand. Lester said you could smell the liquor ten feet away. And there were dozens of others over the forty years of his judgeship. A friend at the bank told Grandmother that there was only ten thousand in his savings account, so it had to be in this house.

"He wants me to put all that cash in the college fund?"

"Those were his last words, that and yours was a love even death cannot destroy."

Now Grandmother really must have thought my mother had gone too far, for everyone knew the old bastard treated Daisy like dirt. But luckily her old sieve of a mind had let that fact sift through. "I'll do it. Wait until I find a suitcase. After all, I do have my insurance every month to keep me and the little one."

Out in the hall, she pressed a spring in the grandfather clock. A side panel in the old clock, which reached to the ceiling, fell open. Inside, the secret compartment was packed tight with brown envelopes tied with twine. The filled space was two feet by two. They helped Daisy put it in the suitcase. Grandmother wanted to do her part and was equally greedy. "Daisy, he said to give the college the Klan funds, too."

"He told you that he was treasurer of the Klan? He told me never to admit he was a member."

"You forget he was dying, and he wanted to go to heaven, where he could wait for you."

Daisy sat on the floor looking like a lost child. She began to sniffle, and Grandmother gave her a handkerchief. "You do know where he put it—I suppose in a box?"

"Oh yes, a metal box behind the books, but it has a big lock on it—I tried."

They were helping her up. "That's all right, dear, we will have the lock cut off."

As Matthew carried the box to the car, and Grandmother and my mother took each end of the suitcase, Grandmother told Daisy, "Now, this is our secret," and my mother added, "Remember, Daisy dear, a good purpose washes bad money clean."

They sat in the back, the suitcase and the metal box between them, smiling like two Cheshire cats.

"How much do you think is here?" Grandmother asked.

"Enough, I hope, to get the plans drawn and maybe a foundation," my mother said.

"How will we get the walls up and a roof?"

"We will find a way. Hughie, don't look at me like that. I'm doing this for you, so you can go to college right here at home where you belong."

"I'm not goin' to your old college, even if you do steal enough money to get it built. I'm going to college in California."

Grandmother looked at me. "Hughie, you think we did wrong, don't you? This is one of those times when the end justifies the means."

"I'll remember that when I steal enough money to go to California."

September 1, 1930

Stanley had been studying with Father Giovanni for over two months before we were all invited to hear him sing. Although he was at his voice exercises full-time, he got up at dawn now to work the horses, and he sang to them as he put them through their routines. Father Giovanni's mass was over by eight, and by eight-thirty Stanley was there. He paid the priest in vegetables and chickens and trout each Friday.

The ladies of Saint Michael the Archangel had a corn beef and cabbage supper to raise money for the church. They were charging a dollar each, and that was a lot of money, even if they were having entertainment. Since the entertainment was going to be Stanley, and he was our contribution, I thought we ought to get a discount.

Since the market crash the year before, the prices on everything dropped every month. You could buy dinner at the Dew-Drop Inn for thirty-five cents, plus ten cents for pie, and a nickel tip, total fifty cents. Even that was half of what men made working in the hay fields all day, so not many people ate out. Even the very rich were taking advantage of the depression. The kind of people who bought dressage-trained horses still had money to burn, yet they argued about the prices and ended up paying only thirty-five thousand each. We sold three horses over the summer. My mother said we would just have to breed more, that was all. The people who bought foxhounds hadn't heard about the depression yet, and they paid the same price they had the previous year for forty hounds.

Stanley paid for all the tickets and invited everybody; everybody, that is, who was white. The good Catholics thought when Jesus said "Suffer the little children to come unto me," he meant white children, so Boobie had to stay home. My mother was the only one who believed blacks were also the children of God, but then she didn't really believe in God, so what did that prove?

We all got to the hall at six o'clock, except Miss Larkin, whose feet hurt, and the third Dutch lady, Erica, who had been sick lately. Helga sat with Mr. Isaac, and Rose sat with Grandfather. They seemed to be pairing off like that these days. My mother sat with Lester. He was at our house more than I thought was necessary now that the Klan was no longer a threat.

The hall was a nice big space with a high ceiling and a platform at the end. It had been the Catholic church until they built the new one. Only a few of the big Irishmen could clean their plates. I didn't try, because Stanley told me there was going to be cherry pie after the singing.

Four fat men in straw hats came out and sang "It's a Long Way to Tipperary" and "Mary, It's a Grand Old Name." They were loud, and so was the applause. I worried about Stanley. If people liked these guys, how were they going to receive two arias sung in French and Italian? Father Giovanni must have worried, too, for he stood and talked Stella up. "Ladies and gentlemen, tonight we are in for a rare treat. A voice so pure and natural, it can be nothing less than a gift from God.

"I have been working with this singer for just two months, and already her accomplishments are as great as some people achieve in a lifetime of training." He sat at the piano and played an introduction, and he nodded to a boy who turned out all the lights. In the dark he said, "It gives me great pleasure to present Miss Stella Fancler."

I heard my mother whisper, "How did he get the priest to do that?"

The spotlights on the platform came on, and Stella stood bathed in a yellow glow. A murmur of expectation went around the room, and then the audience of two hundred or so hushed in anticipation as Stella lowered the black lace fan from her face and parted her red lips in a half smile. She wore the dress she had worn last Halloween, with no jewelry now, only a long scarf of black lace over her hair and shoulders. I glanced at my mother. She wasn't surprised, only pleased, and I knew she had helped with this.

Stella sang the opening notes of "The Bell Song" from *Lakmé*. No hesitation, absolute assurance from the first silver tone. Her posture said, "I came to sing for you and sing I will," and the mien of the audience said, "We have come to listen." Even those who did not understand a word of French understood talent of a rare degree.

The voice had become an instrument, and it set the room to singing. There was not an inch of wood or a pane of glass or a bone in the forehead of anyone in that room that did not vibrate in response. Stella moved with grace from one side of the platform to the other, playing to the upturned faces. Father Giovanni looked as though he were staring at the figure of the Virgin Mary as his hands played from memory. When Stella's voice sent the last clarion bell–like chime across the ceiling, she held the fan up to her chin like a sweet young thing asking for approval, but her amber eyes missed nothing.

It would have been improper to pound on the table in the church, but here these vibrant people did it with a will and stopped only when Father Giovanni twice played the introduction to the aria from *Madama Butterfly*. This time the plaintive cry of the poor betrayed Japanese girl brought tears to the eyes of some of the sentimental Irish. Even Mr. Isaac blew his nose. When it ended, Stella threw her head back and laughed her thanks, and she let the scarf fall to her shoulders. The red-gold hair gleamed under the lights, and the bright freckles glowed on the white skin. This was the look of the Irish dream girl, and that was what she was turning into right before their eyes. There was just the very edge of an Irish brogue to her voice when she spoke: "You good Irish people have been so kind, I would like to sing what I hope is one of your favorites."

As the priest played the opening bars of "Danny Boy," she ran her hands through her hair and loosened it so it fell like a halo around her face. She lowered her voice a whole octave for this one and warmed the sounds to a caressing lyric soprano. She had just gotten past "The pipes, the pipes are calling, it's you must go and oh, it's I must stay," the voice of a father bidding farewell to a son driven from Ireland by the famine, when the sniffles really got started and men who didn't have a handkerchief wiped their noses, unashamed, on their sleeves. By the time Stella got to the second verse, where the son returns to find his father's grave, they would have turned their pockets out for a collection. When she sang Schubert's "Ave Maria" to close, there was absolute silence, except for the outright crying that some could not control.

When the lights were turned back on, Stella was gone. Several people surged forward, feeling sentimental goodwill toward their priest, who had brought them this gift. They patted him and thanked him, and one old woman kissed his hand, and they forgot for the moment that he was an Italian usurper when they had wanted a good Irishman. My mother and Mr. Isaac both wanted to talk to the priest, but this wasn't the time.

Stella was in our car turning herself back into Stanley, but even with the makeup off and his shirt and pants restored, he would never truly be Stanley again.

We all went up to Grandfather's house and had blackberry wine and talked. They had gathered here to talk about Stanley's future. After his performance, they were all convinced he had a future and that it was their obligation to do something about it. They talked about Stanley like he was one of our prize horses. Lester had waited until the crowd cleared at the hall, then brought Father Giovanni, who was the voice expert here, with a valued opinion.

Grandfather gave him a glass of wine and said, "My name is Peter, and this is Leon, and you know the ladies, I believe. We all know that Stanley has this burning desire to be an opera singer and the drive and discipline to shape himself into whatever is possible, but in your opinion, is it possible?"

Father Giovanni settled into a chair by the fireplace with his wine. "This age has not produced a large number of great voices, but I do think we have one here, if carefully handled, and if we can deal with the peculiar nature of this situation."

Mr. Isaac asked, "You mean a man masquerading as a woman?"

Everyone looked at Stanley. In his yellow silk shirt and brown velvet pants, with some of the blue shadow still clinging to his eyelids, he looked more girl than boy, maybe a slightly tomboyish girl.

"Did anyone in your congregation tonight suspect he was not a girl?"

"No one. And they all said what a beautiful girl."

Grandfather asked, "Father Giovanni, I understand you were once a Vienna choir boy and—"

"You want to know if I was castrated?"

"You appear masculine. I wonder if Stanley will—catch up."

"I did not have the operation. I refused. Earlier, young boys were not given an option, and I had no family pressuring me. I became a director of the choir after my voice changed."

"You did know some of the men who had been altered?"

"Yes, many of them lived lives as women; many who fitted into no life anywhere ended it. A few of them were able to go on, and some are quite well known now as female singers."

"Then it is possible that Stanley can make a life as Stella and remain a soprano?"

"I understand there are now hormones that can maintain the status quo, so to speak."

A few of the group looked up at him, surprised that a priest knew such things. He defended himself. "I do not confine my reading exclusively to Vatican directives."

Stanley spoke up for the first time. "I like being a girl. I would like to be Stella all the time now."

My mother didn't think he could. "I don't think I could get you back in high school as a girl. I faked your birth certificate once, I doubt I could do it again."

"I don't want to go back to high school. I want to work on voice and languages full-time. The language teachers there have never been to Europe, their accents are terrible. Aren't they, Rose?"

Rose said, "Yes, and even though my friends and I speak four languages altogether, we speak workingman dialects, not the class needed for opera."

Father Giovanni said, "He should study in Europe. If not Europe now, at least New York."

My mother looked at Stanley the way a mother might. "You can't send a child off to New York."

Mr. Isaac put his hand on Grandfather's shoulder and squeezed it, to say, I'm sorry, friend. "I'll take Stella to New York and stay there at least for her first year. I have the money set aside that I intended to use to send my daughter through Juilliard. I'll be your uncle Leon." He held Helga's eyes until she chimed in, "A pretty girl in New York will need an aunt. I'll be your aunt Helga."

Mr. Isaac added as he smiled at Helga, "One can't just go to Juilliard. I suppose she will have to audition."

Father Giovanni said, "I'm not patting myself on the back as a teacher, but I think the two arias Stella sang tonight would get her into any school in the world." He looked from one face to the other. "I think the saving grace that will make the difference is this circle of concerned friends."

In the next weeks my mother assembled a wardrobe for Stella and taught her how to walk in high heels. Daily Stanley left and Stella appeared. I missed him and was angry that he was so anxious to go and leave me behind. Who would put his arms around me now? The warm body just out of the shower, the warm breath against my neck, the mouth exploring. The wall between me and the opposite sex now came between Stella and me.

Before she left in September, I spent much of my time in my room. I counted my money about two hundred times, and I tried not to talk when I went down to eat. That last morning she came up to my room all Stella, Stanley completely gone. Even the look behind the amber eyes had become the knowing look that women have, a hidden secret. She wore the red Cossack coat with the black fox edging that Grandmother had bought for herself and then given to my mother, as she said it was wearing her. My mother believed that she wouldn't wear it often enough in our small town to justify keeping it, but it was just the thing for an opera singer in New York. Stella strode around in it like she was taking curtain calls. She hugged me in a cloud of perfume.

Everyone was lined up downstairs to say good-bye. The Forrester men and the Thorne boys looked confused, like they might break and run, or maybe they thought it was Halloween all over again. The Miller boys saw it as a preview of the farewell they would get next week when they left for Washington. Handsome had finally grown into the tap-dancing shoes Stanley had given him, and he had learned to stand without holding on to the wall. He did a little tap step as his good-bye.

Boobie said, "If you would let me to go with you, I would change the records for you."

"Oh, baby. I wish you could."

Boobie turned and ran with tears in her eyes.

At the station, Grandfather and Rose and Father Giovanni were loading Mr. Isaac and Helga on the train when we arrived. I saw Grandfather put his arms around Mr. Isaac and kiss him on the cheek as they stood in the space between the passenger cars. There were tears on Mr. Isaac's face when he said, "You know I have to do this because of my daughter. Stella will be my daughter now."

I thought Mr. Isaac had cracked up, but I wouldn't say that to Grandfather. Maybe he would start hugging me with Mr. Isaac gone. Stella had five suitcases and a trunk, and a checkbook that said she had fifteen thousand dollars in the bank, and a birth certificate that had been changed for the second time. The red leather trunk was full of scarves and gloves and wigs. Grandmother had given her all the fancy things that had belonged to Aunt Emma.

Stella brushed my cheek with her painted lips and whispered, "Hughie, I'm scared! Promise that you will always love me."

My mother drove home looking straight ahead. I said, "You did it again, got your nose in somebody else's life. Why?"

"Because he wanted it."

"I bet if I wanted to be Cinderella and go off to New York, you wouldn't let me."

"Of course not. Your foot is too big for the glass slipper."

OCTOBER 15, 1930

THAT AUTUMN IT DIDN'T frost until November, and the leaves stayed green, but everything else changed. The Miller boys went to live with their aunt in Washington, D.C, and go to Howard University. My mother mailed them three checks each month, one to the aunt and one to each of the boys. The Forrester men went to live with Mrs. Thorne, and the two older Thorne boys moved into Uncle Billie's log cabin down in the lower meadow. They never guessed that each evening when they went home, they walked over their father's grave. Bob Marsteller was king of the school bus again, but he had decided that he would copy Stanley, and he had spelling bees and lesson recitals and only once in a while did he throw spitballs. The Thorne twins started to school in town again. They were taller and thinner and had new Tom Mix lunch boxes, but they only lasted a couple of weeks until they were back with Miss Larkin.

Miss Larkin pretended that she was sorry, but she really wasn't, and neither was Boobie. Miss Larkin called the Thorne twins' teacher and explained her theory of manual dexterity and the relationship to mental retention. She told the teacher the boys had been doing fourth-grade work. They knew the multiplication tables and could recite all the battles of the Civil War if she let them keep their hands busy weaving rawhide leather belts. The teacher was nasty and said Miss Larkin should write a book. Miss Larkin said she just might do that and change the way grade schools were taught. She could probably write how she assigned number combinations to letters and taught the Forrester men to read and write.

There was no question this year as to who would house the festival queen. Mrs. Burton's house was all torn up, being reshaped into classrooms and offices, and she was living in Aunt Emma's old room upstairs. It had bad memories for Grandmother, who didn't like to go in there. Mrs. Burton's maid slept in the dressing room because the widow acted funny and had to be watched. Some days she just rode up and down the elevator and sang "There'll Be a Hot Time in the Old Town Tonight." Grandmother was afraid that meant she was going to set the house on fire.

Mrs. Burton's housekeeper, Mrs. Hogarth, had taken over the staff training. She was so good at it that two lazy boys quit. Though the inn wouldn't have its official opening until Christmas, the rooms were finished enough to put a princess in each of the new suites.

The Curtiss house at the end of the long hall now had all of its walls covered with dark green felt or dark brown wallpaper. The furniture was covered in leather, and there were antlers and moose heads and cowhides everywhere, to proclaim this a man's world. The Weirton Steel Men's Choir stayed there, all forty-two of them. They got drunk on bad moonshine and didn't make it to the new brown-fixtured bathrooms. They threw up in six places, including on the new red Persian rug in the dining room.

The festival this year did not bring a lot of money into the town. Nobody seemed to have any. The Baptist ladies who ran the nickel hot-dog stand reduced the price to three for a dime, but with only onions and mustard, no chili.

There were lots of pickpockets in town, and the whole sheriff's department was watchful. Lester couldn't go to the Queen's Ball with my mother, so she didn't go, either. Several Gypsy women had set up tents. Everybody wanted to know when the depression was going to be over, and the Gypsies said it was a curse they could remove for a dollar each. They were as big liars as President

Hoover. But it was true: if everybody gave the Gypsies a dollar, their depression would be over.

November 1, 1930

THERE WAS A CIRCUS set up in the field behind the high school, and my mother took a whole bunch of us. I knew she wanted to see it because the posters all over town said they had the four most beautiful white Arabian horses in the world, and there was a picture: two girls in tights riding, each with one foot on a horse's back. They must have been two queens, as each wore a sparkling crown. I was more interested in the world's largest elephant, now owned by this Beebie-Conklin circus. I knew that was a lie, because the largest elephant's name was Jumbo, and P. T. Barnum had him stuffed and mounted.

We stopped at Aunt Sebe's to pick up Worthy and Harry and see the new baby, Fat Pauline. Harry told me that was going to be her name, and it sure suited her, she was round and full. Aunt Sebe had a story to tell about how hard it had been to push her out. My mother said, "You sure were lucky. If she had been full-term, she might have weighed twenty pounds." To get even with my mother for a remark like that, Aunt Sebe said she should bring the boys home with us for the weekend.

Lester had warned us that there might not be much of a show, because Mr. Beebie had been in his office this morning trying to swear out a warrant for Mr. Conklin. It seemed Mr. Beebie had bought this elephant with the assurance from Mr. Conklin that they could make a lot of money, and now they couldn't afford gasoline to run the generators for the show. You couldn't arrest a man because people didn't have a dollar to buy circus tickets. Mr. Beebie said he was going to take his elephant and go. He could sell elephant rides in the park for ten cents, enough to get out of town.

When we got to the circus, it was evident Mr. Beebie was taking his half and going. His elephant was already loaded on a truck, and a part of the tent was gone, and an old man and a couple of local boys were trying to block the tent opening with a big canvas that held the four Arabian horses painted on it.

There were seven of us—the Thorne twins, Worthy and Harry, my mother and I and Boobie, wearing a yellow wool cap pulled down to her eyes. They weren't very likely to turn a little girl with kinky hair away, for there were only about twenty people here altogether.

The lights dimmed, then blinked off and on like the generators were shutting down. First two zebras came into the single ring. According to the banner, they were supposed to be ridden by monkeys, but Mr. Beebie must have owned the monkeys, because they were gone.

I was sitting at the end of the bench about four rows up when a strange animal came and stood by me. It was a soft, furry-looking thing with a long neck and big, dark calf eyes. It seemed to be half sheep, half calf. It looked over toward me and smiled. My mother whispered, "That's a llama." The old man who was climbing on the bandstand with his trumpet saw it and came over. "That's Eleanor. She's waiting for her cue to join the clowns, only the clowns ran out on us this afternoon. She won't hurt you."

He hurried back to the platform. You could see a flat pint whiskey bottle in his back pocket. He began to blow on his trumpet. The rest of the band must have run out, too, as there were other music stands but no other musicians. He blew a fanfare, and a lady in pink tights and big cloth wings came and stood in the middle of the ring. She looked a little like one of the princesses pictured on the poster, for she wore a crown, but she was older and heavier. She had rolls and bulges that the painting did not, which the pink tights only accented.

By now we had figured out the man with the horn must be Mr. Conklin, because he was the only one left. He introduced the lady in pink as Princess Natasha, the human butterfly. Then he ran out and grabbed the rope that yanked her up into the roof of the tent. She spread out her cloth wings and fluttered back and forth. He tried to hold on to the rope and accompany her aerial antics on his horn at the same time, but the whole thing was kind of funny. At least the twins laughed, but I don't think you were supposed to.

After that was what my mother had come to see, the Arabian horses. There was nothing fake or shoddy or second-rate about them. They were beautiful. They went around in pairs, keeping right against each other so the Russian princess could stand with one foot on each horse's back. This was the same princess who had swung around like a butterfly, only now she had squeezed into bright blue tights, and her jacket had spangles and beads. Mr. Conklin was playing a waltz on his trumpet as they circled. The princess held the reins in one hand to the pair she was riding, and reached back for the reins of the pair that followed. Clearly they should have been ridden by the second princess. She must have belonged to Mr. Beebie.

A couple of times Eleanor reached over toward me and sniffed my neck. The next time she did it, I planned to bend forward and let her sniff Boobie, who sat beside me, her eyes glued on the princess.

The horse act had gone around the ring a third time. I suppose they wanted to give us our money's worth, since this was probably all there was. Just as the horses were in front of us, I saw Eleanor, out of the corner of my eye, aiming her tongue at me. I leaned forward, and she reached across my back and gave Boobie a big slurp. Boobie gave a high-pitched scream of surprise, and one of the horses lunged to the side. The princess lost her footing and fell between them, and the second pair ran over her. I saw one of the horses' hooves step on her head. The horses ran on around the circle, leaving the princess lying in the sawdust. Mr. Conklin continued to play, his eyes fixed on the top of the tent.

My mother jumped into the ring and grabbed the reins of the horses and diverted their path, so they wouldn't trample the poor woman again. Mr. Conklin dropped his horn and ran over. My mother was busy tying the horses' reins to a tent pole and yelling for someone to get to a phone and call the sheriff.

Worthy and Harry and I ran to the lunch stand across the street from the high school, and they called Lester's office. By the time we got back to the tent, we knew the princess was dead. My mother had taken off her coat and spread it over the woman. Just as I got there, Mother was covering her face, which looked pretty bad. Mr. Conklin was sitting on the ground beside her, holding her hand to his lips and staring at her, kind of glassy-eyed.

Lester and the ambulance came, but there was no point in taking her to the hospital, so they took her to Runner's Funeral Home. Mr. Conklin rode with her, his circus forgotten. Lester left a deputy to guard the tent until morning, and we all went home. Eleanor followed us to the exit, and I would have taken her home — she had a very lonely look on her face — but she wouldn't fit in our car.

The next morning my mother and I came back to town and drove up to the circus tent. Mr. Conklin was sleeping in his truck and really smelled like he had tied one on. My mother shook him awake. He needed two hundred dollars to bury his wife and thirty-five dollars for a cemetery plot, and he had only twenty-five dollars. His sole assets were two zebras, four horses, a tent, and a silly-looking llama. He didn't want to sell anything. My mother offered to buy the horses, but he said he loved them and wouldn't sell. She finally agreed to loan him the money he needed and keep the animals at our farm until he could come back and redeem them. She had the right to breed the Arabians, giving him half, and if he didn't come back in two years, she would keep them. She had our attorney write out a contract and got it signed and witnessed. She also gave Mr. Conklin two hundred dollars to get to Florida and be among circus friends who wintered there.

Eleanor stood and watched as the zebras and the four horses were loaded. Mr. Conklin said he didn't care what happened to her, but I did. My mother said she knew nothing about the care of zebras, but Mr. Conklin said just to think of them as mules that had to be kept warm. It turned out we didn't have to worry about them, because in about two weeks, two men came with a truck and a court order that said Mr. Conklin had not paid for the zebras, and took them away. This set my mother to worrying that maybe the bill of sale was fake and someone would come out and claim the horses, but they never did. She used to just stand and stare at them as they went around the exercise ring, the way you might stand and stare at a painting. For someone who really loved horses as she did, these four white beauties were about as good as it gets.

Boobie had the most trouble dealing with the memory of the accident. She felt responsible. She had nightmares and cried out in her sleep and had trouble remembering how to spell in Miss Larkin's class. I suppose if you had to put the blame on someone, it should have been me. I was the one who ducked and let Eleanor lick her. I talked it over with Grandfather Fancler, but he said it was fate, and once an incident was in motion, there was no way you could put your finger on it and say the blame began here or ended there. Grandfather occasionally fell back on his Presbyterian predestination.

If you wanted to get right down to it, it was Eleanor's fault, and she had the right attitude. She just wandered all over the farm, looking at everything with her great brown eyes and smiling. I had a feeling that all along she was really waiting for her troupe of clowns to appear and say the watchword to begin her act.

NOVEMBER 15, 1930

MR. ISAAC WROTE US a letter telling of their good luck in finding a charming little house in Brooklyn, very near the Brooklyn School of Music. It was completely furnished, including a piano. Helga loved it because it had a garden and a chicken coop and a little barn. Stella had been auditioning for various coaches. They had been going from one to another to get a grasp on what voice teaching was all about. They had learned that the jargon of voice teachers sets them apart from music teachers. Mr. Isaac wrote:

> One teacher had been honest enough to suggest that training might jeopardize the special vocal appeal that Stella had. Most teachers were not so honest, and it was hard to separate their enthusiasm from their need to secure a paying student. In the end, Stella has enrolled at Juilliard three days a week and at the Brooklyn School of Music two days, and on Saturdays, she will be coached by Geraldine Farrar, who, I believe, is a very important singer.
> I will write once a week and encourage Stella to write.
>
> *Leon*

Stella wrote that she was including her letter with Mr. Isaac's so she could save a three-cent stamp. It looked like it might be a long time before she had a paying engagement. Mr. Isaac's friend at Juilliard had referred her to Geraldine Farrar. Mr. Isaac was planning to study the history of the opera and the people in it. He felt Stella had made a faux pas. She sang Cio-Cio-San's "Un Bel Di" (One Fine Day) from *Madama Butterfly*, which had been one of Madam Farrar's most memorable roles. But who better to judge, and they were going to work on the whole role together. Mr. Isaac had gotten a lot of opera-history books from the library, and at dinner each night, he recited what he had learned that day. Helga had met several Dutch people, and they were exchanging recipes. Stella was afraid of getting fat, since she had found a doctor to give her estrogen. Every singer Stella had seen so far was fat, but she was determined to stay thin in spite of Helga's good cooking, which included apple dumplings with lemon and cinnamon sauce. She ended her letter with:

> Sometimes I cannot believe the very great good luck I've had in life. The day you took me out of that place and opened for me door after door—I know you think a belief in God limits your possibilities, but I'm afraid I'm beginning to believe. How else can I account for this?
>
> *Love to all. Stella*

My mother shipped a barrel of apples to Brooklyn, carefully packed with the best keepers at the bottom—more apple dumplings. There was no word from

Mr. Conklin, so Lester had his deputies take down the circus tent and pitch it again over Grandmother Curtiss's tennis courts, so she could have outdoor parties and weddings. Lester took the electric generators and the strings of lights up to the poorhouse, so those people could have light other than their smoky kerosene lamps. My mother took the big painted poster of the racing Arabians and put it up in our stairwell. It was the only place where the ceiling was high enough.

When Grandmother came out to the farm, a strange thing happened. She and Eleanor fell in love with each other, and Grandmother took her home. Eleanor decided she was a guard dog and stayed as close to Grandmother as she could. Grandmother bought a fancy red leather leash, which Eleanor didn't need, and took her each morning for a long walk around the park. People in the town said odd things about Grandmother, but then the Curtisses were always subjects of gossip, so she didn't care.

Grandfather Fancler had a new friend in Father Giovanni. The three of them, with Rose in the middle, her arms looped through theirs, took long walks up the orchard's paths and sometimes along the railroad track, all the way out to the tunnel. They were the Three Musketeers. I knew that was the end of me; everyone knows there were not four Musketeers.

When they weren't walking, they were down in the old Hippodrome building, sorting through the boxes of books. Grandfather had opened only about half so far, and he planned to give them to the new college when it was finished. When Aunt Opal heard what they were doing, she began shipping box after box of books that her husband brought home each night from the White House. All the current publications that readers wanted Herbert Hoover to condemn, they mailed to him. Twenty copies alone of Pearl Buck's *The Good Earth*, because the hero was a bigamist; Theodore Dreiser's *An American Tragedy*, and William Faulkner's *Sanctuary*. There were ten copies a day of that one, which made me want to read it. They even sent Robert Frost's *Collected Poems*, which had just won a Pulitzer Prize; Hart Crane's *The Bridge*, and of course, all works by Leon Trotsky, who had been banned in Boston the year before.

Father Giovanni said we were lucky that people only complained about books in this country, because in Germany they were burning them. They burned everything that wasn't neo-Nazi or was written by a Jew, and that was about half of the culture of the country. Hitler got only eleven million votes in the presidential election, but he still influenced fifty million Germans.

Grandmother was on the board to shape the college, as was Grandfather

Fancler, and they intended it to be a liberal college. Most colleges who called themselves liberal weren't. When they discovered how open-minded Father Giovanni was, they added him to the board.

As the men sorted and read, Rose sewed. She had the five machines from Grandmother's Virginia factory and dozens of rolls of fabric. Grandmother had contracted Rose to make all the white jackets and the aprons for her help. Rose hired an unemployed tailor and a woman who knew how to cut patterns, and they were making all kinds of things. Everything was either navy, khaki, or white, since those were the fabrics left from service-uniform orders. There were also dozens of boxes of navy blue peacoats. Almost everyone in town got one after the brass buttons had been cut off and bone ones sewn on. There were none small enough for the kids in the orphanage, so the sewers were busy cutting them down. There were also knitted sea caps on every head in town by the first snow.

Father Giovanni had formed the habit of coming with Rose and Grandfather to our house for Monday night dinner, and everyone shared his latest letter from Mr. Isaac and Helga and Stella. Stella was very busy, but she managed to pencil notes as she rode the streetcars. She had gotten used to the cars by now and no longer feared she would have an accident and someone would see what she had in her bloomers and send her to Bellevue. Father Giovanni read his latest from Stella, a record of the conversations heard in a voice studio:

"Sing as you speak, open your throat, relax your jaw, pronounce your lyrics, don't flat, relax, think happy. Don't lift your shoulders, don't listen to your own voice. Hum in your mask, your tone is too straight. Hit the note on the head, think low, now raise the tone, sing to the back wall, let the breath carry the tone, squeeze your buttocks, too much vibrato, too nasal, cough where the tone starts, if you're dizzy, lean over."

I must confess, dear friend, I am often dizzy, but there is not time to lean over. I read where Amelita Galli-Curci, without one formal lesson, appeared as Gilda at the Teatro Costanzi in Rome in 1909. I do wish I could just skip all this and go right to the Metropolitan. But I am not tired, I am not tired.

Love, Stella

Erica was not well enough to come down to dinner, so after dinner they all went up and had coffee in her room and read Helga's latest letter.

My mother did not breed the white Arabian mares to our stallions, although Big Black and Trojan stood by the fence and watched the female beauties do their dance of seduction. She brought in a pure white Arabian stallion and paid five thousand dollars to keep him a week. When Aunt Sebe heard the figure, she was nastier than usual. Kirby had been pressured to go back to work with his miners again, as the price of coal had dropped to two dollars and a quarter a ton, delivered. John L. Lewis and his crew had been around, trying to unionize the mine for higher wages. If that happened, Kirby would have to shut down.

My mother gave Grandfather five thousand dollars to give to Sebe and not tell her it came from her. Not that she wouldn't have taken it from my mother, but it would have made her more bitter than ever. She seemed to be mad at everyone since Fat Pauline had been born. She had planned on a boy. She was going to name him Lloyd, and that would be another way of getting her son up out of the grave. Kirby was glad he had a girl, even if she was a tub and, Worthy said, fatter every day. Aunt Sebe had only water in her tits, and they had to buy cans of Eagle Brand milk for Pauline. She sucked on her bottle all day long, and they were going broke. Worthy was planning, the next time the Gypsies camped at Cheat River, to take Fat Pauline over there and sell her.

Kirby came late one night to talk to my mother. He thought Aunt Sebe was cracking up, but I heard my mother assure him as he went out that she had always been that way. I doubt if that made him feel any better.

Each day at dawn, my mother saddled Trojan and went racing over the hill to the upper meadows like a madwoman, or a woman on a mad horse. All the fences and gates were down now, clear into the National Forest Preserve. We no longer kept sheep, except for a few to crop our lawns, as it wasn't profitable; the wool storage rooms were packed. Sometimes my mother raced Trojan up the back road, past the Thorne house and back, five miles in about fifteen minutes, but most of the time they plunged up the steep hills. She said Trojan preferred a challenge. She thought she knew what he was thinking, because she could stand down by the barn with his bridle in hand and he would come up from the lower meadow, as if he heard her call. Maybe he did.

CHRISTMAS 1930

GRANDMOTHER'S CHRISTMAS OPENING was a big success. She had sixty guests, and it cost her a lot of money. Everything was first-class, as she had learned to understand it. Syrie Maugham had helped her assemble a guest list that was a real Who's Who. Even rich people like to eat and drink for free. Some of the people were social and some just interesting. The Morgan twins, Gloria and Thelma, were there, and Mrs. Maugham thought they would bring the Prince of Wales, but I guess his mother, the Queen of England, was having a party, too. Thelma brought Aly Khan, who was even richer, and he came out to our farm to see the Arabians. He wanted to buy them, but my mother explained she couldn't sell them until Mr. Conklin's two years were up. She didn't really want to sell them, anyway.

Marion Davies came. She was a blond actress who stuttered; William Randolph Hearst was trying to make her into a movie star. She had her bodyguard with her, a Captain Brown; he took his job very seriously and never left her side, even at night. Elsa Maxwell had brought a whole group of people who were called "café society." Grandmother was paying her a certain amount per head. Cole Porter had brought his boy lover and kissed him openly under the mistletoe. Elsa Maxwell played one of his latest songs, "Anything Goes," and these people meant it. She had begun her career playing piano for silent movies, and had parlayed that into being New York's number one party giver. She must have known an awful lot of dirt on a lot of people, for she looked like a fat, ugly pig.

I awoke at four o'clock Christmas morning. A half-moon lighted the icy crust on the snow, and the stars were still bright. I wasn't the first one up; the lights were on in the hall downstairs, and the whistling teakettle in the kitchen was shrill. My mother caught me before I had opened my first package. She was already dressed in pants and boots and a sheepskin jacket.

"Hughie, run down to the barn and tell Mr. Brownie and Mr. Talbot to put the chains on my car."

"As soon as I open my boxes."

"No, now; and I want you to go with me. Dress warm."

Mr. Brownie and Mr. Talbot were the new men who had moved into Stanley's room. I didn't go up to wake them, I just banged on the metal stair with a broomstick. They leaned over the opening in their long red underwear.

My mother wanted to make her assigned rounds in town with the Christmas baskets before the children were up. The food baskets had been going out all week, but these were the toys and clothes from Santa Claus. I was sure these kids knew there wasn't any Santa Claus, unless it was Billy-Pearl Curtiss, and why she felt compelled to be him, I didn't understand.

Grandfather had divided the list in two, and he and Rose took the narrow roads that went up into difficult hollows because Mr. Isaac's old truck with its big tires and heavy chains could go places we couldn't in Mother's old touring car. Even then, we got stuck twice and needed a push. We came back to the church at about nine o'clock for the last load, but Rose and Grandfather were just loading it up, so we were done. Grandfather had on a red Santa Claus hat and looked silly. His beard wasn't long enough yet. He had vowed not to shave it until Mr. Isaac came back home.

I was really tired, since I had climbed up and down a lot of snowy steps, but my mother thought we should go by and say Merry Christmas to Grandmother. We didn't buy her a present, because she wanted the money to go into the Christmas baskets. My mother had looked at me, but I hadn't volunteered the same; I had spent too much time working on my Christmas list and leaving it lying around where everyone could see it.

The street had already been plowed, so we could pull up in front of Orchard House Inn. Grandmother, with Doris Duke and Eleanor in tow, was just crossing over into the park. We joined them. I was going to remember to tell Boobie that I got a Christmas hug from the richest woman in the world. I would have gotten a slurp from Eleanor if I hadn't ducked. The hair between her ears was brushed up into a tuft and tied with a red velvet ribbon.

My mother said, "What's the matter, Virginia? That is not exactly a 'Merry Christmas' face you're wearing."

"Does it show? Doris and I had to get out and breathe some fresh clean air."

"You're tired of the perfumed air of your Orchard House Inn?"

"Billy-Pearl, I've made a horrible mistake. I thought I could gather around me all the smart, sophisticated people, the kind I thought I wanted to spend the rest of my life with, and this—the inn—was the way to do it. I listened to their empty chatter last night as they all got drunk on my champagne, and I did not hear one person say one worthwhile thing, not one plan that benefited anyone but their shallow selves. I have built a house of vanity. Oh, Billy, what will I do?"

We had reached the bandstand, and we went up and sat on the cold benches.

"There's a whole world of wonderful people out there, people equally able to support this lifestyle. You've just made the wrong choices."

Grandmother told us how a man was pounding on her kitchen door at dawn. He apologized, but the five children in his broken-down truck were cold and hungry. As she fed them and put them in beds up over the carriage barn, she thought of all the guests in silk pajamas under eiderdown comforters—useless, shallow people—and felt like going up and down the halls and yanking them out. These people who would never know anything of hunger and yet had not earned one bite that went in their mouths. "Do you know that fourteen million people are now unemployed in this country?"

Grandmother was shaking with emotion. Miss Duke and my mother put their arms around her from either side and assured her they were out there, these worthwhile people, she just had to find them.

APRIL 1932

WE NEXT SAW STELLA and Helga in 1932 at Eastertime, when they came by train to Erica's funeral. Erica had died of pancreatic cancer and was buried up at Mount Zion cemetery. There wasn't much room left in the cemetery, so my mother bought an acre of adjoining land from Mrs. Thorne.

I felt awkward when Stella hugged me. It wasn't the same as when Stanley hugged me, but he was gone. Stella moved gracefully, like a dancer, on her high heels. And she had the assurance to call Father Giovanni and volunteer to sing in Handel's *Messiah,* planned for Easter morning in his church.

Grandfather was disappointed that Mr. Isaac had not come, but there were lots of robberies in Brooklyn these days, and he had stayed home to guard the house. Charles Lindbergh's baby had been kidnapped in New Jersey, and Mr. Isaac feared anarchy had begun here as it had in Germany. Besides, they had bought a cow who had to be milked.

Stella had brought me a bank shaped like the new Empire State Building. When it was full of dimes, it would be enough to go to New York, but I wasn't going to waste my dimes going there—I was going to California!

THE MILLER BOYS came back to spend the summer. Raymond and Donald had four-point averages their first year in college, and Miss Larkin was very proud of them. Stella and her new aunt and uncle stayed in New York; she had a summer job singing in a chorus.

That summer Franklin and Eleanor Roosevelt stayed at my grandmother's inn twice, on their way back and forth across the country campaigning for the presidency. They were part of a new group of people who had started coming, friends of Doris Duke's. Worthy and I helped to get Roosevelt elected because we went all over town and painted mustaches on Herbert Hoover's posters. Roosevelt won in a landslide, 472 electoral college votes to Hoover's 59.

Grandmother was embarrassed when the Roosevelts were there. Her llama was eating the roses from her garden, and Grandmother had gone out yelling, "Eleanor, Eleanor, how many times have I told you not to eat the roses?" Mrs. Roosevelt, who was pushing her husband through the orchard in his wheelchair, appeared on the path and said, "Once will be enough."

The two Eleanors were introduced, and it was hard to tell who had the toothier smile. Mrs. Roosevelt said, "I wonder which of us would make the best first lady."

APRIL 1933

THERE WERE LOTS of changes in 1933. Franklin Roosevelt came into office, and with him, the New Deal. Change was the watchword. The economy where we lived didn't change much, for it took a while to get the government-work projects going. In the meantime, many of the men in our town jumped into open boxcars as the trains passed through, planning to work in Florida or California and send money home. Most of them never even wrote. It was easier to start a new family somewhere else than to come back and feed eight or ten they already had. Relief programs didn't amount to much; the average was nine dollars a month per family.

Many who knew how and could afford the setups—the mash, the still, the copper coil—made bootleg liquor. You could sell good moonshine (it was so named because most stills were tended at night, when the revenuers could not see the ascending smoke from the still fires) for two and a half dollars a gallon jug. The retailer in town added half as much water, some burned sugar to bring the color back, and bottled it at a dollar a pint. Many a man with hungry kids at home spent his last dollar for a pint. There was a side industry that occupied Harry and Worthy. They picked through the city dump just below town for empty pint whiskey bottles and sold them back to bootleggers for a penny each.

When Herbert Hoover left office, he went to Wisconsin, and his secretary did not go with him, because his wife, my aunt Opal, would not leave Washington. She had rented Aunt Almeda's ball gowns to the ladies in Franklin Roosevelt's inaugural ball, and she liked her new business. Democratic ladies thought it was wise to rent for onetime affairs. Republicans were too snobbish to do that, but they were out for at least four years.

Aunt Opal said life was too short to put up with crap, and though she loved Aunt Almeda, she couldn't stand her constantly getting ready to greet Senator Burton when he returned. Aunt Almeda had to go to a home. She lived there only two months.

While Aunt Opal was cleaning house, she threw out her husband and his mother and got a divorce. She liked going to the White House, so she found a man in Roosevelt's cabinet, and when her divorce was final, she married him. Now that she had the hang of it, she married and divorced three more times in the next ten years. She wasn't marrying these guys for a house, because she had Aunt Almeda's house and her money, except for her bequest to Burton College—that was an embarrassment to Grandmother. It didn't bother Mrs. Burton, because she was over at Weston in the crazy house. Grandmother had put Mrs. Burton in Dr. Butt's hospital because she wouldn't come out of the elevator. In the hospital, she set her mattress on fire and threw it out the third-floor window, and Dr. Butt sent her to Weston. Daisy Brown went in the same ambulance, because she had been pregnant for two years, according to her, and wanted Dr. Butt to perform a cesarean.

Aunt Almeda left a hundred thousand dollars for scholarships to girls who, without her help, would have become mistresses to married politicians. All the girls interviewed said that was their case exactly.

I had my eleventh birthday in March, and I was already five feet eleven, so I thought I might just reach my goal to be as tall as Grandfather.

Three of the four Arabian mares produced colts. When they were born, they were black, and my mother feared that Grandfather's Big Black had had at them. She didn't know then that pure Arabians were black for the first two or three years. Turned in with the other colts, they all looked alike. My mother thought she could hide them there if Mr. Conklin did return. It had been two years this fall, and she was too much in love with the horses to give them back.

A man came and wanted to buy all our bottomland to build an airport. He said it was progress and we shouldn't stand in the way. Tuck Marsteller said he wouldn't stand in the way, took his money, and went to Florida. Already they were scraping and digging and leveling right up to our lower fence. Our horses stood behind their fence and watched like curious children. When the little one-motor propeller planes started landing, the horses ran back and forth but were not really afraid, as my mother was. She was afraid they would expand it, and she had heard that airports all over the country were putting lights around runways so planes could land at night. One good thing about it: an airmail letter to New York would get there in two days, but it cost nine cents, so I doubted many people would be using airmail.

AUGUST 25, 1933

ALL MY MOTHER'S FEARS came true. Mr. Conklin pulled into our drive the last week in August in a truck with a double horse trailer, and he had beside him what must have been his new Russian princess. My mother always said sometimes you had to lie for the sake of courtesy. I guess that was what she was doing, as she went toward him with her hand extended. "Why, Mr. Conklin, how nice to see you again." I don't know how she recognized him. The bleary-eyed drunk of the circus was gone. There was a word used at the time for men who looked like this: "natty." He was dressed in a white linen suit with plus fours over brown and white golf shoes, and over his thinning hair, he wore a white panama hat. He was gracious to a fault as he helped down the lady who rode beside him. She did look like as much of a lady as you could buy at a good store. Her name was Mabel Dodge, and he introduced her as his fiancée. He said he had come to pick up his racehorses. Not a word about the circus.

He was now the proprietor of a string of racers, and they were on their way to Hialeah, Florida, where the good and obviously rich Mrs. Dodge lived. She was wearing dark glasses and white gloves. He mentioned twice that she was a member of the Dodge Motor Car family. He said he had come to pay his board bill, as he remembered the agreement, two hundred a month for twenty-three months, and he added a thousand-dollar bonus for goodwill. He said not a word about colts, and my mother said nothing. He paid in cash, counting out hundred-dollar bills. When the mares were brought up from the meadow, they seemed to remember him, and one of them nuzzled against his neck. When they were loaded and Mrs. Dodge was in the truck, he took my mother's hand and said, "I thank you for everything." He whispered, "Especially your discretion."

I suppose if Mother was the crying type, she would have cried. Instead she just stood and stared down the road long after they were out of sight. I said, "Now you have three Arabian colts that are all yours."

"Yes, and I'm going to train them to be the finest horses in this country."

SEPTEMBER 1933

IN SEPTEMBER WE WENT to New York for Stella's debut. Geraldine Farrar had made it possible for her to appear at Carnegie Hall and had ensured ticket sales by appearing as well. Mother, Grandfather, Rose, and I stayed at the Algonquin Hotel. It was the showbiz thing to do; besides, they didn't have room for us at the house in Brooklyn. At the last minute, Grandmother Curtiss came with Doris Duke and Mrs. Maugham and Father Giovanni, and Aunt Opal arrived from Washington with some fellow named Perry, who had a funny English accent and had just won the world tennis championship. Every seat was sold or given away, and the place was full of people in fancy dresses and tuxedos. Grandfather and Mr. Isaac looked like the Smith brothers in their beards and black coats. I knew my mother had wanted Lester to come so she would have an escort. She said she was delighted to go with me in my new blue jacket, but I knew it wasn't the same.

We didn't see Stella before the performance, for fear of making her nervous. I don't think we would have. It was like at the church social. Stella came to sing, and sing she did. It was her evening, and everyone said how generous Geraldine Farrar was; she even wore black to Stella's white beaded gown, and she sang only secondary roles. She gave Stella "One Fine Day" and sang the role of Suzuki, maid to Madama Butterfly, instead.

The Gerry-flappers in the audience were disappointed that their heroine hadn't starred, but they wanted what she wanted, and obviously she intended to launch Stella Fancler into orbit. After each aria, there was applause that grew more intense as the evening progressed, until the final number was followed by a five-minute standing ovation. Stella came forward and looked out over that sea of approval and said, after her thank-yous, "I have dear friends in this audience tonight, who first heard me sing 'Flow Gently, Sweet Afton.' For them I will close with that song." She stood in the pale green lace she had changed into for the second half and charmed this hard-nosed New York group with only the harps from the orchestra accompanying her. She did all the right things, handing her sheaf of red roses over to Miss Farrar.

We all waited at the Tavern on the Green in Central Park, where Grandmother Curtiss was hosting the after-theater party. Stella arrived with the orchestra leader and Miss Farrar, and we all waited there until the reviews came out in the morning papers at three A.M. I was asleep in a back booth but was awakened by the yelling and applause after each critic's review was read. Each seemed to top the one before. Finally Mr. Isaac read, with fatherly pride:

> A new era in opera was launched tonight in the person of Miss Stella Fancler. Now the beautiful young heroines of Puccini, Verdi and Gounod can be cast as they should be: young, slender, with the voice of love; the face of love . . . The most remarkable sound of this or any season. A voice with the strength of a man; but with a charm that is all woman.

When Stella found me in the back booth and put her arms tight around me, I said, "You don't need me to love you anymore, you have everybody."

"That will never be true, Hughie, never, never, never."

That fall, when the Miller boys went back to Washington, their mother went with them. She was going to work for Aunt Opal, and there was plenty of room for all of them in the big old Georgetown house that had once housed Senator Burton and Aunt Almeda. I had always played king of the hill, but I didn't know how much I would miss Boobie until I saw them loading up to go to the train. She was ten now and tall and slender and, I realized for the first time, quite pretty. She would be able to go to public school in Washington, and Miss Larkin was sure her placement tests would put her in the sixth grade.

Mrs. Miller went up under the aspen trees to say good-bye to Mr. Miller. She had transplanted azaleas and rhododendrons from the woods all summer until the whole hillside would be a flower bed next spring. She planned to come back when they bloomed.

I would even miss Handsome. He was five and could dance like a windup toy. He held on to the box that contained his collection of hats that Stella kept sending him. Tuba wanted to go, too, but Aunt Opal had bad memories of her from childhood and didn't want her. Tuba mostly just sat in the kitchen and rocked, anyway, and sometimes she struck out at me with a broomstick when I passed.

After they were gone, our house seemed really empty. Miss Larkin was holed up back in her room most of the time, writing her book. The Forresters and the Thorne boys went about their chores and pretty much kept to themselves. I started taking piano lessons from Petey Bender, but that wasn't a full-time game. Grandfather had given me a lot of books to read, including one about how to read faster, and it helped.

I had written my father a letter, thinking he might write me to come up to Buffalo, but he didn't. He didn't even answer for a month.

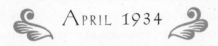

April 1934

In 1934 Max Baer became heavyweight boxing champion of the world. Some woman up in Canada had five babies all at once; the FBI shot public enemy no. 1, John Dillinger; I started to high school, and Stella went to Europe with Mr. Isaac and Helga, who got married. They were afraid to go to Germany or Italy. People there were doing terrible things to Jews. In Switzerland, Stella got the final operation that turned her into a woman.

When she came home the next summer, she explained to me exactly what they had done. They had turned the little cock wrong side out and tucked it inside, and what had been the outer skin was now the lining. She could get fucked and feel good about it. She didn't invite me to try, though I had grown pretty good.

September 1935

Stella appeared at the Metropolitan the next fall. We went, and if there had been any doubt as to her place in the opera world, her reviews removed it. She was established, celebrated, lionized. The only dark place in her life: Mr. Isaac had died. Grandfather went to New York and got his body and brought it back to bury in his family plot at Mount Zion. After that, Helga traveled with Stella as her dresser, her maid, her mentor, her mother.

April 1937

In 1937 American Airlines made our town a regular stop. The runway came right to the edge of our meadow, and though there were only two flights a day, they were disturbing. The world was encroaching.

I didn't know who was bothered by it most, my mother or Trojan. They tried to time their rides up into the mountains so they would be out of range when the planes landed. I liked them because you could go to either Washington or Pittsburgh in ninety minutes. We flew for the first time to Aunt Opal's wedding, her third, to General Openheimer.

Grandfather was eighty-eight years old in 1938. He hadn't really changed too much in the last ten years, except for a sadness when he spoke of Mr. Isaac. He still rode Big Black. He had built a stable in the orchard behind his house, and my mother had given Hannah to Rose so she and Grandfather could ride together. Rose had her hand in as many activities as my mother and Grandmother Curtiss. She had a sewing factory and a business of farming out quilts and rugs to be "handmade Appalachian-folk products" that Aunt Opal arranged to sell in a shop in Washington.

April 1938

My mother was now in charge of the county relief organization. Although there were several government-sponsored work projects here, there were still bootleggers sent to the Moundsville penitentiary for a year and a day, leaving wives and children behind for the county to feed.

My mother's office was next door to Lester's in the county courthouse, and she checked his schedule to see which bootlegger was to be raided at dawn and sent messages for them to dump their stills and be gone. There was a limit to how many the county could carry on its relief rolls. Lester was careful to leave the schedule out where she could find it.

Grandmother's inn was at least half full most of the time, and her prices were still high. Quite often the whole place was taken by groups of politicians, brainstorming secret deals that were supposed to keep our world on track. Eleanor Roosevelt was a regular visitor and brought with her the kinds of women's groups Grandmother admired.

The Curtiss women, Virginia and Billy, were not admired by everyone. They were called "do-gooders" and a lot of things less flattering, but they didn't care. They had combined the old people in the poorhouse and the children in the orphanage into one group. Children now had adoptive grandparents to read them to sleep.

Miss Larkin was a director of the reorganized school there, and she was putting some of her theories of learning into practice. The Thorne twins were a shining example of her success. Richie and Lou were now in public school in eighth grade.

The training of the three Arabian colts consumed most of my mother's waking hours, and by the time their dark coats had faded to white, they were like three beautiful, well-oiled machines who responded to the mere tightening of a muscle. She said they were the culmination of her life's efforts, the fulfillment of her every dream. And I had thought I was.

BY 1939 BURTON COLLEGE had an enrollment of 1,250, but they were not going to get me. My mother had enrolled me five years before, when the school opened, though nobody had asked me. She and Grandmother had it all worked out. I would become a teacher and teach here at Burton College. I could live in town and run the inn when Grandmother was gone. I could surely manage the two things, since you could walk up the hill from the inn to the college, and I could run the horse ranch with a good manager by going out only two or three times a week. And, they added, "God willing," I would be president of the college one day. They mentioned God only as a courtesy; they knew if the two of them put their minds to it, they didn't need Him.

The week after high school graduation, I took a list of colleges that still had open enrollment to Grandfather's to talk it over with him. He agreed with me that I should go away somewhere.

"I love your mother, but if you are ever going to learn to be your own man, you're going to have to get away from her."

Rose was making navy bean soup with little hot sausages, and corn bread, so Father Giovanni arrived for supper. He brought a big bunch of green onions, the season's first. After supper we went over my list and checked the locations on a big map on the floor. I favored Santa Clara University, because it was in California and the farthest school from home. Father Giovanni said it had other things to recommend it, not just that it was Catholic. It was taught by Jesuits, who, he thought, were the best educators in the world, though many Protestants viewed them as crafty schemers.

Grandfather said they would have to go some to be a better schemer than I was. He also said, "I think a world of men might be good for Hughie. He's been raised in a world of women, except for me."

So I told my mother where I was going, and her response was "I won't pay for it, and that's the end of that."

But it wasn't. I called my father in Buffalo and reminded him he had never done anything for me, and I wanted him to pay my tuition. He agreed reluctantly, even if he had to get a loan on his automobile business.

We had been mostly silent at dinner, then my mother said, "I don't know how you can do this to me. You know I love you."

"No, I don't know you love me. You love those horses more than me."

"I have tried to manage the best life for you I could."

"You try to manage everybody's life, and not everybody's grateful. I don't know why you do it."

She sat a long time and moved the trout around with her fork. "I don't know, either."

The next day she got on the phone, and by Saturday she had sold her three Arabian darlings.

I went to California to school, and I was a lot more lonely than I admitted to anyone.

September 1940

Stella was in London when they began evacuating women and children because the Germans were dropping bombs. It all seemed remote and unreal, even when we read that Hitler had invaded Holland, Belgium, and Luxembourg. We went to Chaplin's film *The Great Dictator,* and thought Hitler was some comic who would go away. I was glad I had learned to play the piano. I played "You Are My Sunshine" and "When You Wish Upon a Star," and the boys sang with me, and we didn't really think the war was a reality until we had to go home and register for the draft.

December 1942

I could have stayed out longer than my junior year, because my grades were good, but Grandmother Curtiss tripped me up. She was determined to keep me out, so she got herself appointed to the draft board. I was the last of the Curtisses, and she was not going to let me get my procreation parts shot off until I had produced an heir. But other mothers and grandmothers didn't want their sons to go, either. If I wasn't going, then they weren't going. She had to draft me by the end of 1942 as an example.

I had to go back to West Virginia to leave for the induction center. I stood by the bus with all the other country boys, waiting to get on. All around me, anxious mothers were bidding sons good-bye, hugging and kissing, crying and patting. My mother stood beside me saying nothing, her face a mask of despair; her eyes were like blue ice, but her arms remained at her sides. I wondered, right up to the moment they began calling names and we lined up at the bus door, Will she hug me? Will she hold me for even a moment?

She put out her hand and shook mine and said, "Take care of yourself." She bit her lip until it bled, and I got on the bus and didn't look back as we pulled away.

MARCH 1943

I HAD BEEN AT BILOXI, Mississippi, for four weeks of basic training when I passed the test that qualified me to be a tail gunner. But when I reported and they discovered my six-feet-four-inch frame could not be folded into the plastic bubble under the B-17, they sent me on to pilot training. I received a letter from my mother saying that she had been forced by the government to sell the farm so they could extend the airport to accommodate army transport planes. She had known about it when she last saw me but couldn't bring herself to tell me. The money was already in the bank in my name. She was moving her furniture into Grandfather's old farmhouse on Craven's Run, the house where she was born. She and Lester were going to live there together. She said, "After all, I'm still a young woman. I'm only forty-three." All the horses were gone now except Trojan. It all seemed so final.

I was in my fourth week of pilot training and had almost forgotten it was my twenty-first birthday. The commander sent for me and said the Red Cross representative had a message for me. I thought, Somebody is going to a lot of effort just to wish me happy birthday.

People don't usually ask you to sit down just to tell you happy birthday, but they do to tell you your mother is dead. They gave me a four-day leave.

My mother's funeral was all arranged for the next morning, after I arrived, and the church was full of people she had pushed in one way or another. The eight remaining sisters were there. I could see they had already been through my mother's wardrobe. Aunt Sebe was wearing my mother's green velvet suit and her mink coat. Other pieces of her clothing were divided around the room. Fat Pauline, who at thirteen was enormous, pushed Kirby in his wheelchair. He had the white-faced look of miners who had black lung. Mrs. Miller was there, but she told me Boobie couldn't get a plane from Oberlin College in Ohio, where she was a junior. Stella didn't make it to the church service but pulled up in a chauffeur-driven limo at the cemetery.

I didn't really feel anything. I didn't know what to feel. I studied Grandfather's face for a clue, but he was as confused as I. He said only, "It's a terrible thing for a man to follow his children to the grave, and I never thought it would be Billy. I never thought death would find Billy—she was too alive." I guess that was my feeling, too.

I took one of Grandmother's trucks and drove the Forrester men and Mrs. Thorne home. I wanted to hear how my mother had died. The Forrester men had found her and removed her from Trojan's saddle after he had thundered down from the hill, knowing something was wrong. They took her to the hospital, but she was dead before they got there. The doctor said it was a heart attack, but they looked at each other and nodded as though they knew better. Mrs. Thorne said what they wouldn't: "She died because she couldn't give up the farm." The men added, "It was seeing the barns torn down."

When we came over the last rise before the farm, I saw what they meant. There was nothing left but the house. The barns, the chicken houses, everything, even the apple trees were gone, and there were several pieces of heavy equipment down in the meadow, leveling the ground. There was a chain-link fence just behind the house. They had not yet decided whether to retain it for storage. I looked for Trojan, but the Forresters said he had stormed back up over the hill, and no one had seen him since. He could go thirty miles before he reached the first fence.

I walked through the empty house, a ghost house now, only spectral reminders here and there. My mother had taken most of the furniture to the old farm. Here and there were marks on the wall where the old family portraits had hung. There were a few pieces of furniture that none of the scavengers had wanted. The poster of the four Arabian mares still hung on the stairwell. The big blue rocker from Stanley's old room stood in the hall.

In my mother's office, I pulled the bookcase away from the wall to check the safe. It was still there, and I knew no one had the combination except my mother and me. Now, if she hadn't changed it, only I knew it. I opened it and was surprised to find its contents still intact. Why had she left it for last? Maybe she was having it moved to the old farm.

I laid its contents out on the floor. Her jewelry and the opera-length strand of pearls were on top. There was an envelope, old and brown, marked "Uncle Billie"; it contained twelve hundred dollars. The shoe box, with the last of the Millers' loot, contained twenty-three thousand dollars. Mrs. Miller was still at Grandmother's, and she cried when I gave it to her. I'm sure she thought my mother's death meant the end of her income. But Boobie could stay in school now.

I didn't take time to count the rest; whatever it was, it was mine, and I would put it in Grandmother's old safe. I heard the outside door open and knew a moment of panic. I covered the money with an old newspaper until I heard Stella call out, "Hughie, Hughie, are you here?" She hugged me and cried a little for both of us, and a little more when I gave her the strand of pearls and told her the lie that her name was on them. The only other thing she wanted was the blue rocking chair.

"You do remember, don't you, Hughie?"

"Some of the best memories of my life."

Stella's driver tied the chair on top of her car and they were gone. She had a performance tonight in Pittsburgh.

It seemed everybody was taken care of. The Forrester men had the start-up of a still and would soon be full-fledged bootleggers. The Thorne boys were all in the service, and each was sending twenty-five dollars a month to their mother.

I walked up the hill to see the newly made grave beside Uncle Billie's. I had forgotten about old Tuba, who was here. The old liar! She had said she was a hundred and ten, but according to the marker, she was only ninety-eight. I looked down on the house, and it cried out to me, "Hughie, do something. Don't leave me like this." I thought of all those arrogant strangers who wouldn't understand the feelings of a house that had been in one family for 140 years. I was the last; it was my responsibility. I found the old lamps in the kitchen and the back hall and splashed kerosene down the halls, under the stairs, over the kitchen. Then I lighted the fire. I watched for a minute as the flames quickly ate through the poster of the Arabians, and then I ran. I parked on the rise of ground south of the house and watched it burn until the roof fell in.

I went up in Grandmother's elevator to tell her good-bye. She had gone to bed after the funeral. I opened her door and stopped, surprised. I knew she loved

Eleanor, but I didn't expect her to be in Grandmother's bedroom. She didn't move, and as I looked closer and saw her glass eyes, I knew she was stuffed.

"Grandmother, how could you?"

"She died of pneumonia last year, and I just could not give her up. You know, Hughie, God doesn't give us very many things we can really love."

"I'll remember that."

1944

THE NEXT YEARS, Stella seemed to be everywhere. She made a movie in which she sang and danced. Her picture was on the cover of magazines and everywhere else the image of a beautiful woman reminded men what they were fighting for. One naval base voted her the girl they most wanted to come home to. She entertained at bases everywhere, singing what servicemen wanted to hear: "You'd Be So Nice to Come Home To," "The White Cliffs of Dover," "Praise the Lord and Pass the Ammunition."

I saw her twice during that time. At the Blythe airbase one night so hot that the tarred runway was too sticky to use, she climbed on the wing of a B-24 and sang for an hour. She put her arm around me as she sang "People Will Say We're in Love," and I had added prestige for at least three days.

The second time was at a base in North Africa. She was there with Bob Hope and Martha Raye. This time we didn't say anything. We just stood and looked at each other. We looked at the burning sand with the old Roman aqueducts in the background, and we both understood. I could read her mind. How did we get from a farm in West Virginia to a world like this? There was nothing to say.

Grandfather Fancler died while I was making my way through the toe of Italy, with Rommel on the run. Rose's letter did not reach me for two weeks. I cried because there is no way to keep from getting old. He had held together better than most, he was ninety-one.

When the war was over, I didn't go back to West Virginia. I was afraid if I did, I somehow would not be able to escape. I went to California.

1967

IN 1967 MY DAUGHTER was twelve years old, and my grandmother Curtiss died. I went back to bury her and to sell the inn, since I was her only heir. My ex-wife went along, to show our daughter where her ancestors came from, she said, but it was really to latch on to a share of the sale. She wasted her time; when the will was read, Grandmother had left me the inn with instructions that it could not be sold. I was to run it and live here, or it would go to Burton College as a sorority house. Even from her grave she was reaching out, trying to rule my life. She was carrying on the tradition for my mother. I told the college they could have it as soon as I cleared out what I wanted.

My ex-wife and my daughter went through the inn like kids in a candy store. My daughter won my heart when I heard her arguing with her mother to take the moth-eaten grizzly bear back to California. And then explaining why she just had to have the eighteen dining room chairs that Grandmother had saved for me. They would become a standard, and she wouldn't marry unless the man could provide a house suitable for those chairs. We had packers working for a week; they filled three vans that were sent to California, and still the place seemed full.

I had to get out in the air, so I took a walk up over the hill to the old Curtiss cemetery. There were now houses built almost up to the fence, and the trees and shrubbery had overgrown until there was a green canopy over the whole thing, with only the shaft of stone commemorating the old general piercing the middle. I walked between the rows of my ancestors and read their names. They didn't seem familiar anymore, the way they had when I walked through here as a child with Grandmother Curtiss. They no longer seemed to be my exclusive history; more like books whose copyright had run out and were now in public domain.

I was startled to see someone down at the end of the row of flat stones that capped the graves nearest the shaft. I stood and looked at her. She was standing on the stone, tapping a booted foot impatiently. It was against all rationale, but it was Aunt Almeda as she had been that first day coming from Washington, dressed in her riding habit, complete with derby hat. I looked away, then looked back, knowing it was a trick of the mind and thinking she would be gone.

She slapped her riding crop across the headstone. "Well, Hughie, it took you long enough to get here. You promised me that you would visit and we would talk."

"I'm here now."

"Finally. You owe me."

"You mean that hundred dollars you sent me?"

"No. For love, Hughie. I did love you."

"Only for a little while. Nobody seemed to love me for very long."

"It wasn't easy, Hughie. You weren't very lovable."

"What do you want?"

"I want my grave moved to the Curtiss plot over in Maplewood. We can only get so far away, and there's nobody here worth talking to. And that idiot Booth, who's buried down there in the corner, gets up twice a week and shoots at me."

"You just want to get over there by old Senator Burton."

"Poor dear. Think of him trapped over there with that boring woman for all eternity."

"I'll do what I can."

"That's no answer. You're a Curtiss, you can do whatever you really want to. Oh, damn, someone's coming!" She snapped her riding crop against her boot and was gone.

Someone was indeed coming through the gate. A tall black woman carrying flowers. She was somewhere in her forties. I can never tell the age of black people, and this one was very well groomed. She was making her way toward me, reading the names on the headstones.

"Can I help you?"

She was so startled, she dropped her flowers. I went and helped her retrieve them. Up close, she had good eyes, smart and appraising. She was looking closely at me.

"Dear Lord, can it be Hughie?"

"Yes."

"I'm Helen Miller. Boobie."

There wasn't really anything funny, but we stared into each other's faces and both began to laugh until we had to sit down on the headstones.

"I don't know what's so funny about finding you here in a cemetery after all these years," Boobie said.

"What are you doing here?"

"I'm looking for your mother's grave. I wanted to say thank you."

"She's buried at Mount Zion with my grandfather."

"I've got a car, do you want to drive with me?"

I found that I did, and I wanted to drive across the country to California with her. She was on her way to Claremont, where she was the new dean of women at a prestigious school. The old house I had bought in Pasadena wasn't that far away.

I did have Aunt Almeda moved to Maplewood. When I decided to write this book, I went back to Elkins and lived in the old farmhouse on Craven's Run. I thought it would be easier to remember everything from there, and it was. I had owned it all these years, and after Lester's death, various family members who needed a home had lived there. Fat Pauline was living there now, all two hundred and fifty pounds of her. She cooked and cleaned and talked and talked, spewing out venom and ill will against everyone. Both Worthy and Harry had died in the war, and Aunt Sebe had spent the years berating the fates until Pauline had moved out here in the country to a solitary life. I arranged an income that would keep her fed. It had to be fairly generous, for she was a big eater.

AFTER STELLA READ the book you have just read, I waited a week before I went back up to Santa Barbara to see her.

"Hughie, you son of a bitch! No, I take that back. I don't want to call your mother a bitch, she was one of the few women in my life who wasn't. I thought you were going to tell our story, but you have told the story of everybody in West Virginia, although I have to admit you have hidden my true identity admirably — and those of a few scoundrels you should not have gone to the trouble to disguise.

"I was mad as hell when I read my beginnings, the Stanley part. And then I thought, Dammit — it's all true. Why not?"

"Do you want me to start over, just tell the pretty parts?"

"Hell, no. We are what we are because of, no, in spite of, all of this. I come off in your story a pretty special dame."

"You are a special dame."

"You didn't have to tell the part about the blue rocking chair."

"That was a part of you. Do you still have it?"

"Upstairs in my bedroom. Many an ambitious boy singer started his career in that chair."

She was laughing now, and the years fell away. The amber eyes sparkled, and she ran the tip of her tongue across her red lips.

"Do you think I've grown too big to sit in your lap?"

She led the way up the stairs.

Epilogue

AFTER I FINISHED THIS BOOK, I gave it to my agent, who sold it to my editor, who liked it very much. She, in turn, began sharing my story with many people, both inside her publishing company and out. A number of people felt they wanted a little bit more—a few loose ends tied up.

I really thought I had done it with that one sentence to Stella: "Everyone involved is dead now, except you and me."

Well, that's not exactly true. There are all of those cousins, of course, third- and fourth-generation descendants of Peter Fancler. They must have bred like rabbits, for there are now seven hundred and fifty of them. They had a convention last year to count their numbers. Granddad Fancler, wherever he is, must be laughing his head off.

I made my own journey back to Elkins not so long ago. I hadn't been back in fifty years, and I decided to return, if for no other reason, to walk through the cemetery and read my history as it's written on the family tombstones. I wasn't sure, but I thought this might inspire me to tell some truths that I hadn't told in my book.

There is an old joke about not being able to get there from here and that was pretty much true of my trip to Elkins. The airport is closed down—there's not even a shuttle in from Washington. The nearest place to fly into was Pittsburgh, where a car could be rented for the drive. There are no buses and no trains. In fact, not only had they stopped train service; they had taken up the tracks. What had once been a thriving town of ten thousand was barely two. The hotels had been replaced by a couple of motels.

I walked the streets all over town, but nothing looked familiar; nothing jarred my memory. I went to each of the three cemeteries where my ancestors lay. I read their names and tried to remember the faces of those I knew. In my youth, the graves were always well tended, but now there were only a few badly with-ered flowers here and there ... with the notable exception of Aunt Almeda's grave, which was adorned with an expensive, professional arrangement. That was a mystery. Who on earth would do that?

I had left to the last my visit to the Oldfellows Cemetery, where my mother is buried. Someone had been there only that morning. The grass was newly clipped and moist, and a tin bucket held a fresh bunch of black-eyed Susans. Another mystery. I tried to think who my mother might have touched in her life who would feel such gratitude. Of course, as soon as I began the list of pos-sibilities it grew long; who had she not touched?

From her grave site you could look down across to the airport runway, now overgrown with low brush. What had once been the seemingly unending rich meadows of our farm had been transformed into waste. There were whirlwinds of dry dust where once thick, red clover had been alive with bees. I wondered if it made my mother's spirit weep to see this, but then I remembered that my mother seldom wept. She would have considered weeping over this to be a waste of tears. Were I a younger man, however, I could be persuaded to start a revolution against stupid, self-centered politicians who destroy fields of clover to no real purpose. May they never know the taste of clover honey on their tongues.

I sat on my mother's gravestone and tried to conjure up our house, tried to see it again as it was. On the last day of the four-day leave I had taken from the army in order to journey home and bury my mother, I had stood very near where I was now and watched the flames devouring that wonderful old structure. There was no fire brigade to put out the flames; they had already gone to war.

I have already told you what I can remember of my young life, but I haven't really told the whole truth of that last day home. Since finishing my book, I have given it a lot of thought, and here is what I can tell you. I walked those empty rooms that day, trying to remember which ancestor's portrait hung where. I didn't want to remember the safe, but I couldn't help myself. I could feel the tumblers falling into place as I worked the combinations. There were the pearls and there was the money, but I guess I didn't want to remember what else I found. There was a small tin box that normally contained two cyanide capsules, kept for emergencies like putting down a horse that had gone lame; but only one capsule remained. Where was the other one? I really didn't want to know, but a sure, steady sense of dread enveloped me.

I walked upstairs and found a bucket of orange paint in the hallway, the brush drying on top of it. I followed the trail of paint drops into my bedroom. She needed a whole wall for the message she'd left me:

Forgive me, Hughie, you won't need me anymore. I have lost my world;
I'm left with a headache and a lifetime of headaches I can't live with.

Mother

AND I WAS LEFT WITH a lifetime of anger toward you, Mother, because you killed yourself on my birthday.

I don't think she meant it as a message to me — I think she didn't remember, and that hurts the most. At long last I can forgive her. Maybe, after writing this book, I have finally grown up, but nothing is ever really over.

I got kerosene on my hands as I drenched the hallway with it, then I turned my mother's farewell to ash. If my mother could end it like that — a cyanide capsule in her mouth, on the back of her favorite horse — then I could bring the history of a house and the records of six generations of Curtisses to an end. I ran like a madman, emptying files and boxes of pictures on the floors. I opened doors wide, so that no room would escape. I worked until the smoke drove me out.

I sat down the road in my pickup truck and waited until the roof collapsed. I had hoped by burning every bit of evidence that we had ever been here, that that would be the end of it. Of course, as long as I have a brain in my head such a thing is not possible; nothing really ever ends, nothing can be fully erased. I guess I thought writing it all down would free me, but it hasn't.

It is not difficult to remember what spectacular beauties my mother and all of her golden sisters were. To me, they were the most unique group of women this country has ever seen. My daughter has inherited a great deal of what I call the Look. I watch her swing aboard her horse with such style and sweep her silver-blond hair back over her shoulders, and it makes my heart quicken: she looks exactly like sister number seven.

No one ever told me what happened to Trojan. It was wartime and our valley was full of strangers. Surely someone would have taken him in and prized him, for he was the most beautiful of horses, a dappled gray the color of platinum. I think of him now in heaven, racing madly from cloud to cloud, with my beautiful, proud mother on his back.